SISTERS *of* NIGHT *and* FOG

ERIKA ROBUCK

Berkley
New York

BERKLEY
An imprint of Penguin Random House LLC
penguinrandomhouse.com

Copyright © 2022 by Erika Robuck
Readers Guide copyright © 2022 by Erika Robuck
Penguin Random House supports copyright. Copyright fuels creativity, encourages
diverse voices, promotes free speech, and creates a vibrant culture. Thank you for buying an
authorized edition of this book and for complying with copyright laws by not reproducing,
scanning, or distributing any part of it in any form without permission. You are supporting
writers and allowing Penguin Random House to continue to publish books for every reader.

BERKLEY and the BERKLEY & B colophon are registered trademarks of
Penguin Random House LLC.

Library of Congress Cataloging-in-Publication Data

Names: Robuck, Erika, author.
Title: Sisters of night and fog / Erika Robuck.
Description: First edition. | New York: Berkley, 2022. | Includes bibliographical references.
Identifiers: LCCN 2021026573 (print) | LCCN 2021026574 (ebook) |
ISBN 9780593102169 (trade paperback) | ISBN 9780593102176 (ebook)
Subjects: LCSH: Szabo, Violette, 1921–1945—Fiction. | Albert-Lake, Virginia d', 1910–
1997—Fiction. | World War, 1939–1945—Fiction. | LCGFT: Biographical fiction. | Novels.
Classification: LCC PS3618.O338 S57 2022 (print) | LCC PS3618.O338 (ebook) |
DDC 813/.6—dc23
LC record available at https://lccn.loc.gov/2021026573
LC ebook record available at https://lccn.loc.gov/2021026574

First Edition: March 2022

Printed in the United States of America
1st Printing

Book design by Alison Cnockaert
Interior art: map of Europe by Peter Hermes Furian / Shutterstock

Praise for

SISTERS of NIGHT and FOG

"Following her triumph *The Invisible Woman*, Erika Robuck returns with an even more powerful book. . . . Inspired by true stories, this incredible book tells of American Virginia and Violette, each swept up in the current of World War II and forced to choose whether to risk everything for the things in which she believes. Their lives collide in powerful and irrevocable ways that will hold readers spellbound. In a crowded field of books set during the Second World War, *Sisters of Night and Fog* stands head and shoulders above for its meticulous research, heart-pounding storytelling, compelling relationships, and important message. Bravo!"

—Pam Jenoff, *New York Times* bestselling author of
The Woman with the Blue Star

"A novel of duty, sacrifice, fate, and hope, set in a world steeped in courage and madness. Searing, powerful, and told through the lens of two overlooked historical figures who gave up nearly everything to fight against tyranny in one of the twentieth century's darkest hours, Erika Robuck's *Sisters of Night and Fog* soars. Two women—connected at the outset by fate, chance, and little else—hurtle toward a tragic date with destiny in the infamous Ravensbrück concentration camp, where prisoners are starved and tortured, and not all will make it out alive. Based very closely on the true stories of two incredible twentieth-century women in the shadows who risked their lives to save others, this novel, devastating in its truth and power, will break your heart and stay with you long after you've turned the final page."

—Kristin Harmel, *New York Times* bestselling author of
The Book of Lost Names and *The Forest of Vanishing Stars*

"Few writers are as skilled as Erika Robuck at the exacting art of spinning the raw truth of history into the vital tapestry of fiction. . . . She takes the well-documented stories of [Violette Szabo and Virginia d'Albert-Lake], whose courage under the most harrowing circumstances almost defies description, and she makes us *believe*. This impeccably researched and profoundly moving novel will stay with readers long after its devastating and heartfelt conclusion, and they will marvel, as I did, at the valor of its heroines and the artistry of its author."

—Jennifer Robson, *USA Today* bestselling author of
Our Darkest Night

"Erika Robuck has once again proved her mastery of biographical fiction, respecting the historical record as she weaves together the true stories of two endlessly courageous women whose daring and sacrifice helped defeat the Nazis. Utterly compelling, beautifully written, and meticulously researched, *Sisters of Night and Fog* is a book you sink into, one that becomes your world as you read it. I loved this book madly."

—Tasha Alexander, *New York Times* bestselling author of
The Dark Heart of Florence

"Evocative and intimate, here is an unforgettable dovetailing of the real-life stories of two remarkably brave and inspiring women. A World War II tale that has surely been pleading to be told."

—Susan Meissner, bestselling author of *The Nature of Fragile Things*

"Robuck delivers an enticing tale of two women who risk it all to help the French Resistance. . . . Robuck lures the reader into the mud and the muck alongside the protagonists as they face the dangers and destruction wrought by the conflict. Fans of World War II dramas are in for a treat."

—*Publishers Weekly* (starred review)

OTHER TITLES BY ERIKA ROBUCK

Receive Me Falling
Hemingway's Girl
Call Me Zelda
Fallen Beauty
The House of Hawthorne
The Invisible Woman

For Patrick and Tania

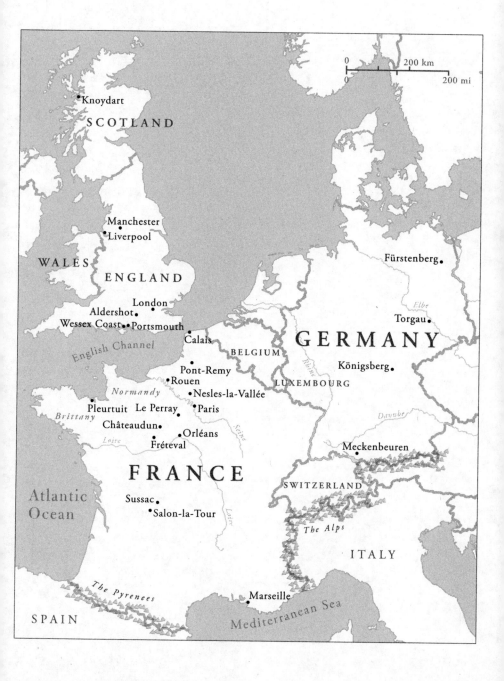

SISTERS *of* NIGHT *and* FOG

HOW COULD I think returning to this place would be a good idea?

Of the two hundred fifty of us women on that final prisoner transport to Ravensbrück concentration camp, only sixty made it out alive. Fewer still are on this bus with me. We said we'd meet here after the war to burn the camp to the ground, but after incinerating thousands of women, the Nazis burned the camp down before we could, destroying every file of every prisoner possible, trying to erase us.

My love had cautioned me about returning, but when have I ever obeyed him?

"You're able to smile," says my companion.

"Was I?" I ask, twirling my wedding ring. "I can't help it when I think about my husband."

"Lucky," she says. "When I think of mine, I want to spit."

"Which one?"

We laugh, wrapping our wrinkled arms around each other a little tighter. I think back to when our arms were smooth and young. Now, we have more padding, and the skin from our forearms to our knuckles looks like the roots of an old tree that has weathered many storms to keep the trunk upright. It's difficult to reconcile the withering body

I inhabit with the woman I am in my mind, especially because will and care were once enough to resurrect me. There can be no resurrection from age.

"There," my companion says.

The sight of the looming brick wall is a blow, and I feel as if I've been struck by the crop. A wave of nausea rises. I hear the breathing increase in tempo around me, and the crying. I squeeze my eyes shut. I will not allow tears. Nor will my companion. We used to say the ones who cried didn't live through the night.

Was I foolish to think I'd be able to rise to this occasion, to face the place—about which I've barely uttered a word all these years—that almost destroyed me? It's easy to talk about the successes, the thrills, and the adventures, but the consequences are another story. I've locked the memories deep in a box at the bottom of my heart, buried with the women it hurts too badly to remember.

Though I have my friend with me, I don't know if I'll be able to get off the bus for the remembrance ceremony. If there's any hope, I must compose myself the only way I know how. I open my eyes and lean my head against the bus window, looking up to the heavens, hoping my love can see the same sky. My heart lifts when I notice the quarter moon in the dawn. I can almost see back in time to my child's plump finger pointing at the moon, surprised to see it during the daytime.

A day moon is called a child's moon because only young, fresh eyes can see it. In spite of my advanced age, I can still see the day moon.

I am one of the only ones left to see it.

I

1940 – 41

Some people have suggested that we should never have sent women on these missions at all. I cannot agree. Women are as brave and as responsible as men; often more so. They are entitled to a share in the defence of their beliefs no less than are men. . . . I should have been failing in my duty to the war effort if I had refused to employ them.

—*Colonel Maurice Buckmaster,*
SOE, F Section (France), They Fought Alone

1

PONT-REMY, FRANCE

—— VIOLETTE ——

VIOLETTE IS SHAKEN awake, Tante Marguerite's wild-eyed face inches from hers.

"Réveille-toi!"

Disoriented, Violette feels a stab of panic. Did Tante discover what Violette did last night?

"Why so early?" Violette asks her aunt, keeping her voice as innocent as possible.

"For once in your eighteen years, Vi, obey," says Tante. "Pack!"

Tante Marguerite hurries to wake Violette's eight-year-old brother, Dickie.

With a sinking feeling, Violette realizes the day she's been dreading has come. She and her little brother are being sent back to London.

The siblings have been staying in France with their mother's sister to give Maman space to mourn their littlest brother, Harry, who died last year from diphtheria. Violette and the rest of her family had grieved Harry hard and fast, but even after months passed, Maman could barely tread water.

In spite of war making fire of the French horizon, Violette has no desire to return to London. France is her mother's home and Violette's dearest love. She's spent every summer of her life here, and half her school years, and knows it's where she belongs.

"I don't want to go," she says.

Ignoring her, Tante tells Dickie to dress at once.

Violette is about to argue, but the look of sheer terror on Tante's face silences Violette. Her aunt is not one for hysterics.

Violette looks out the window and sees a flurry of motion on the street. Refugees pass, with trunks and valises and frightened children loaded on carts and on goats' backs and whatever else they could find. A distant rumble calls Violette to action. She throws back her sheet and pulls their suitcases from the closet. She stuffs her clothing, toiletries, and magazines into one. As she heads for Dickie's drawers to pack his suitcase, Tante grabs Violette's arm.

"*Une* valise. And your passports. Hurry!"

Violette rolls her eyes but obeys, putting her and Dickie's necessities into one suitcase and dressing as quickly as possible. While Tante leaves them and bangs around the kitchen, muttering about someone getting into the cupboard, Violette sneaks out of the house and to the shed. She pulls open the door and looks for her pilot, but he's gone. She'd think she dreamt him if it weren't for the heart he drew for her on the dirt floor.

Last night, Violette had snuck out for a midnight bicycle ride, when she'd stumbled across a Belgian pilot sleeping along a ravine. She'd poked him awake—scaring him half to death—and once he calmed, he explained he'd been shot down and lost his crew. He was trying to make his way to Spain so he could get to London and back in the air fighting Nazis. Violette had set him up in Tante's garden shed with a blanket, half a loaf of bread, directions south, and prayers for his safe travels.

Violette touches her chest and sighs. Resolved, she hurries back to the house. Once she escorts Dickie safely back to London and places him in her mother's arms, Violette will find a way back to France to do whatever she can to fight the Nazis.

IF VIOLETTE STARES at the gulls gliding overhead, she can remove herself from the chaos. She imagines looking down on the dock at Calais from a great height, from heaven.

Does it look like a pretty, breezy day, a single ship remaining on the quay, a line of merry travelers waiting to board? she thinks. *Is this how it looks to God? Is that why he doesn't help?*

Dickie's sweating hand jerks Violette back to where they stand among a mass of weary, frantic travelers. He sobs so hard he shudders for breath. He's been crying since they dragged him from the house and pushed him on the crowded train. They had to walk the last kilometer of the journey because the tracks were blown out by the Luftwaffe.

A terrible growling sound starts. Violette again lifts her eyes to the sky. These are not gulls coming in, but Heinkel bombers, flying so low she can see the pilots. As soon as they're overhead, the shooting begins. Great splashes erupt from the water, coming closer and closer, until the first blast hits the crowd along the dock. Luggage and limbs erupt in a red spray of fire and blood. Violette watches in shock, and her gaze finds a little girl of no more than five lying in the sand, whose dead glassy stare matches that of the dolly in her arms.

Violette feels as if a gun has gone off in her head. Though Dickie is almost as tall as she is, she lifts her little brother in her arms and races toward the dock. With Tante at Violette's heels, they push through scores of French, Belgian, and Dutch refugees making for the last ship out at one o'clock. Violette and Dickie will be given preference because of their British citizenship, but they have to get to the Royal Navy destroyer first. If they miss the boat, Maman will never recover.

Tante keeps up with Violette, plowing a path through the crowd with the suitcase. Sweat soaks through Violette's dress to her jacket. The voices around them are angry, scared, and speaking many languages. The sailors look panicked. They've stopped checking passports. With just a few yards to go, a gendarme in the French police closes the gates and locks them.

"No!" screams Tante.

At the barricade, Tante bangs the bars, begging, while Violette scans the fence for an opening through which she might squeeze Dickie.

As the next wave of bombers arrives, the crowd drops to the ground. Tante continues to beg, from her knees. When Violette sees the planes taking aim farther down the docks, she stands with Dickie and moves toward the gendarme and the remaining sailor. Dickie has stopped crying and stares blandly before him. Tante joins Violette.

"Please," Tante says, grabbing Violette's cheeks. "Look at my beautiful, British niece. Will you leave her to the filthy *boches*? Do you know what they'll do to her?"

While the sailors pull off the lines, the gendarme looks from Violette to Dickie to the remaining sailor and back. Violette knows she can take care of herself, but Dickie is defenseless. Violette looks up, imploring the men with her large, violet eyes, the ones that inspired her name.

Please.

The gendarme looks back at the sailor and receives a curt nod. He unlocks the gate and pulls Violette and Dickie through.

Amid Tante's crying and well-wishes and the angry shouts of the crowd, Violette runs to the ship with Dickie. She forgot their suitcase, but there's no time to go back. A sailor helps them aboard, and when the one from the gate follows and they push off, Violette kisses him on both cheeks.

The passengers are instructed to go belowdecks, but Violette refuses. She won't allow them to get trapped if the ship gets hit. She'll swim back to shore with her brother if necessary.

The destroyer accelerates. The waters roil and churn. The wind blows. They're not traveling straight, but in sharp zigzags, like a tacking sailboat.

As the bombers return, Violette covers her brother's body with her own and prays as she never has.

2

LE PERRAY-EN-YVELINES, FRANCE

——— VIRGINIA ———

AT DAWN, A rumbling sound draws the American woman and her French husband out of bed, to the window. Buses file past the house where the couple are billeted. At first glance, the buses appear empty, but upon closer look, they can see the silhouettes of many small heads.

"Paris is sending away her children," Virginia says, touching her stomach.

She hasn't yet told Philippe her suspicion, and she doesn't know how or when she will. Her cycle, which usually runs like clockwork, is four days late. They've longed for a baby since the moment they got married, three years ago, but knowing Philippe is about to join the fighting, Virginia thinks he'll be crushed with worry. Not only that, with war erupting, her mother has been begging Virginia to return to the family home in Florida, but she refuses. If she's expecting, she knows her argument will lose weight.

Philippe comes up behind his wife, wrapping her in his great arms. "The poor *bébés*," he says. "How has it come to this?"

Refugees have been on the march for days through the village where Philippe's cavalry unit is stationed. The pair are in a lovely house on the main street, where an officer's wife keeps them in a set of beautiful, well-equipped rooms. Virginia has been following Philippe and his men like a lamb from town to town, creeping toward the front. Both of them know she'll be able to go only so far, but they refuse to face the truth. Until the river of weary refugees began running, Virginia could pretend she and Philippe were on a second honeymoon, touring French villages, enjoying each other in the growing warmth and lengthening days of spring. Right or wrong, they have resolved to live only in the moment. There's no other way to live in war.

Virginia turns her back on the scene out the window and stands on tiptoe to kiss Philippe. Philippe's late father was French, but his mother is British, and that side of the family is where he gets his height. Virginia presses herself into Philippe, noting the soreness in her breasts through her nightgown, wondering if she should tell him. It's his thirty-first birthday, after all. The words are on her lips to share the news, when a banging at the door to the sitting room outside the bedroom makes them jump.

"Sergeant!" comes the voice. "Maréchal d'Albert-Lake?"

"Is it even six in the morning?" Virginia whispers.

Philippe hurries to pull on his uniform. While he buttons his shirt, Virginia grabs his blue cap with the red stripe from the nightstand. Philippe strides over to allow her to top him off, kisses her forehead, and rushes from the room, leaving the door slightly open in his haste. Virginia creeps across the floor and eavesdrops from the shadows.

"Why haven't your men reported for duty?"

Virginia bristles, looking through the crack to see who berates her husband.

"My apologies," says Philippe to a haggard general. "We were not told to expect you."

"Everything's falling apart. Men abandoning posts. Not enough uniforms or weapons. It's pandemonium."

Virginia is filled with dread.

"First, Poland," the general says. "Now Denmark, Norway, Belgium, the Netherlands, Luxembourg. We're next."

Philippe leaves, and Virginia hurries back to the window to watch him escort his superior to the house where the region's commander is staying.

They soon disappear and, sure enough, in the slowly moving tide of refugees, there's a sprinkling of soldiers. Filthy, shell-shocked, disoriented men are mixed throughout the throngs, moving away from the action.

"No," she whispers.

Where are they going? If they aren't fighting the enemy, what can this mean?

Virginia thinks of Philippe's grandmother at the family estate in Pleurtuit, near Saint-Malo. His mother, in Paris. Their own Paris apartment, and the country house they've just had built, thirty miles north of the capital. They call their little love nest Les Baumées—balm, respite, sanctuary from the world—their happily ever after. Will Les Baumées be safe from the Nazis? Will any of them?

Of all times to get pregnant, she thinks.

She runs to the bathroom and gets sick.

LIGHTING A CIGARETTE, Virginia forces a smile, trying hard to pay attention to Philippe's words.

He updates her on news of the soldiers woven into the tapestry of refugees. The villagers have been giving them side glances and cold shoulders all day, but Philippe assures her the men are not deserters—not exactly. They got lost in the chaos of retreat. Their commanders abandoned them, and they're trying to find units to join. Philippe has a good hold on his men here and will be able to assimilate the new arrivals. Virginia is relieved to hear it, but her mind is not entirely on war.

"Honeybee," Philippe says, placing his large hand over her small one, where her fingers drum the table. "Are you all right? You haven't touched a morsel."

They celebrate Philippe's birthday at Au Coq de Bruyère, a charming restaurant with outdoor seating at the town's hotel. The stone walls are thick with climbing vines, and their plates are full of roasted chicken, lemon-rosemary potatoes, and asparagus, on which they've splurged knowing the days of such eating are likely coming to a close.

The light of sunset saturates the village in lavender, but the beauty and serenity of the scene remain apart from Virginia. She feels as if she's a black-and-white image on a painted canvas. Philippe stares at her a moment longer. Then he sets his brown eyes as stern as she's ever seen them and throws his napkin on the table.

"That's it," he says. "As your husband, I order you to return to Florida."

Virginia can't help but giggle. It's the first time she's done so in days, and it releases untold tons of pressure from her chest. He jerks back as if she's slapped him.

"I've allowed this American *free will* of yours to run rampant for too long," he continues.

Her giggle has turned into a laugh.

"In France, women obey their husbands," he says.

Amid her amusement, he throws up his hands and then crosses his arms over his chest, but a grin soon breaks the faux stone veneer he tried to put on his face. Virginia stubs out her cigarette and lays her hand over Philippe's arm.

"That was adorable," she says.

"I tried." He shrugs.

"It was a good effort. But it isn't war that's made a bundle of nerves of me."

"Then what is it? For the first time, there's something between us I cannot access."

She won't keep the secret from Philippe any longer. Besides, maybe the news will inspire him with even more will to come back to her, if one can will such things in war. A lump forms in her throat, preventing her from speaking the words, so she takes his hand and lowers it to her belly. It takes him only a moment to understand. He pushes back from the table and lifts her into his arms.

VIRGINIA REGRETS TELLING Philippe about her suspected condition. He was already worried about their impending separation; now he's in agony.

Yesterday he saw Virginia picking flowers in the garden and begged her to lie down. Then he came upon Virginia polishing Madame's silver and asked her to sit while attending to chores. Virginia doesn't feel at all tired, and she hasn't gotten sick since the day the general arrived to warn Philippe. If anything, she feels energized. She has new purpose—something to protect and fight for. It's not as if she's asked to drive ambulances like the women in uniform heading toward the front. Now she's worried Philippe's mind will be too much on her and the baby to attend to his duties.

In the evening, Virginia, Philippe, and Madame eat their ham dinner, but the endless footfalls and squeaky wagon wheels along the road silence their conversation. Virginia chews each bite slowly, savoring the salty meat for which she has been ravenous all day. Philippe keeps looking between his plate and the window. Madame moves her food around without eating it. Virginia places another bite in her mouth, thinking, *This is for the baby*, but no matter how much she chews, it's difficult to swallow. She has to force the food down with coffee.

Seeing the others have stopped eating, Virginia meets Madame's gaze, then Philippe's. Without a word, they stand and carry their unfinished plates to the kitchen. Philippe hauls the kitchen table outside, while Madame and Virginia return the ham and carrots from their individual plates back to the large serving dish. They fill as many cups as they can with small servings of coffee and carry out the provisions.

A swarm gathers. Philippe makes order, setting up a queue, while Virginia distributes ham and carrots to the refugees. All she can see are many hands—young and old, elegant and rough, masculine and feminine—grasping for meat and vegetables, lifting morsels to mouths. They swallow so quickly the taste might not even touch their tongues. An old man refuses food but is grateful for coffee. A young mother takes a piece of ham but, as she walks away, pulls it apart to give her children another serving. An old woman arrives for the last piece, but insists Virginia tear the small serving in half again so the person behind her might have a little. Virginia marvels that they didn't have much to distribute but, like the multiplication of loaves and fishes, it fed more than it should.

Maybe one only has to be willing to reach out with empty hands for God to fill them, she thinks.

Virginia and Madame return to the house to wash dishes while Philippe stays on the side of the road, stopping those lucky enough to still have cars with fuel, reminding them to dim their lights so they don't make a target of the refugee road. When the women finish and Madame retires, Virginia joins Philippe. She feels strangely alert, as if she's been jerked awake from a long sleep. The night air is thick with the smell of goat droppings and the last liters of petrol burning in the cars that will have to be abandoned once they run dry. On the shiny blue hood of their Fiat—the dear little car they call the "blue baby"— Virginia sees a wink of moonlight.

"I'm fetching Mum tomorrow," Virginia says.

"No," says Philippe. "I don't have a good feeling."

They've been around and around about Virginia taking a day-trip to Paris to collect some of their belongings from the apartment, and Philippe's mother from hers, but they can't agree on when. Paris is only about forty kilometers from Le Perray. Getting there will be a snap. Moving with traffic on the way back could take a while, but it must be done.

"Now's the time," says Virginia.

"The Germans are advancing too quickly."

"Then I should have gone today."

Philippe rubs his eyes. Virginia leads him by the hand into the house. She draws him a bath, helping her exhausted husband remove his uniform and insisting he get in the tub. She pours warm water over his head and uses a cloth and fine French soap to wash his back and arms.

"I should be doing this for you," Philippe says.

"Do it for me on my birthday," Virginia says. She'll be thirty in two days.

As she continues to wash and massage Philippe, he allows himself to relax. She places a towel under his neck and enjoys the smile she gets when her arms reach deep under the suds.

How long will we have power and hot running water? Virginia wonders. *Ham, and coffee, and cigarettes? How long will we have each other?*

She soon feels as tired as Philippe looks.

After Virginia takes Philippe to bed, she returns to the bathroom to shower, a thoroughly modern luxury. She tries to enjoy each experience in ordinary living—if one can call this ordinary—as if it will be her last for a long time. Though she knows she should turn her attention to those worse off than she, Virginia can't help but resent the Nazis for disrupting her life.

She and Philippe have had a charmed three years dancing between abodes, enjoying France and all it has to offer. Their friend circles are being torn apart as the men are sent away to fight. Her dear mother-in-law—widowed just last year—is still trying to navigate life without her beloved, and now has the stress of war. They've spent every summer Virginia has lived in France at the family estate on the Brittany coast. Will they be able to get there this year? And if so, how can Virginia enjoy the water, the sun, the long walks, and the game nights knowing Philippe is fighting?

And the baby—will he or she even get to grow up with a papa?

Her worry turns to despair. Virginia leans her forehead against the tile, unable to move until the hot water runs cold.

3

WESSEX COAST, ENGLAND

———— **VIOLETTE** ————

VIOLETTE SURFACES, GASPING, from the icy waters of the Solent, churning under Chilling Cliff.

One of the boys from the Marines who man the searchlight battery dared one of the girls from the Land Army to race to the buoy. Violette beat him on the way out and knows she will on the way back, so instead of racing, she decides to have a little fun. Holding her breath as long as possible, she swims along the shore. About thirty yards from where the girls fret about Violette's well-being, she slips from the water, allowing the night to cloak her in its shadows. She scales the cliff, creeping to the lookout where the Marines are supposed to be on duty. Once there, she crouches down, lowers her voice, and shouts at them.

"Where are the boys who are supposed to be in this tower? I'll have you flogged!"

A rush of apologies ensues as the three Marines scurry toward the stairs and up the cliff. When they appear at the door and catch sight of Violette hiding—grinning and shivering in her two-piece bathing suit—their mouths open. Amid the laughter and cursing, one of the larger boys pushes forward, throws Violette over his shoulder, and carries her back to the beach. Once he reaches the tide, he heaves Violette into the water as far as he can throw her. She resurfaces to the shrieks of delight of her two girlfriends, who congratulate her for outsmarting the boys.

The girls hold towels around Violette while she slips off her bathing suit and dresses, finishing by tying the bottom of her buttoned shirt at the waist of her shorts. She wrings out her shiny black hair, and combs it.

The boys have hauled a portable gramophone to the beach. They put on American jazz records, and pair off dancing with the girls as best they can over the large, slippery pebbles.

It's been a strange, rainless, restless spring. Violette's mother is beside herself with gratitude for Tante's smarts and Violette's bravery getting herself and Dickie safely home, but Violette's father is angry they waited so long. He forbids Violette to return to France, and Violette doesn't know how she could anyway, seeing as the fighting has intensified, and every day they wonder when the Germans will try to invade Britain. Knowing the storm fronts of her and her father's personalities wouldn't fare well in the same atmosphere, and desperate to make a difference, Violette signed up for the Land Army.

"Vi," says her dance partner.

She looks at him but can't remember his name. They're all Johnnies or Willies or Charlies.

"The boys at the pub say you helped smuggle a pilot out of France," he says. "Is it true?"

"*Oui,*" she says, knowing they love when she speaks French. "A Belgian. He was dirty and starving. I practically had to carry him to safety. And all while Nazis were advancing."

Or something like that, she thinks.

"I bet he fell in love with you," the boy says.

She's sure his ears would be pink if she could see them.

"He did," she says. "Drew me a heart in the dirt and promised to find me after the war."

"Well, for my sake, I hope he don't."

She grins at him and pulls him closer while they dance to "Moonlight Serenade." Violette gazes over his shoulder toward distant shores.

As the waves crash and the wind blows her hair dry, a darkness settles over her. She thinks the laughter of the young people around her should lift her spirits, but she has the unsettling feeling that she's surrounded by ghosts. Their voices seem very far away and from another time, and they appear as but shadows and memories of those lost in the war.

"You all right, Vi?" the boy asks. "You stopped dancing."

She pulls back and looks at his large brown eyes, his smooth skin, and downy, shaved hair. He's almost eighteen, when he'll become a real soldier, which she knows she'd be better suited to than this fawn. She has an urge to kiss him, to give him a memory to treasure, because she's suddenly certain he won't survive the war. She presses her lips into his clumsy kiss, and when they separate, he beams like a searchlight.

"Time to go," says Violette.

In spite of the boys' protests, the girls obey Violette, grabbing their bags, blowing kisses, and giggling off toward the path that leads to camp.

The June air is sweet from the endless strawberry fields, glowing blue in the enchanted night. Violette thinks back to how strange and disconnected she'd also felt with the girls, earlier that day. Picking strawberries is not what she had in mind to help the war effort. It's in the fields that sprawl in endless quilts of overripe produce, bees stinging her, sun beating on her hat, fingers sinking into bruises in the seedy, red pulp where she's stopped with disgust a thousand times a day. In her mind, she keeps seeing the child mowed down by the Luftwaffe, staring from death like her glassy-eyed doll, and it fills Violette with rage.

The girls around her haven't seen war up close. They're maddeningly cheerful, singing songs and saying patriotic things. They're good girls, and in the saccharine glow of their goodness, Violette senses that she's what they might consider a bad girl. This gives her a thrill, but it leaves no lasting happiness. Violette doesn't want to pick fruit; she wants to shoot guns. She wants to aim them at the Nazis and watch the red pulp splatter from their thick skulls, tallying boches instead of berries.

On their way back to camp, the girls have reached a stretch of path that leads through the woods. Violette's two companions walk faster—warnings from their warden about the "gypsies" who live there echoing in their heads—but Violette's legs feel leaden.

"Hurry," the girls whisper.

They know from their short acquaintance with Violette that she does only what she wants to do. Their forms grow smaller as they pull away from her. Violette can still see them about fifty feet ahead. She tracks them as she would her little brothers, as she would if she were hunting grouse with her father, always keeping her targets in sight.

The woods normally teem with peepers and creeping things, but Violette notices it's grown deadly quiet. The hair on her neck rises and she scans the undergrowth, allowing her eyes to adjust to the darkness. In a moment she detects motion, a shadow of several forms, moving irregularly, approaching the path. She quickens her pace as the shadow separates into three distinct outlines stumbling toward her friends.

Violette shoots forward, reaching the girls as a man wraps his arm around one of them. Her friend struggles while the other shrieks. The remaining men hang back, taking turns swilling from a bottle. Violette is relieved to see it. Drunk men will be easier to fight than sober men.

"Let her go," Violette says, deepening her voice. She puts her hand to the comb in her pocket, acting as if it's a weapon. "Now, if you know what's good for you."

The man looks at her a long moment before removing his hand.

"S'just looking for a friend to share a drink."

"Looks like you've had enough of that," she says.

The girls watch with wide eyes, drawing together.

The wind picks up, allowing the moonlight through the overstory in shafts. The men shrink from the light. Violette moves toward it, glaring at them, making herself as fearsome as she's able.

"Get on your way," she says. "Now."

One of the men still hanging back calls the one in the front and he obeys, receding into the shadows. Violette tells the girls to start walking, and follows soon after, keeping an eye on the road behind them all the way. Violette releases her breath once they're out of the woods. The girls take off running for camp, but Violette continues to walk, even when a rumbling begins. Upon her return, she's greeted by the frantic, angry warden.

"Where have you been?" she says. "Report to shelter!"

There's a flurry of activity surrounding Violette, but she feels as if she's still apart from it, in a slow-motion film. Even the scream of the air raid siren is muted and slow to her ears. The girls urge Violette to hurry, but she can't. A cocktail of fatigue, apathy, and bewilderment roots her.

While they run to the shelters, Violette walks to the tent and curls up on her cot. Though she's aware of a distant explosion and the earth trembling under her, sleep overcomes her. She's soon shaken awake, startled by a masked face pleading with her to put on her gas mask. Violette smells burning oil and surmises the nearby refinery must have been hit, but she still feels paralyzed. She couldn't move if she wanted to. She hears the woman mutter, "Good riddance," as she leaves.

While Violette falls back asleep, she wonders in a curious, detached sort of way if she'll live to see the morning.

4

PARIS

—— **VIRGINIA** ——

WHEN THE BOMBING starts, Virginia and Mum are eating lunch at Chez Bosc on place Vendôme. They stare at each other, forks of sautéed eggplant poised at open mouths, their eyes wide.

"Was that . . . ?" Mum asks.

"I think so," Virginia says.

Mum places her fork on her plate and stands in unison with the panicked diners around them. The owner, Madame Bosc, gestures for everyone to sit.

"Please," Madame says, with sangfroid. "We mustn't allow them to upset our lives. Carry on."

Virginia doesn't know if this is wise during actual air raids, but her hunger urges her to obey. She can't be certain if it's because of the baby or because rationing and guilt prevent her from eating everything she wants, but her appetite is monstrous. Each day it grows, taking up more space in her head, dominating her thoughts. There's a constant pang in her belly that wants to be filled.

Mum sits and resumes her dainty bites, though more hurried than before. Virginia is embarrassed by how quickly her food disappears, but she can't help it. When she finishes, she motions for the waiter and settles the bill. As the noise of airplanes increases, Mum stands, picks up her pocketbook, and starts for the door. Seeing Mum left a bite on her plate, Virginia stabs it with a fork and shoves it in her mouth. Her eyes catch the waiter's, and he averts his gaze. Virginia's face burns on her way out of the restaurant.

Outside, the blue baby is loaded down with their belongings.

"Careful, Mum," Virginia says, helping her mother-in-law into the Fiat.

As Virginia closes the passenger door, an explosion shakes the ground under them. Virginia runs around the back of the car, and a wave of heat rolls over her. She opens the driver's side door, puts the key in the ignition, and throws the Fiat in gear.

As she navigates the streets of Paris, it's as if she's watching a moving picture on an enormous screen but, unlike her dinner with Philippe, this time the world is in black and white and she's in color. The air is thick with smoke, and Luftwaffe bombers roar over them. With each flyover, her heart races faster.

I've got my baby inside me and Philippe's mother next to me, she thinks. *I'll be damned if I don't get us all safely back to him.*

Glad for the three years she's called Paris home, Virginia knows the side streets and alleyways, and she drives as quickly as she's able away from the heart of the city she loves. There isn't much traffic on the way out of town, and there are no pedestrians; all have disappeared into the metro stations and basements, bunkers and catacombs.

Virginia says a prayer as she passes the American Church, where she first met Philippe at the dance that would change her life. By the time the Fiat breaks free of the shadows of the buildings and emerges into the open air, Virginia's knuckles ache from holding the steering wheel, and she's soaked through with sweat. Once she reaches a turn-off where she feels safe to stop, Virginia puts the car in park and she and Mum climb out. Great plumes of smoke rise from the capital. Whole facades are ripped off buildings, lampposts are blown from their pedestals, and craters now gape from where, just moments ago, there were gardens and walkways.

Mum covers her face, and Virginia wraps her in an embrace. But they don't linger. Once Mum is calm, they return to the car and, as Virginia races on, they pass the bombed Citroën plant and Versailles, which is mercifully untouched.

A makeshift village of refugees soon appears. Virginia weaves the car through a maze of wandering, half-starved animals, noting the tents made from bedsheets along the forest edge. Her gaze soon finds a woman, sitting alone, staring into space while an infant screams at her exposed, shriveled breast. Virginia pushes the accelerator and tries to clear her head of the image, driving as fast as she's able back to Philippe.

THROUGH EYES BLURRED with tears, Virginia stares at the blood in the commode. She holds her stomach and winces through another lightning bolt of pain, followed by a release. As the cramps subside, guilt rises.

This is my fault, she thinks. *I never should have lamented the timing of the baby, and I shouldn't have made the trip yesterday.*

Philippe slipped away from his unit's village headquarters earlier that morning to tell Virginia he and his men are being called to the front. He had to hurry back to prepare, and almost as soon as he left, a terrible pain started in Virginia's lower back, reached around to her abdomen, and began its relentless cramping. She barely made it to the toilet before the miscarriage started.

Thank goodness Mum is in the kitchen helping Madame prepare lunch. Virginia can't bear for Mum to hear what she suffers, and the thought of telling Philippe when he returns fills Virginia with despair.

What if we're never able to have a baby? she thinks.

A fresh wave of cramping keeps her in place for a few moments more. Though it makes her sick to do so, once Virginia thinks she's through the worst of it, she pulls the handle on the toilet and watches as the mess is replaced with clean water. At least this house has a flushing toilet. The last village place where they were billeted did not.

With shaking hands, she cleans herself up, arranges the sanitary napkins she was hoping not to have to use for a long while, and stands to look in the mirror. Dark circles hang under her large green eyes, and her auburn hair is limp from sweat. She washes her face, rolls and pins back her hair, and takes time with her makeup. It's the last day she'll have with Philippe, and she wants him to remember her looking her best.

VIRGINIA PULLS PHILIPPE into the walled garden, where she can pretend, for one last moment, that her husband isn't going to war, and she's not about to embark upon a dangerous journey, and she didn't just lose their baby. Nature conspires with Virginia's need for solitude and sweetness, perfuming the air with roses. They walk, holding each other's hands, until they're cocooned in a hedgerow with fat, white, lemon-scented roses all along its base. It smells woodsy and clean, and Virginia inhales, trying to press the good parts of the moment in her memory.

Philippe takes out his pocketknife and cuts a rose from its stem, stripping it of thorns and placing it behind her ear.

"I hoped to have something more beautiful for you on your thirtieth birthday," he says.

"I can't think of anything I'd want more," she says.

He sits on a wrought iron bench and pulls Virginia into his lap. She rests her head on his chest and allows him to cradle her, running her fingers along his palm, tracing where the lines meet at the bottom. She says the ugly words.

"You're sure?" he asks.

Virginia nods. She's unable to hold back her tears any longer.

"It's my fault," she says. "You were right. I should've gone another day."

"No," he says. "Don't say that."

"The strain was too much."

"No. It's God's plan," he says. "Who wants a baby to be born in a world like this? Better we wait until after we defeat the Germans, *oui*?"

Her relief at his reaction is enormous. If only she could siphon his optimism. Philippe holds her tight until she's spent. Then he lifts up her chin to look at him.

"We'll be reunited," he says, running his thumb along her lips. "We'll have a baby one day."

He leans in and coaxes a kiss, gentle at first, then building in passion. It's agonizing when they have to separate, but the clock is ticking. Before Philippe departs, he wipes Virginia's tears and takes her face in his hands.

"Courage," he says. "Take care of yourself and the others, and I will come back to you."

Virginia gazes into his eyes, desperate to believe him and to reassure him. But she has no feeling left in her save the cramping in her stomach.

THE JOURNEY TO the coast that should take four hours lasts twenty-seven.

When news of the bombing of Paris reaches the local population, it's as if all come out of hiding. Virginia and Mum crawl by caravan in two lanes, inching so slowly Virginia never gets the car out of second gear. With Nazi fliers roaring overhead, they feel as if they're trapped in a beehive. They've only just left Chartres when it's bombed. As they pass the weary on foot, Virginia feels guilty she can't offer the refugees a ride, but what can she do? There isn't a centimeter of space in the car.

With nowhere to change her pad, Virginia has to place a towel under her to absorb the leaking blood. She doesn't tell her mother-in-law she's having a miscarriage, leaving Mum to think the curse is especially bad. The cramping continues in waves, some so sharp they take Virginia's breath away, but when she sees the exhausted women with babies strapped to them, and tired, dirty, crying children trailing them, she realizes the loss of her little one may have been a severe mercy.

When night arrives, Virginia thinks she'll go mad from sitting in the car. She pulls off down a lane and raises her eyes to heaven in thanks for finding a swiftly running stream. She wades in to let the water rush over her, rinsing her body. Virginia has never experienced filth like this. She scrubs her skirt, underclothes, and towel, and pulls on fresh clothes and a new pad. It's heaven to be clean, if only for a few hours. The women try to sleep in the moss outside the car, but rain drives them back into the dreaded prison. Mum soon dozes, but Virginia can't grab an ounce of rest. The moment the first light appears at dawn, she resumes the drive.

As the barricades and checkpoints force two lanes to one, the volume of traffic multiplies. Virginia's anxiety rises. The needle approaches empty, and each station they pass has CLOSED signs hanging, showing the pumps have run out of fuel. Virginia and Mum still have a long way to go, and the lines at the stations are impossible. When Virginia knows she can't go much farther, she pulls into one of the endless queues. While they wait, she continually turns the Fiat on and off so she doesn't waste fuel idling. It takes hours for them to get to the pump, and with one car ahead of them, they see the driver call the attendant and motion to the hose. The station owner shakes his head and disappears inside for a short while before returning with a crudely written sign.

FERMÉ.

"No," says Virginia.

Exhaustion permeates every cell in her body. If she didn't have Mum next to her, Virginia thinks she might pull off the road, curl up on the seat, and give up.

Courage.

Virginia takes a deep breath and turns the wheel, setting off for the next station.

"How will we make it?" asks Mum, wringing her hands.

"Pray," says Virginia.

They manage to cover another twenty kilometers before a petrol station appears in the distance. The car sputters and, as they take their place at the end of the line, the blue baby dies. Virginia puts her forehead on the steering wheel. In seconds, a honk startles her, and she sees the line crawling away from them.

"Mum, can you take the wheel?" Virginia asks.

Mum nods, her face a mask of anxiety.

Virginia climbs out of the car, moving the soiled towel to the back seat so Mum doesn't have to sit on it. Virginia is thankful her dress is midnight blue so no blood is easily visible. Once she helps Mum into the driver's seat and instructs her to put the car in neutral, Virginia walks around the back of it. She looks up to the sky, takes a deep breath, closes her eyes, and pushes.

It takes all of her diminished strength, but the car begins to move. There's a slight incline, so this is harder than she thought it would be. She's dizzy from all the blood loss, but there's no other way. Mum couldn't manage this. Virginia pushes harder, imagining Philippe at her side, and suddenly, the pushing gets easier. She opens her eyes and is surprised to see a woman of about forty years on her left. Then, on her right, a teenaged girl joins them. Through their obvious fatigue, they smile at her, and tears spring to Virginia's eyes. The women help her all the long way to the pump and, thankfully, she's able to fill the tank. Before she drives away, she presses two cans each of vegetables Madame had packed for Virginia into the women's hands.

The last leg of the journey is endless, and when they make the final turn leading them to the family château, the women cry out with joy. They beep the horn and practically leap from the car before it's fully stopped. Philippe's grandmother and his cousin Michel's wife, Nicole, run out to meet them. Azeline, the housekeeper, follows. The women laugh and cry and embrace one another.

Azeline takes Virginia's face in her rough, wrinkled hands.

"You're peaked!" Azeline says. "You must have soup. And bread. Come."

"I'll put it back on the stove," says Nicole, rushing ahead of them. "We just finished dinner. It won't take long to heat."

Grandmère and Mum walk arm in arm into the house, and the

women settle around the table while Mum tells them how Virginia got
them safely out of Paris and then to the coast, with bombs hot on their
tails. Azeline fetches bowls and plates. She even spoons the first bite
of onion soup into Virginia's mouth. Virginia closes her eyes, savoring
the hearty sweetness of the broth, and greedily consumes the rest.

"You don't look well," says Nicole.

Virginia doesn't know what to say. Her exhaustion makes it so she
can barely form words.

"A bath," says Azeline. "Then bed."

While Azeline draws the bath, Nicole fetches the women's suitcases.

Numb, all Virginia can do is follow Azeline's orders, but Virginia
doesn't allow Azeline to bathe her. Virginia is ashamed of how filthy
she is.

The water is so hot it stings, but she's grateful for it all the same. It
turns murky from her mess, and once she has washed, she drains the
tub and turns the water back on once more to rinse her skin and the
porcelain. The cold is a shock, but she endures it.

Azeline tucks her into bed like a child but, as bone weary as Virginia is, she can't sleep. She feels a need to breathe the fresh air and
look up at the same moon she knows Philippe can see from wherever
he is.

In her nightgown, Virginia crosses the back lawn, thinking she must
look like the ghost of a corsair's wife from centuries past. She walks to
the shore and has to sit on the stairs leading down to the beach to allow
the dizzy spell to pass. Listening to the clanging of the sailboat halyards,
gazing up at the quarter moon, she inhales great gasps of salty wind and
thinks of Florida.

Should I go home? she thinks. *Back to Mother and Daddy?*

No one here would fault Virginia. Philippe would be relieved. If
her mother knew what Virginia had just gone through, Mother would
be devastated she wasn't there to care for Virginia. But the thought of
leaving Philippe makes Virginia feel sicker than the miscarriage has.

No, she could not live that far away from Philippe. Even if he can't be with her.

Virginia returns her attention to the Rance. She's hypnotized by the strange, terrible, surreal beauty of the searchlight hunting for German bombers, reflected in its waters.

5

LONDON

~⌇~

———— **VIOLETTE** ————

THE QUARTER MOON is shrouded in mist, and Violette thinks the strains of her mother's voice coming through the open window, singing "La Marseillaise" between bouts of tears, are the saddest sounds Violette has ever heard.

The papers scream that France has surrendered to Germany. The Germans will occupy a zone in the north, while the south will remain unoccupied, where the new French State government will operate out of the spa town of Vichy. To humiliate them, Hitler made the French commander sign the documents agreeing to pay for the German occupying army and the near dissolution of the French military, among other punishments, in the same railway car where the Germans had surrendered in the Great War.

While Violette paces along the fence, her father sits smoking at the wobbly table behind her in the claustrophobic backyard of their terraced house. The Bushells live in a working-class neighborhood in northwest London. The blackout has hit their neighborhood, unused to quiet and dark, hard. Unable to gather as freely at pubs and cinemas after hours, they feel like trapped animals. Thank goodness they have the late, lingering light of summer to keep them from going completely bats. Violette shudders to think how they'll all cope if this war lasts until winter.

The tiny backyard is the only place Violette can escape the darkness in the house, yet here her father is, breathing down her neck. Since leaving the so-called Land Army, Violette has been anxious to find her place in the war and in the world. There's a profound restlessness in her that Violette knows her old job at the perfume counter of Le Bon Marché won't satisfy. With the looming threat of attack on London, Maman sent Violette's younger brothers, Dickie and Noel, to their country relatives. Violette's nineteen-year-old brother, Roy, is in the army, and her sixteen-year-old brother, John, has joined the engineers. So, she's left with her parents. Atrophying.

"How could France just roll over and cave to the boches?" Violette says.

The slur for Nazis has become the norm in their speech. *Boche* is for *caboche*: blockheaded, stupid thug.

"Funny how the young, who've never fought," says Papa, "have so many opinions about the leaders who try to keep another generation from walking through hell."

"How can you say that? You don't believe it."

"No, but it's not black and white."

"It is. We're handing our country to the Nazis without even trying."

"France isn't my country."

"It's Maman's. And it's mine."

"Sorry, Vi. Much as you'd like to think otherwise, you're me—Britain—through and through."

Violette groans. Papa met Maman while driving ambulances in France, in the Great War, and it's difficult for Violette to imagine her darling, regal mother falling for her cheeky, crass father. He is terribly handsome—a thick crop of dark hair, light eyes, tall, and substantial—and is everyone's favorite at the pub, but he takes up an enormous amount of space. Maman draws out the best in him, but he behaves only for her.

Violette sees the flash of Papa's teeth through his grin. She hates when he laughs at her.

"You're just pressing my bruises," Violette says. "I know you think the Germans are monsters."

"I hate to tell you, they're not monsters," he says.

"What're you saying?"

He sighs and stubs out his cigarette. Violette is startled to see there's no more twinkle in his eye, no more joke on his lips.

"The most frightening thing about the Germans is they're not beasts," he says. "They're plain men with plain interests. The worst thing I've learned is that once men deem others less than them, they're capable of committing unimaginable horrors just before taking the tube home, kissing their wives, pissin' in their toilets, and picking their teeth with toothpicks."

At that, he stands, scraping his chair over the stones, leaving Violette brooding in the dark.

"'BASTILLE DAY PARADE.'" Violette reads the newspaper headline through clenched teeth. "In London!"

"The first time in years we haven't been able to celebrate at home," says Maman. "At least Marguerite is all right."

Maman holds the letter Tante managed to smuggle to the family. Tante's words are brief, but she gives assurance she's alive. At least, she was when the letter was sent.

"'The morning after the swastika was hung over the town square,'" Maman reads, "'a tricolor appeared. Someone had not only removed and defecated on the Nazi flag—had not only hung France's flag—but then wrapped the pole in barbed wire.'"

Understanding Tante's glee between the lines, they snort with laughter.

"I wouldn't be surprised if Marguerite did the deed," says Papa.

"What's that say on the back?" asks Violette.

There's a PS written in pencil. The rest of the letter was written in ink. Maman turns over the paper and reads aloud. "'Tell my niece, the shed has been full since she left. There will be plenty of gardening to do when she returns.'"

Violette's heartbeat quickens while Maman looks at her with a question in her eyes.

So, other pilots have heard about the shed, thinks Violette. *And Tante is helping them.*

It feels like a tiny victory and makes Violette even more desperate to get back to France.

"Gardening. Ha!" Papa says. "Vi's never picked up a rake in her life."

"I have all sorts of talents you don't know about," Violette says.

Maman puts the letter on the table and turns back to her daughter.

"Vi, will you go to the parade at the Cenotaph?" she says. "Find a French soldier missing home and invite him to dinner. They need French solidarity."

"You'll send your daughter to collect a strange Frenchman to bring home?" says Papa. "What if he's a spy?"

"Charlie," Maman says.

"Or what if someone tries to scoop her up?" Papa continues. "There's practically a line out the judge's door for quick war weddings. No one wants to die a virgin."

"Charlie!" Maman says.

"Sorry." He gives Maman a sheepish shrug.

"You don't have to worry," says Violette. "I'm not marrying until I'm at least twenty-five."

Violette sees all the work and fretting Maman does to care for the family. She's a gifted seamstress—an artist with a needle and thread—but she uses up all her time and talent on practical sewing and repairs. Papa has jumped from job to job, driving taxis and vans and repairing automobiles, never able to hold steady for any length of time. It's Maman's income that keeps the family going, and she never complains. Violette is in no hurry for that kind of life, and she's definitely not one to keep quiet.

Though Violette doesn't want to walk among hot parade crowds to bring a stranger home, it's preferable to remaining in the small house and being annoyed by Papa. She steps into her heels, touches up her lipstick, and spritzes herself with perfume. On her way out, she looks at the letter on the table, making a mental note to erase the PS when she returns. Tante surely wrote it in pencil for a reason, and that reason must be to make it disappear.

Violette makes sure to slam the door good and hard on her way out on Papa's grumbling about what kind of man she's trying to attract. It takes many blocks for her shoulders to relax, and the parade concludes as she arrives.

Columns of exiled French soldiers march amid great fanfare and music, and she finds her spirits lift in spite of herself. As the fog of her foul mood dissipates, Violette spots a bench and sits to observe. She wants to find someone with polish to appeal to Maman, humor—to take Papa for what he is—and, for herself, she'd like one easy on the eyes. In spite of their tidy uniforms, most of the French soldiers are haggard and warworn. While it's good to have British support, no Frenchman wants to spend Bastille Day in England. Violette admires those men who still stand alert, courageous, and hopeful. That's the kind who'll win the war. But these are few and far between, and if Violette finds them, they don't meet her other requirements.

"Mademoiselle."

She turns to see a French soldier has approached from the direction she wasn't looking. He's dark, stocky, impeccably groomed, and though he looks tired, his posture is confident.

"May I have the time?" he says in poor English.

Under his sleeve peeks the band of a watch. Violette reaches for his arm, slides up his uniform, and replies in French, "Half past two."

His laugh is deep and sexy. It shatters the air around them and touches her skin in a thousand places.

6

PLEURTUIT, FRANCE

─── VIRGINIA ───

CHÂTEAU CANCAVAL. SEAT of Philippe's family for three centuries. Place of Virginia's heart.

Arriving at Cancaval has torn a seam in time for Virginia. It wasn't so long ago she first set foot on its enchanting grounds. It wasn't so long ago that the dance at the American Church in Paris changed her life.

It was the summer of 1936. Virginia had just turned twenty-six and was a schoolteacher at the Country Day School, the private primary school her mother ran out of their family home in Florida. An education conference in England gave Virginia her first opportunity to travel abroad, and she took it. She even booked a side trip to France, a lifelong dream of hers. She'd studied the language in school and had a decent grasp of it. Her mother sent her with admonitions about pickpockets and cautions about the reputation of Frenchmen, but Virginia laughed her off while promising not to bring one home.

"A pickpocket or a Frenchman?" her mother had asked.

"Either."

Love hadn't entered Virginia's mind. She'd always had a life plan: graduate from high school, pursue higher education, marry, and have children. Everything had proceeded accordingly until the marriage part. Boyfriend after boyfriend passed and things never worked out for one reason or another. So now her plans involved teaching and travel, and while stimulated, at the end of each day, she felt a certain emptiness without someone to share her life.

In Paris, the ballroom at the American Church had a stage where a band played Gershwin, a pine-paneled floor for dancing, and a wall of graceful, Gothic, pointed-arch windows that let in the evening light. A small group of educators had made the side trip, and their leader had gone to search for the man who would serve as their guide—Monsieur d'Albert-Lake—a French travel agent with a steamer company, who was fluent in both languages and whose English mother attended the church. While the song "The Man I Love" began, Virginia had wandered away from her group and stood at the windows, gazing out, trying to comprehend that she was actually in Paris and it was every bit as magical as she'd hoped it would be, when someone cleared his throat.

She'd turned, lifted her gaze to meet the warm brown eyes of the tall, handsome man before her, and thought, *There you are.*

Clear as day, the thought came from both inside and outside of her. Philippe later told her he'd thought the exact same thing at the same moment.

Philippe d'Albert-Lake's guided large-group tours around Paris and Versailles quickly became small-group tours of Giverny and the villages special to locals. Finally, Philippe invited Virginia alone to his family's estate on the Brittany coast, and she'd fallen in love with all of them, and on a sunset sailboat ride on the Rance, Philippe kissed her for the first time.

Virginia now stands at the Rance, arms wrapped around herself, lost in the thought of Philippe's lips on hers. As the memory evaporates, she feels empty and aches as she did when she'd had to leave Philippe to return to Florida.

The rest of that summer and fall of '36, Philippe's letters came with such frequency, she was forced to tell her parents about the relationship sooner than she'd planned. Her mother had thrown her hands to the sky.

"I told you about Frenchmen and their terrible reputations!"

When Virginia admitted she and Philippe planned to marry, Mother took to bed for an entire week in protest. But Philippe crossed the ocean for Virginia, and he so thoroughly charmed her parents, her brother and sister, and every person of her acquaintance, that he single-handedly made Francophiles of half the state of Florida. He'd dazzled Virginia with a stunning, antique, wide-banded, platinum and diamond ring that fit her finger perfectly. It came from Monsieur Fruchter, a jeweler on the rue de Sèvres, who claimed it may have been the actual jewel worn by courtesan Valtesse de la Bigne, in the painting by Henri Gervex. In May of 1937, Virginia and Philippe married at the First Presbyterian Church of St. Petersburg, honeymooned in New York, and set off for France immediately thereafter. Virginia had never looked back.

From where she now stands along the river walk, Virginia stares up the long green lawn to Cancaval. Just across from Saint-Malo, Cancaval is a three-story beauty constructed of ecru plaster, bordered in irregular, gray stone. The house is considered a *malouinière*, a holiday home of Saint-Malo, built by French corsairs to watch for enemy ships to plunder. Abundant in Cancaval's gardens and grounds are poufs of purple agapanthus and pink hydrangeas, strong magnolia trees, and delicate roses. Curved, columned porches grace the facade, and ivy climbs the walls to the four chimneys that rise at regular intervals along a slate roof, and to a lookout terrace in the rear, where one can watch over the surrounding land and stables all the way to the Château de Montmarin.

Along their beach runs a stone wall topped by a now vacant dovecote, a rectangular structure that once housed pigeons for meat, eggs, and communication, but is now haunted by the ghosts of Philippe's childhood. Philippe and his cousin Michel would hide in it, and skin their knees on its stairs, and play soldiers in the tower until the sun set on their adventures. She'd imagined their child doing the same, but now it's not to be.

Virginia has been trying to cry out the ache left in her empty womb and in the empty tomb of her heart, growing colder each day that passes, especially without her love. Marriage grafted Philippe to her. With him wrenched away, she feels as if she's lost all the limbs from one side of her body. Where she's anxious, he's calm. Where she's lively, he's quiet. She's small; he's large. He's the sun to her moon. Their dance of opposites brings them each in perfect balance. Without the other, they're not complete.

If Virginia could only have a word from Philippe—just a breath on his whereabouts, especially now that France has surrendered—she thinks she could do this. She could press on. But she doesn't even know if he reached the fighting. And her crippling worry makes it so she can barely put one foot in front of the other. She knows Philippe would want her to wear a brave face for his family, to take care of the women in this house of husbandless wives, but that feels impossible.

God, don't let me be a widow, she thinks.

Her feet are bare and wet, the grass brushing the sand from them as she walks up the lawn. A figure bursts from around the side of the house. It's Nicole, gesturing wildly. If it were a year ago, Virginia would think Michel was about to appear behind his wife, chasing Nicole, hoping to catch her to toss her in the water. But they are beaten by the Nazis, so Virginia knows Nicole's gesturing is not joyful, it's frantic.

The thing they have been fearing has come.

Virginia drops her shoes and runs up the lawn.

THE SOUNDS OF motors and the clopping of horse hooves grow louder. Nicole is on her knees, digging with her hands in the dirt like a dog, while Virginia embarks on a fruitless search for a shovel. They collected all the jewels they could find in the house, shoving Mum's, Grandmère's, and their own in the wooden box with the silver.

"Help me!" Nicole says.

Virginia tries to hide her disgust as she gets on her knees and pulls the soil away with her hands, the hole deepening quickly under their joint efforts. Breath coming fast, lock of hair in her face, Virginia can barely see from the sweat putting a stinging film over her eyes. Her arms are sliced with cuts from blades of sea grass they've pushed aside to conceal their treasure. Once they place the box in the bottom of the hole, Virginia starts to push the dirt back over it, but Nicole grabs her arm.

"Your ring," Nicole says.

Virginia looks down at the wide platinum band, the round diamond poised above it, caked in dirt but still glinting.

"No," Virginia says.

"What if they steal it?" asks Nicole.

"I'm not taking it off."

Virginia hasn't done so since Philippe slid it on her finger, and she won't while she has breath in her lungs. Besides, the enemy needs to know they're married. Virginia doesn't know if it will protect them, but at least it can weigh on the Nazis' consciences—if they have consciences—if they do to them what the rumors say about soldiers of the Wehrmacht and pretty young women.

They arrange the sea grass back over where they've dug. When Virginia stands, she has a dizzy spell and has to grasp Nicole's arm for support. Nicole knows about the miscarriage—Virginia needed someone to talk to—and that Virginia is still anemic from all the blood loss. When Virginia confessed her guilt to Nicole over thinking the timing was bad to have a baby, Nicole said, "Virginia, if women's thoughts and worries over the timing of children had any effect, there would be a lot fewer people on this earth."

How true.

"Are you all right?" Nicole asks.

Virginia nods.

The women brush themselves off and hurry to the pump to wash up as best they can. As they dry their hands on their skirts, the clop of horse hooves on Cancaval's gravel drive takes Virginia's breath. She wraps her arm around Nicole's, and creeping around the barn, they look out.

God help us, Virginia thinks. *It's them.*

7

LONDON

—— VIOLETTE ——

"I FOUND A soldier," Violette says, leading her Frenchman into the house.

Violette can hear only the ticking of the grandfather clock and the drip from the leaky faucet in the water closet.

"Maman?" Violette calls. "Papa?"

There's no response.

"They're probably at a neighbor's," she says to her soldier in French. "I'll put on a pot of tea. You can smoke at the table in the backyard."

Violette feels his eyes on her every move. She knows she should be wary of being alone with this clearly enamored stranger, but she's not afraid. In fact, she gives his stare right back, and flashes him her brightest grin. He smiles with relief—like he has walked many, many miles and has finally found a place of rest—and obeys her.

The Frenchman is named Étienne Szabo. He's thirty, though he looks older because he's weathered, quite literally. A Legionnaire, now in the ranks of Brigadier General Charles de Gaulle's Free French Forces, Étienne has just come from the icy, frozen region over the North Sea, where his unit had tried and failed to protect Norway. On their walk to Violette's home, he told her about the merciless mountains, the frostbite, the long nights, the lack of food, but shuddered at the remembrance and stopped speaking of it. The French who've made it to England are forming a new army, and Étienne has training coming up at Aldershot, where Violette's older brother, Roy, is stationed. Étienne is eager to enjoy his short leave, seeing the sights of London.

Violette watches Étienne sit in a chair at the wobbly table and turn his face to the sun. She can hear his deep sigh through the open window, feel the pleasure he gets from the warmth, how it must thaw the ice from his bones.

How kind of London not to rain on his parade, she thinks.

A blackbird lands on the wall and chirps at him. He opens his eyes and watches it sing. After a few moments, he unfastens his top collar buttons and again lifts his chin to the sun, exposing his throat. He sits with his legs open, his dark, rough hands on his knees. Violette gets a sudden image of straddling him, kissing his neck, feeling his hands running up the backs of her legs. She indulges the fantasy until she jumps from the kettle whistling.

"Get ahold of yourself, Vi," she whispers as she hurries through tea preparations.

Before she steps out on the patio, the letter from Tante Marguerite catches Violette's eye. She quickly erases the PS. Then she stops by the mirror, smooths her hair, and checks her lipstick. In spite of the heat Étienne has stirred in Violette, she arranges her face as serenely as possible and goes out to meet him.

VIOLETTE THINKS A cloud has covered the sun, but it's only Papa.

"I can barely see, from the glare of all those medals," says Papa. "Well done, sir."

Étienne stands, shaking Papa's hand and apologizing in advance for his poor English.

"*Enchanté*," Étienne says to Maman, bowing deeply and kissing her hand.

"When I saw the two of you," Maman says in French, "your dark heads leaned toward one another, conspiring, as the butterflies flitted around your heads, I thought you could be an Émile Friant painting."

"*The Lovers*," says Étienne.

"You know it?"

"Of course. Have you seen his work *The Small Boat*?"

"*Oui.*"

Maman takes the seat next to Étienne, and the French talk to the French. After a few moments Violette looks up at her father, expecting a frown, but instead sees a small smile playing at his mouth. Papa joins them at the table, eager to hear Étienne's military exploits through Violette's and Maman's translations.

As they talk of France and their families, the afternoon passes into evening. Étienne grew up in Marseille and entered the military after losing his parents at a young age. He's an orphan, his only family found in the men of his regiments. He has been steadily climbing the ranks for over a decade and is already an *adjudant-chef* at the tender age of thirty. In English, Papa tells Violette how impressed he is with Étienne and how he'll be a major before the war is done. But it's hard for Violette to pay attention to anything but the deep, gentle cadence of Étienne's French and the regular return of his warm gaze to hers.

It's only when Étienne's stomach growls that they realize they need to eat dinner. Étienne buries his face in his hands in embarrassment, but Maman reassures him she's glad his stomach reminded her to feed him since he was far too polite to say it himself. Violette rises to help Maman prepare the salade Niçoise, for which she already boiled the eggs and potatoes. Unable to converse without their translators, Papa and Étienne soon follow.

"We have a French-British balance," says Maman, once they're seated around the dinner table. "Étienne and Vi, me and Charlie."

"We work well together," says Étienne, Violette translating for Papa.

"You need the British now, eh?" says Papa. "A little cold water thrown on that French ego."

"I'm not telling him that," Violette says.

"Come on. He's a good sport."

"Now's not the time to tease," she says. "He still has chapped hands from frostbite. He has friends who died."

Unable to follow the conversation, Étienne continues to smile innocently. Maman hushes Violette and Papa and places a record on the gramophone. The sultry voice of Germaine Sablon fills the room.

Violette can't take her eyes off Étienne. He's seen and lived so much. His confidence and ease in his body are a stark contrast to the silly boys in the Marines and the neighborhood. Though Violette has only just turned nineteen, she feels older than her peers. She thinks perhaps she's been dating boys who are too young for her. Maybe she needs a man.

When the blackout curtains have been pulled, and Étienne has missed the last bus, Maman writes him instructions for taking the tube back to the hall in West Kensington, where he and his men are billeted. After Maman hugs him, Violette is shocked to see tears on Étienne's face.

"I'm sorry," he says. "I'm not used to the sweetness of a family dinner. Today has been an unexpected gift, and one I didn't realize I needed."

Maman and Violette look at each other, placing their hands over their hearts and sighing. When Maman translates Étienne's words, Papa rolls his eyes.

Étienne reaches for Violette's hand and kisses it, his eyes squeezed shut. Papa flinches at the intensity and moves forward to intervene, but Maman holds Papa back. Étienne opens his eyes, kisses Maman on both cheeks, and then—much to their amusement—does the same with Papa. Before leaving, Étienne gives Violette one more look of longing, then disappears into the night.

It takes a great act of will for Violette not to follow.

8

PLEURTUIT

——— VIRGINIA ———

VIRGINIA FLINCHES AS the Nazi officer takes his smooth white hand and turns the clock forward one hour to German time. She feels the hair on her arms rise as he runs his finger over the mantel, inspects his fingertip, and nods at the women to show his approval of the lack of dust.

Virginia stands in a stiff line in the front parlor with Nicole, Mum, Grandmère, and Azeline. Unsure of how to interact with the enemy, Virginia keeps her face neutral, her eyes fixed straight ahead of her. The other women do the same, except for old Azeline. Arms crossed, she stands defiant and snorts at the Nazi as if to say, "What else did you expect?"

The officer looks at Azeline a moment, but does not react, only slides his gaze over the group until it rests on Nicole and then Virginia. At thirty years old each, they are the youngest women on their peninsula. Azeline had warned they should hide when the Germans came, but—not fully believing it could be possible—they were caught unawares. Now, standing unkempt before the officer's inspection, Virginia feels naked. It's unbearable.

The man is impressive, with perfectly combed blond hair, broad shoulders, a narrow waist, and the kind of haughty air that shows he comes from money. He takes in Virginia's dirty dress, scratched arms, and bare feet, and then looks back up at her face, where her auburn hair still hangs in sweaty ringlets over her eyes. Her body betrays her need to remain aloof by burning hot, the heat of her shame climbing her neck and reaching its flames up her face. Under his thin mustache, the corner of his mouth twists into a smile, making her burn hotter.

"*Parlez-vous Allemand?*" he asks, looking from her to the group.

"*Ja,*" says Mum. She speaks some German from her school days and travels.

Virginia catches the word *stall* in his reply.

Mum nods.

At that, he bows, gives Virginia a strange look, and leaves.

The women watch through the front window as he returns to the four soldiers on horseback, points in the direction of the stables, and mounts his own horse, leading them there. Their collective breath releases once the Nazis are out of sight.

"At least he has good manners," says Mum.

"Manners?" says Azeline. "You call the way he looked at Virginia good manners?"

"And having to endure it in bare feet," Virginia says, covering her face.

"Thank goodness we got the jewels hidden," says Nicole.

Virginia looks at her dirty ring, wondering if it was foolish to keep it on her finger.

"First the clock," Azeline says. "Then the stables. I wonder what they'll think they're entitled to next."

"God help us," says Grandmère.

With no knock and no warning, they startle when the officer returns, stepping into the doorway behind them that leads to the kitchen. It has been only a few minutes, and his so-called manners are already weakening. In his utterance, Virginia catches the word *Auto*.

"They need the keys to move the car," says Mum.

Virginia bristles. She doesn't want him inside the blue baby, touching the steering wheel, fondling the gearshift.

"*I'll* move the car," Virginia says.

Mum translates and, to Virginia's consternation, her insistence appears to delight the officer.

The keys hang on a hook in the pantry. Virginia has to walk by the German to get there, and he doesn't move a centimeter as she passes. When her arm brushes against his uniform, she can smell his aftershave and has an almost physical pain at the thought of Philippe and his delicious cologne and his beautiful uniform and his perfect manners. The ache hardens and turns cold.

It's the Nazis' fault she lost the baby. They've torn apart this country and her family. They've destroyed her happily ever after, and she may never again see her husband. Virginia knows she has been raised in luxury. Her marriage has been a fairy tale. But now, she feels like a peasant girl who has to serve the conquering enemy in a castle. She has a sharp desire to strike this man, to claw out his eyes for how he and his army have reduced her. She balls her fists to keep from doing so, digging her nails into her skin until it hurts.

The officer follows Virginia too closely, his presence an oppressive shadow. Shocking though the feeling is to her, she has a sudden desire to watch him die. How quickly war has tugged her animal instincts to the surface. She's never been violent, but she thinks she would enjoy seeing a bomber mow him and his men down, especially if it meant Philippe could come home to her.

But the Allies have gone. Their planes are silent. Philippe and Michel, and all French soldiers—if they're alive—are in limbo, awaiting their fates. As are the women.

Mum's wellies are by the back door. Virginia steps into them, covering her naked feet so she no longer has to be the object of this Nazi's amusement. She exits the house and, when Virginia reaches the stable, the officer rejoins his men. Whatever he says to them elicits crude laughs. Virginia climbs into the car and starts the engine, wanting to run them all down but knowing that would get her nowhere. She revs the engine when she passes them, and drives to the old, vacant farm cottage behind the stable. Once the car is parked, she starts back for the house.

The officer intercepts her. He points to the Rance and then between the two of them, making motions with his arms as if he's swimming.

"*Schwimmen?*" he asks with a smile.

How dare he, she thinks. *Does he really think I'll go out for a frolic with him in the water?*

Instinct and upbringing command every cell in her body to behave with good manners, to be diplomatic. But there can be no diplomacy with the enemy. She stands tall and speaks clearly.

"*Nein.*"

THE WORD HAS become her refrain.

While Nicole and Virginia teach themselves to mend old fishing nets so they can add to their scarce food supply, the officer joins them. He makes rowing motions and points at the Rance.

"*Nein,*" Virginia says.

He meets her frown with a smile. Then he takes the nets and makes his men fix them while Nicole and Virginia watch, dumbfounded.

The next day, he crosses Virginia's path while she carries baskets of asparagus, green beans, and blueberries. With the groundskeeper off with the army, the women have to work the gardens. The soldier points from Virginia to the horses. He makes a riding motion.

"*Nein,*" she says.

Then he removes the basket from her grip and carries it into the kitchen.

"*Kaffee?*" he says to Azeline.

"*Nein!*" she barks at him.

He shrugs and leaves, helping himself to a handful of blueberries on the way out.

The Germans are pushing in closer, day by day, taking over a little more at a time. With no word from Michel, Nicole wants to go home to Paris, to her mother. Grandmère and Mum also want to return to their Paris apartments, where they won't have to live with Germans. But there are whisperings that the Nazis in the capital are not nearly as cordial as those here have been. Reports of roundups and beatings and a general air of oppression and cruelty come to the women from neighbors with Paris relations.

In spite of the rumors, a strange thing is happening. Virginia doesn't know if it's from surprise that the Germans aren't trying to beat them into submission or the general state of exhaustion and fear, but the residents of the region are coexisting with the Germans in relative harmony. Some locals have even gone so far as to praise how well-mannered the soldiers have been. It's a confusing, unsettling state of existence, both in town and at the estate.

Further disorienting is the beauty of Cancaval, somehow even more lovely in this time of worry and uncertainty. The waters of the Rance are gentle, the sky is Madonna blue, and the air is perfumed by flowers. Bees and butterflies populate the gardens. The leaves of every plant and tree are green and shiny, absorbing the warm light of the sun, giving them good air to breathe. In the enchanted atmosphere, Virginia finds her health returning. With the chores that must be done outdoors, her skin has tanned and her hair has lightened. Though she feels stronger in body, her spirit remains dormant, as it will as long as she's separated from Philippe.

One morning in town, when the postmaster has an envelope for her, Virginia is given a brief high followed by a crushing low.

"All the way from America," he says, handing her a letter from her mother.

Of course, Virginia is happy correspondence from her family has gotten through, but she wants Philippe's words.

That evening, as the sunset glows above them and the scent of sweet alyssum rises from the white carpet in the garden beds around them, the women sit in a semicircle, gazing out over the lawn toward the water while Virginia reads her mother's letter aloud.

"'My bridge club is anxious that you choose to remain in France,'" Virginia says, translating as she goes. "'They say your husband should insist you return to Florida. I can't say I disagree with them.'"

Virginia purses her lips. Mum touches Virginia's arm and smiles at her.

"They don't understand your love," Mum says. "Or Philippe's disposition, for that matter."

The women laugh, and Virginia feels the prick of tears behind her eyes. How fortunate she is to have a mother-in-law she loves as deeply as her own mother, one who can even transcend the role to be a friend. Virginia swallows the lump in her throat and continues reading.

"'I have some good news for you. The *St. Petersburg Times* is going to publish the letters you mailed earlier this summer. I took the liberty of sending them to a writer there, and she was so taken with your descriptions of life as the Germans pressed in that she immediately asked if we could get your permission. I gave it on your behalf. I hope you won't mind.'"

Mind? Virginia thinks. *Published letters. In the* Times. *Heavens, no! I'll be the talk of the town.*

The good cheer of the women evaporates the moment the German officer rounds the corner. Virginia folds her mother's letter and tucks it in her pocket, as if hiding it away will protect her privacy from a man bent on invading it. At least he doesn't speak French, so he can't have understood whatever he overheard. He throws up his hands as if to look surprised to find the women there and has the audacity to point to an empty chair next to Virginia—the last in the row—gesturing to it as if asking permission to join them, as if he won't just do what he wants. Mum gives him a stiff nod, and he takes the chair. He gestures toward the sky and starts jabbering.

"*Schön,*" he says, leaning across Virginia, for Mum to translate.

Virginia shrinks from him, trying to contract into herself.

"Ah, *bella?*" he says. "*Belle?*"

Mum nods.

Virginia keeps her eyes fixed ahead on the sunset, but he touches her arm, demanding her attention. When she turns to him, his face is inches from hers.

"Belle," he says, no longer looking at the sky.

As Mum shifts closer in her chair toward Virginia, she can feel the soldier's aggression crashing up against Mum's protective instinct. Virginia turns her gaze back to the sunset, doing her best to control the heat she feels rising in her neck. How can she mute her emotions? She doesn't know. She's never before had to do so under such circumstances.

After a few moments, the officer leans away from her and settles in his chair. He speaks in German, eyes moving between Mum and Virginia, impatiently awaiting Mum's translations.

Are they pleased that his men manured the garden? Did the women see, they fixed the missing boards in the stable? Did they enjoy the fish they caught for the women?

It's as if he's desperate for them to think well of him, especially Virginia. The more blank Virginia keeps her face, the more it appears to drive him crazy. He shifts in his chair, rubs his hands together, even reaches for Virginia to touch her arm, looking for her approval. As he rambles, she finds that his agitation is a source of strength for her. The more ill at ease he behaves, the more power she feels, and this power gives her a certain measure of control over her emotions. The heat leaves her neck, her skin cooling like the air from the swiftly falling sun.

When the women sit like marble statues, unresponsive to him, he gets the message. Almost midsentence, he stands, gives them a curt bow, and leaves. But the next night, he and his soldiers edge their way into the house.

"Just for billiards," he says.

Which becomes coffee in the mornings, on the garden patio, occupying the chairs in which the women used to sit. Then the soldiers start drinking champagne at night on the terrace. They take excursions in the boats, inviting Nicole and Virginia each time.

"Nein," the women say, over and over, refusing them, always.

One morning, Nicole and Virginia are on the beach catching shrimp, their skirts tied up between their legs. Virginia is surprised how much she's come to enjoy this smelly task, which she never would have tried before the war. The women make a competition of seeing who can grab the most critters, and Virginia's bucket is filling at a fantastic rate. Her attention is taken, however, when she hears a frantic whinny. She shields her eyes with her hand and sees one of the Germans' horses running along the seawall, frightened and unsure where to go. Virginia hurries toward him. She takes the stairs two at a time, and when the horse catches sight of her, she slows and holds up her hands.

"Easy," she says. "You're a handsome boy."

The horse becomes still, regarding Virginia with suspicion, but as she gets closer, he bucks and tries to dodge past her up the lawn. She reaches out and grabs the rope flying loose beside him, getting jerked, but she's soon able to slow him. Once he's under control, Virginia looks up and sees the German officer running toward her, the worry on his face changing into delight. He laughs, claps his hands, and bows to Virginia. Before she remembers to check herself, she smiles in response.

From his beaming, triumphant face, Virginia knows she's been unwise to let down her guard. When she looks over her shoulder and sees how Nicole glares at her, Virginia is filled with shame.

9

ALDERSHOT, ENGLAND

── VIOLETTE ──

"WHAT JUST HAPPENED?" says Papa as the Bushell family poses for the reporter's photographer.

Moments after the civil ceremony—five weeks after they met—Violette and Étienne are in a giddy, if somewhat bewildered, line outside the registrar's office, with Maman and Papa, Roy, and the esteemed captain Marie-Pierre Koenig, who's standing in as a father for Étienne. Just promoted by de Gaulle, Koenig has known Étienne for many years, and commanded his unit in the north. Koenig was also a soldier in the Great War. Between Koenig's and Étienne's decorations, and the emerald-and-diamond rock on Violette's finger, Papa is starstruck.

The local paper heard an English girl was marrying a French soldier, and now calls them the toast of two countries, brought together in war. With the flash of camera bulbs, the laughter, and the chatter of a dozen men from Étienne's unit, it takes the group a moment to hear the air raid siren. The unmistakable blasts from the antiaircraft battery, however, leave no confusion, and Captain Koenig leads as the men form a tight ring around Violette and Maman, herding them to the shelter across the street.

They rush down the stairs and into the bunker—a long, dark tunnel, with crude wooden benches running along either side. The door is pulled shut, and though only a few seconds pass before lighters flicker and candles are inflamed, Violette feels suffocated by the total blackness and being crammed underground with so many bodies. As the minutes tick by, the new thought rising in Violette's mind is that she'd rather not die before she's consummated her marriage. She whispers her desire in Étienne's ear, and he throws back his head and laughs, exposing that sexy neck, sending shivers all over his bride. He kisses the side of Violette's head and pulls her close.

The men are a rowdy, raucous lot. They sing "La Madelon," a French song even Papa knows, about a group of soldiers in love with a young waitress. Roy reaches for Maman's hand and dances her around the cramped space. Étienne does the same with Violette. Papa takes Roy's place with Maman. They bump one another and laugh their way through song after song, passing two hours belowground as best they can.

When the guns cease and the all-clear siren sounds, they stumble out—hot and disoriented—and head to the restaurant for the reception. The party continues with shepherd's pie, sea bass, and ale. The group grows quite drunk, and Violette and Étienne feed each other strawberry cake, and there are many sloppy kisses on cheeks before the newlyweds rush out through a tunnel of men holding their arms together overhead.

When they say their goodbyes, Maman and Papa are the last to wish the newlyweds well. Maman showers them with blessings and praise. While she tells Étienne how much she loves him already and to take good care of her daughter, Violette turns to Papa.

The day went better with Papa than Violette expected. Two weeks ago, when Étienne had stumbled through an awkward meeting with Papa to ask for her hand, her father had been outraged by the speed of the courtship, not to mention the eleven-year age difference. Maman tried to reason with Papa, drawing connections to their own wartime romance, and citing how well suited the French-British marriage could be. But for the first time in their lives, Maman couldn't persuade Papa to relent. Violette had left home to stay with her best childhood friend, Vera Maidment, and when Papa didn't go after Violette, she marched Étienne back the next day and told Papa it was the last time he'd see either of them if he didn't give his blessing.

What could Papa say to that?

"I don't know why you protested in the slightest," Violette says, reaching up to straighten Papa's tie. "You're finally going to get rid of me. At least, once we've won the war."

"Right you are," he says, giving her a strange look.

"Why're you ogling me like that?" she says.

"You just look so pretty and grown up. I hadn't realized."

Violette beams. It might be the first time Papa has recognized Violette is an adult.

"Maybe Étienne will have more luck reining you in than I have," says Papa.

"Unlikely," says Violette.

"Knowing how Étienne's moving up through the ranks, at least someday you'll have a cushy, luxurious life. Maman and I'll visit you in your château in France or your villa in Casablanca."

"I'll see if we can squeeze you in. The life of a major's wife is quite full."

He grins and pulls Violette into a rough, drunken hug. She enjoys it while it lasts. It's rare to get this level of affection from Papa, and she knows it's only a matter of time before they'll be arguing.

Captain Koenig interrupts them to kiss Violette on both cheeks, followed by Étienne, Maman, and then Papa. Amid the laughter, the newlyweds leave the reception, the shouts and well-wishes warming them all the way to the hotel.

And they can't get there fast enough.

After five weeks of courtship, the long day—including two hours underground—and the slow check-in process, they're practically at a run to the hotel room, the door barely shut before they come together, kissing and pulling off each other's clothes. Once Violette is down to her slip and Étienne to his undershirt and pants, Violette pushes back against his chest.

"Wait," she says.

She leads him to a chair, slides his legs open, and forces his hands on his knees.

"From the first day I saw you in our garden," she says, "I've wanted to do this."

Violette straddles Étienne and places his hands on the backs of her legs. She pushes back his head, exposing his neck, and kisses it slowly. When he can stand it no more, Étienne lifts Violette into his arms, and takes her to bed.

THE DAYS OF their honeymoon take on a dreamlike quality.

The music of the army marching band, parading through the streets of Aldershot, seems very far away from where Violette and Étienne hold hands, walking along the road, gazing at each other in wonder, silly grins on their faces.

When the heat and the people become too much, they slip away, walking the country lanes that lead to sunflower fields. They cut a path through the stalks, taller than they stand, floral heads heavy with yellow petals and seeds over them. Violette and Étienne come together in the shade and shelter of the flowers, wishing they could forever hide from everyone and everything in the private, earthy kingdom of which Étienne crowns Violette queen with a chain of yellow moonbeam flowers.

When night falls, they beg the guard at the observatory to let them in to look through the telescope. Under the dome, in the womb of the little tower, they lean their heads together, taking turns looking through the eyepiece at the magnified heavens, the shimmering constellations, the startling white waning gibbous moon.

Étienne takes Violette's face in his hands.

"Every night we're apart," he says. "Look at the moon and know I do, too, and send your love to me as I send mine to you."

Violette didn't know a man like Étienne could exist. He's of another mold entirely from the men in her family and the boys she has grown up with and dated. Étienne is a gentleman. He's strong, powerful, and in control, but he's not a bully. He's not crass or aloof. He doesn't lord his strength over or dominate others. He uses it to support them, to support her. Yet she doesn't feel subordinate to him. Étienne looks up to her. He respects her. He defers to her. In the gaze of his admiration, she feels herself growing in stature, becoming the best version of herself.

She doesn't know what she did to deserve love like this, but she will drink every drop from it, every day that she can.

A WEEK LATER, on the docks at Liverpool, Violette feels a cold like a kind of frostbite, spreading over her skin and her heart the smaller Étienne's waving form grows on the decks of the SS *Pennland*. Étienne travels on a Dutch ship, one of a large convoy, including General de Gaulle, on their way through U-boat-infested waters to West Africa, where they'll try to persuade the Vichy French traitors to join the Free French.

Once Étienne is gone, Violette travels back to Burnley Road, to her parents' house. Standing before it, she feels as if she had a cancer she lived with many years that was removed for a time but has returned. Maybe she shouldn't have married Étienne so quickly. To have tasted love like that only to have it torn away is unbearable.

That first night home, Violette doesn't say much. She can't bear the awkwardness of how Maman and Papa look at her, trying not to think of the nights she spent with her husband. After dinner, in her bedroom, Violette looks over her pink coverlet while flashes of memory of the things she has done with Étienne in bed—and how much she loved them—come at her. Tiny ballet slippers hang from her mirror, and a shelf of dolls with glass eyes stares at her. She shivers when her thoughts turn to the little girl the Nazis murdered on the dock at Calais.

Violette looks away from her girlish things with disgust, flops on her bed, and stares at the ceiling, thinking, *What just happened?*

10

───── **VIRGINIA** ─────

IT TAKES MANY cuts before she comprehends the truth: France is bleeding out—sliced with a mortal blow—and with it, Virginia's old life is dying.

Like the early days of grieving a loved one, Virginia awakens each morning not knowing, but rather having to remember. That remembering brings fresh pain with each wave, and the waves are drowning her. She thinks it will be better when she simply *knows* the world has turned upside down—to have the thing dead and buried and not have to recollect. Then maybe she can move on. But there's no knowing, at least not now. There is no certainty and no timetable, and that's the hardest part. Though she knows it's not for her ultimate good, Virginia continues to grasp the ever-vanishing vapors of the memories of *before*, but they're getting increasingly hard to hold.

The armistice was the beginning of the end, the gate opening to Nazi infestation. Now, as restrictions on everything from travel to eating and drinking are added by the day, the death of the old life becomes final. The conquering enemy has stopped asking before plundering the cupboards. They're no longer shy about reaching out to grasp arms, no longer polite about trying to fumble with the French language, instead telling the women to learn German.

Virginia finds Mum's old French-German dictionary in the library. Virginia feels an urgent need to master a particular set of words, not to obey the enemy but so she can speak plainly to the officer who's always looming. The opportunity comes almost as soon as she has perfected them.

"I have a husband I love," she says to the officer in German. "He will be home soon."

The officer's expression turns cold. She feels a chill from the draft he leaves in his wake.

Virginia wants what she says to be true, but she doesn't know if Philippe is alive. If he saw combat. If he's injured or a POW. Every day that passes without word of his well-being is agony, and she doesn't know how much longer she can endure.

When Nicole receives a letter from Michel, the women rejoice. Michel is being demobilized and is heading to Paris. Nicole will join him as soon as he sends word of his arrival. Virginia forces a smile for Nicole, but at night, Virginia weeps. Michel didn't have news of Philippe's regiment.

And the Germans press in.

Virginia and Nicole have to register at the town hall, presumably for German slave labor, somewhere at some future time. By decree, Azeline, not from this region, must return to Marseille, her place of origin, breaking all their hearts. The Nazis have taken over the house entirely, pushing the women to the farmer's cottage. Grandmère and Mum have been forced into peasants' quarters. As they are too well-mannered to complain, Virginia only knows their discomfort when they rub their aching backs upon awakening in the mornings from sleeping in such poor beds. Virginia tries to learn from them, but her bitterness overwhelms her, a scowl ever on her face.

It rains nearly every day. Leaks in the cottage roof drip into metal buckets. Hair refuses to lie smooth. Clothes cling, damp and musty, never drying. The Nazis strut about, splashing through puddles in their black boots, tracking mud over the Aubusson rugs in the house, complaining about such unfortunate weather. If it had been any other summer or any other guests, Virginia would have apologized for the rain, but it's a summer of mourning, and these men are not guests, they're thieves. They are invaders and murderers. And God is weeping over all of them.

Since Nicole has such life back in her, she hardly notices the miserable weather, and pulls the heaviest weight with the chores. Virginia can see that Nicole is doing all she can not to gloat. Though Virginia knows it's wrong, she secretly resents Nicole's happiness. Virginia had to wait so long to find love, and now it has been taken from her. Her husband and their baby—gone. She's never believed in a punishing God, but now the thought plagues her, a torturous temptation to doubt she's having a hard time ignoring.

The German officer has changed tack with Virginia. He still puts himself in her path a dozen times a day, but he no longer cares for her good opinion, making him more dangerous than when he did. It's clear he wants Virginia. How long before he takes her, as he has taken the stables, the house, the gardens, and the beach?

They're almost out of coal and laundry soap, and Virginia's hands have grown rough from all the scrubbing. Mum and Grandmère daily debate returning to Paris with Nicole, and Virginia thinks they're resolved, but she doesn't want to go with them. She spends her days longing for Philippe, fantasizing about returning to their country cottage, Les Baumées. If all the women go to Paris, Virginia knows she can't stay at Cancaval, alone with the Germans, but maybe she can go to Nesles-la-Vallée. The village is tiny and tucked out of the way. She could hide at Les Baumées and wait for Philippe. And if there is no more Philippe, she thinks she'll simply fade away until she's a ghost at the place they had such plans to fill with life and children.

Virginia and Nicole ride bikes to town each day to check the post and see what goods and news they can procure. It chills them to pedal by the houses full of Nazis—listening to their radios spewing the horrid voice of that madman, Hitler—pretending not to hear the whistles and crude shouts of the soldiers. When the women arrive in town, they start at the post office, standing in the long queue of people who look utterly devoid of feeling.

The postmaster is a kindly old man who tries to give everyone a word of cheer, even though he almost never has any news for them. Virginia sees his sad headshakes for those in line ahead of her and prepares herself for disappointment. Mother's letters aren't even coming anymore. This time, however, when the postmaster sees Virginia, his face brightens. Virginia's heart quickens, but she keeps it in check, in case the letter isn't from Philippe. The postmaster hurries to the box and returns with a trembling hand.

"It's a good day, *l'Américaine!*" He kisses the envelope and hands it to her.

When she sees the handwriting, a heavy weight lifts from her chest and she feels as if her dead lungs fill with air.

"Philippe!" she cries.

Nicole and Virginia hug and cheer and hurry back to Cancaval to give Mum and Grandmère the good news. They find the dear ladies in straw hats, picking vegetables in the garden. There's much celebration, and Virginia goes straight inside to pack a bag. She'll need permission to travel to Bussière-Galant—five hundred kilometers south of them, in the Unoccupied Zone, where Philippe awaits demobilization—and she wants to get it first thing in the morning.

In the letter, Philippe said the Frenchmen who didn't reach the fight—as Philippe did not, *thank God*—won't be punished. POWs will remain in German custody, and many in the French Navy will be retained for German service, but cavalry units like Philippe's are being sent home. She has a hard time believing there won't be any consequences, or he won't be called up later to serve the Germans, but she won't worry about that now. All that matters is Philippe is all right, today, and he asked her to come to him.

"Why would he request you travel all that way?" asks Mum. "It's so dangerous."

Mum has been fretting since she realized Virginia intends to travel alone, all the while helping Virginia fix food for the journey and pack a knapsack.

"I'm American," Virginia says. "I can travel freely. And Philippe could be stuck there for weeks. We can't bear to be separated any longer."

"You can't ride a bicycle for five hundred kilometers. You haven't been well."

Mum has noticed, Virginia thinks.

"I won't have to," Virginia reassures her. "I'll take buses and trains as far as I can."

"They won't let you pass into the Unoccupied Zone. I just know it."

"They will."

Virginia doesn't sleep a wink that night, and she's up before the sunrise to finish preparations. In their bathrobes, with tousled hair and worried frowns, the women hug her and try to convince her one last time to wait at Cancaval and leave for Paris when they do.

"Philippe can come to you, there," says Mum.

Virginia won't hear of it.

She doesn't linger over goodbyes, and she doesn't cry. Knowing she and Philippe will soon be reunited, she feels as if she has wings on her feet, the wind at her back, unlimited stores of energy. She pushes off with a "toodle-oo" and races toward the gate, only to have to slam on the brakes and slide to a stop once she reaches it. The officer who has been circling her these weeks blocks her path. He holds up his hands like a question.

Virginia points to her ring and to the road.

He stares at the ring, his face darkening. Virginia catches the chill from him and stiffens her posture. He runs his eyes slowly over her. It cannot escape his notice that her hair is done up, her makeup is impeccable, and her ring has been polished, scrubbed free of garden dirt. Will he try to defile her before she can reunite with her love?

In the minutes that pass, her heart beats fast and it becomes hard to breathe. She has to keep her mind settled, to stop it from imagining the worst, what he could do to her, what that would do to her marriage. It's a terrible thing to know she's completely at the mercy of one she doesn't trust.

Real panic rises in her as he takes a step forward, but something catches his eye that stops him. Trembling, Virginia glances over her shoulder and sees Grandmère, Mum, and Nicole, hastily dressed, and watching like stone gargoyles. While the sight of these great women stills and strengthens her, it throws a bucket of cold water over the officer. If he is going to harm her, he'll have to do it in front of her family.

It feels like an eternity, but he finally moves aside, allowing Virginia to pass.

THE RED-FACED NAZI at the Kommandantur in Dinard refuses Virginia the pass she'll need to get through the barricades to the Unoccupied Zone.

"Why?" she asks.

He stops stamping papers and narrows his eyes, looking her up and down as if to say, "Who do you think you are?" He waves his hand at her like he's swiping away a fly and calls for the next person in line. Virginia steps aside. There will be other chances along the way. She'll have to try her luck at the next stop.

But the bus ride to Rennes takes four hours—making her think she should have ridden her bicycle the seventy kilometers—and she's refused a pass at the Kommandantur there, too. She takes the train to Nantes but is again discouraged by the seven hours it takes to go one hundred kilometers. The next morning, Virginia is again denied the pass, but is able to buy a train ticket to Saintes. And so, all the long, tedious, sweltering journey goes. Travel. Scurry for a room. Denied pass. Repeat.

The smaller the distance shrinks between Virginia and Philippe, the more elated she feels, but the crushing lows of pass denial, and the trip taking much longer than it should, weigh on her. The German soldiers overrun the Occupied Zone, and they're rowdy and flirtatious. Virginia does her best to try to blend in, but she's a solitary woman with bright green eyes the Nazis keep remarking on, and there's nowhere to hide in cramped train compartments.

At the final Kommandantur before the Unoccupied Zone, just eighty kilometers from Philippe, Virginia is denied the pass. She still heads for the rail station. What else can she do? She'll buy the train ticket and pray for a miracle. When she reaches the head of the ticket line, the stationmaster asks to see her pass to the Unoccupied Zone.

"I wasn't able to get one," she says.

"Then I can't sell you a train ticket."

"Monsieur, please. I've been traveling for days. My husband has been demobilized. I'm going to meet him."

"It's pointless. The Germans will never let you cross the check-point."

"I'll deal with that once it happens."

"No. It's madness. And it could put you in danger. Without a pass, I won't sell you a ticket."

Crushed, Virginia steps away from the window and scans the waiting area, her eyes finding a window that has just opened. She pretends she's going to walk out of the station but, once the stationmaster is occupied, she slips into the new line. When it's her turn, as casually as possible she requests the train ticket to Limoges. She hears the buzzing of the machine and is shocked when the man slides the ticket to her without a second glance. Virginia stutters her thanks, and it's all she can do not to run to the train. When it starts moving, she prays with all her might.

The closer the train gets to the line, the faster Virginia's heart races. Desperate for a cigarette, she spins the ring on her finger and chews her nails. She snuck her last cigarette a week ago, back at Cancaval. Women are no longer allowed tobacco in the Occupied Zone.

The train comes to a stop at the demarcation line. She sweats while she waits. In a few moments, she stiffens as she sees the green uniform, the shiny metal plate necklace, and the iron cross patch of the German MP. He steps in and demands her ticket and identity card, but she doesn't hear the word *pass*. She prays he doesn't notice how her hand shakes when she presents her documents. Squinting his eyes, looking from Virginia to her picture, his face suddenly brightens.

"Amerikanerin?" he asks.

She stammers a yes.

"You, New York?"

"Nein." She shakes her head. "Florida."

"Oh, *gut. Heiß,*" he says, fanning himself.

"Ja. Hot."

He smiles, pleased with her attempts at German.

"Why go?" he asks in broken English, pointing at her ticket.

"Husband," she says, pointing to her ring. *"Mann."*

"Gut."

He hands Virginia's papers back to her, and bows, before leaving her.

Stunned.

He must have thought the station checked for her pass. Or he likes Americans. Or he's stupid. She doesn't know why, and she doesn't care. She's going to get to Philippe!

As the final train pulls into Bussière-Galant, she practically leaps from the compartment and onto the platform to fetch her bike from the storage car. It's a relief of unimaginable proportions to have those horrid green uniforms everywhere replaced with khakis and blues. Virginia can breathe again, and she didn't realize she'd been holding her breath.

Once she has her bicycle, she sets off. Crossing the bridge into town, pedaling past red-tile-roofed houses, she stops at the first group of men to ask where Philippe d'Albert-Lake is. They shrug, and so does the next group. She grows increasingly impatient, and it takes her many queries, before, at long last, a soldier's face brightens at the question. He points to a little house with a sweet, grassy yard, not a stone's throw from where they stand.

"Philippe!" she calls.

Virginia pedals, yelling, not caring that she must look like a madwoman. As she gets closer, she spots him. His head pokes out an open upstairs window.

"Honeybeeeeee!" Philippe calls, before disappearing from the window.

At the yard, Virginia jumps from her bicycle and runs with all her might. She tackles Philippe when he reaches her, and they roll on the grass, laughing, crying, hearts pounding again to the same beat.

IN THE DREAMLIKE days in Bussière-Galant, while they await Philippe's demobilization, they scarcely stop touching. At night, the moonlight comes in the circular bedroom window like a boat porthole. Unwilling to disentangle to get a proper rest, they wrap themselves around each other, waking up a hundred times in the small hours to reassure each other they are together. But all too soon, it's time to go. They decide to travel to Cancaval first, to see Philippe's family and fetch the blue baby. Then they'll settle at Nesles.

Knowing public transport is a nightmare, they procure a bicycle for Philippe. Though Virginia tries to prepare her husband for what it's like in the Occupied Zone, he can't understand how completely the Nazis have taken over until they cross the line, and he sees it with his own eyes.

German signs replace the French. German language assaults their ears. The cold, suspicious glares of Nazi soldiers are directed at Philippe, and they disrespect him when they grin and whistle at Virginia. On the last night of the humiliating, exhausting weeklong journey, they have to stop in Rennes, seventy miles from Cancaval, and spend their last francs on a hotel room to do so. They don't even remove their dirty clothes when they fall into bed. Virginia doesn't reach for Philippe. She can't bear her own filth.

"I'll burn these clothes once we get home," she says.

Philippe doesn't respond, and she wonders if he hears her. When she looks over, she sees that he stares up at the cracked ceiling above them.

"What is it?" Virginia asks.

Philippe doesn't answer.

Virginia pushes up on one elbow and looks down at him. He won't meet her eyes.

"I'll ask you once more," he says. "I beg you. Go home to your family in Florida. You'll be able to find a way. You're American. Please."

"Stop."

"What kind of man am I to let you put yourself in unnecessary danger? The way those boches whistled at you."

"You aren't putting me anywhere. I belong at your side."

"If anything happens to you, it will destroy me."

"If I'm separated from you, it will destroy me. It almost did already."

They stare at each other a long moment before Virginia lies back down on the bed. For the first time Virginia can remember, Philippe doesn't wrap himself around her to sleep. It feels like a strange, new country in so many ways.

The next morning, the first half of the day is agony on their aching legs, but as they grow closer to Cancaval, they find new energy to press on. At the final turn, the road is downhill, and the familiar, beloved sights rise around them. Traveling at breakneck speed, they round the bend to Cancaval and the back road to the peasant house behind the stable. They leap off their bikes and run to the door, but when they throw it open and rush into the cottage, they see the beds have no sheets, there are no dishes in the sink, and the windows have grown grimy.

A cold pit forms in Virginia's stomach. Philippe scowls and walks out, striding toward the main house with Virginia in his wake. Her fear grows with every step. Philippe is as angry as she has ever seen him. When they arrive at the kitchen, they see kettles bubbling, baskets overflowing with produce, and hear voices. They open the door, creep into the dining room, and stop at the entrance, where their eyes are greeted by a table full of laughing Nazis. One stands and points his Luger at them. Philippe sweeps Virginia behind him, while a voice barks a command for the soldier to lower his gun. Virginia's eyes find that of her German admirer. He glares from Philippe to Virginia.

"*Où les Frauen?*" Virginia says, in a blend of French and German.

The officer stares at Virginia a long moment before a sneer touches his lips. Clearly glad to deliver the news, he speaks the words that bring Virginia and Philippe fresh heartache.

"Die Frauen sind weg."

The women are gone.

AFTER THEIR INITIAL panic, Virginia and Philippe are relieved to learn the women went to Paris, voluntarily, shortly after Virginia left. They spend a fitful night in the cottage on the property and leave the next day, with permission to take the blue baby. Missing the women, unsure if they'll get to see their beloved Cancaval again, they shed quiet tears the first half of the journey and sit tense and silent the second.

All along the way, Virginia can't believe they traveled these very roads the previous year, touring with Virginia's mother and sister on their summer visit. How charmed they'd been by France. Virginia had been so pleased by the visit, especially when Mother had taken Virginia aside, held her face in her hands, and said, "You've made a wonderful choice, my dear." They'd hugged and Virginia felt closer to her mother than she ever had. Virginia's father, a surgeon, and her brother, studying to be a doctor, couldn't get away but promised to come next time.

Will there be a next time? Virginia thinks. *Will anything be left standing for them to see?*

Virginia tries to make conversation along the journey, but her man of few words becomes a man of fewer. She knows Philippe is sick with the shame he and his men carry over the defeat, sick the men had to turn over their healthy horses to the Germans while the rest were set loose to starve or be eaten, sick with worry over how long he'll have a paying job before he's forced into some kind of servitude to the Germans. But he doesn't want to talk about any of it, so she won't force it. It's not until they turn onto their winding, wooded driveway that Virginia and Philippe are able to exhale.

Nestled in gently sloping hills, Les Baumées is a timber-framed cottage—like those of Normandy or Alsace—set on forty hectares. Known as the Valley of the Artists for a small colony that had formed there after the Great War but fizzled out during the Great Depression, Nesles-la-Vallée feels a million miles from civilization but is only forty kilometers north of Paris. Even the train station is a village away, making Nesles too provincial for the Nazis, who want to exploit the landmarks and tourist attractions. Nesles has no brothels, no fancy dining or high-end shopping—only a bakery, a tiny hotel, a boarded-up restaurant, and a church. Before the war, the market teemed with farmers selling beets and potatoes, rabbits and chickens, but now the strings of peppers and beans and cured meats that once decorated its rafters have been taken over by cobwebs.

They park the blue baby under the overhang outside the barn. After Philippe unties their bicycles from the roof and locks them up, Virginia follows her husband to the house. He puts the key in the door and pushes it open, bringing the smell of fresh wood and plaster to their noses. Their steps echo on the floor, making the sparsely furnished house feel very empty.

Philippe walks to the window in the living room and gazes out over their land. Virginia crosses to the other window and does the same. She spots a buzzard pulling gristle from a deer carcass at the edge of the forest. Averting her eyes, she longs for some words of reassurance or wisdom from her husband, but he doesn't speak.

"This is good," she says, finding her voice. "We have each other. We're sheltered. We'll just wait out the war. Nice and safe."

The words fall from her lips, thin and brittle as birch bark. She can almost see them littering the sawdust piles on the floor.

11

———⟨⟩———

—— VIOLETTE ——

CROSS AND BITTER, resenting the war for taking Étienne from her, Violette pushes the food around on her plate.

The sporadic, polite communication full of censor strikeouts Violette has been receiving from her husband leaves her wanting. In her correspondence with Étienne, Violette mentioned she was searching for a job to fill her time—there are enough vacancies now that most of the workforce is militarily employed—only to get reminded she doesn't need to work because his pay will go directly to her. Violette doesn't care about money. She cares about usefulness and industry. She won't bring up the subject again, and if Étienne tries to forbid it, he'll find out exactly what kind of woman he married, though Violette's quite sure he learned that on their honeymoon.

Violette's brother Roy is home on leave for the weekend. He is older by only one year, so they're practically twins. Roy—now her second-favorite dance partner, since she has Étienne—is her first-favorite partner in mischief making. But she's not laughing at Roy's jokes, nor is she keeping up with his attempts at conversation. It's hardly conversation, really. Just him and Papa shouting at each other about the state of the world.

A napkin hits her face, causing her to jump.

"Hallo, Vi," says Roy. "Come in."

She throws the napkin back at Roy.

"Manners," says Maman.

"Vi's the one with bad manners," says Roy. "Playing with her food. Ignoring me."

"Don't talk back to Maman," says Papa, slapping Roy on the head.

"You're moping," Roy says to Violette, ignoring Papa. "Stop feeling sorry for yourself."

"Can't a wife miss her husband who's off fighting a war?" asks Violette.

"No. She needs to keep her chin up. Stay hopeful. So the war isn't being fought for nothing."

Violette sighs and rolls her eyes.

"That's it," Roy says, pushing back from the table and standing. "I'm taking you out."

"No," she says.

"I'm not asking. I insist. Get your dancing shoes on."

"I don't want to. I won't dance until my husband is home safe."

"Then you can smoke at a table while I dance. I need to find a pretty girl who'll marry me, quick, before I ship off like your Frenchy."

"Find a rich one," says Papa. "I'm not paying for another wedding."

Roy crosses around the table, pulls back Violette's chair, and yanks her to standing.

"Hurry up," he says, pushing her toward the stairs. "Before the bombardment starts."

"Must you go out?" asks Maman.

In this first autumn of war, more bombs than leaves have fallen on England. The Nazis have started with a blitz—showers of bombs each night. Two thousand Londoners were killed in the first bombardment, and countless since. Yet they've learned to live with it the way only a people as practical as the British can. Violette, for one, would be content to sleep through the assaults at home, but Maman's pleading urges Violette to follow each night, yawning, belowground to the tube stations, to sleep on puffy down mats Maman has sewn for them. It's not bad, really, for one like Violette, who sleeps like the dead. She's lucky that's always been a talent of hers.

"Come on," says Roy. "I don't want to miss all the pretty girls."

VIOLETTE TAKES A long draw from the flask—the booze making her nose and throat burn. She grimaces and passes it back to Roy, before lighting a cigarette.

The Locarno Dance Hall in Streatham is a popular nightspot, where she learned all the dance crazes, including the jitterbug and the strolling dance that was born here, the Lambeth Walk. She won't admit it to Roy, but it does give her heart a lift to be here. He's spent most of the night dancing with a pretty redhead in a Women's Auxiliary Territorial Service—or ATS—uniform but has pardoned himself to check on Violette.

Violette thinks back to the night of her debut. She'd just turned sixteen, and Roy took her to a ball at the Savoy Hotel, where he worked as a porter. Maman had sewn Violette a dress of white silk, trimmed in bright red. Roy had taken her to a photo booth for pictures and had twirled her all over the dance floor, until the boys started lining up one after the other. Until she met Étienne, it had been the happiest night of Violette's life.

She remembers the first time she danced with Étienne. Her neck grows hot just thinking about how he'd pulled her into his lithe, warm body on this very dance floor, and how his lips had grazed her ear while he spoke French to her. How they'd laughed at how silly he'd looked doing the Lambeth Walk.

"There's a smile," says Roy. "Let's dance."

"Won't your future wife be upset?" Violette says, nodding toward the redhead.

"Nah, I told her you were my sis. Come on."

Violette sighs, stubs out her cigarette, and follows her brother to the dance floor. Singer Jessie Matthews is tonight's entertainment and, seeing her up close, Violette can't help but think she's prettier and more talented than the star.

"If Matthews can get into the pictures, I can," Violette says.

"You're pretty enough, but you've got too much of that Cockney-French accent."

"Oh, shut it," she says. "I can speak proper. I'm just too lazy most of the time. And you're not worth the trouble."

"Right you are," he says. "You might think of it, actually. I hear they want girls for propaganda films. But now that you're hitched, you might have to take yourself out of the pool."

"Why?"

"Shouldn't you be tending house, or something?"

"Do I seem like the type?"

"Hardly."

Roy leads Violette around the dance floor to "Over My Shoulder," Matthews's most popular song. Violette tries to enjoy herself, but she has that terrible feeling again, the one that she's surrounded by ghosts.

"It's too bad you can't suit up and fight with us," says Roy. "I'd take you covering me with that shot over half the boys in my regiment."

"I might just do it. If you see a new guy with purple eyes and a fresh buzz cut turn up at the barracks, just keep your mouth shut, will ya?"

Roy laughs.

Matthews takes a break, and the pounding of a drum announces a jitterbug. Cheers erupt and the floor is soon flooded with couples, kicking and spinning and tossing one another around the hall. Roy looks at Violette with a question in his eyes, and she nods. The mad energy around them allows Violette to forget her cares. But all too soon, Jessie Matthews returns with a slow number. The chandeliers are dimmed, and the crowd is more ghostlike than ever. Melancholy creeps over Violette. She passes Roy back to the redhead and pushes through the crowd to get out of the hall.

It's disorienting to step into the cool, black quiet. She wonders if the Germans will give them a rest tonight. An air raid warden stops a car foolish enough to have its lights on, and after the reprimand, the driver inches away, navigating the shadows. The door opens behind her, and a giggling couple emerges. Violette feels a pang thinking of Étienne.

When she hears a rumble, she utters a curse and reaches for the door to the dance hall, just as it slams open and the crowds emerge. Roy soon finds her, and they hurry to the nearest tube entrance, seeking cover from the bombs.

12

⤜⥈⤛

—— VIRGINIA ——

THE EVENING BRINGS the first autumn wind to the valley, and with it the sweet, decaying scent of dying vegetation. Windows thrown open during the warm afternoon now let in breezes that make stirring ghosts of the filmy white curtains and bring a chill to Virginia's arms. She rubs her skin and continues dressing for dinner in the master bathroom, listening to Philippe chop wood in the backyard. He's been out there for hours—no ceasing to the endless hacking and splitting— and he'll be sore tomorrow.

Virginia has been at housework all day, sweeping and dusting, removing furniture covers, arranging what pieces they have, and un-packing their suitcases and the limited groceries they purchased on the journey home. She used a healthy portion of their stores to make a quiche for dinner and an apple pie for dessert. She knows the meal is extravagant, but she wishes to celebrate their return home with a little fanfare before the deep rationing of war and winter. Besides, they never had a birthday dinner for Virginia, so this will have to do until they can return to the beautiful, mirrored, high-ceilinged restaurants of the capital. Oh, what a glorious day that will be.

They'll need to make a trip to Paris soon. They have only summer clothes here, and it's getting chilly. They could use some of the dishes and furnishings from their apartment. They also want to check in on the women in the family.

Virginia thinks back to her lunch with Mum in Paris, the day before the miscarriage, when Madame Bosc told the diners not to let the Germans disrupt their lives. Honoring this spirit, Virginia sets the dining table with their wedding linens and china—white-and-gold-embossed Limoges with tiny blue forget-me-nots along the rim—and dons a dinner dress, blue as the sky at Cancaval, with a jewel neckline and three-quarter-length sleeves. While she puts on her diamond earrings, she thinks Philippe should have washed by now. He's been at work for hours, and he'll be filthy and exhausted. Not only that, the quiche will be out of the oven soon, and it will become dry if she leaves it in too long, or cold if she places it on the trivet.

Heels clicking, Virginia crosses the terra-cotta tile floor to the window. Looking down on Philippe, she sees a sheen on his shirtless torso. He's in as fine a shape as he's ever been, and she takes a moment to admire her husband before calling to him. His eyes are dark, and he doesn't respond to her. It takes her three tries before he stops working and looks up, glancing around in bewilderment, as if he's just realized where he is. He nods at her, his face shadowed and serious, and leans the ax against the substantial woodpile he's made before heading toward the house.

Virginia hurries downstairs to light the tapers in the brass candlesticks on the dining table. She smooths her dress and arranges a smile, looking forward to Philippe's pleasure when he sees the tableau she's arranged. So it feels like ice water dumped over her when he appears in the doorway to the dining room and scowls.

Philippe's gaze travels from her dress, to the table, to the kitchen, where the apple pie cools on the white marble countertop, its aroma rising with steam to the exposed wood beams on the ceiling. In the rustic dining room mirror, Virginia looks from her sweaty, dirty husband to herself. She feels a rush of shame but shoves it quickly aside to allow for indignation.

"It's only to celebrate," she says. "We're safe and we have each other."

Philippe doesn't reply, dropping his gaze to the floor.

"I never even had a birthday dinner," she continues, crossing her arms over her chest.

It's his silence that wounds her. It would be better if he scolded instead of wearing this heavy look of disappointment.

The timer goes off, saving both of them.

THERE'S NO WINE and the quiche has grown cold. At least she found a half pack of cigarettes in Philippe's jacket. He's always been able to take or leave them, so she'll most certainly take his. She'll smoke one cigarette a day until they're gone.

She savors the last draw and watches with great longing as her final exhalation dissipates. She thinks of all the years she took cigarettes for granted. She took wine for granted. Quiche and pie. Steak. Coffee. A pantry full of choices. Freedom to travel. Summer estates and Paris apartments. The theater. Dining out. Cafés and book stalls and antique shops.

She and Philippe have a shared passion for wandering the aisles searching for old treasures. In her perusals, she's drawn to dolls. Silly as it sounds, she thinks of dolls as little orphans who need homes. She loves their precious features and their tiny clothes. She has a small collection of them at their Paris apartment. Virginia lovingly cleaned and restored each one and hopes to be able to display them in a wall cabinet someday. Philippe loves old furniture and the stories each piece holds. The oak trestle table where she sits, for instance, came from a sixteenth-century monastery plundered by Henry VIII. There's a moisture ring that the dealer told Philippe came from a monk's beer tankard, and a burn mark he said dripped from the torch of one of Cromwell's thugs. The stories are often preposterous, but always amusing, and make for a good dinner conversation.

Virginia thinks of how she took frivolous dinner conversation for granted.

A noise at the entrance to the dining room silences her thoughts. Philippe is dressed in a suit. He shaved and oiled his brown hair, and the scent of his cologne fills the room with its warmth. He pulls a bouquet of wildflowers tied with twine from behind his back. Virginia rises from the table and crosses the room to bury herself in his arms.

"I'm sorry," they say at the same time.

"I know what you were trying to do," Philippe says. "I shouldn't have made you feel bad."

"No," says Virginia. "I should have discussed it with you. I was frivolous and wasteful."

"Stop," he says. "We both have to learn how to live in new ways. One minute I'm worried. Then I feel hopeful. Then I feel guilty. Then grateful. It's an exhausting cycle, and when I came in from chopping wood, I was on the worrying part."

"I go through the same cycles."

"Then let's be patient with each other."

He leans down and kisses her. It feels like a new kind of kiss, one more meaningful, a deepening of their affection. One she will no longer take for granted.

When they pull back, Virginia carries the flowers to the kitchen. She hunts around until she finds a canning jar, fills it with water, and returns to the dining room. Philippe has moved his place setting from across the long table to the spot next to hers. He has pushed the fine plates aside and set the serving dish between their two seats. He takes the silver forks from their linen napkins, shoves them directly in the quiche, and looks up at her with a grin. She returns it, and knows she'll never forget this night.

She will no longer take any of these moments of peace for granted.

THE NEXT MORNING, a phone call shows them just how fleeting moments of peace are in war.

Philippe's fear has come true. Because the steamers at his travel company have been conscripted, his employer has shut its doors. Virginia and Philippe leave for Paris immediately.

Days later, their beautiful apartment in the seventh arrondissement is sold. Their landscape paintings, the blue settee where Virginia loved to read, the crystal candlesticks and wineglasses and vases. Philippe's precious antique dining chairs and prized first-edition books. Virginia's furs, her doll collection, and most of her jewelry.

Everything frivolous: sold.

There's a select number of pieces of sentimental value they won't sell—Philippe's family piano, for one, and Virginia will never, ever part with her wedding ring. They've sent some things to Mum's and Grandmère's apartments for safekeeping and have hired movers to transport the rest of their belongings to Les Baumées.

It was an emotional reunion with Philippe's family. Even though it had only been months since they last saw one another, the strain was evident on all of them, none more so than the grand old ladies, who appeared much diminished. But at least they're alive and safe, for now.

Fidgeting with the ring on her finger, craving a cigarette, Virginia stands with Nicole staring at the practical furnishings left in the apartment. The floorboards by the window, where the gleaming black grand piano has always stood, now reveal a dark brown outline of the instrument, while the hardwood around it is bleached from the sunlight.

"Well," Virginia says, a false note of brightness in her voice. "It certainly feels larger. If we'd done this years ago, I wouldn't have had to suffer so many bruises from the maze of furniture."

Nicole glances from Virginia back to the room.

"Why aren't you taking all of it?" Nicole asks.

"The movers have packed everything we need for Les Baumées," says Virginia. "Besides, the concierge also owns the building. He bought back the place from us but said we can leave what furnishings we want and stay here when we come to the city. Nightly rental, like our own, personal hotel room. We can even keep a key. He'll send word if someone wants to buy the apartment, but he doesn't think that's likely."

Who can afford places like this now? she thinks.

"That's kind of him," says Nicole.

"I think he's holding on to hope this will all be over soon, and we'll be able to buy back in."

It gives Virginia a spark of joy just to say the words aloud. *Oh, if it were only true.*

"I pity those who can't see the writing on the wall," says Nicole. "This will all be much harder for them."

Virginia doesn't answer, the meaning of the words hitting their mark. She can't help but bristle. She doesn't appreciate Nicole's judgment, which she feels has hung over her since the incident at Cancaval with the German officer's horse. Last night, at Nicole and Michel's place, there had been a tense exchange when Virginia had asked Michel to stop speaking about a resistance movement of which he'd gotten word.

"Can we talk about something else?" she'd said. "It makes me uneasy."

"We can't ignore it," Nicole said.

"No," Virginia said. "But if we play by the rules, we all might make it through the war alive."

"The rules get worse every day. The noose tightens. Will you be saying that on the way to the hangman's platform?"

After an awkward silence, Philippe joins the women and places his hand on Virginia's back.

"Ready?" says Philippe.

"No," Virginia says. "But here we are."

The men embrace and switch off to kiss the women on both cheeks. Nicole gives Virginia a stiff hug that leaves her cold.

"Think of coming to Les Baumées for Christmas," Virginia says. "Mum and Grandmère hope to join us. We'll make room even though the place is small."

"We'll think about it," says Nicole.

She's polite, but Virginia hears in Nicole's voice that they won't.

After Nicole and Michel leave them, Philippe gives instructions to the movers, who will lock up the truck in their storage garage for the night and meet the couple at Nesles tomorrow. Then he and Virginia make their way to the Gare du Nord, where they'll take the train to Verville. It's the closest stop to Nesles and, without buses or taxis, from there they'll have to walk almost five kilometers to Les Baumées.

They leave and start for the station. Philippe threads his arm through hers and pulls her close to his side. As they turn the corner onto the rue Royale, they're startled by a German shepherd bounding toward them. Philippe pushes Virginia behind him as the dog stops short and bucks back, as scared by the appearance of the pair as they were of it. Frantic, dirty, and skinny, the dog runs back and forth across the street several times before collapsing, exhausted, in an alley, pushing itself against the stone of a building for some measure of security.

"Poor thing," Virginia says. "It's a stray."

"Do you have any food?" Philippe asks.

Of course not, she thinks, giving him a look.

Philippe walks to a nearby café and uses a ration ticket to buy a piece of the foul gray stuff they're calling bread. Virginia keeps an eye on the dog, who alternates between sitting and lying. It's a female, and one that has clearly been abandoned and possibly abused. When Philippe returns, they crouch down and whistle to her. The dog looks at them with her sad, tired eyes, but she won't cross the street.

While an old woman in a shop door looks on, Virginia and Philippe move slowly toward the dog. Once they're within a meter of her, Philippe holds out the bread. The dog pulls herself to sitting but won't come near them.

"You want some filthy boche mongrel?" the old lady asks.

"It's not her fault where she came from," Virginia says.

The old woman shrugs.

Philippe tears off a piece of bread and places it on the ground a few inches from the dog. She sniffs it but turns her nose up at it, drawing smiles from Virginia and Philippe.

"Who can blame her?" Philippe asks.

They stand to leave.

"We tried," Virginia says.

They give the dog sad looks before walking away but, in a few paces, they sense they're being followed. They stop and look over their shoulders to see the shepherd. She looks up at them with her large black eyes and flattens her ears.

Overwhelmed with affection for the pitiful animal, Virginia approaches her, holding out the back of her hand. With caution, the dog leans forward and sniffs. Then she allows Virginia to pet her. The dog's coat is thick, but her frame is thin. Virginia feels a release of tension in the animal as she strokes her. A noise calls their attention, and the old woman hurries to catch up, holding out a loop of twine.

"A leash," she says. "So the boches don't stop you."

Philippe thanks the old woman and takes the twine, fashioning a slipknot and carefully placing the leash over the dog's head.

Now three, the little group heads to the station, and though the dog is still skittish, she jumps toward Philippe's leg, cowering into him instead of away from him when frightened. Virginia is filled with an unspeakable joy. She loves animals, and adopting this scared, abandoned dog feels like a small good in a dark world. She can tell Philippe feels the same way. He keeps looking between her and the dog with a smile.

"We'll get her loved and fed and trained," Virginia says.

"And she'll be a great protector once we have her loyalty."

"I think we already do."

At the station, they're questioned by a German MP while he checks their papers.

"Where did you get this animal?" he says.

"We found her in the street," says Philippe.

"How do I know you didn't steal it?"

"You're welcome to have her," says Philippe, holding out the makeshift leash. "Keeping her fed will be a problem in these lean times. Also, I suspect she has a nasty case of fleas."

The MP shrivels his nose in disgust. German soldiers shrink back from anything they deem unclean. The MP waves them on, and Virginia gives Philippe a grin once they board the train.

Filled with new hope, they chatter and pet the dog all the train ride home. They decide to call her Nan, after Philippe's nursemaid when he was little, and discuss how she can help them hunt rabbits and alert them in case of any intruders. They're both as animated as they've been in a long while, so they scarcely notice that it has grown dark outside on the journey.

As soon as the train stops, Nan jumps up from where she slept and paces. She practically pulls Philippe off the train. To their horror, as soon as they step onto the platform, the whistle screams, startling them and making the dog shoot forward, snapping the thin leash. As she disappears into the night, they run after her and call her, but it's no use. She's too fast and she doesn't know her name.

Though it feels ridiculous to cry for a dog she's had for only an hour, Virginia can't help it.

Can there be no lasting joy? she thinks.

Philippe wraps his arm around her, and they start the long walk home. It's frightening in the cold and the dark without their protector, and Virginia imagines all sorts of terrors that could await them. Every breaking stick and shivering leaf causes her to jump, and when they make the final turn onto the road that leads to Les Baumées, she thinks she'll just crawl into bed and stay there until the holidays are over. What's the use in celebrating during so awful a time?

A noise on the road behind them makes Philippe stop. The hair on the back of Virginia's neck rises when she hears the footfalls. She and Philippe creep to the side of the road and look through the night in the direction of the sound, which gets closer. Virginia is about to scream, when suddenly, she makes out the outline of a dog, trotting down the road. Even in the shadows she can see the pointed ears, the full coat, and the spindly legs, moving ever faster toward them.

"It's her," says Philippe. "She must have followed our scent."

Elated, Virginia calls out. "Nan!"

The animal breaks into a full run toward them, and when they meet, Nan accepts their hugs and pats and praises with jumps and a wagging tail.

Their little family of three is now established at Les Baumées.

13

—— **VIOLETTE** ——

VIOLETTE'S WEDDING PHOTOGRAPH is sellotaped at eye level on the shiny switchboard at the telephonist station. In the picture, Étienne, Papa, and Roy are uniformed, a smart line of past and present soldiers who have fought or now fight the enemy. How she envies them.

She looks down at her ring.

"Come in, Violette," says her friend Vera. "Mayday."

"Sorry," says Violette.

"More honeymoon fantasies?"

"No, murder fantasies. Of Hitler," says Violette. "Étienne is off in Africa, making a real difference in the war. So are my brothers. And I'm stuck here in a converted post office, sitting on my bum for hours every day, connecting phone calls."

"Excuse me, I'll have you know I think we're making quite a difference. Keeping people connected is of the utmost importance in times of war."

"You sound like a propaganda poster."

Vera gives Violette a petulant look with her large brown eyes.

Violette grins and grabs Vera's face, planting a kiss on her cheek, leaving a stamp of bright red lipstick. How Violette loves her childhood chum, who has always gone along with whatever Violette asks her to do, including getting this job. While Vera giggles and swats Violette away, their boss—a steel-eyed woman in horn-rimmed glasses—peers across the room at them with disapproval. Violette and Vera quiet down and lean their heads together.

"Churchill should send her to meet with Hitler," whispers Violette. "She'd scare him into submission."

Vera snorts, but one more stern look causes her to sit upright.

"In all seriousness," says Violette, "there must be something more we can do."

"We can stay alive," says Vera. "So our men won't have fought in vain."

There's a rumble, and the floor of the station trembles. The clock reads six fifteen.

"Oh, not tonight," says Vera. "I so wanted a full night of sleep."

"Disperse," shouts the boss.

As the girls prepare to leave, an explosion causes the windows over them to shatter. Violette throws her coat across her and Vera and pushes her friend to the ground. Amid screams, glass rains over them, stinging their backs like tiny needles. When the barrage is finished, Violette helps Vera stand, grabs the wedding photo, and ushers Vera toward the door.

The frigid December night has become an inferno. Violette is stunned by the sight—the terrible beauty of the lights dropping from the sky and leveling the city like the devil's fireworks.

She returns to action, pulling Vera toward the nearest tube station. Violette has done this so many times it's possible even through walls of smoke and ash—fourteen paces forward, turn right, twenty-six paces, feel for the railing on the right. When they find the entrance, they stumble down the stairs to the stinking mass of humanity waiting out another night underground. Men and women whimper, children stare through the dark, wide-eyed.

This is their life, thinks Violette. *This is all they will remember of their short lives.*

The thought fills her with rage. She deposits Vera against a wall, but Violette cannot sit. Not for one more moment. She paces, cursing her impotence, until a man comes down the stairs.

"St. Paul's," he cries. "They hit St. Paul's."

A collective gasp goes around the crowd. Seeing the dome of the cathedral still standing over the rubble each morning has been the heart, the spine, the will to go on each day for Londoners. It's their hope.

Violette feels a crack in her foundation. All that she's been holding in, the tears she has refused to shed, the fear she has demanded stay at bay, comes rushing to the surface. A bomb drops nearby, rumbling the floor under their feet while dust falls on their heads. A crack slices across the ceiling of the station like a black lightning bolt. Violette pulls Vera up and they merge into the crowd as it rushes to the stairs. With bodies pressing against her, squeezing the breath from her lungs, Violette struggles against the crush until she hears a mewing sound, like a kitten.

"Don't stop," says Vera.

Violette can't help herself. People push all around them, desperate to escape before the ceiling collapses, but Violette can't get the sound out of her ear, the awful mewing. But it's not mewing, it's crying. There's a young child who can't be more than six standing under the staircase, trembling so violently he can't move. He reminds her of Dickie.

"Meet me at the lampstand," Violette says.

Without waiting for Vera's reply, Violette rushes against the last of the mass, pushing toward the child. In the vacancy, she's finally able to catch a good breath.

"Where's your mum?" she asks.

The ceiling makes a groaning sound.

Violette grabs the boy and lifts him, taking the stairs two at a time now that the station is empty. Outside, the city is so lit with fires, they can see everything and nothing. The obliteration renders the crowds dumbfounded. Where buildings stood just minutes ago are great holes and mountains of smoking rubble. A crater gapes where the telephone exchange used to be.

"Dragon," the boy says.

Violette's gaze follows where his finger points at a building choking fire out its windows, writhing as its frame bends in the conflagration. The boy whimpers, and the voice of a woman can be heard screaming.

"William!"

The boy begins to squirm so violently Violette has to put him down. The hysterical woman draws nearer, dragging two little girls, and when she sees the boy, rushes to him and grabs her son.

"I told you to stay with me!" the woman says, shaking him.

Violette finds the mother's raw terror uncomfortable to witness. The woman pulls the child away and is swallowed by the black haze. With the sound of roaring planes overhead, Violette's thoughts take her back to the dock at Calais. The little girl lying dead in the sand, her eyes matching her dolly's. Violette holds her head, wishing the memory would go away, when someone takes her arm and calls her name. It's Vera.

Again alert, Violette joins her friend, moving in the direction of St. Paul's. They hurry along Pilgrim Street, choking on smoke, fighting through a stinking cloud of smog and ash until they climb Ludgate Hill. From their vantage, they're able to take in London. It glows with an ungodly fire. Red flames light up the night, revealing the destruction.

How many have died tonight? thinks Violette. *How will we ever rebuild?*

It takes Violette a moment to realize she hasn't heard a bomb in many minutes, and a quiet begins to settle around them. A slight stirring of wind nudges away the heat and begins to dissolve the smoke. As the night clears, an exquisite sight awaits her eyes.

St. Paul's Cathedral still stands.

Violette and Vera hug each other and the strangers around them, cheering with joy. As they rejoice, a gentle snow begins, cooling the heat, suffocating the fires, covering the broken city in a white blanket. Violette holds out her arms in her torn, burnt coat, allowing the snow to cover and soothe her.

Under the glowing white of snow, the cathedral seems to rise even higher: a stubborn, towering beacon of hope still daring to stand in the face of evil.

14

NESLES-LA-VALLÉE

—— VIRGINIA ——

SHIVERING, HANDS BLUE in spite of wearing gloves, Virginia enters the house with her scant market provisions and curses when she sees the woodstove isn't lit. Philippe should have been back from the train station with Mum by now. Because of the difficulties of travel, not to mention the unholy cold, Grandmère decided to stay in Paris for the holidays, but Mum wanted to join her only child and his wife. They were due in around ten, and it's now one o'clock in the afternoon.

Virginia pauses to respond to Nan's greeting and walks to the kitchen with Nan circling. Virginia found a few cans of food and some biscuits for the dog. It seems not many people are using their resources for pet care. Virginia makes Nan sit before presenting her with a biscuit treat.

"You made out better than we did," Virginia says.

Each outing to the market gets worse than the last. Four hours. She waited four hours in lines today, frigid wind assaulting her, only to come home with one-fifth of a pound of butter, a carrot bunch, some rutabagas, and an octopus. For Christmas dinner. She'd cry if she didn't laugh when she saw that it was the only fish left.

Virginia places the octopus in the icebox and the rest of the groceries in the pantry, shaking her head at their ever-dwindling stores. Now that the apartment is sold, she and Philippe are on better financial footing than most, and she's thankful for it. But better footing or not, food selection is abysmal. The Nazis take everything for themselves and withhold the rest to force France's government at Vichy and the population at large to cooperate. And it's only the beginning.

An envelope on the counter catches Virginia's eye. When she sees the name and address—Edith Roush, St. Petersburg, FL—she can hardly believe it.

Mother!

Philippe must have gone to the post early. The envelope is dated November 25, almost a month ago to the day. Virginia tears it open and devours the words, racing through it so fast she has to read again, the second time around her sister's good news sinking deeply into her.

> *Eleanora's baby arrived! A fat, healthy boy they've named Marshall. Eleanora looked ready to pop at Thanksgiving dinner, but she went until November 24. We're so happy to have a baby to spoil at Christmas. How we all wished you were with us. You could still get out. The news from Europe is terrifying. My darling, please don't say never.*

"Never," Virginia says.

I will never leave Philippe.

Virginia stuffs the letter back in the envelope and tucks it in her pocket. Try as she does to be fully happy for her sister, the news pokes fresh scars. She never told her mother about the miscarriage. Who can put that in a letter? She's glad Philippe isn't here to see her reaction. At least she'll have time to compose herself before he and Mum arrive, time to work through the shameful emotions of envy and bitterness that plague her. Virginia's only consolation is that having a child under these conditions would be terribly strenuous. She keeps repeating that to herself over and over. Maybe one day she'll believe it.

Virginia hurries outside to fetch wood and returns to the kitchen stove. She wastes match after match, but the damp logs won't ignite. Philippe can't keep up with their demand. They burn fires all day and all night, giving the freshly cut wood no time to properly dry or air out. They even have to sleep with Nan between them, drawing warmth from her fur.

Poor Mum will be frozen.

Another match runs out, burning Virginia's fingertips. She shakes her hand and blows on it. Her nails are thin and brittle, and her skin is rough and chapped. She's run out of lotion, but no amount of it could keep up with what the cold and the washing and scrubbing do to her. She tries another match, but it's useless.

Virginia leans against the cabinets and slides to the floor, no longer able to see through her tears. Face in her hands, she doesn't register that Nan has gone bounding and barking toward the door, at least not quickly enough to compose herself before Philippe and Mum enter, their smiles quickly evaporating.

"The wood is wet," is all Virginia can manage to say.

Mum and Philippe give each other worried glances. Philippe holds up a bundle of dry logs wrapped in netting.

"Dr. Lebettre traded me these and more in exchange for four pounds of pasta and beans. And something else I think you'll like. It's your Christmas present. Come."

Philippe places the logs on the floor and helps Virginia to stand. Mum crosses the room and hugs her disheveled daughter-in-law, tapping a new reservoir of Virginia's tears.

"I'm sorry," says Virginia.

"Please," says Mum. "There's no need to apologize. I have to pick myself up off the apartment floor at least once a day."

But at least you pick up yourself, thinks Virginia.

"And how's my pretty granddog?" says Mum. "Will she let me pet her?"

"As long as I assure her you're safe," says Philippe.

He proceeds to introduce Mum to Nan, and Mum makes a fuss

over the dog for a few moments before the little group heads outside, leaving Nan whimpering at the door.

"Why can't Nan come?" asks Virginia.

"You'll see."

When they get close to the barn, Philippe covers Virginia's eyes with his hands, and they shuffle inside and to the stalls. Virginia hears her present before she sees it, and the sound gives her such joy she's almost dizzy from the extreme fluctuation of her emotions.

"Une poule!" Virginia says. She throws her arms around Philippe and kisses him.

The hen is a mottled black and white with a fluffy crest and beard. She's making a big fuss, sweeping piles of straw backward with her claws. And, lo and behold, in the corner they see a fat, glorious egg. The group laughs and exclaims over the bounty. Virginia picks up the precious treasure and, after they lock the hen in the barn, they return to the house, planning how they'll cook the egg.

Virginia falls behind Philippe and Mum, gazing upon their dear forms with love. She takes a deep breath and lifts her gaze to the sky. It's steel gray and smells of a coming snow, which would have filled her with misery earlier today, but now she fixes her eyes on what she has. Her husband and her mother-in-law. Her dog and her chicken. A letter from her mother. A new nephew. A home and health and a bundle of dry wood. If only for a night, that's all she needs.

MUM SPLATS THE slimy, wet octopus on the wooden cutting board. It looks as if it has just slunk in from the sea.

"Cut off its head and beat it," Mum says.

Virginia has stood in kitchens taking cooking instruction from Mum countless times, but Virginia thinks today will be the most memorable. She raises her eyebrows.

"Go on, dear," says Mum. "Imagine the enemy."

Virginia fixes her stare on the creature, and the German officer from Cancaval comes to mind. She picks up the knife and brings it down, hard. It's not a pretty cut, but it's clean.

"You were generous in your execution," says Mum. "I was hoping you'd hack at it a bit."

Mum uses surgical precision to remove the vital pieces, leaving only the tentacles and some edible parts of the head. She passes Virginia the tenderizer, which Virginia employs with violence. When she looks up from her task, Mum smiles at her, great pride evident on her face. She wipes a splatter off her cheek with the grace of a queen.

"Remind me never to get on your bad side," Mum says.

"I didn't know I had it in me," Virginia says.

"You have a great deal of *it* in you."

Virginia lowers her gaze and shakes her head, all of her fear and shame and anxiety churning like the water in the pot that's coming to a boil.

"I'm glad you think so," Virginia says. "I always was good at keeping up appearances."

"Give yourself more credit," says Mum.

Virginia doesn't know how to answer. She's been sulking inwardly since the war began, lamenting the loss of her fairy-tale life. For every step she makes forward, she finds she falls that much farther back. She envies her own sister for having a baby. She envies the others around her, who soldier on without hesitation, while she can barely keep up with the march.

"Where are you?" says Mum.

Virginia looks up at her mother-in-law, then around the kitchen.

"What do you mean?" Virginia asks.

"Where are you—my American daughter-in-law, who is free to go home to the safety and care of her family in warm, sunny Florida—as war ravages cold Europe?"

Virginia stays quiet.

"I'll answer for you," says Mum. "You're in France, with your husband, standing in the middle of the fire, voluntarily. My American daughter-in-law, who drove me through an air raid to safety, who cared for me on the long journey to Cancaval, while losing a baby, and never saying a word about it."

Mum knew. Virginia blinks back her tears.

"My beautiful American daughter-in-law," continues Mum, reaching for Virginia's hands, "who defied Nazi officers in whatever ways she could, who's learning to make a home on a farm where there are no workers, who keeps my son cared for and happy in spite of terrible conditions."

A little pilot light in Virginia's heart flickers to life.

"You're generous," says Virginia. "I feel like a spoiled child sometimes. You and Grandmère never complained about having to sleep in a peasant cottage after getting displaced by Nazis."

"Yes," says Mum, "because we lived through the Great War and the Spanish flu. We have calluses. But don't forget, it takes the skin breaking and bleeding many times before calluses are formed."

AFTER THE OCTOPUS dinner, which turned out much tastier than Virginia could have imagined, they decorate the little pine tree Philippe cut down, and exchange gifts. Mum and Virginia present Philippe with Mum's father's car coat—salvaged and hidden by the women during the thinning of the estate and lined with rabbit fur by the village seamstress in Nesles. Philippe's eyes roll to heaven when he pulls it over his large frame.

"Was this Granddad's?" Philippe asks.

"None other," says Mum. "He was as big as you are."

Next, Philippe and Virginia present Mum with her prize: the last pound of real coffee Virginia was able to buy at the market, months ago.

"No," says Mum. "I can't accept this."

"We insist," says Virginia.

"We'll at least share it while I'm here."

Mum hushes their protests and brews them each a cup. It will help them stay awake for midnight mass, which is actually at nine because of curfew. Philippe's father was Catholic, but the rest of them are Protestant. Saint-Symphorien is the only church in the village.

After coffee, they make their way. Candles illuminate the nave of the church. The spicy, pungent incense calls to mind the wise men. Abbé Rabourg, a former missionary, is like a star burning in the chancel.

"Hope is not a flimsy thing based on an outcome," says Abbé Rabourg. "It's a deep well—its source in God—from which we can draw in any situation."

Virginia thinks her life has always been about outcomes: degrees, marriage, children. She realizes she has a mindset that tells her, "You will finally be happy when this or that milestone is reached." But perhaps that's why—in spite of times of happiness—there has never been peace. Maybe peace is an illusion. Or maybe she has been looking for it in the wrong places.

"I beg you to find courage," the priest continues. "We're at the beginning of the winter of our lives. We can no longer delude ourselves by placing hope in the temporal. We must become new creations, acting out of love for our fellow man. Each act, no matter how small, is noticed by our Lord. And those acts will look different for each of us."

Virginia gazes around at the parishioners, mere shadows in the dark. She notes those closest to her. Their widowed neighbor, Madame Fleury, who with her late husband helped find the land for them to build Les Baumées. The baker, Marcel Renard, and his wife. Dr. Noël Lebettre, the earnest young village physician. It's good to be with people. It's good to be warm and safe, if only for a night.

"'Be not afraid,'" says Abbé Rabourg. "The most oft-repeated phrase in the Bible. Make that a prayer and keep it always on your lips. Some of my brothers are afraid to say it—and I understand—but I will not stay quiet any longer. The Nazis are evil. They are the enemy. Find ways to resist. Do not be afraid of those who can kill the body but not the soul."

Virginia is stunned at his pronouncement. The parishioners whisper around her. This is the first time she has heard a priest or minister speak so boldly from the pulpit. She looks at Philippe and at Mum, who raise their eyebrows.

Is it Virginia's imagination or does the congregation sit up a little straighter? Sing a little louder? By the time the service concludes, walking out through a dark cloud of incense, she feels wide awake.

The people file like soldiers down the dark streets, but a sudden sound causes them to look to the skies. Panic ensues when the airplane engine roars closer. Philippe shepherds Mum and Virginia toward Les Baumées, but as the plane crosses overhead, it doesn't fire upon them. It looks like a blizzard begins. Falling from the sky, what Virginia thought were snowflakes materialize into the papers they are. She reaches up and catches one, while those around her do the same.

It's a newspaper: *Le Courrier de l'Air. Joyeux Noël!* reads the headline. Underneath is a cartoon of Hitler getting punched in the face.

Virginia laughs aloud. She hears laughter around her. As the Allied plane leaves them, she looks back to the heavens, uplifted, as papers continue to fall gently over the village like snow.

15

LONDON

~≫≈~

—— **VIOLETTE** ——

TIME DURING WAR is a strange, altered, uneven thing.

As long as individual days drag, the months move at an astonishing speed. It scarcely seems any time has passed since Violette stood in the snow, back in December, crying tears of joy to see St. Paul's Cathedral had survived that unholy night of one hundred thousand bombs. The telephonist station, however, did not survive, forcing them to relocate to a cellar that reached its damp fingers deep into Violette's lungs, plaguing her with a cough, ending her employment.

It's now summer, a second summer of war. It seems as if a century has gone by since Violette's honeymoon, since she looked through the eyepiece of a telescope, cheek to cheek with sweet Étienne, hair littered with sunflower petals, skin flushed with the heat of love.

That was a year ago, not a century. And it has been six months since the telephonist station was bombed. And it has been two months since Étienne's last letter, which makes Violette chew her nails, and run to meet the postman each day, and scowl every time he has nothing for her.

When Étienne's letters do make it to her, they look as battered and aged as they're all becoming. Greedily, she reads and rereads them, particularly enjoying how he's taken to giving her secret messages. The last letter had read, "Are you reading your Bible like a good girl? Ex. 21."

She'd laughed aloud at the words, but then she'd grown quiet.

While pondering the strange question, she sought the family Bible and opened it to the passage Étienne had noted. It was when God parted the Red Sea for Moses and the Israelites. It was then Violette realized Étienne was telling her where he was, and it gave her a thrill.

Then he'd written, "I'm staying well fed on lots of pasta. I'm devouring it." Violette took that to mean Étienne was fighting the Italian Army. News reports supported it.

She's going mad worrying all the time about Étienne and living by the endlessly disappointing mail delivery cycle. Seeing women in ATS uniforms, while being unable to walk ten feet in London without coming across a poster for the service, convinces Violette what she must do.

100,000 WOMEN WANTED URGENTLY FOR THE AUXILIARY TERRITORIAL SERVICE! reads one poster.

NO WOMAN WILL EVER HAVE PEACE IN HER HEART UNLESS SHE HELPS THESE MEN! reads another.

Since April, women in the ATS have full military status. Duties used to be solely domestic—cooking and washing for the men— which held no interest for Violette. But now women are drivers and mechanics, and they staff searchlights and antiaircraft batteries, though they still aren't allowed to fire the guns. Violette has no doubt she'd be able to get off a round if she had the opportunity. The question is, will Étienne support her wishes? Like her parents, he wants her tucked snug within her family, keeping the home fires burning.

On her one-year wedding anniversary, Violette's mood is black. She should be in Étienne's arms, not at her parents' house, wondering if her husband is alive or dead. She had to get out for a walk, but she's been brooding so heavily, she's back home before she knows it. The poster closest to her house infuriates her.

COOK FOR THE TROOPS! GREAT RESPONSIBILITY IS BORNE BY THE ATS COOKS WHO NOURISH OUR MEN!

She tears it from the wall, crumples it into a ball, and throws it in the nearest rubbish bin. On her way inside, she slams the front door behind her.

"Vi, *s'il te plaît*," Maman chastises from the kitchen.

"*Je suis désolée*," Violette says.

When Violette enters the kitchen, her parents turn to her with smiles. Her mother steps aside to reveal a three-tiered cardboard wedding cake, with a real strawberry tart as its crown. Papa promptly tops it with the bride and groom from Violette's wedding. She's so touched by the gesture, her anger evaporates. Maman holds open her arms and Violette falls into them.

A knock at the door calls Papa away, but he's soon back and beaming.

"A telegram," he says.

Violette pulls away from her mother and snatches the envelope from Papa. Her hands shake as she devours the words that lift her from her misery and send her whooping and shouting all over the house. She can hardly believe it.

Étienne!

ÉTIENNE RUNS A raven feather down Violette's side, from her breast to her thigh, and back up to her neck, which he punctuates with a kiss. He slides the feather in her hair and brings his lips to hers.

For days they've barely left the Liverpool hotel room. Étienne's week of leave is almost concluded, and aside from surfacing for the necessity of food and drink, they've stayed in bed consuming each other. Even after the long year apart, Violette feels no shyness, not a breath of hesitation. Remarkable, really, since their courtship had lasted only half a summer. How can this man she has known in person for three months of her life feel as if he has been in it forever?

"My love," Étienne says in French. "In Egypt, there are ravens in the desert they say bring good luck. There was one I saw every day. Its shiny blue-black wings made me think of your hair."

She kisses his neck while he whispers to her.

"When we won the last battle," he says, "I saw the raven, and as it flew from me, it left a feather on the ground. I can't tell the difference between it and your blue-black hair. Your violet eyes. My Violette."

She bites his ear, and once he is fully relaxed, lying across her body, she tickles him. He squirms, attempting to get out of her grasp, but she wraps her legs around him, continuing her assault. He's able to grab her wrists and pin her to the bed, but she quickly pushes him over until she's on top of him. She pins him down and nuzzles his neck.

"Woman. You're an animal."

She bites his ear in reply.

When daylight fades, she pulls the shutters, ties the blackout curtains, lights candles around the room, and two cigarettes, one for each of them. He sits up to smoke in bed and pats the place next to him, but she walks to the vanity, sits, removes the feather, and brushes her hair. Their gazes meet over her shoulder in the mirror.

"I need to ask something of you," she says.

"Anything."

"I want your blessing to enlist in the ATS."

"Why must you keep up with this? I have one day left."

"One day. Then you'll be gone. Maybe for another year. And I'll be stuck here, idle. Doing nothing but worrying. Wasting my talents."

"Preserving yourself. For me. For us."

"Not preserving. Dying a little. Each day."

"Then move. You get my pay. Rent a flat. A sweet little place for me to come to when I'm on leave. Where we can start our life after the war."

"And do what in that flat? Stare at the four walls? Pace like a caged panther?"

"You could go back to a different telephonist station."

"I'm made for more!" she says, slamming the vanity with her hand.

Étienne puts out his cigarette, throws off the covers, and rushes to her, kneeling at her feet.

"I beg you," he says. "Keep yourself out of danger."

He buries his face in his hands. She stands and paces away from him.

"Nowhere is safe, Étienne. When the station was bombed, glass shattered over me and my lungs weren't right for months. I'm not going to the front; I just want to help however I can. Shorten the war however I might."

She crosses back to him, pulls him to standing, and presses herself to him. Their kisses are like gasps of air. She pulls him to the bed, and when they're spent, he lays his head on her breast and she strokes his hair. He holds her so tightly she can barely breathe.

"I want you to voice your blessing," she says.

"How can I permit my wife to endanger herself?"

She stops stroking. He lifts his head to look into her eyes.

"I did not say 'permission,'" she says. "I said 'blessing.'"

THE BANQUET HALL is hung with streamers and garlands, cigarette smoke, aftershave, and chatter. Rows and rows of young men and women sit in smart uniforms, pretending they're not preparing for war.

The moment Étienne had left, Violette had dragged Vera to the recruitment office for the ATS to complete their applications. Violette had proudly presented hers to the woman in charge.

"Violette Reine Elizabeth Bushell Szabo," the woman read. "Are you some kind of royalty?"

"Hardly. Just a wife of a serviceman who wants him home as soon as possible."

"Then you've come to the right place. I see your talents lie in languages, athletics, and shooting."

"Prizewinning."

"I also see you've listed your weaknesses. We did not ask for those."

"Yes, but stating clearly I'm not meant for strawberry picking, sewing, cleaning, or cooking should help in the placement process."

The woman had lifted her gaze to Violette's face, scanned her from head to toe, and returned it to the application, where she made a note.

"How long till training?" asked Violette.

"Watch the mail, dear. You'll know in a week if you'll be assigned."

SISTERS OF NIGHT AND FOG

As Violette turned to leave, the woman said, "Then you'll find out what you're made of."

It had delighted Violette. She knew exactly what she was made of. And now, she's at the head of her class in the ATS.

Weeks of antiaircraft training with the mixed battery in Shropshire have been intense and exhausting. Teams of men and women have become experts in seeking and setting the course to destroy Luftwaffe fighters, and they await their assignments with impatience.

Violette taps her foot, eager to get on with the awards ceremony so the fun can begin. She's been preparing her dance all week for the evening's mixed revue, and the performance is sure to set tongues wagging.

As the final awards conclude, Violette leans toward Vera. "You up for a late-night mission?"

"No," says Vera. "If we get caught again, we'll have to run for hours. I've just got over my blisters from last time."

"Oh, come on. You know the bombardier was amused that we found his cigarette stash."

"But less so that you depleted it by half. What d'you want to risk punishment for this time?"

Violette points to the streamers overhead.

"For our bums," says Violette. "It looks softer than the tissue in the toilet."

Vera snorts.

"Gunner Szabo!" the emcee calls, followed by applause.

Violette has no idea why she's been named but stands and waves at the crowd as if she does.

"Gunner Violette Szabo," the commander says. "Sharpest shooter of the bunch, achieving one hundred percent of all targets."

She goes to the podium and bows to allow him to hang the award around her neck. She can't wait to tell Papa—the man who has taught her everything he knows, who takes her out poaching pheasants at night, when they stay in the country with his sister, Aunt Florrie. Their shooting is a sticky subject with Maman. She almost divorced Papa the time he shot an apple off Violette's head with an air rifle. But shooting is one of the only things they have in common, and she knows Papa will be proud.

Once they're dismissed from the ceremony, Violette hurries to the dressing area to change. Vera helps her into the belly dancing costume Maman made from old curtains and adds beaded combs to Violette's hair. Violette applies another layer of red lipstick and stands back to admire herself.

"Goodness! Look at me," says Violette.

"This brassiere deserves an award if it holds you up during your performance," says Vera.

"Maman will be delighted to see I've finally bloomed," says Violette. "I've never had buzzies my whole life. Hey, what's taking so long back there?"

"I can't get these buttons fastened. Suck it in."

Violette pulls in her breath and looks down at her stomach.

"You're up!"

Violette shoos off Vera and hurries toward the stage. The lights are dark, and the audience hushed. Vera cues up the record, and the sultry music begins. Violette closes her eyes and imagines herself in a desert, Étienne before her, incense perfuming the tent while she dances. There are soon whistles and howls, and as the speed of the music increases, she builds to more acrobatic moves until the climax, when she makes a backward somersault ending in a split.

She's exhilarated until the air hits her and she realizes her newly ample bosom has freed itself from the brassiere. As she quickly rights her costume, she receives a standing ovation, and she finds herself blushing, perhaps for the first time in her life. She pretends she doesn't care that she has exposed herself to a full auditorium and bows, accepting the applause. Back in the dressing area, Vera meets her, laughing while she helps Violette back into her uniform.

"How d'ya think Étienne will react when he hears you've joined the Moulin Rouge?"

"I think I'll hold this little secret close to my heart so *his* won't stop."

"It'll be hard to hold anything close to that heart, with those breasts popping out from it."

Violette and Vera laugh all the way back to their chairs. They arrive as a tap dance number starts and, with the cadence of the men's powerful stomps, it's all they can do to stay in their seats. It's during a ventriloquist act, however, that a sharp wave of nausea sobers Violette. With each act in the show, Violette grows more unsettled.

Could it be? No.

She doesn't allow the thought to fully form itself, even telling herself she imagined the nausea until another wave rolls over her.

For the last performance, a baby-faced young man with red hair takes the stage, singing "Paper Doll" in a smooth voice, earnest and sad.

Violette's body feels strange to her, embedded with a fatigue the likes of which she has never before experienced. She closes off all thought of why—refuses to allow her mind to travel that road.

I must listen to this song, she thinks. *Live in this moment.*

The summer they had courted, she and Étienne had danced to "Paper Doll" at the Locarno. How close he had held her, humming in her ear. She feels an actual ache in her from all the places on her body he can't touch from so far away.

The song undoes her. Like that night on the beach, she can't help but think that all these boys and girls dressed up as men and women will die. And all the sharpshooting and belly dancing and mixed revues, the quarrels and dreams and honeymoons will be nothing. Memories burned to ashes, drifting away on the winds of war.

Ignoring Vera's whispers, Violette leaves the hall. Once outside, she looks to the sky, but there's no moon, and her head aches, and she can't get a good breath. She feels as if she's suffocating. She gasps and presses her hands to her chest.

It hurts.

Violette staggers away from the hall, across the field, until she finds an empty army canister by the railroad tracks. She sits and turns her gaze back to the sky. The stars pulse overhead. With lights blackened, every constellation is revealed. Looking up helps her breathe better.

Violette recalls the night she and Étienne fell in love. They had watched *A Midsummer Night's Dream* at the open-air theater in Regent's Park, and he'd kissed her for the first time. His mouth had traveled from hers, down her neck. She'd opened her eyes because she wanted to remember the enchantment, and the moon and stars were twinkling for them. She'd said, *Stop*, and Étienne had pulled away, concerned he'd gone too far. She reassured him she was speaking to time. His laugh had vibrated down her neck and embedded itself in her bones. The people around them laughed at the play, at Bottom's absurd portrayal of the death of Pyramus.

"Now am I dead, Now am I fled; My soul is in the sky. Tongue, lose thy light; Moon, take thy flight. Now die, die, die, die, die."

Laughter around. Laughter within. Laughter in spite of war. Because of it. Aren't we absurd?

It was not Étienne's kiss, but his laugh, that made Violette fall in love with him. If she could only hear it now.

God, to be back at that night, watching that play, kissing Étienne, laughing with him.

Somewhere on the periphery of her consciousness, Violette senses the hall behind her emptying, ghostly shadows of future soldiers slipping back to their barracks, happy and safe, if only for a night. She longs to fold in with them. But with each wave of nausea, certainty grows. She doesn't return to join the others because she knows—almost as soon as she's become one of them—she'll have to leave them.

Though she knows Vera will worry, Violette remains outside alone—but not alone—all night. She watches the sky until a rim of light begins to glow at the horizon, bringing in a new time.

APRIL 1995
FÜRSTENBERG

I SHOULDN'T HAVE come.

I stare out the open bus window over the lake, unable to move. I hold my breath so I don't breathe in the cold wind blowing off the water, because I know what's under it. A man rows a yellow canoe over the surface. A vessel out for a pleasure cruise. Does he know what lurks in the depths, what was dumped there?

Our guide, a woman of about forty, stands at the front of the bus. She's German but speaks to us in French. The German accent still makes my palms sweat and my body shake. It's an involuntary, uncontrollable response I've had since the war. The woman calls our attention to the large statue of two emaciated women presiding over the lake—one holding another with a shaved head, gazing up to heaven.

"*Tragende* (*Woman with Burden*), by sculptor Will Lammert," the guide says. "The Pietà of Ravensbrück."

The statue is ugly. As ugly as we were. It could have been made of me. Of any of us.

Our guide is plump and fresh-faced, with a thick, blonde chignon. She could be one of the guards who tortured us years ago. One would think the tour organizer would have been more thoughtful about such things. But the younger generation doesn't understand. They can't because we haven't spoken about the war. It occurs to me, if we don't start talking soon, it will be too late.

"Let's get this over with," says my friend.

Fine. We've come this far. We might as well go farther.

It's a horror to step off the bus into the throngs being ushered through the gates. It could be now or fifty years ago but, instead of being sorted by SS guards, we have sorted ourselves. My friend and I stand amid the French. There are Russians around us. Poles. Belgians. Austrians. Hundreds of Jewish women arrive wearing blue and gray headscarves. Some of the women have worn their old prison garb.

Why would they do this?

I'm overcome with nausea, but I'm able to suppress it. Others around me aren't so lucky.

My friend and I hold each other a little tighter and force our legs to take us, one step at a time, back through that horrid gate. Back to a place we'd hoped never to return.

II

1942–44

In my view women were very much better than men for the work. Women, as you must know, have a far greater capacity for cool and lonely courage than men.

—*Captain Selwyn Jepson,*
British SOE senior recruiting officer

16

PARIS

——— VIRGINIA ———

PRETENDING EVERYTHING IS all right is still Virginia's greatest temptation. The serpent is ever at her ear, whispering to her that the path of least resistance is best.

It's easy to pretend at La Coupole, an American bar in Montparnasse, where the art deco walls echo with the laughter of many years ago, where the black-market alcohol flows freely, where the mirrors reflect endless faces that merge in the change of the light, the tilt of the head, one face becoming another. The bar feels like a gilded incubator, a place apart from the dark, angry world, though it is not safe. Nowhere in Paris is.

Virginia runs her eyes over the beveled glass whose edges break and twist the iron crosses and swastikas on the sprinkling of Nazi uniforms in the crowd into black versions of the yellow stars now stitched on the lapels of every Jew in Paris. She laughs darkly in her drink at the irony.

"I love to hear you laugh, my darling," says Philippe. "So rare these days."

His voice is thick with alcohol. He leans heavily on her from one side, pushing her toward Nicole and Michel, where they're crowded into the booth. Philippe throws off a lot of heat, and that, combined with the temperature in the bar and her perpetual uneasiness, makes Virginia feel queasy. The many glasses of wine she's consumed aren't helping. Tomorrow will be unpleasant.

"What's tickled you?" Philippe asks.

"She's laughing at the boches," says Nicole. "They look a little shaky. They know the Allies are taking the air."

In their secret broadcasts, the BBC had reported a thousand British bombers had rained hell on Cologne, displacing over forty thousand of its German residents. It had cheered them all to no end, though it makes Virginia nervous to play the radio program that could get them arrested.

"Let's toast to the RAF," says Michel.

The group raise their glasses, then drain them.

A Nazi across the way erupts into a laugh.

Virginia worries they'll be heard.

"We need to find a place where the pigs don't gather," says Nicole.

"In Paris?" says Philippe. "If you find it, let me know, will you?"

"We better go," says Nicole to Michel.

They lean over to kiss Virginia and Philippe before departing, and weave their way through the crowd, disappearing out the door into the night. Philippe looks back toward the toilet and sighs at the substantial line.

"We have a long walk," he says. "I must. Pardon."

Philippe leaves Virginia at the table. She feels blurry, like a sketch with smudged edges. She could use a glass of water. She searches the miniature skyline of alcoholic vessels along the table, illuminated in the flickering candlelight. There's a low pool of water at the bottom of one of Philippe's bourbon glasses, where the ice has melted. She drains it, wrinkling her nose at the medicinal taste but grateful for the small relief of cold liquid on her tongue. She closes her eyes to savor the feeling.

"It's good, *ja?*"

Her eyes snap open.

A Luftwaffe fighter stands before her, red tips on his collar over columns of flight decorations. His hair is black and shiny, and his eyes are so brown they also appear black. He smiles at her, and his dimple softens his intimidating appearance. Her instinct is to return the smile. She's pleased she's able to suppress it.

"May I?" he asks in English.

Can she refuse? Nicole would. In fact, Nicole's entire aura would have put him off to begin with. Virginia fumbles for a response.

"My husband is just . . ." Her voice trails off, but she nods in the direction of the restroom.

"Oh, I'm not being forward," he says. "I'm married. To an American, which you clearly are."

I am? she thinks.

"I heard you speaking earlier," he says in answer to her thought.

She stiffens. Did he hear their German slurs and talk of Allied successes? Is he trying to trap her? He doesn't seem to be, but one must be careful.

He looks around as if he doesn't want to be heard, then leans toward her.

"I confess," he says. "I'm homesick for America. I lived there before I was mobilized. In Miami."

Before she can censor herself, she blurts, "Florida! That's where I'm from."

He grins and slides into the booth.

When will I learn? she thinks.

While she inwardly curses herself, he begins rambling about his wife and his favorite beaches. She's so ashamed to have let down her guard, and to be seen sitting with a Nazi. What will Philippe think?

"Have you been down to the Keys?" he asks.

She nods.

"It's a good little spot. Lots of promise. I try to think of it when I'm in battle."

A waiter comes by and the Nazi orders three glasses of champagne. Over his shoulder, Virginia sees Philippe returning. She widens her eyes and glances at the Nazi. Philippe's face darkens. He stands up taller and waits for the waiter to leave before approaching. When he reaches the table, he stands over the Nazi, throwing his shadow over him. The Nazi begins to rise to introduce himself, but Philippe waves him down with a grunt and slides in next to Virginia. She squeezes Philippe's thigh under the table.

"I was just telling your wife that my wife is also from Florida," the Nazi says.

"What a small world," Philippe says, his voice low and joyless.

"Were you in the army?"

"Cavalry," says Philippe.

"Good. I'm a gunner for the Luftwaffe. Terrible thing to be."

The waiter arrives with the champagne. The Nazi insists on treating but also insists they raise their glasses to Nazi victory. Virginia and Philippe stiffly obey, but neither of them drinks. The Nazi drains his flute and runs a hand through his smooth black hair.

"You can't imagine the terror of being in a dive-bomber," he says. "I'm on leave for a few more days, but then it's back in the air for me. Are you going to drink that?"

He points to Virginia's glass, and Virginia shakes her head.

"Good," he says, reaching for it. "A temperate wife. Nice work."

He nods at Philippe, as if Philippe has groomed her. She feels a flare of anger and squeezes Philippe's leg tighter.

"Would you also have mine?" says Philippe. "I'm afraid I've already had too much to drink. I won't feel well tomorrow. You should indulge as much as possible before your return to war."

Virginia fights to keep the smile off her face. She knows that Philippe means that the gunner should indulge before he dies. She's no expert, but survival odds for a gunner can't be good. Savage though it is, she hopes this man's plane goes down in flames.

After the third glass of champagne, the gunner goes over the edge into drunkenness. His eyelids grow heavy, and he begins to blather about the necessity of German victory for world order. He sounds like he's memorized a propaganda film. It's all Virginia can do to sit still, listening to this man spew such evil, but she doesn't have to wait long.

"It was good speaking with you," says Philippe, excusing them from the booth.

Virginia can hear Philippe's thoughts. She knows he means it's good to know the gunner is scared and will likely die.

The Nazi is so consumed with his own rambling, he barely notices them leave.

Philippe holds Virginia's hand so tightly it's painful. They walk faster and faster from the bar, nearly bursting from the door at a run. Once outside, they take great gulps of the fresh night air.

17

LONDON

—— **VIOLETTE** ——

WRITHING AND GROWLING on the table, Violette gasps, taking a great gulp of air before pushing. She harnesses all her fury and bears down.

Étienne is not here. He promised, and he's not here for the birth of his child.

It's not his fault, but in the chaos and pain of labor—alone—she hates him. She hates all men for never having to tear themselves in two to bring a baby into the world, especially her father, for doing this to her mother six times. She hates all men because they make the wars that keep the fathers from their children, the husbands from their wives, and sisters and friends and lovers apart. They have made war since the first murderous set of brothers walked the earth and will until the end of time, and she hopes every last one of them burns in hell.

She falls back on the pillow, sweat clinging to her neck.

Violette almost hadn't made it to St. Mary's Hospital in Paddington, and it's only a mile from her new flat in Notting Hill. She'd rented the one-bedroom place two months ago, back in May, so her growing family would have a home of their own. In bombed and broken London, Pembridge Villas remains reassuringly intact. Her flat has high ceilings with tall windows to allow for maximum natural light in the daytime and heavy draperies already installed for nighttime blackouts. Building amenities include an enchanting walled garden and a basement shelter.

Étienne wrote to Violette that one day he would surprise her with a knock on the door there, which turned out to cause her severe strain. There are many knocks at the door, but he's never on the other side when she opens it.

The unbearable pressure returns, and she again rises to push. She harnesses her hatred of the Nazis for this round.

After months of Allied superiority, German general Rommel and his forces broke the British defensive line and took Tobruk, forcing the Allies back to Egypt. This does not bode well for Étienne's unit, which has to be exhausted beyond comprehension.

She can relate.

"Too bad we didn't have time to sedate this one," the doctor mumbles to the nurse.

Violette fires a string of curses at him he won't soon forget. Then she bears down one last time. Her scream is eclipsed by the baby's cry, a banshee shriek that startles the room to silence. The doctor holds up the howling, bloody infant.

"A girl," he says, eyes wide over his mask at the wriggling child in his hands. "Like her mother."

Though Violette is half out of her mind, the meaning of his remark isn't lost on her. But the small, dark squall of a girl is so feisty, and so new and fresh and pure, Violette bursts out laughing. Her daughter is placed on her chest and the girl quiets. She looks toward Violette's face with heavily lidded infant eyes, and Violette feels as if a supernova explodes in her heart, bathing the room in its light.

"*MA DOUCE PETITE fille*," Violette whispers, her lips on her daughter's dark, downy head.

Violette refused to let the nurse take the baby to the nursery, so the infant sleeps on Violette's chest. She needs sleep but she's never felt so awake. She cannot comprehend the fact that she has a child, that this human is utterly dependent upon her, that such dizzying heights of hope and light and love are possible in wartime.

Violette has named her little girl Tania for the fairy queen Titania from *A Midsummer Night's Dream*, the play from the night she and Étienne fell in love. She hopes he likes the name. She knows he will.

Tania burrows into Violette and makes a little grunting sound, and Violette feels such a rush of love that it takes her breath and leaves her with a rising sense of panic. She thinks of the girl on the dock at Calais, of Violette's dead little brother, Harry. She knows she couldn't live if anything happened to this child, and they've only just met. She can't stand the world she has brought Tania into, and the restlessness Violette hoped would dissipate with the birth of her baby has multiplied.

Tenfold.

When the nurse returns, Violette climbs out of bed and pushes Tania into the nurse's arms.

"You should lie down," the nurse says.

"If I'm still another minute, I'll go mad."

"You just gave birth."

"When can I go home?"

"In a week."

"Like hell."

Riffling through her suitcase, Violette hardly knows what she's doing.

"It's midnight," the nurse says as Tania fusses. "You're certainly not going anywhere now."

Violette looks at the clock and sees the nurse is right. Vision blurring the numbers, she squeezes her eyes shut and leans on the chairback. She vaguely registers the nurse's call for help and the baby's crying before everything goes black.

18

∼⚬∼

—— VIRGINIA ——

A WHISTLE YANKS Virginia from sleep. Glad for a moment to be wrenched from the nightmare, she's quickly reminded by grim reality that waking is no respite. She opens one eye and feels the headache pulsing through it. Her mouth feels like it's full of cotton. She reaches for the glass on the nightstand but it's empty.

Virginia regrets last night's alcoholic overindulgence, something they're engaging in more and more as their anxiety rises. An unsettling visit they all made yesterday afternoon to Mum's had put them on edge and required an antidote, even knowing the antidote would later make the pain sharper.

Madame Mollet, a friend from Mum's church, had visited Mum. A widow of a Frenchman, Madame had recently been released from an internment camp for Englishwomen at Besançon, near the Swiss border. Her once luxurious crown of white hair had thinned and yellowed, and her emaciated, clawlike hands trembled on the teacup, causing an unnerving clinking every time she placed it back in the saucer.

"The day of the roundup," Madame had said, "they called me to the town hall and told me I had thirty minutes to pack. If I didn't return, I'd be hunted and executed."

They'd all looked at Mum in horror, wondering if she'd be next.

"She'll be all right," Madame Mollet had said, seeing their alarm. "I was released because I turned sixty-five. They don't want any old women."

Thank God, Virginia had thought.

"The conditions were odious," Madame Mollet continued. "Filth left in puddles. A diet of old potatoes washed down with cloudy water. Sick women and children defecating in the dirt. Manual labor. I became ill and was sent to the hospital there, which turned out to be a godsend. It was warmer and we had soup. I never thought I'd be so happy to be old and sick. It was my exit ticket."

That night, along with Nicole and Michel, Virginia and Philippe had drowned their worries about the ever-tightening Nazi noose, about Mum's safety, and about the looming threat of American internment, now that the United States had been sucked into the war. It made them all feel guilty, but the thought of a few hours' drunkenness to numb the pain was a temptation none of them could resist.

Virginia and Philippe hadn't even made it home. They crashed at Nicole and Michel's apartment. But the only sleep Virginia got was plagued with nightmares where she was the one called to the town hall and imprisoned. She kept seeing images of her hands as they were pulled from Philippe's, as dirt caked her fingernails, as her young skin became old and shriveled and as clawlike as Madame Mollet's.

A shrill whistle again slices through the air. Philippe groans and covers his head with his pillow. Virginia drags herself out of bed and crosses to the window, opening the heavy curtain only enough to see out onto the street. In the building's shadows, she's startled to see motion. Gendarmes herd groups of disheveled people illuminated by the yellow stars on their clothing.

Michel had told them the stars were only the beginning for the Jews. Virginia hadn't wanted to listen. She tried to curate the bad news. She thought there wasn't enough space in her head or her heart to process all of it. She had better make room.

"Philippe," she whispers.

He rises and comes up behind her, looking down over her head at the street. Families are pushed and prodded. Few hold suitcases. Some still wear their nightclothes. Philippe utters a curse.

"Women and children," she whispers.

Large numbers of Jewish men were rounded up in May, but many said it was only foreigners, as if that were any consolation. Now it appears they're arresting more, and sheer numbers would indicate there are French men and women being taken.

Virginia sees a woman whose beautiful wavy hair is pinned up at the sides. On one arm, she supports an elderly lady—perhaps her mother—while grasping a little boy's hand with the other. The woman walks as stiff and tall as she's able, her face alert and strong. She lifts her eyes up to where Virginia stares. A gendarme also catches sight of Virginia watching. She sucks in her breath and closes the curtain, shame washing over her.

Philippe withdraws to the room and pulls on his clothing.

"Where're you going?" she says. "You can't go out there. It's too dangerous."

"I'm not Jewish."

"But you don't know what's happening."

"I need to find out."

"Then I'll come with you."

"No!"

She's startled by his tone.

"No," he says, more quietly. "You know you're an enemy. They could take you, too."

The truth they've been avoiding, uttered aloud.

Philippe breaks her stare and looks down to tie his shoes.

She's surprised to find that the pressure of this unsaid thing is released in the saying. Naming it hasn't made her more afraid. If anything, she feels less so.

While Philippe watches her in silence, she dresses, brushes her teeth and hair, and pulls on her shoes. She grabs her handbag, scribbles a note of thanks to Nicole and Michel, and hurries to the door.

Philippe hangs back, torn—she knows—between his need to gather information and his fear that something will happen to her. While she holds the doorknob, he stands in the middle of the living room, staring at her. She meets his gaze.

"When we were separated," she says, "I thought I would die. And I know you felt the same. You know as well as I, we're not complete if we're not together. From now on, as long as we can control it, there will be no more talk of you doing things separately from me. So, we either walk out this door together, or we stay in the apartment together. But we're not taking separate paths. No matter what. And you must stop suggesting it. Now, are we going, or not?"

He remains still. Immobilized in a way she has never before seen in her husband.

Fear can be more powerful than love, she thinks. *Fear of what will happen to those we love. To ourselves. What will happen if we act? What will happen if we don't act? Fear can keep a person firmly planted even when the soil has run dry, even if it means withering away alone.*

Philippe loves her too much to decide, so she'll have to decide for him. She opens the door with one hand and holds out the other to him.

He takes it.

PARIS HAS NEVER felt so inhospitable.

As quickly as the human tide below them swelled, it recedes, leaving the dark, empty streets haunted. The faraway cries and shouts grow faint, but the air still buzzes from the terror that has coursed through it.

Virginia and Philippe hold each other's hands. They move swiftly toward their apartment, hating the noise of their shoes clicking on sidewalks, echoing off buildings. The humidity is already oppressive, and the sun hasn't even risen.

Faraway sirens pierce the morning air, compelling them to walk faster. Along the way, they note broken windows and open doors in places that are usually tidy. Anti-Semitic posters are plastered on store-fronts owned by Jews. There's a smattering of trucks being loaded with furniture and artwork.

Virginia and Philippe look at each other in shock. They knew things were getting bad, but this is incomprehensible. Jewish families are being rounded up, their homes ransacked. And where are they being taken—to camps like the one at Besançon? In France or in Germany? When will they be able to return?

When Virginia and Philippe turn onto the rue de Sèvres and reach the jewelry shop where Philippe bought Virginia's engagement ring from Monsieur Fruchter, they stop short.

A gendarme yanks Madame Fruchter out of the shop by her long gray hair. Her nightgown is splattered with blood, and her screams are punctuated by the sounds of glass shattering and wood smashing. While she's forced into the waiting truck, a gendarme uses a knife to slash through the black-and-white awning over the store.

Virginia and Philippe hide in an alleyway and peer out, horrified at the scene before them.

Monsieur Fruchter soon appears, dragged by two gendarmes. He has a gash on his forehead that sends rivers of blood down his face and pajamas, and he can barely walk. He's shoved into the covered bed of the truck after his wife, and after a gendarme shoots the beautiful oval of etched glass out of the shop door, the vehicle rumbles into gear.

As it nears Virginia and Philippe, they flatten themselves against the alley wall, praying they aren't seen. The noise of the engine recedes, and they're left with the sounds of faraway sirens and their own ragged breathing. They stay there a long time, immobilized.

How could we hide? Virginia thinks. *How could we let our friends get dragged away without trying to help?*

Following their honeymoon, after they had returned to Paris, Philippe had taken Virginia to meet the Fruchters. Madame's gray hair was pinned in a stylish chignon, and she'd worn a sleek lavender dress with gleaming silver buttons. She'd lifted the cat-eye glasses on the chain around her neck, taken Virginia's hand, and held the ring close to admire how it looked. Monsieur had offered to clean it for free, and they'd had espresso while they waited, Madame taking Virginia through the provenance of the ring and telling her it had finally found its rightful owner.

Virginia looks at the ring on her left hand, gleaming in the shadows, but the vision of Madame's bloodstained nightgown and Monsieur's battered face assaults Virginia. She pulls away from Philippe and runs as far into the alley as she can before getting sick.

19

LONDON

——— VIOLETTE ———

SINCE THE BIRTH of the baby, Violette has experienced a severe depression of spirits. Refusing her mother's offer to come stay with them, Violette insisted on taking Tania to her flat in Notting Hill. But Violette had no grasp of the demands of a newborn, the sheer relentlessness of their needs, and how hard it would be without another adult around for support.

Étienne was heartbroken to have missed Tania's birth, and admitted in his last letter that he'd barely survived a recent battle. Between the newspapers and the BBC, Violette has pieced together Étienne's unit was at Bir Hakeim in Libya, where Rommel took another victory.

"I look forward to the day when this is all over," Étienne wrote. "When the three of us will walk into L'église de la Madeleine in Paris. We'll light candles, and hear Mass, and thank God for our survival, and for our blessings. I can *see* it, Violette, and that vision assures me all will be well. Can you see it, my love?"

She cannot. All she sees are images of war and annihilation. All she feels is guilt for bringing a baby into this broken world. And the news from France brings fresh despair.

The paper says thirteen thousand Jews were rounded up by French police in Paris, held at the Vélodrome d'Hiver, the arena where Tante

Marguerite had once taken Violette and her brothers to watch the circus. The men, women, and children were crowded like cattle in a stadium whose mirrored ceiling had been painted for blacking out, making an oven of the place. There was one water tap and no lavatories, and attempted escapees were shot. A pregnant woman had to give birth on the dirt.

Violette still bleeds from childbirth, but she has running water, and a home with a soft bed, and a crib for Tania. The thought of that poor mother and infant makes Violette weep.

Tania wails in the other room, but Violette can't lift herself from the couch. She doesn't know how much time passes when there's a knock at the door.

"Étienne!" Violette says.

She rushes to the door and throws it open, but it's not her husband.

Maman looks at Violette with pity and escorts her daughter back to the couch. Then Maman goes to Tania, consoles her, carries her to Violette, and helps get Tania latched onto Violette's breast. The let-down stings but, once the pain passes, she feels the relaxation. She can't stop crying.

"I know, *chérie*," Maman says. "It's hard at first."

Maman's gaze finds the newspaper open on the table. Her eyes skim the words before she closes it.

"Come home, Vi. Just for a week."

Violette shakes her head.

"It's not good for you to be alone with the baby. Let me help you."

"Papa's too much."

"I'll send him to Florrie's," says Maman. "I'll tell him to take Dickie for a holiday, so you can nurse the baby in peace and privacy. Would you like that?"

Violette nods.

"*Bonne fille.* Now, let's get you girls packed."

AT THE MERE mention of breastfeeding, Papa takes Dickie away not one but two weeks. With Roy and John deployed, and Noel enlisted in the navy—he lied and said he was seventeen instead of fifteen—all the men are gone.

Violette soon feels the haze lift. The baby sleeps more regularly, giving Violette better stretches of rest. At twenty-one, her young body heals quickly, and the nursing takes the weight right off her frame. She can move freely again, has started gentle exercise, and with her mother preparing meals, helping with the baby at night, and showing her off to neighbors in the day, Violette has some time to herself, making her more refreshed for the times with Tania.

Once Papa returns, Violette is out her parents' door, but she does better on her own now. Her mind and body are sound, even if she's still restless. She has correspondence from Vera, who consoles Violette over her absence from the ATS by complaining about the infernal heat and grumpy commanding officers. Vera is at her wit's end, and thinks she'll soon leave.

Though there's no regularity, Étienne's letters come, reassuring and giving Violette slivers of hope, but in the nights, in the dark, looking at the stars from the tiny garden, there is a thing growing in Violette—a black hole of silent rage. Though she bikes and runs and shoots when she can, she feels she will explode if she doesn't find an outlet soon.

Distraction comes in an unexpected way.

One afternoon, when the weather is fair and the garden is in full bloom, Violette lays Tania on a blanket in the grass. Violette talks and sings to the baby, eliciting the sweet little smiles Tania has just begun to give.

"We're not complete yet," Violette says. "We need your papa. And his laugh. It makes everything right."

Tania smiles as if she understands, breaking Violette's heart the way she does a hundred times a day. Violette turns her gaze to the sky and closes her eyes, but soon, the hair rises on her neck. She feels watched. She snaps her head in the direction of the entrance leading to the garden.

A man stands there. He's the quiet, middle-aged bachelor from upstairs. She passes him frequently and he always nods politely, but they've never spoken.

"I'm sorry to bother you," he says, with Italian-accented English. "May I?"

She nods and he takes a seat at the bench beside the yew tree. He offers her a cigarette, which she accepts.

"You like to smoke out here," he says.

Though it's jarring to think he has watched her, she doesn't get a predatory feel. Still, it's a strange thing to say to a woman he's just met.

"I must sound odd," he says. "Apologies. I watch people for a living. I'm a film producer."

He has her attention.

"My brother owns the building," he continues, "but I'm looking after it while he's interned on the Isle of Man with the other so-called enemy aliens."

"Why aren't you there?"

"Because I know the right people," he says. "And I'm outspoken in my hatred of fascists."

"That's good to know. I wouldn't want a spy living in my building."

He smiles, his eyes crinkling under his glasses. Then he extends his hand.

"Filippo del Giudice."

"Violette Szabo."

"Has anyone ever told you about your striking resemblance to Ingrid Bergman?"

"No."

"It's uncanny." He takes a long drag of his cigarette. "Anyway, I have to go, but here is my card, and you know where I live. I'm working on a film, *In Which We Serve*. It's good old British war propaganda. We need extras for goodbyes at railway stations, theaters, crowd scenes. It doesn't pay much, and the hours can get long, but it will get your foot in the door. And with that face, you should consider acting. It could help provide for you and your daughter."

Violette's heartbeat quickens as he speaks. It would be just the thing to keep her busy during the war and might lead to something afterward.

"Thank you," she says. "With my husband in North Africa, I need distraction."

"I'm glad to hear he's alive and well. It sounds like you would be a perfect fit for a war film. Think about it."

"I don't have to think," she says. "When do I start?"

A WEEK LATER, Violette finds herself in Portsmouth, elbow to elbow with dozens of extras, at a poorly lit mirror, applying lipstick. Tania is at a nearby nursery in the care of a naval officer's wife. Papa was horrified, and so was Maman—who felt hurt at being rebuffed in her offer to care for the baby—but Violette wanted Tania both away from the dangers of London and close enough to visit on Violette's days off. Besides, it's only for a few weeks. They'll be back in London in no time.

The air around Violette is heavy with powder and hair spray, chatter and cigarette smoke, and she hasn't felt this alive in a long time. She's part of a lively, lovely bunch. It's like the ATS, but more glamorous.

"That color red makes you look like the ultimate femme fatale," one of the extras says to Violette.

"Thanks," says Violette. "I hope it makes someone important notice me."

"I heard not only are there movie scouts on set, but also spy scouts."

"Spy scouts?" asks Violette.

"Yes, you have to be a good actor to be a spy."

"You don't say. And I was just thinking about how to get in front of the director."

The girl at Violette's left gives her a side glance and rolls her eyes.

"He'd turn away as soon as you open your mouth," she says.

"Why?" asks Violette.

"That accent. What is it? Cockney meets *la classe populaire?*"

Violette stiffens, and finishes blotting her lipstick. On her way out, she knocks into the girl's shoulder so her lipstick smears across her cheek.

"Blimey," says Violette, in her thickest Cockney accent. "I'm such a klutz. Sorry!"

Amid sniggers and cursing, Violette leaves and heads to the set. Though she's angry at the girl for saying it, Violette knows it's true. Her French is good, but her English is plagued with her father's influence. If she is going to become an actress, she must work on her polish.

The closer she gets to the set, the more Violette's aggravation is replaced with excitement. She loves getting lost in the imaginary world of cinema. The lighting, the direction, even the tension is thrilling. The days have been long and tiring but rewarding. It feels good to be a part of something outside of herself, something that might inspire others.

In Which We Serve is based on Lord Louis Mountbatten's experience on the HMS *Kelly*, which was sunk the previous year during the battle of Crete. There are many former servicemen as sailor extras telling their recent war stories, and some of them even got to meet the royal family, who visited the set in Buckinghamshire. If only she could have been there to see King George, Queen Elizabeth, and Princesses Elizabeth and Margaret.

But almost as soon as Violette arrives, she's finished. The director didn't notice her, and for now, her only claim to fame is walking solo across the background of a train platform.

With a heavy heart, she withdraws Tania from the nursery and begins the journey back to London. She regrets promising her mother she'd stay with her parents the first night back. She and Tania could use a little one-on-one time, and she wants to thank Mr. del Giudice for the opportunity and assure him she would like more of them.

Exhausted from the long day of travel, she's distressed when she arrives and finds her mother has stepped out to the market, leaving Violette with Papa. Bracing herself for his admonitions about putting Tania in a nursery while she worked, Violette is surprised when Papa lifts Tania from Violette's arms the moment she walks through the door. He carries the baby back to the garden, while showering her cheeks with kisses. Dickie is there and breaks into a grin at the sight of his big sister and his little niece. While he plays peekaboo with Tania, Papa turns to Violette.

"Are you finished with all that film nonsense?" he asks.

She rolls her eyes and sits in the chair where Étienne sat the first day she met him. She has a flash of memory of Étienne with his head turned toward the sun, and the ache for him turns physical. She takes a deep breath and steels herself for sparring with her father.

"Filming has wrapped up, if that's what you mean," she says.

Papa narrows his eyes at her.

"Why so uppity?" he asks.

"What makes you say that?"

"Why're you speaking like some toffee-nosed royal?"

"It must be from the good influence of actors."

While Papa grumbles, she turns her attention back to her little brother.

"You look well, Uncle Dickie," she says. "Taller and healthier."

Dickie beams while she ruffles his hair.

Papa retreats, walking Tania around the garden, naming every tree and flower until he circles back around to Violette.

"And here's your mummy," Papa says. "Do you recognize her, after weeks away from you?"

"Three weeks, Papa," says Violette. "Not including weekends. Fifteen days."

"That's a long time in baby time. And what'd they feed her?"

"Bottles made from dried milk, like all the babies of women in service."

"I'd hardly call making a film 'service.'"

"It is a war film, one that inspires and celebrates courage."

To Violette's relief, Maman soon arrives.

"Look at her!" Maman says, lifting Tania from Papa's arms. "She's doubled in size since I last saw her."

"From those bottles she's been eating, little cow," says Papa.

"Hush," says Maman. She kisses Violette on the head and stands back to regard her. "You look different. I feel like we have a Hollywood star in our garden, isn't that right, Charlie?"

He grunts as he lights his cigarette.

"Étienne will fall in love all over again when he sees you," says Maman. "Have you heard from him?"

"Last weekend. Forwarded mail," Violette says. "He said the spots on the paper were his tears upon receiving the photo of his little girl. It hurts so badly that she doesn't know him, and God knows when she'll get to meet him. He hopes for leave in October."

"Not too much longer," says Maman. "And Tania's so little, she'll never remember this time without him."

Maman passes the baby back to Papa and enlists Violette to help her bring the food outdoors. It's a lovely night to eat in the garden. Dickie pours glasses of water for them, and when Violette offers to take the baby so Papa can eat, he waves her off.

"You go 'head," he says. "Till she starts fussing."

Violette widens her eyes in surprise but is happy to indulge him. He continues to walk with Tania, gently jiggling her and whispering in her ear.

"Reminds me of how he was with you," says Maman.

"Really?" says Violette. "When did the tides turn?"

"When you could defy him."

"Oh, so age one?"

"About that," Maman laughs.

When Violette finishes her dinner, she relieves Papa. As he passes Tania to Violette, she gets a sudden urge to kiss her father on the cheek.

"What was that for?" he asks.

"Just enjoy it," she says. "Before the feeling passes."

He smiles and sits to eat his dinner.

Birds sing their summer song, and butterflies flit among the flowers, while the rest of the evening passes peacefully. When Tania is asleep in the bassinet in Violette's old room, and Dickie has put himself to bed, and Maman dismisses Violette from trying to help wash dishes, she returns to the garden for a smoke with her father. Though the moon is only a sliver, the stars are beginning their evening show. She closes her eyes and sends her good night wishes and prayers to Étienne.

"I've been thinking," says Papa.

"How dangerous."

Papa flicks her on the ear.

"Cheeky," he says. "What I was trying to say was, the baby's doing well, but you need more."

"You don't say."

"And what your mum says might be true. Tania's too little to notice if her parents are gone for spells."

"And?"

"There's a position at the Rotax factory, where I'm working. Making switch gears for aircraft. Real service, not some silly film. You interested?"

"Is this a joke?"

"I'm trying to help you," he says. "Why do you have to turn it into something ugly?"

"Is it really wise to suggest working in the same place with each other? We can barely get along through a dinner."

"It's a huge complex. You might not even have to see me. I promise I won't embarrass you."

"Papa."

"No, if you hate me that much."

"Stop," says Violette, reaching for his arm. "I'm sorry. It's hard to know when you're being serious. I appreciate you thinking of me."

He nods but grows quiet. Violette tries to imagine working in the same place as her father. If they don't have to work directly together, it might not be a failure. In fact, maybe it will give them something in common.

"Yes," she finally says.

"Yes, what? I do embarrass you?"

"No, Papa. I love you. And I would like to work at the factory with you. It would keep my mind off Étienne and help the war effort."

"Good, then," he says. "It's settled."

"It is."

"God help me," he says.

"God help us both."

20

NESLES-LA-VALLÉE

——— **VIRGINIA** ———

IT WAS LOUIS Fruchter's blood that snapped them closed and rendered them impotent. Virginia and Philippe are awash in shame and guilt for not intervening. But they don't know what that would have accomplished, aside from their own blood on the wall, their own lives sucked into the black hole of the enemy, consumed by an appetite for destruction that only grows. No one is safe. The enemy will come for all of them. It's a matter of *when*, not *if.*

Yet, in this third autumn of war, somehow the world still turns. Relentlessly.

Virginia thinks the sounds she'll most remember from this time in her life are Philippe's tools against wood. Ax slicing. Hammer banging, cracking, nailing. When Philippe isn't chopping, he's digging, hacking at earth instead of wood. He breaks through the crust of the dirt and destroys the knotty tangle of weeds. He tills the soil and makes neat piles of pale French limestone in a border around a kitchen garden, where he plants cabbage and garlic, root vegetables and winter onions. Hearty things to supplement the ever-tightening rationing. The sounds of his industry are the background to hers. Clothes washing. Canning. Cooking. Cleaning.

She never imagined this life for herself, but here they are. The former belle and beau of the ball are now farmers at a country cottage. Their cheeks are pink, their muscles are strong, their bodies are sharp and lean. If only their souls felt as healthy.

They've added five chickens to the flock, and they've started trapping and breeding rabbits. They already have four, and with monthly litters, it will be their best hope for keeping up food supply with the ever-shrinking ration offerings. Virginia doesn't relish the thought of Philippe killing bunnies for them to eat, but she's also hungry, and hunger makes one desperate.

Virginia and Nan head to the forest to check the rabbit traps. Philippe has built a line of cages concealed along the forest edge so the German soldiers—who now sometimes pass through town—and the French collaborators, keen to get rewards for reporting subversive neighbors, can't see them. As much of a threat as the Nazis are, it's the French turncoats who are becoming an even greater problem. Virginia thought they'd be safe at Nesles, but nowhere is safe. The *collabos* can put their horrid little eyes and ears in many places the Germans can't, and it sickens Virginia and Philippe to have to be so paranoid.

Paranoia. Disgust. Fear. Impotence. These are the states in which they find themselves, and it's wearing them thin. There's no longer much to say at meals. Little joy to be found. No romance. There's only the farm work to lose themselves in, and they feel increasingly like they are lost.

The shadows of the trees raise the hair on Virginia's arms, and the leaves that have begun to fall cause her to make more noise than she would like. After that day of the roundup in Paris, running through the streets, heels clacking on the stones, Virginia had scrounged through the village rubbish yard until she found rubber to nail to the soles of their shoes. Philippe didn't have to ask her why she wanted to erase the sounds of their footfalls, why she works at muffling them to help them disappear. But all the things Virginia does to try to increase their safety leave her feeling increasingly exposed. The impulse to hide doesn't feel like it's saving them. It feels as if it's killing them.

Nan bounds forward and paws at the ground where she sees the wooden trap box quivering from the frantic animal inside it. Virginia looks through the wire at the rabbit and feels a pang of sympathy. She lifts the heavy box and returns to the cages. As she's about to transfer the rabbit, a movement near the house stops her. She sees Philippe speaking with a man, the truck parked nearby revealing that it's the baker, Marcel Renard. It's unusual for Renard to make deliveries, especially because she's already collected their bread ration for the day.

Once he's gone, Philippe strides toward the forest, his usual look of worry deepened and darkened to reveal total anxiety. With every step he takes toward where she hides, she wants to contract into the woods. She doesn't want any more bad news, but as soon as she allows the thought, her constant companions of shame and guilt return. She forces her feet forward to meet him. Nan greets Philippe, circling his legs. He pulls Virginia back into the woods.

"I have to report to the town hall by the end of the week to register," he says.

Virginia's mouth goes dry.

"For what?" she asks.

"For work. Wherever the Nazis see fit. Vichy has said all Frenchmen between the ages of eighteen and fifty who work less than thirty hours a week have to 'volunteer' for service. For every man who's selected, the Germans will allegedly release a French prisoner of war. But it sounds like a dirty trick."

Virginia feels a rising panic.

"Philippe, you can't volunteer. If they send you to Germany, you'll never return."

"If I register our home as a farm, I may remain exempt. We'll need to disclose and turn over more of what we grow and raise, but it might keep me here."

"Might." Virginia covers her eyes with her hands.

"Virginia," he says, pulling her hands back into his. "I haven't told you everything."

She tries to brace herself.

"They've begun arresting Americans for internment. Including women. Renard told me you must be careful. Not everyone in the village is an ally."

Virginia feels cold. She looks from Philippe to their sweet home on the hill, the rolling fields, the beautiful trees. After she resolved not to, she has taken the days for granted, the endless, boring days. *Boring* is a gift, and one that she could soon lose.

Not *if* they lose all this, but *when*.

Like the Fruchters, it's inevitable she or Philippe will be taken at some point, and their lives might end. But right now, they're not living. They must live until they may not. They mustn't allow the numbness to kill them before their time. Otherwise, evil wins.

"You could survive without me," she says, allowing her thoughts to expand outward, forcing herself to imagine the future and all its possible dangers. "But I have to learn a few things if I'm forced to survive without you."

As soon as she speaks the words, Philippe's eyes clear, and his shoulders lift for the first time in weeks. She sees that most of his burden lies in worrying about her, and that will no longer do.

Virginia looks at the rabbit she's just caught. She lifts the box and heads to the barn, Philippe and Nan following. Once there, she closes the door on Nan. Pulling a handful of alfalfa hay from the mound, Virginia places it on the ground a couple yards away from the trap. She opens the lid and waits until the rabbit feels safe enough to creep out and eat. While it nibbles, she reaches for the broom and rests it over the rabbit's neck, as she has seen Philippe do. After taking a deep breath, she stands on either side of the broom, pinning the rabbit before pulling its legs up, breaking its neck.

Virginia steps aside and lifts the dead rabbit by the feet.

"Show me what to do next," she says.

21

──── VIOLETTE ────

VIOLETTE COULDN'T HAVE anticipated working with her father at a factory would fill her with such purpose, but it has. She's surviving, even thriving, and knows her little daughter is doing the same.

Violette's home is filled with her loved ones—Tania, her parents, Dickie, and Vera, who left the ATS and now helps with Tania's caregiving. They're carving a pumpkin and eating apple pie and bread from the fruit Aunt Florrie sent. All that's missing is Étienne. Violette had a dream he showed up at the door, like he promised to try, and she thinks today might be the day.

"The Yanks make a big fuss over Halloween," says Violette. "An American soldier invited me to a costume ball, but I refused, out of respect for Étienne."

"Good judgment, Vi," says Papa, kissing his daughter on the side of her head.

Since they started at the factory together, they have experienced a new closeness. They see each other just enough to remain on pleasant terms, but not so much that they suffocate each other. Since her promotion last week, her father has been bragging about her to anyone who will listen.

Vera feeds Tania tiny pieces of apple bread, which the baby dribbles out all over her bib. Dickie thrills over the slimy mush of the pumpkin. Maman pours tea for everyone and remarks on how she hopes the weather will hold. The sky has been threatening rain, and it's only a matter of time before they're forced indoors.

"Vi has her girls singing their way through every workday," says Papa. "They're more productive when they're happy. I should get my own promotion for bringing Vi on."

"I'll put in a good word for you," says Violette.

She picks out the pumpkin seeds and rinses them in a bowl of water before placing them on a roasting pan to toast later. Papa helps Dickie get the final scrapings out of the pumpkin and pulls out his pocketknife to begin carving.

"Should we give it a little mustache, like that Hitler?" says Dickie.

"And then beat it to bloody smithereens," says Papa, nudging his son.

The boy finds a stick in the corner of the garden and pretends it's a sword. When Papa finishes carving, they have quite a pulpy likeness of the despicable Führer.

"Now, where's a candle?" says Vera.

"I'll go fetch one," Violette says.

She wipes her hands on her apron and heads toward the door. In her flat, she rustles through the drawers until she finds what she's seeking. On her way back to the garden, the sight of the people she loves arrests her. It was just months ago that she felt frantic and bereft. She had looked out this window and imagined herself, the baby, and Étienne laughing in the garden. The vision had given her hope and purpose, and now, though the vision is incomplete, she somehow feels Étienne with her. She imagines him coming up behind her and kissing her neck, and wraps her arms around herself, indulging the fantasy.

A knock startles her, breaking the spell.

Étienne!

Heart racing, she runs to the door and throws it open.

At first, she doesn't register the significance of the uniformed man with the sad face.

She can't remember reading the words on the telegram.

All she recalls from the afternoon she found out her husband was killed in the Battle of El Alamein was her father dragging her— through sudden torrents of rain—away from the pumpkin she could not stop beating.

VIOLETTE DOESN'T KNOW what day it is. She doesn't know where Tania is. She wears the same sweaty, stinking, pumpkin-splattered dress and apron she wore the day her heart was torn out of her chest.

Her mother comes to make her drink and eat.

Violette doesn't know where Tania is.

Violette hears footsteps in the hallway, outside the flat.

"Étienne?" she whispers.

No, he will never be there again.

He lied to her. He had to have known he'd never return from hell. She hates him. She hopes he's in hell. She wishes she never met him.

How could I allow such thoughts?

She hates herself.

She weeps.

The footsteps recede.

Where's Tania?

Wherever her daughter is, it's better than here. Violette is not fit to mother Tania now, or maybe ever again. At least not until the war is over.

How can I make the war end?

She sits up, fighting the dizziness.

What if that was Mr. del Giudice in the hallway? What if he wanted to offer me a new role?

She stumbles out of bed toward the toilet, but when she sees her greasy hair, sunken eyes, and sallow skin, she's horrified. She scrubs her face, brushes her limp hair, and puts on her red lipstick. The effect is worse than before. She looks garish, like a porcelain doll dressed up as a clown.

She wipes the lipstick with her arm, smearing it across her face, and laughs. What else is there to do?

Kill Nazis, she thinks. *Prevent them from stealing Tania's future the way they've stolen mine.*

She breathes deeply, trying to compose her erratic emotions, and again scrubs her skin clean. When she lifts her face to look back at the mirror, she's startled by the cold, hard fury she sees. She's almost unrecognizable to herself.

VIOLETTE WALKS INTO her parents' home without knocking to find Dickie coaxing Tania to roll over on a blanket on the floor. Dickie's eyes find Violette's and light briefly before worry transforms his face. He glances over his shoulder toward the kitchen, where Violette hears her parents' voices.

"Disgraceful," says Papa. "To walk out on the factory without giving any notice. Leaving all she's achieved without a second glance."

"Charlie, her husband was killed."

"Do you think she's the first war widow? I got three women in my detail alone, in that same situation. And they have more kids than Vi does!"

His words are a sucker punch to Violette's gut.

"It just happened," says Maman.

As Maman continues to plead with Papa, Violette curls her lip in disgust, picks up Tania, and walks out of the house. In a few moments, her mother's heels click on the sidewalk behind her.

"Violette!" she calls.

Maman overtakes her and wraps Violette and the baby in a hug. Violette stiffens.

"Why didn't you say 'bonjour'?" Maman says, pulling away, a false note of brightness in her voice. "Come, eat with us. Lunch is ready."

"I won't eat with him."

"He didn't know you were there."

"Does that matter? He has no heart."

"He does. And it's broken for you. But he's worried, and his worry comes out as . . ."

"Judgment."

"Vi, you've been in bed for weeks. Papa has helped care for Tania all this time. He loves that baby. You caught him at a bad moment."

"No, it was helpful to hear it. Because now I know she'll never be in his care again."

Her mother's panicked look weakens Violette's resolve. She hates to keep Tania from her mother, but she won't have the baby around her father, not if he's there spewing his poisonous opinions. One day, the baby will understand. Violette won't let him turn Tania against her.

Tania is fully crying now. Violette walks around her mother, but Maman pleads.

"No," Violette says. "If you want to see us, you'll have to come to me. I'm done with him."

22

—— **VIRGINIA** ——

"STARTING TODAY," PHILIPPE says, upon returning from the post office, "it's no longer voluntary to sign up for German work. Every Frenchman, age eighteen to fifty, and every unmarried Frenchwoman, age twenty-one to thirty-five, is required."

Virginia receives the news with stoicism, while wringing out Philippe's damp, threadbare car coat, the one his mother had given him last Christmas. No, the one before. Or was it the one before that? She doesn't know what day it is, let alone the year. She shakes her head to clear the haze.

"Will our farm status protect you?" she asks.

"I don't know."

"And I've not hidden my American status, so they can come after me anytime, too."

"Yes. And we've witnessed arrests with our own eyes."

The memory of the Fruchters being tossed in the back of a police truck like rubbish rises in Virginia's mind.

"Nicole said the rumors are, the work camps aren't work camps at all," Virginia says.

"They're death camps."

"When they come for us," she says, "do you think we should go willingly?"

Philippe doesn't answer. He excuses himself to chop wood, leaving Virginia alone to finish the wash. But all she can do is stare out at him through the window, and all he can do is stare back at her. They soon meet each other on the lane, take each other's hands, and walk. They walk in silence past the barn, noisy with laying hens, past the garden empty of its recent harvest, past the cellars of canned goods, and to the rabbit cages, lively with game. They look back over the farm together and then at each other in silent agreement.

No.

VIRGINIA WIPES HER sweaty forehead with her arm and takes a deep breath, drawing in the rich scent of pine while surveying their work.

Though the air is crisp, they've removed their coats, and their clothing is damp from exertion. They've been digging a hideout in the wood nearest the house all day. Thankfully, they've not yet had a frost, so the soil is soft under their shovels.

After applying brown stain to the plywood box the movers used a lifetime ago to transport their grand piano from their Paris apartment, Virginia pressed moss and pine needles all over its wet surface. While that dried, she and Philippe dug a deep pit with room enough for the two of them to hide, with a kind of dirt shelf along the top where the box will rest, flush with the ground. They'll arrange the box so the oblong hole in its side faces the house and the road, allowing them to be on the lookout for any approaching danger.

Virginia rests her shovel against a tree and touches the box, noting that the stain has dried. She and Philippe lift it and place it on the dirt ledge. Then, they take a step back to assess their work.

"Hmm," says Virginia. "It needs something."

She spots a scattering of rocks, and heaves several of them—and a bundle of fallen branches—around the shelter to better camouflage it. When she stands back, she smiles at Philippe and says, "Voilà!"

He stares at her in the most curious way.

"What is it?" she asks.

His eyes twinkling, he breaks into a grin.

"I never thought I'd see you covered in dirt, whistling your way through digging and hauling boulders for a hideout, but here you are. And I have never loved you more."

"I feel alive when I do things to subvert the enemy," she says, returning his smile.

"Then maybe you should do more."

"Maybe I will."

"Maybe I will, too."

DRESSED, PRESSED, AND fresh, Virginia takes the seat at the piano for the first time since they've settled at Nesles. She hasn't felt like making music in a long time, but today is different. It feels as if she and Philippe have claimed some small parcel of land—some tiny but meaningful territory of power in this war—and it has given them a vitality they've not felt in ages.

After they dug their shelter, they went right to the telephone. Heads leaning together around the earpiece, they'd called Michel and Nicole, who had indicated on their last meeting that the Resistance kindling was aflame, growing like a forest fire. Michel said whenever Philippe and Virginia were ready to leap into the flames, they just had to let him know and their names would be given to the right people. They might be called upon to distribute subversive papers or get contact from Allied spies, though what exactly that will lead to, they aren't sure.

"Count us in," Philippe had said on the call.

"You're sure?" Michel asked.

Philippe had looked at Virginia, and she'd nodded.

"Oui."

Hearing the whoop Nicole gave from the background when Michel relayed the news to her gave Virginia a deep and abiding joy.

"When you're in Paris next," Michel had said, "come to our place, where we can talk more."

They've made plans to return to the capital in the coming weekend. Virginia's hands feel as dusty as the piano keys. They're sore, and her fingernails are cracked and brittle. Though her nails are grimy, and her bones are sharp beneath her skin, her hands are strong and useful. They're hardworking hands. She's proud of them. She's proud of the new work they'll start, whatever that will be.

While the aroma of Philippe's rabbit stew perfumes the air, Virginia plays, stirring the embers of her musical memory. She starts "The Man I Love," by the Gershwins, the song that she and Philippe danced to the first night they met. This song has punctuated their lives at romantic intervals. It was on a July night in Paris—in 1937, when they'd just returned from their honeymoon—when the papers announced the sad news of George Gershwin's passing from a brain tumor. Virginia and Philippe had walked in the sultry summer air, fanning themselves, when a man rolled an upright piano onto the boulevard Saint-Germain. Throngs of pedestrians on the sidewalks and in the cafés stopped and listened as he played "The Man I Love." Philippe had taken Virginia in his arms, and they'd danced, other couples joining them. The moon glowed over the entire enchanting scene, many lifetimes ago.

The piano at Nesles is out of tune, but it coughs to life, and soon, under the increasing pressure of her fingers, the instrument quivers with a new and shimmering vitality. In moments, Virginia feels Philippe's hands slide down her arms. He kisses the side of her neck. She stands and says to him, "Oh, there you are," the way she did on that first night of their life together.

He grins and lifts her into his arms—her feet off the floor—and dances her around the dining room to the music they can hear in the echoes of their memories.

23

⟨⟩

—— VIOLETTE ——

VIOLETTE DANCES WITH one man after another through the smoky hall. She's trying to numb the pain of losing Étienne, to fill in the great craters blasted in her heart, if only for a few hours. She knows the guilt will rise with the hangover in the morning, but she pushes that thought out of her mind.

The soldier she's dancing with is rough and sweaty, and his breath stinks from beer. She tries to push him off, but he's got her tight, and the amount of gin she's consumed has dulled her. Her squirming makes him hold her tighter, so she relaxes just long enough to lull him into thinking she's resigned before shifting backward and kneeing him between the legs.

Amid the sounds of his cursing and the laughter of his peers, Violette stumbles to the table where she left her drink. She doesn't remember emptying it but sees the evidence. She's not used to drinking so much. She usually likes to have her wits about her, but there's only so much reality one can take. She picks up her pocketbook, wobbles to the bar, and tries to order another. The bartender doesn't hear her.

He does, she thinks. *But he's pretending he doesn't.*

"*Va brûler en enfer,*" she says, riffling through her bag until she finds her cigarettes. She pulls the last one from the crumpled pack and attempts to light it, but—vision swimming—it looks as if two cigarettes point out of her mouth where there should be one.

A hand with a lighter appears before her and puts a flame to her cigarette. She inhales, slips her lighter in her bag, and looks up to see a tall, square-jawed, serious fellow, wearing a British Expeditionary Force uniform. He's with another uniformed man, though that man looks like he's a teenager dressed up in his father's clothes. A woman on the dance floor calls to the younger one—"Jack, come on!"—and he leaves them. Violette watches him hurry away before returning her attention to the man who lit her cigarette.

"*Merci,*" she says.

"*De rien. Êtes-vous française?*"

"*À moitié.*"

"*Et l'autre?*"

"British. You?"

"Same, actually. British born. French raised. Henri Peulevé," he says, extending his hand.

"Violette Szabo."

He notices her ring.

"Married?" he asks.

The darkness she carries threatens to overwhelm her. Her vision blurs and she wavers. Henri grasps her arm and helps her to sit on the stool, taking the seat next to her.

"Widowed," she says. "The Battle of El Alamein."

"Just a few months ago," Henri says. "Horrible."

The way Henri glowers, it transforms his already serious face into one that would make the enemy tremble. She reads Henri's uncensored hatred for the Nazis, and it electrifies her.

"Royal Armoured Corps?" he asks.

"No, he was a Legionnaire. Étienne was French."

She's surprised to find that saying Étienne's name aloud releases a large amount of pressure from inside her.

"I know many Legionnaires and have heard of their bravery," says Henri.

His voice is deep and sounds like a radio announcer's. Both his British and his French are impeccable.

"I don't have any details," says Violette. "Only that he'll never come home. He never got to meet his daughter."

Henri's eyes darken further, and he clenches his jaw. She meets his gaze with her own scorching bitterness, and he's unable to keep his eyes on hers. He turns away and blows smoke toward the dance floor, where his friend Jack is cutting a rug with a dark-haired beauty. Henri returns his gaze to Violette's.

"I'm sorry," he says. "There's nothing I can say."

She's grateful he doesn't give her a look of chivalrous pity.

"I'll ask around about Étienne in my French circles," Henri says. "See if I can find any details."

She searches his face, trying to ascertain if Henri has an agenda, but there's only fury and camaraderie present. The inky, dark circles under his eyes and the line in his forehead between them make him look older than he must be, but there are also smile lines down his cheeks, so that serious face must know how to laugh. She can't imagine it.

"If you want me to, that is," he says.

"*Oui,*" she says. "I'd be grateful."

She digs through her purse and finds a pen but has only the empty cigarette pack on which to write. She scribbles "Bayswater 6188" and passes the box to him. He nods and tucks it into his uniform pocket.

"Now, will you buy me a drink?" she says. "The bartender's ignoring me."

"Might I suggest I walk you home, instead?"

I don't want to go home, she thinks. *I want to drink away my pain. But Henri's impulse is correct.*

"All right," she says. "I should probably go to bed, anyway."

"Bed? It's only half past two in the afternoon."

IT'S THE FIRST of many walks home. The first of many conversations and meals together.

Henri is twenty-seven, but he looks older. The war has aged all of them beyond their years. This unexpected friendship has rekindled a spark of happiness in Violette and made the first winter of her widowhood livable. In addition, the constant joking and sweet exuberance of Jack, Henri's twenty-one-year-old friend, lightens both Violette and Henri. Jack claims he's a British officer, but his look and accent are French, so Violette knows there's more to that story. She suspects there's more to Henri's story, too. But he's reserved, rarely revealing anything about himself.

Vera provides childcare for Violette whenever Henri and Jack invite her out, which isn't too often. They're busy with some kind of training about which they're maddeningly vague. When Jack begs Henri and Violette to accompany him to the dance halls, they can't refuse his charming pleas. Sober, Violette won't dance because of the emotional pain of missing Étienne, and Henri doesn't because of the physical pain in his leg that he broke in some past incident he won't discuss. But once Jack is set loose on the dance floor, Violette and Henri can enjoy a quiet smoke together, watching their friend carouse, and reminiscing about what it felt like to be so carefree.

Violette likes being with Henri. There's a stillness in him that calms her. In the intensity of his gaze and the growing frequency of his calls, she knows he's developing feelings for her, but there's no pressure from him. His admiration is a gentle, pleasant pulse, like the warmth of spring sunshine, coaxing but never oppressive.

On Saturdays, he's started bringing Violette brunch from a nearby bakery that makes the most out of wartime ingredients, and books and stuffed toys for Tania. He sits on the floor next to Tania, and she places her plump little hand on his arm, while he reads to her. It makes Violette's heart ache to see her little girl so starved for a father figure. Violette still hasn't seen her own father since that day he'd raged about her leaving the Rotax factory, and she wonders if he'll ever try to make amends.

One Saturday in early March, when Henri's at her place, Violette points out Mr. del Giudice through the window and tells Henri she was an extra in a film. Henri surprises her by admitting he was a camera operator before the war.

"Ah, you've finally revealed something personal," Violette says.

Violette has told Henri everything about herself—including her stay with Tante Marguerite, and the pilot she helped at the start of the war—making it clear that she wants to get back to France, to somehow fight the Nazis. She has asked Henri if he knows anyone who might help get her into war work, but his answers are always vague, and he quickly changes the subject.

Henri's face colors.

"You're blushing," says Violette. "How endearing. What else can I get out of you, besides details of your unreserved love of France?"

"Only that I think you would make an excellent actress."

"Thank you. My father doesn't approve. He thinks I should just take care of Tania. Or at least go back to my respectable job in the war factory."

"Acting is perfectly respectable," says Henri. "Especially films that contribute to good."

"That's what I think. And acting jobs are short-term. I wasn't apart from Tania long enough for her to miss me."

"When you become a big star, you'll be able to hire a full-time caregiver who'll watch Tania in your trailer, where you can visit her between scenes."

"Now you're talking."

Violette thinks how refreshing it is to hear a man support her wishes for employment outside of the home. Even Étienne didn't like Violette's working. It's nice that Henri recognizes how happy it makes her.

A noise draws Violette's attention to Tania, on the floor. She's been sitting there, between Violette and Henri, banging stacking cups together. When one rolls away from her, Tania pivots onto her hands and knees and rocks back and forth. The cup is just out of reach.

"She's getting close to crawling," Henri says.

"Yes, then I'm in big trouble."

Tania continues to rock, but then she makes a jerky, hesitant scooting motion toward the cup. Concentrating hard, Tania's able to crawl two paces forward to reach her goal. Violette whoops and claps and gets on all fours in front of her baby.

"You did it! Big girl!"

Tania grins, showing all four of her new front teeth.

When Violette looks up at Henri, he beams at her.

THE NEXT WEEKEND, Vera watches the baby, while Violette accompanies Henri and Jack to Kensington, to the Studio Club, a favorite military watering hole. The unseasonably warm evening lifts her spirits and makes her feel more like herself than she has since Étienne died. Inside, there's is a sea of Allied military uniforms and pretty dresses, dulled by a smoky haze. Once they find a table, the band starts a rollicking tune. Jack asks Violette to jitterbug with him, as he always does for his first dance, which she always refuses.

Until tonight.

Jack puts his hand over his heart and pretends to fall backward. Violette rolls her eyes and allows him to lead her to the dance floor. She winks at Henri over her shoulder as she goes.

Dancing gives Violette a boost of energy. Jack is thrilled to find that she's an excellent partner, so skilled he can barely keep up.

"You've been holding out on me," he says, breathless. "Now, if you can just get that old grump on his feet, you'll really be talented."

"I thought his leg hurt too badly."

"He's healed."

Violette glances over at Henri and sees how intensely he watches them, a smile playing on his lips, but his eyes wear a new kind of look, one of hunger. She has a hard time tearing her stare away from his, but she does to finish the dance. She and Jack hug when it's over, and the band goes into a slow song, "I'll Be Around."

"Think I can get Henri to dance for this one?" Violette asks Jack.

"I think he'll do whatever you tell him, Vi."

Violette gives Jack a long look, before walking back to the table where Henri is seated. When she reaches him, she holds out her hands, and he takes them. When their skin meets, Violette shivers. They hold hands as they walk to the dance floor, and once there, Henri pulls her into his arms. Feeling uncharacteristically shy, she moves closer into him so she doesn't have to look him in the eye. He rests his cheek against hers and glides her around the floor to the music.

Guilt, relief, desire, confusion. Violette's emotions rise and fall like a procession of horses on a carousel. Is she betraying Étienne's memory by feeling drawn to another man? It's only been half a year since Étienne died. But she knows she wouldn't have wanted Étienne to be alone forever, mourning her. Still, as much as she likes Henri, as much as he clearly likes her, she knows so little about him. And the very fact of his uniform tells her he'll be pulled into the undertow of war sooner or later, though he hasn't said when.

But, oh, he smells good, she thinks.

Henri's aftershave is spicy and clean, and his cheek is smooth against hers. He leans closer to her ear and hums along with the chorus, bringing a smile to her face. She takes a deep breath and commands herself to relax, to enjoy the moment. She's doing nothing wrong, and she might even be doing something right.

They dance to every slow song, Violette growing more relaxed all the time, but all too soon, Violette has to leave to relieve Vera from babysitting. Henri offers to walk her home, and on the way out they wave at Jack, leaving him on the dance floor with his crush of the moment.

The night is still—not a bomber in sight. Violette and Henri walk arm in arm, following the lines of white paint on the sidewalks to help them find their way.

"Someday I'd like to take you dancing in Paris," Henri says in French.

He slips into the language whenever he speaks of France. He talks about it with passion and melancholy, like remembering an old lover.

"Count me in," she says.

"There's a boutique hotel where I like to stay when I'm in Paris," he says. "The Reine Marie. Just off the boulevard Saint-Germain. Have you been to the hotel?"

"No, but my mother's name is Reine, so I'll remember it."

"Maybe we'll stay at the Reine Marie together someday," Henri says.

Violette raises her eyebrows.

"Maybe we will," she says.

He smiles and casts down his gaze. After a few moments, he continues.

"We'll have real coffee under the red awnings at Fouquet's."

"And buy secondhand novels from the bouquinistes along the Seine," she says.

"Yes, we'll look for Hilaire Belloc's *Cautionary Tales for Children* for Tania, to scare her away from trying dangerous things. Though it never worked for me."

"Me neither. Dreadful stories. Do you remember Matilda, the liar, burned to death?"

"Or Algernon, who shot at his sister, but was only reprimanded."

"Hideous," laughs Violette.

"And we could go shopping for you. For your mother."

"Where would we go?"

"The Trois Quartiers on the boulevard de la Madeleine."

"Yes," she says. "And we'll light candles at L'église de la Madeleine."

The words slip from her mouth before she thinks, conjuring Étienne and depressing her mood.

They're quiet the rest of the walk home. When they reach the front steps, Henri kisses her hand, and watches to make sure she gets safely inside before he leaves her.

THE NEXT WEEK, Mr. del Giudice surprises Violette with two Saturday night tickets to a screening of *In Which We Serve*. He'd been asking her if she'd seen it, but the opportunity had not yet arisen. He finally took matters into his own hands.

"I think you'll love the film," he says. "You're only in the background at a railway goodbye scene for a few moments, but you left an impression. You should get some formal headshots made. I think you have a bright future ahead of you in acting."

Since it's a late show, Vera kindly agrees to keep Tania for the night. Violette doesn't know what she'd do without Vera, especially because Violette still won't bring Tania around her father. Maman has been over to plead with Violette on his behalf, but Violette refuses to budge. If Papa cared, he would come over to see Violette himself.

"You pay me too much," says Vera. "I'd watch Tania for free."

"Don't be silly," says Violette. "You're a lifesaver. The best friend I've ever had."

"I love Tania. And keeping her every now and then means I can watch your adventures from a safe distance instead of being dragged along for a change."

Violette laughs and hugs her friend, then she kisses Tania and heads to the theater to meet Henri.

She spots him first. Glowing in the golden light of sunset, his face lights up like a marquee when he sees her. He bows and takes her arm.

"Escort to a star," he says, drawing a laugh from Violette.

When they arrive at the top of the walkway to the theater, Violette stops and inhales. It's been so long since Violette has been to see a movie, she'd forgotten the pure thrill of the moment the lights go out and the picture begins, the way reality dissolves, allowing one to enter into a world of fantasy, enchantment, and imagination. Knowing that she's some small part of the fantasy world about to unfold before her makes Violette feel as if she'll burst with excitement. Once they're in their seats, she leans over to whisper in Henri's ear.

"I hope you've enjoyed your time with me before the start of my film career. It's all going to go straight to my head, making me insufferable."

Violette sees the crinkles at the edges of Henri's eyes and the lines in his cheeks becoming deep. How she loves to see that rare smile. He turns toward her, his face inches away, and stares at her.

"Violette?" he whispers, like a question.

She leans in, cutting off the request with her lips. Her entire body warms, and she's surprised by the depth with which he meets her passion. He's been so reserved with her—only kisses on the cheeks or hand until now. She may have initiated the kiss, but he's taking it to the next level.

The laughter around them soon breaks the spell. They pull apart, still intoxicated from each other, to see the newsreel that has inspired the audience reaction. The reel is footage of Nazi soldiers in their ridiculous windup-doll marching formations with the music of "The Lambeth Walk" spliced in, making it look as if Hitler's puppets are dancing along to the tune. The audacity of it draws Violette and Henri into the laughter and gives Violette another thrill. Belittling the demons that stole her husband is sweet revenge. She hopes the boches will get their hands on this to see how the world mocks them.

When the movie begins, Henri wraps his arm through hers, his touch filling her with heat. Throughout the showing, he leans in to kiss her many more times, each one leaving her more breathless than the last. The movie is action-packed and inspiring and—though her cameo is so quick she almost misses herself—she feels a great deal of pride in being a part of something the audience receives with applause. She's grateful for the unexpected sweetness of the night, and knows she'll remember it forever. So it's especially painful when Henri walks her home, and she invites him inside, but he refuses.

"I'm sorry," he says. "I have something to tell you. I should've told you earlier."

"What?" she says, pulling her hands out of his and crossing her arms over her chest.

"I have to go."

"Where?"

"I can't tell you."

"Why?"

"Please, don't ask me any questions. Just know I feel sick leaving you. And Tania. And I have every intention of coming home to you when I return."

"When do you leave?"

"Tomorrow."

Another sucker punch.

Must I always get them? she thinks. *Why do they still take me by surprise?*

"Don't bother," she says. "I won't be waiting."

A sudden downpour begins. She doesn't step back so he can join her under the overhang but lets him soak through. Henri doesn't flinch. His stare bores into hers and his jaw clenches. She feels a pang for being so cold with him, but he could have told her something. He could have prepared her earlier that he would leave her before kissing her the way he did.

"I understand," he says.

His eyes convey such agony that she can't help but soften. She searches his face, and his look tells her everything she needs to know. He didn't want to start an affair with her because he knows how she's suffered from losing her husband. Henri doesn't think he'll return to her, either.

She sighs, steps into the rain, opens her arms, and takes him into them.

24

$\sim$

—— VIRGINIA ——

THE RUE DE Bellechasse is heavy with mist and sodden from the overnight rain, its puddles frozen at the edges. Two days into spring, the trees remain bare and the sky is the color of used bathwater. Through the puff of Virginia's breath hitting the morning air, Virginia sees her shoes are scuffed and dirty, and her legs—revealed through a run in her last wearable pair of stockings—are ghostly pale.

We're living in a black-and-white film, she thinks.

The sharpness of a German accent calls her attention a block ahead of her. She now hears German as much as she hears French. Radio Paris plays only German musicians. Swastikas defile every flagpole. Europe allowed itself to fall asleep and has awoken to a Nazi-saturated nightmare.

Virginia pauses, watching a soldier reprimand the florist—a little blonde slip of a thing—whose shop is a two-minute walk from Virginia and Philippe's apartment. The neighbors here don't like the young woman, who sells flowers to Nazis for their mistresses, but Virginia tries to reserve judgment for those who engage in such transactions. People have to eat. Not only that, but appearances can be deceiving.

The florist nods and bows to the soldier, bobbing her head like a chicken pecking the dirt. When he leaves her, she hurries to carry the bunches of flowers—almost as big as she is—back into the shop, though she had clearly just moved them into displays in the street. From the effort, her cheeks are dotted with red circles like doll rouge, and strands of the wavy hair she has loosely pulled into a bun cover her eyes.

Virginia's own arms are empty. With butter now at five hundred francs a kilo and sugar at two hundred fifty, she didn't bring enough to cover their grocery needs, and she won't bother returning to the market. The line is already wrapped around the building. It looks as if they'll have to endure another day in Paris with growling stomachs.

Not long after Virginia and Philippe contacted Michel about starting with the Resistance, he said there had been a betrayal that resulted in arrests and instability in the network. They were to hold tight while the structure reconfigured. The waiting is like holding one's breath. It makes motion difficult and the mind unsteady. Worse, with the knowledge of arrests, and the longer they wait, the more she and Philippe doubt the wisdom of involving themselves with Resistance work, whatever it might be.

The florist stumbles on her next trip into the shop, nearly spilling the entire container of flowers on her way. Virginia looks up and down the empty street before crossing to help. She lifts a heavy vase of purple tulips and starts for the door, nearly colliding with the young woman.

"It looks like you need a hand," Virginia says.

The florist lowers her eyes to the wet pavement and mumbles a thank-you, before hurrying around Virginia to get the next bunch. When Virginia steps inside, she draws in her breath.

The fragrance is the first enchantment. Somehow the shop doesn't have the funeral parlor smell of rotting stems in water. Instead, there are sweet fragrances of blossoms coming in wafts through the rich undertones of the dried bunches of lavender and sage hanging from the wood beams. The glass cases, wooden shelves, light fixtures, and green-framed mirrors glisten as if they're covered in dew. A fire roars in a large, marble-manteled fireplace, and the lush, zesty aroma of freshly brewed tea gives the shop an air of cleanliness and health.

"Oh," is all Virginia can think to say.

The florist takes the tulips from Virginia's arms and sets the vase down in front of a door, closing it with her bottom as she does so. When she stands up straight, she smooths her hair.

"Merci," she says.

"Avec plaisir."

The silence expands between them, but Virginia is so taken by the place, she can't make herself leave.

"Your shop is beautiful," says Virginia. "I've never seen anything like it. I feel as if I'm in a rain forest."

The florist looks around as if seeing it for the first time. Virginia notices the stiffness leave the young woman's shoulders for a moment while she takes it all in, but it returns when her gaze arrives back at Virginia's.

"May I ask," Virginia says, "why did the German tell you to put away the flowers?"

The florist doesn't reply right away, and when she does, it's not to answer the question.

"Are you American?" she asks.

"I am," says Virginia, extending her hand. "Virginia d'Albert-Lake. I'm married to a Frenchman."

The florist takes Virginia's hand but releases it quickly.

"Michelle," she says.

"It's a pleasure to meet you, Michelle. I'm sorry if I'm making you uncomfortable. I don't mean any harm. I think I would like to buy some of your tulips."

"You don't have to do that."

"I want to. I can't remember the last time I had fresh flowers. And since butter was too expensive this morning, I'll settle for this. Though my husband might not be pleased at the substitution."

Michelle attends to Virginia the way one would observe a wild animal by which one is both intrigued and frightened, but she soon gets to work.

"I'll mix you a bouquet of red and blue tulips," Michelle says. "The red is for love. The blue is for peace. Also, loyalty."

The way Michelle looks at Virginia, she senses the young woman is feeling her out, wondering if Virginia is an ally. But which side is Michelle on? Virginia can't say exactly why but, in spite of the fact that the florist sells to Germans, Virginia feels certain Michelle is on the side of good. Maybe she's even a resister. She'll have to ask Michel and Nicole if they know anything about the florist. For the time being, all Virginia has are her instincts. And if Michelle is going to make her a red and blue bouquet, there only needs to be one more hue to represent the colors of not only the American flag, but also the tricolor.

"Could you throw in a few white tulips?" asks Virginia, her eyes twinkling.

A grin flashes across Michelle's features, which she quickly stifles.

"White tulips mean forgiveness," Michelle says. "Your husband is sure to be pleased."

Fetching four of each blossom in her slender hands, she arranges the flowers in alternating colors, sliding in foliage to make the blooms stand out, wrapping it all—taking care to cover the tulip tops—in brown paper, and tying it with a thick, waxy sliver of green leaf.

"Did you know," Michelle says, passing the bouquet to Virginia, "there's another American who lives nearby, above the patisserie on the rue Champ de Mars?"

"I didn't. How interesting."

"You'd like her. Madame Jacqueline Blanc. Her husband, Paul, is a good man. Your husband would get along with him. I think you'd have much in common."

"I'll be sure to tell him," says Virginia.

Michelle nods and the heavy silence returns.

After scanning the prices on the chalkboard written in script, Virginia reaches in her pocketbook to pay Michelle, giving her a generous tip, for which the young woman is grateful. As Virginia turns to leave the shop, Michelle's voice stops her.

"The boche said we must keep the finer things in the back."

Virginia turns to face the florist and is struck by how her appearance has changed. Michelle is no longer the awkward, young, fumbling girl, but a solid and powerful woman.

"It upsets the Nazi soldiers on leave from the Russian front," Michelle continues. "Many of them are dying, and he said such luxurious displays are vulgar and offensive."

"*Many* Nazis are dying?" Virginia asks, feeling a level of hope she hasn't felt in some time.

"Thousands," Michelle says, eyes blazing.

"You'd never hear that on Radio Paris," says Virginia.

"I hear all kinds of things Radio Paris doesn't report."

25

LONDON

∽⟡∽

—— **VIOLETTE** ——

IN THE DRIZZLE, Violette riffles through her purse, searching
for the address to which she's been summoned. It's at the Sanctuary
Buildings on Great Smith Street, near Westminster, and she's to meet
with an "E. Potter." The letter that had arrived at her parents' house—
Maman delivered it to Violette at her flat—was vague, mentioning
something to do with the war effort. Violette assumed that meant the
widow's pension she was set to receive had come through. Still, why
make a widow come in to get it? Couldn't they just send it through
the mail? Worse, she forgot her umbrella—a ridiculous mistake for
one who has spent half her life in London—and she's soaked through.
She dips under an overhang and continues the search until she pro-
duces the soggy paper that tells her which office she needs in Building
Three. She hurries a few blocks farther and enters the imposing brick
structure.

Within the massive lobby, men and women in uniform zip about
like subway cars in the tube. There's an air of productivity and importance in the place that makes Violette stand up straighter and attend
to everything around her. She wipes a wet strand of hair out of her
eyes and crosses to the front desk, where she asks for Mr. Potter in
room 531. The attendant tells her to fill out the guest log with her

personal information and then directs Violette to the elevator, where a slender operator with eyes like beady black marbles and a small tuft of white-blond hair waits. As he pulls the door shut, Violette feels as if hands are squeezing her throat.

While the lift rockets them to the fifth floor, Violette stands as far from the man as she's able, watching him while he watches her. The squareness of his jaw, his posture, and his efficiency of movement have her suspicious he's a German spy—Brits are certain they're everywhere—and when they arrive at her floor and he says, "Five," with a distinct *fff* sound at the end, the way a German would say *Fünf,* she's downright alarmed. When she sees his name tag—HARTMAN—she's convinced. He's using the British spelling, but adding another *n* to the end of his surname would make it Germanic. She takes a final look at him on the way out and tries to think why a spy might be at the pension building and where to report him without appearing paranoid.

When she arrives at room 531, she notices the number one is facing in the wrong direction, and the sign for E. Potter is handwritten on a paper that has been slid into the holder. A small man wearing a gray suit, who looks to be in his midforties, gives her a warm greeting and invites her into his office. He motions to a chair, closes the door behind her, and takes his seat on the opposite side of the folding table.

Because of the blackout curtains and the boarded window, the light of the single electric bulb overhead casts the room in shadows. There are no photographs, plants, or personal touches of any kind, and there's only a sheet of paper and a pencil on the table. On the wall nearest the door are air raid instructions, but someone must have thought it amusing to add to the list of prohibited items allowed in the shelter. Under the directive that "no birds, dogs, cats, other animals, or mailcarts" are allowed, the jokester penciled in "also mothers-in-law, mistresses, and Krauts."

The corner of Violette's mouth lifts in a half grin, and she turns her attention back to Mr. Potter, curious but unalarmed.

"Miss Bushell?" he asks in a quiet voice.

"Mrs. Szabo."

He widens his eyes.

"Apologies," he says. "I was told you're Violette Bushell, of the Land Army and the ATS."

"I am, formerly. My married name is Szabo."

"Married," he says, picking up the pencil and scribbling on the paper. "And your husband?"

"Was killed. At the Battle of El Alamein. He was a French Legionnaire."

Now she can say it without choking on the words. It makes her sick that she's already becoming used to her widowhood when she's not even used to her motherhood.

"I'm terribly sorry," he says. "The loss is unimaginable. Is that why you were given release from the ATS?"

No, she thinks. But she feels an instinct not to reveal that she has a child.

"Yes," she says. "Pardon, Mr. Potter, but was I called here to get my widow's pension?"

"No, I'm afraid not," he says.

He regards her a moment before continuing to speak.

"May I confirm, will you be twenty-two years of age on June twenty-sixth?"

"Yes."

"Please tell me about your upbringing, specifically the French parts."

Her heartbeat quickens and she sits up in her chair.

I'm being interviewed for war work, she thinks. *Henri, did you arrange this?*

"*Ma mère est française, mon père anglais. Je suis née à Paris,*" she says.

Mr. Potter grins. As he continues asking her questions, he slips between French and English, as she does with her replies, neither of them missing a beat.

"How many years did you live in France?" he asks.

"Eleven. And most summers since."

"When were you last in France?"

"Nineteen forty. As the boches ran her over and beat her into submission. Just after hiding a Belgian pilot on the run. I evacuated during an air raid. I've been desperate to get back ever since."

"And you're an actress now?"

"I am."

"Has anyone told you about your uncanny resemblance to Ingrid Bergman?"

"Once."

He continues to scribble on the paper.

"Was it Henri?" Violette asks.

Mr. Potter pauses a half second before he continues writing. When he finishes his notes, he looks up at her, his expression neutral.

"Was what Henri?"

"Did Henri Peulevé tell you about me?"

Mr. Potter places his pencil next to the paper and folds his hands on top of it.

"Acting," he says. "Intimate knowledge of French culture and language. Service in the Land Army and the ATS. Proficiency in shooting. These are some of the many *details* that have brought you to our attention from a number of sources."

"Who are you? And who do you work for?"

"Mrs. Szabo, before I continue, I must stress the importance of the confidentiality of everything I'm about to say to you. You are not to tell a soul. Not your parents, your brothers, your cousins, or your friends. For the good of the Allied cause, in this godforsaken war, this is top secret. A matter of life and death."

"You have my solemn oath," she says, nearly breathless.

"You've come on the radar of an elite clandestine organization. I'm the first of a long line of people who recruit, vet, train, and send forth a select group for covert work behind enemy lines."

Violette lets out her breath and rises from her chair.

"Yes, Mr. Potter. I'll do it."

He motions for her to return to her seat.

"You don't know what you're saying," he says.

"I don't have to know more. You want to see if I'd make a good spy. I'm telling you, I'd make the best spy."

"Confidence is essential in this line of work."

"I have it. To spare."

"Delusions of grandeur, however, are not. Nor is a naive ideal about service to God and country. This kind of work is looked down upon by many members of our very own war department. Our tasks are unsavory and dangerous. We sometimes operate under the idea that the ends justify the means."

"Nothing you say deters me."

"I see that and, frankly, it concerns me. You've no real idea what you're walking into."

"Mr. Potter, my husband was murdered by Nazis. The criminals who stole my birth country, who mowed down a child before my eyes, who force women to give birth in the dirt, and who are set on eliminating Jews from the face of the earth, under the direction of a madman. The ends do justify the means if they lead to their destruction. I do understand how dangerous the work is, and I'm not afraid of dying."

"We don't send out our people to die. We send them out to live."

"I have every intention of doing so. But every soldier has to know death is a possible outcome. And this is the only way, as a woman, that I can be a soldier."

Mr. Potter puts his elbows on the table and rubs his eyes. When he pulls his hands away, he looks older than he did a few moments ago. She has the feeling he somehow regrets meeting with her, and she feels desperate to reassure him. As she starts up again, he cuts her off.

"I've long been an advocate and supporter of women in this organization," he says. "But there are some within who don't agree. And it's not easy for any of us to send any of you into the field."

"I've been competing with boys my whole life. Why stop now?"

He releases a laugh before his face returns to a mask of concern. He stares at her a long time before speaking.

"Is there anything or anyone who you should think of before you agree to move forward?" he says. "It's best if personal connections are severed before going into this very lonely, very intense, incredibly taxing line of work."

She thinks of her darling Tania. Unless Mr. Potter is testing Violette, in spite of all the homework he has done, he doesn't know she's a mother. He hadn't even realized she was a wife. Tania will already grow up without a father, and Violette knows she's splintered in a thousand pieces. There's only one way she can become whole again—to become a good mother to her child—and that is by helping avenge Étienne's death and the Allied cause however she can.

I will succeed, she thinks. *I was made for this. And I'll be back before Tania is even old enough to understand I left her.*

"No," she says. "There's nothing holding me back."

VIOLETTE'S MIND HASN'T stopped racing since Mr. Potter dismissed her. He didn't promise her anything. He said he had to think more, and she should, too. She didn't need to think and was becoming frantic pacing the small flat, with Tania crawling and getting into absolutely everything.

One night, a week after the meeting, as Tania reached her plump little hand under the couch, searching for a dust bunny to eat, the phone rang. Violette had swept the baby's mouth, scooped her up, plopped her in the crib, and was breathless when she answered the call.

"Mrs. Szabo," said the quiet voice she recognized as Mr. Potter's.

Violette had shrieked with joy, startling the baby.

Desperate that Potter not hear Tania fussing, Violette squeezed her hand around the phone, pushed the door to the baby's room closed with her foot, and stretched the cord across the kitchen so she could hide in the pantry. It was crouched under the shelves in the dark that she heard the words that were to change her life.

"We'd like you to come back for another interview."

So elated she could hardly see, Violette had barely heard a word he said following, and had to ask him to repeat the meeting place instructions.

"Mrs. Szabo, there's often not time to repeat important information in dangerous situations."

Furious with herself, Violette had apologized and assured him she wouldn't let him down.

"I hope not," he'd said.

But she again fails. In her single-minded eagerness to do well at the meeting, she's almost run down while crossing Northumberland Avenue, where she's scheduled for an interview at the Hotel Victoria, which has been requisitioned by the War Office. As the car horn blares, she jumps back, placing her hand on her heart to steady it. Cursing herself for her carelessness, she sets her posture straight, takes a deep breath, looks *both* ways, and walks as smoothly as she's able to the hotel.

In spite of its boarded windows and the sandbags along its base, the grand structure of pale stone is still a beauty. Violette walks under the arched entrance into a lobby with a soaring ceiling crowned with enormous circular chandeliers. The fixtures are darkened, the furniture is covered, and there are no travelers—just a single man at the now-dusty pub who waves her over and asks her name. He directs her to the lift, and she stops in her tracks when the operator is none other than Hartman. His name tag now says WOLF.

Is this a test? she thinks.

She arranges her face as neutrally as possible, steps in, and says in a steady voice, "Second floor."

When he closes them in, the claustrophobic feeling she had the first time with him is amplified. They have fewer floors to travel but it takes twice as long, and she can't get out of the lift fast enough when it arrives. She keeps an eye over her shoulder until the man closes himself in and leaves her. She proceeds, and notices the hallways are narrower than she would have anticipated in such a grand place. She can hear her heartbeat in her ears. Once she arrives at room 238, she knocks. A woman in uniform appears behind a veil of cigarette smoke and motions Violette in, closing the door behind her.

All traces of hospitality have been removed from the hotel room. It's a dark, smoky war office, hung with blackout curtains and maps, with file folders everywhere, including one lying open that contains a picture of Violette pushing Tania in a pram through Holland Park. Violette swallows, but her throat is dry.

"Mrs. Violette Reine Elizabeth Bushell Szabo," the woman says with a British accent befitting a royal. "A name fit for a queen."

"Given to a pauper."

A smile flares over the woman's face but is quickly extinguished. She's slender and has perfect posture. Not a strand of her beautiful glossy black hair is out of place, and her pretty mouth is turned down in a slight frown that matches the slant of her eyes, under which there are deep shadows. She motions for Violette to take a seat, and crosses the room, closing Violette's file folder as she sits on the opposite side of the table.

"May I ask your name?" says Violette.

"I'm not ready to divulge that," the woman says.

"But you already know so much about me," says Violette, her gaze flicking down to her file folder and back to the woman.

"Yes, even the things you didn't mention in your first interview."

"Mr. Potter asked if there was anything holding me back. There isn't."

"Tania isn't?"

Violette flinches to hear her daughter's name on this stranger's lips.

"No," says Violette. "In fact, she's the reason I want to be a part of this."

"You don't even know what *this* is."

"Then tell me what it is."

"I have my own questions before you ask yours. First, which number was backward at Mr. Potter's office?"

"One."

"In addition to animals and mailcarts, what should one never take to a shelter during an air raid?"

"Mothers-in-law, mistresses, and Krauts."

"What color was the stone in Mr. Potter's pinkie ring?"

"He wasn't wearing one."

The woman grins.

"Tell me about the lift operator," the woman says.

"Hartman. Wolf. The same one here as was there."

"Good."

"I'm afraid he's a German spy."

"I assure you, he works for us."

"Disappointing. I was hoping he'd be my first Nazi kill."

The woman narrows her eyes.

"Potter mentioned you have a bloodlust. You're motivated by revenge. This doesn't sit well with either of us."

"Revenge is not my sole motivation. Making the world better for Tania—that's what I desire."

"You're acting. Some might say lying. But you do it well, and that would be an asset."

"Thank you."

"As is your excellent French accent, according to Potter."

"Merci."

"I hear you almost died while crossing the street to this hotel."

Violette swallows. This woman has eyes everywhere. Violette makes an excuse, but the woman holds up her hand to silence her.

"Also, an asset," the woman says.

Violette looks at the woman, a question in her eyes.

"You looked left first, instead of right," the woman says. "Left, as if you were in France, where they drive on the opposite side of the road as we do here. One of the things we have to hammer into the heads of our British recruits in training is *not* to look right first when crossing the street in France. Such simple missteps have gotten our agents captured and killed."

"Your agents?"

The woman stares hard at Violette before pulling a pink container of Passing Clouds cigarettes from her breast pocket, and offering one to Violette, which she eagerly accepts. The woman uses a silver lighter for her own cigarette first before passing the lighter to Violette. The way the woman inhales, it's as if she draws strength from the act.

"Early in the war," the woman says, "Churchill found out about a network of clandestine nonmilitary groups across Europe who had been gathering intelligence and sabotaging Nazi efforts at advancement. He organized the forces and set the wheels in motion for them to grow, officially creating the Special Operations Executive, or SOE, in charge of coordinating and supplying local Resistance groups and engaging in espionage and sabotage in enemy territory. I am with F Section, for France. We work with the RF—de Gaulle's Free French Forces—and the OSS—the Office of Strategic Services, our American counterpart—to undermine and make the Nazis in France as miserable as possible. We also provide safe houses along escape lines for downed pilots, wanted Resistance members, and Jews."

"I accept. What do I need to do? I'll do anything. Where do I go for training?"

"*I* will decide if you head to training, and honestly, I've never felt so divided about a recruit."

"I beg you, don't let the fact that I'm a mother hold me back."

"While at the forefront of my mind, that's not my only reservation. You see, Violette, we are the smallest war organization with the highest casualty rate. Because of double agents, we've recently had massive roundups and arrests that have decimated our networks and resulted in the imprisonment and murder of many of our own. There's a good chance you will never come home."

"My home is France. My husband's home was France. So is my mother's. I want to take my daughter there when this is all over, and there will be no France to take her to if the Nazis win."

The woman slides a large pile of file folders stamped MIA and KIA across the table.

"So many of ours, lost. Their relatives get letters full of lies. The lucky ones died quickly from a bullet. Many, however, were tortured first. The women are nearly always raped."

For the first time since the process began, Violette pauses.

Rape? Torture?

She tries to imagine her parents receiving the news that she has died. Her parents have already lost one child. Maman couldn't endure losing another. Even Papa, for all their troubles, would break if he lost Violette. She knows he loves her fiercely. His temper with her is really his temper with himself, because they are so very much alike.

Her thoughts return to her cherubic little one. How could she leave Tania to grow up without either parent? Violette couldn't leave Tania to her own parents. She wouldn't subject Tania to her father's mercurial personality. But her friend Vera is good with Tania. Vera and her mother, Alice, would care for the baby if something ever happened to Violette. She knows they would.

"I see you have finally sobered," the woman says. "This pleases me. This is the kind of careful, mature, measured thought you need to give this."

"I do worry about my daughter," says Violette. "She would be an orphan. But if I may be totally honest, caring for a baby while the world burns, knowing that I could make a serious difference in the outcome of the war, with all of my talents, is making me go mad. I believe—I know—I was made for this. I will be successful, and I will come home to my daughter as a woman she can be proud of. A woman who inspires her. But if I don't come home, I know she'll still be proud of me."

An Oscar-worthy speech, Violette thinks as the woman's face softens. Violette can't be certain, but she thinks the woman blinks away tears. She finishes her cigarette, stubs it out, and stands, extending her hand.

"My name is Miss Atkins. Allow me to welcome you to the Ministry of Ungentlemanly Warfare."

26

PARIS

~≈~

---- VIRGINIA ----

THE FAIR AMERICAN woman and her dark French husband greet Virginia and Philippe at the door of the apartment on the rue Champ de Mars. Virginia presents the couple with a bouquet Michelle, the florist, said they would appreciate—red, white, and blue aster. The symbolic colors of the arrangement feel risky, but the bright smiles it brings to Madame Jacqueline and Monsieur Paul Blanc's faces reassure.

Much has happened in the short time since Virginia and Philippe told Nicole and Michel about Michelle the florist and agreed to become a part of the Resistance machinery. Now that the Nazis have taken over all of France—dissolving the demarcation line and spilling over into what was once the free zone, while forcing Frenchmen into work in Germany by the thousands—there has been a definite and palpable shift in the national mood. Like the majority of the population who had initially tried to keep their heads down and cooperate, now Virginia and Philippe can no longer pretend the writing isn't on the wall. The Nazis don't want cooperation; they want domination. And part of that domination is extermination of everyone they deem "lesser than," which turns out to be everyone who is not of "Aryan" stock. Not only that, the French population are rationed to hunger while the Germans remain fat and happy.

Along with Nicole, Michel, and even Mum, Virginia and Philippe are beginning to make connections with others, seeking to create a web of trusted allies who might find ways to help the growing Resistance. Michelle has been vetted, and now they're seeking more friends and helpers. Their duties are unclear, but they've been charged with laying a foundation of men and women who might be called upon for things they don't yet understand. Creating these relationships is a delicate and dangerous exercise, but it's also exhilarating, and Virginia understands that's why they've been introduced to the Blancs.

Inside the sixth-floor apartment, through the tall arched windows lining the living room, there's a clear view all the way to the Dôme des Invalides. Virginia is surprised to see a toddler in a playpen and a newborn in a bassinet. And here their mother is, polished and coiffed in a way one would not imagine a woman could look so soon after giving birth, especially during wartime.

"I hope we're not imposing, Madame Blanc," says Virginia. "Michelle didn't mention you had two such little daughters."

"It's no imposition," says Jacqueline. "We're desperate for adult company. And please, call me Jessie-Ann."

The woman stands eye to eye with Virginia. She has dark blonde hair, brown eyes, and an open, warm smile. Paul, her husband, gazes on her with obvious love. They look like they could be a couple in a Veuve Clicquot magazine advertisement.

While Jessie-Ann fetches a vase for the flowers, Paul invites Philippe to the bar. Virginia walks over to the babies. The newborn in the bassinet is wrapped in a white blanket and wears a pink cap. She has puffy eyes and sleeps heavily. The toddler clutches the edge of the playpen. When Jessie-Ann joins them, the toddler reaches for her mother. Jessie-Ann lifts her out and allows the little one to explore along the oval coffee table in the living room, where the women settle.

Watching Jessie-Ann and her daughters, Virginia feels a pang, but she holds no envy or bitterness, only the quiet sadness to which she and Philippe have resigned themselves. In truth, Virginia can't help but feel a measure of terror for this woman, having two such little girls during such an excruciating time. Virginia's own mother's letters no longer get through, but the last were full of anguish for her daughter. Virginia wants to assure Mother she's well, but that opportunity is not likely to come anytime soon.

"It's good to meet another American," says Virginia. "To speak English."

"Yes," says Jessie-Ann, pouring them both a glass of champagne from the bucket on the table. "I thought I was the only one of us reckless enough to stay. Paul begged me to return to Minnesota, but how could I leave him? Then I started having babies. I spend half the day on my knees in thanks for the girls and half wondering what kind of mother I am to have brought them into life in Nazi-occupied France. But I'm glad I stayed here with Paul. And the girls give us hope and something to fight for. Though I can hardly call living this way 'fighting.'"

"Yes, Philippe also wanted me to go, but I couldn't. We belong together and we're in this together, whatever we do, whatever end that brings."

"That's exactly where we've arrived," says Jessie-Ann. "Paul kept worrying about me. But hiding, keeping our heads down, has taken a toll. We thought we were preserving our lives, but we realized it was eroding us. If we can't be proud of ourselves, what kind of life are we living?"

The women look over at Paul and Philippe, whose dark heads are bent together.

"It looks like the men have made fast friends," says Virginia.

"Like us," says Jessie-Ann with a smile. "We feel a rising urgency to contribute to the cause."

"We also feel that urgency. We're speaking of resistance, yes?"

Virginia surprises herself by uttering the word so plainly, but with Michelle's recommendation, and the ease with which the couples have fallen in with each other, Virginia doesn't feel the need to proceed delicately.

"We are," says Jessie-Ann.

The toddler has worked her way around the table and now looks up at Virginia, touching her legs and smiling. Virginia takes the girl's hands and helps her to step carefully over the plush rug as she finishes her short journey back to her mother. Virginia touches the girl's downy blonde hair, and a prayer rises in her heart for the child's well-being.

"When this is all over," says Jessie-Ann, "I want my girls to look up to me, not feel ashamed that I didn't do anything while others were being destroyed by evil."

Virginia reaches for her glass of champagne. "I'll drink to that."

27

———— ✦ ————

—— **VIOLETTE** ——

VIOLETTE COULD USE a drink.

"Just a wee dram?" she asks, putting on a thick Scottish accent.

Though the giant at the bow of the boat doesn't reply, she sees the corner of the large man's mouth twitch. The surly, grumbly Scotsman now in charge of her ever-shrinking team of SOE recruits pretends to be exasperated with her, but she knows she'll win him over.

She and her peers—two women and six men, total—row through the darkness of the Loch Nevis to the Knoydart peninsula. Though autumn has just begun, the predawn air is frigid. The lodge where they'll stay can only be reached by boat, and they set out from Mallaig an hour ago, with three other boats full of recruits promoted to the next round of training. Violette's hands sting with blisters, and the damp coldness reaches her bones, but in spite of the unpleasant conditions and knowing how much worse they're about to get, Violette feels exhilarated. After years of pacing around a figurative cage, escape into her new world happened in a flash.

Once Violette received her security clearance, and got Vera Maidment to agree to Tania's continued care, Violette began training. Her cover is that she's enlisted with the FANYs—First Aid Nursing Yeomanry. FANY allows women uniform, rank, and pay, and serves as a front for female SOE agents. When Violette called her mother to share the news, it was harder than she'd imagined to keep the secret. Violette still hasn't reconciled with her father, but it would be hard to keep it from him, too. She thinks he'd be proud of her if he knew.

For the first round of SOE training, Violette spent several weeks at Winterfold, a requisitioned country house in Surrey. Since her group was destined for F Section, the four women and fifteen men had to speak French at all times and underwent intelligence, psychological, and physical tests that acted as a screening for further eligibility. Like her schoolgirl days, Violette found the time in the classroom setting grueling, but she, along with seven others, passed the tests and had been sent on to paramilitary training in Scotland. If she succeeds, it will be on to the next phase, whatever that is. If she fails, she'll have to report to "the cooler"—an estate in remote Scotland under the guard of the Cameron Highlanders, where she'll be exiled until she forgets everything she's learned, or until the intelligence becomes outdated enough for her to return to civilian life.

She's determined that will not be her outcome.

Violette soon spots the lodge of their destination: a solitary white dwelling nestled amid mountains, rolling and rising as far as the eye can see. It's a simple and lonely place, wild and weathered, but it looks solid, like a sturdy boat on a tumultuous sea. Violette feels a kinship with it.

I'll come here with Tania, after the war, Violette thinks. *I'll show her all the places her mother learned to be a soldier.*

The thought gives her such joy, it takes her a moment to master the sudden rise of emotion she feels.

In the weeks while she waited to hear if she could advance, Violette spent every waking moment with Tania. Violette was astounded at how changed the child was after such a short while. Now a year old, Tania chatters like a little bird, adding new words daily. Lively and inquisitive, Tania reminds Violette very much of herself, but without the edge that so curses her. Whether it was Violette's father who gave her that edge—inherited or learned—she doesn't know, only that she won't allow Tania to get it. Maybe Tania will have enough of Étienne in her to subdue that restless-tiger nature Violette has wrestled her entire life.

One area that continues to worry Violette is Tania's care in the event of Violette's death. Miss Atkins said the child would get a pension equal to that of Violette's service rank of ensign, section leader, but she has nothing in writing. Miss Atkins promises she'll obtain it if Violette makes it through training.

"Glaschoille," the instructor growls as they beach the boat. "Bordered by Loch Nevis, which ye've just navigated, and Loch Hourn, which ye'll see later. Hourn means 'hell,' which is an apt name for the waters along your home for the next month, where we'll separate the boys from the men. We keep a cemetery round back for the ones who don't survive the training."

Violette grins as nervous laughter rises from the group. The recruits climb out of the boat, tying it to a post and lining up as the other vessels in the fleet do the same. It's impossible to see the men and women in the predawn light, but she doesn't miss the flash on the spectacles of the man leading a swarm of Scotsmen in camouflage and kilts coming toward them.

"Major Sykes," says Violette's instructor. "He'll be taking ye off my hands. Don't be fooled by his kind face. He's the deadliest man I know. And ye don't need to know the name of the men who'll shadow him. Only that they're of the legions of hell, in charge of your torture."

With that, her instructor strides toward the lodge. After having so quickly taken to him, Violette is sad to see him go, and sadder at the look he gives her when he passes. The stern set of his forehead relaxes, becoming one of worry. Doesn't he believe she'll make it? She thinks she'll find him later, at mealtime. She'll convince him that she was made for this.

"Did ye not hear your command?" a tall, dark Scotsman shouts in her face. "Fall out!"

Disoriented, Violette realizes she missed the order, and stumbles to catch up, last in the group, cursing herself for her inattention. She's being evaluated and scrutinized at every moment, and now she's in the hole.

Quite literally.

All morning long, in and out of filthy holes, her team jumps and crawls. Muscles burning from exertion, as the sun rises over the recruits, she thinks she might not make it through this after all, especially when she realizes they haven't been fed in twenty-four hours. Dirt in her eyes and her teeth, she joins the formations told to spread out at the edge of the loch. The recruits' breath is ragged, and there's a general groan when they're told to swim out to the little island across the way—fully clothed, including boots—touch the flag there, and swim back, touching the flag here. It's a race.

The moment the gun is fired, Violette darts forward, flying into a diving leap that plunges her into the icy water, taking her breath away. Fully awake, she strokes and kicks with all her might the hundred or so yards out to the island. Once her boots hit the opposite shore, she darts up the hill toward the red flag, aware of a man who has emerged parallel to her and determined to beat him, which she does. But her step falters when she hears a voice she recognizes say, "Good job, Vi!"

The moment of her hesitation and recognition of Henri's friend Jack—her young dance hall partner—costs her the lead, and she curses as she races to catch up. Just after him, Violette leaps into the loch and swims with everything she has in her, invigorated by the confirmation of what she suspected: Jack and Henri are in the SOE.

No longer tired or hungry, Violette feels like a sea sprite, like a woman reborn. She and Jack emerge on the other shore, neck and neck. They race forward, laughing, gasping, shouting at each other, until Violette sticks out her foot to trip him, taking the lead and reaching the flag first.

The scowling Scotsman waiting at the flag shows no emotion. She only gets applause from Jack, the close second, while he collapses next to her on the sand. They can't catch their breath from being so spent and laughing so hard at the absurdity of meeting there. When they finally do, Violette pushes up on one elbow and looks down at Jack.

"It was you and Henri who recommended me, wasn't it?" she asks.

He gives her a boyish smile but doesn't speak. It's all the answer she needs.

VIOLETTE'S ELATION AT seeing Jack is short-lived. They're largely kept apart, especially after their successful sneak raid.

On Major Sykes's whisky stash.

Their punishment was running up and down the mountain until they vomited, a consequence Violette does not want to repeat.

The recruits aren't staying in the lodge and given downtime at the cozy fireplaces as Violette would have hoped. They sleep in tents made from parachutes, under scratchy wool blankets that have never seen the washtub. They're worked to the bone and must eat salmon and trout they have to catch themselves in the loch. They rise before the sun they never see fully, only glimpse through billowing clouds, fog, and stinging rain in the world of green, gray, and brown they inhabit. They crawl through buggy marshes and muddy peat bogs, hoist themselves up sharp cliffs, march, run, and hike until dusk. When they can barely stand from exhaustion, they're given rudimentary Morse training.

Unlike Jack, Violette has not been tapped for proficiency in operating a wireless transceiver—the sole communication of their networks with London once behind enemy lines. She'll be a courier or saboteur, but she still has to learn the basic skills. Wireless operators only have a life expectancy of six weeks in the field, so the others have to be ready to tap out at least a crude message to HQ if their operator gets burned.

Somewhere along the line—as the days blur into nights, her body covered in bruises, her stomach empty—Violette forgets the brief joy of seeing a friend. She forgets why she's there. She forgets everyone and everything, except her assigned task at hand. Whether it's a mock raid, wiring a temporary structure for demolition, an exercise in silent killing, or a thirty-kilometer hike in the rain, all she knows is that she must accomplish her mission, and she must do it better than those around her.

She doesn't always succeed.

Among the staff of trainers and evaluators, she feels the tension of those who are rooting for her, and those who want to weed her out. Though they all have faces of stone, Violette catches the looks among them, the disappointed shakes of the head, the whispers through clenched teeth that precede furiously scribbled notes. She's seen their eyes light up for other recruits but not yet for her.

Further distressing are the extremes of emotion she's having difficulty controlling, which she knows a lack of sleep is exacerbating. The recruits are awakened around the clock by their hellish commanders and forced to wade through icy streams without adequate dress and memorize area maps under nearly impossible time constraints. In Violette's mind, she knows the torture of commando training is not personal—it's designed to break the weak so only the toughest remain—but in the nights, she loses all reason and becomes paranoid. Miss Atkins told Violette to expect discrimination. Many of the men, even in their own rebellious ranks, don't approve of women in training, and they certainly don't want pretty young widows with children. Especially when those widows beat them at shooting.

It's on a morning after a failed raid—Violette turned left instead of right at a boulder and ended up getting lost, having to be found—and a long, painful night being tormented by self-loathing that she rises before the others, before the sun, before the wake-up call, and walks to the edge of the loch wrapped in her scratchy blanket. A sea eagle screams above her, and she imagines she's the eagle looking down on herself: a lonely, broken woman, impossibly small against the large, uncaring world. She thinks back to that day on the quay, when she and Dickie were trying to get out of France. How small they must have looked from the gulls' height, from the bombers', from God's.

She's furious at God. Étienne taken from her. An opportunity of a lifetime, slipping through her fingers like water from the loch. She tastes the salt of her tears, running in her mouth, and turns her fury from God to herself, to her weakness. How could she ever think someone as unimportant as she is could make a difference? Maybe she shouldn't go to war. She isn't cool and calm like the rest of them. Her passions rise and fall like mercury in a thermometer.

Despondent, she turns back for the tent, thinking maybe today she'll tell Major Sykes to send her to the cooler—at least she'll have a bed and a hot meal—but a panting sound stops her. Through the dissipating fog, a stag appears. It's regal in bearing. Its chest is puffed, its coat is thick, and it has a rack of antlers worthy of a king's wall. The stag watches her for a moment before stomping its foot and releasing a deep bellow. Then it nods its head and thunders up the hill.

Étienne comes to Violette's mind. He arrives so suddenly and so wholly she feels as if her blanket falls away and it's his arms wrapped around her.

Courage, he says.

28

NESLES-LA-VALLÉE

—— **VIRGINIA** ——

VIRGINIA STANDS ON the terrace, wrapped in a blanket, staring out through the moonlit night at a stag. The thought of venison chili makes her stomach growl—she's tired of eating rabbit—but she doesn't know if she could kill a creature as majestic and substantial as a deer. Though the Germans required all firearms to be turned over to them, Philippe kept one of his guns. It's stashed in the piano bench under a pile of Reich-approved sheet music, including Bruckner's Adagio of the Seventh Symphony and selections from Wagner's *Tristan and Isolde*.

Yes, she thinks. *I could kill the stag. I'm hungry enough.*

The sound of a gunshot, however, would call forth the German officer—a tall, bald man with a linebacker's build—who has requisitioned a room for use on the weekends at Madame Fleury's home. He hunts whenever he's here, and his presence casts a heavy shadow over their sanctuary. Worse, Nan is becoming used to him because Madame Fleury keeps Nan when Virginia and Philippe travel to Paris. When Nan sees the German pass by, she leaps forward with greetings instead of growls, and he never fails to pet her and give her a meat treat from his pocket.

The stag sees Virginia watching it and stomps its foot at her.

That soldier will kill you, Virginia thinks. *Will he kill all of us? Will he move in on me the way the one at Cancaval did all those years ago?*

She sometimes thinks of that officer and his men. Mum and Grandmère have heard from Cancaval neighbors that the house and area remain overrun, but recent upticks in Resistance sabotage have created trouble for the Nazis there, who are already uneasy, aware that their extended holiday will eventually come to an end, if the Allies ever invade the coast like the rumors say.

Invasion can't come soon enough. It's the autumn of 1943 and, like a cancer, the Nazis have infiltrated every cavity of France's marrow. German patrols have even started in their sleepy village, and French betrayers and collaborators are joining the ranks of the *milice*, the French militia, to be extra eyes and ears for the Nazis, to help ferret out the growing Resistance.

Philippe comes up behind Virginia, wrapping his arms around her. The stag bucks toward the forest. Virginia burrows into Philippe, tilting her head to the side while he kisses her neck.

"What did I do to deserve you?" he asks.

"I ask myself that question every minute of every day," she says.

"Come to bed."

She has a hard time tearing herself away from watching out over the falling night—she feels something coming and wants to be awake for it—but Philippe's pull overtakes her, and she joins him in bed.

After their intimacy, even as Philippe falls into a heavy sleep, Virginia's eyes are wide open, staring through the dark. She hears the ticking of the clock, and Nan's pacing in the kitchen, the dog's nails clicking over the floor. Virginia rises, pulls on her bathrobe, steps into her slippers, and walks to the kitchen. Nan leaps with relief when she sees Virginia and rubs against her legs while Virginia sinks her hands into the dog's fur, patting her back.

"I know," Virginia whispers. "I feel it, too."

Virginia is plagued with a constant restlessness. Each new Resistance relationship they add strengthens their growing network's foundation, but it's taking so long to build she doesn't know if they're doing it correctly. Michel assures them they are, but Virginia's stomach is always upset, and the lines in her forehead are deepening from being creased with worry. Many of the people they meet are strangers, which makes one feel out of control, even with strangers who are vetted and deemed "trustworthy." Philippe is losing his hair by the day, and just last week in Paris, Virginia was taken aback to see how stooped Grandmère had become, how she no longer felt strong enough on her own, so she'd moved in with Mum.

Virginia motions for Nan to join her in the living room, sits on the sofa by the window that faces the forest, and pats the cushion so Nan knows it's all right to climb up in her lap. The warmth of the dog is a comfort, but the wind howling outside, making great, dancing skeletons of the nearly bare trees, raises goose bumps on her arms. The light of the waning gibbous moon gives an eerie blue glow to the landscape, like the pilot light on a gas stove, and her eyes play tricks on her, making men of the shadows along the wood line.

As she starts to nod off, she hears the unmistakable sound of a vehicle's brakes squeaking outside on the driveway. She jumps from the sofa. Nan races toward the door, barking. Philippe is there in seconds.

"What is it?" he says.

"Someone's here," whispers Virginia.

Nan continues barking as Philippe and Virginia hurry to the kitchen, where they can watch the walkway, unobserved. Virginia's heart pounds in her ears. With few exceptions, the Nazis are the only ones driving about in cars—especially this late. Have they come to take Philippe? Or her?

"The shelter," whispers Virginia, pulling Philippe's hand. "Let's go."

"Wait," he says. "It looks like Renard."

"What would he be doing here after curfew?"

They watch as the baker climbs out of his truck and glances over his shoulder, down the wooded lane. He pulls off his beret, wipes his forehead, and climbs back in the vehicle. Then he pauses and steps back down. He takes a deep breath, leaves the door open, and hurries toward the house.

Virginia and Philippe greet Renard before he has time to knock. Virginia holds Nan back and hushes her as Philippe allows the man in, closing the door behind him. When Renard sees both of them standing there, his forehead contorts with worry.

"Pardon," he says. "May I have a word with Monsieur?"

"You may say whatever you need to in front of my wife," says Philippe.

The baker's face falls, conveying his further distress. He's mute with indecision. He doesn't seem disrespectful, only afraid.

"J'y vais," Virginia says.

She takes Nan to the bedroom and closes the door. In a short while, Philippe enters in a hurry and dresses.

"What is it?" she whispers.

"I'll tell you as soon as I can," he says, energy buzzing from him like a live wire.

She throws up her hands. He kisses her on the head and leaves her. She falls back on the bed and stares at the ceiling. As the sound of the truck recedes, she turns her head to watch the clock. The second hand ticks by five minutes, ten, fifteen. At twenty, she's pacing the room. At twenty-five, she chews her fingernails. Thirty, and she pulls on her clothes in case she needs to go to the shelter. Thirty-five, and she starts for the door. As she heads downstairs, the shrill ring of the telephone cuts through the silence. Her heart pounds while she runs to answer it.

"Honeybee," says Philippe. "Come to the bakery. Right away."

SHE'S TOO EXCITED by Philippe's tone of voice to be afraid.

Stepping out into the night, hurrying through the forest, creeping along the road to town, Virginia arrives at the back door of the bakery in less than ten minutes. She raises her hand to knock but is pulled into the dark before she can, the aroma of bread enlivening her senses. A match is struck, a lantern lit, and there before her, seated at a table, with Renard standing beside them, are three strangers.

She looks at them a moment, then at Philippe with a question in her eyes, before darting her gaze back to the men.

They're clearly not Frenchmen. Two of the men are fair and the other is Asian. All wear ill-fitting, dirty clothes, but their faces are young, fresh, and open.

"Bon jure," says one of the fair men, with a toothy smile.

Virginia gasps.

"You're Americans!" she says in English.

"So are you!" says the Asian man.

Faces lighting up, the men stand, knocking back their chairs as they do. Virginia rushes toward them, embracing each one of them, laughing, fussing over them like a mother hen. Philippe looks on, beaming.

"I needed interpreters," says Renard, in French.

"You've got it," Virginia says.

Madame Renard tiptoes in with a smile on her face, carrying a tray with wine, bread, and cheese, and the group settles around the table. She encourages all of them to help themselves, and they devour the food, talking with full mouths through the night, Philippe and Virginia translating back and forth as quickly as possible.

These men of the US Army Air Corps were part of a vast configuration of Flying Fortresses bound for industrial targets in Germany. Their B-17, the *Yankee Raider*, was shot down by enemy fire near Normandy. They lost one of their gunners, and these three were separated from the rest of their crew. They've been on the run for weeks, relying on the kindness of strangers, being sent from house to house, working their way slowly toward Spain, where they hope to find a guide to help them escape over the Pyrenees.

"It's been especially hard to hide me," says the man they now know is Hawaiian. "I'm so thankful for anyone willing to do so."

The enormity of what he says settles over the group like fog over the Channel. Every person in the room could be deported, or worse, if the Nazis find out.

When the cock crows, Virginia shakes her head, shocked by how quickly the night passed.

"You better get going," Madame Renard says to Virginia and Philippe. "The bakery line will form soon."

They stand and say their goodbyes, Virginia giving each American a hug and kisses on his cheeks. She hadn't realized what a boon seeing her own countrymen would be. They're so young and brave and vulnerable it brings tears to her eyes. She has to work to keep them from falling.

But all the way home, she and Philippe can't keep the smiles from their faces.

29

MANCHESTER, ENGLAND

── VIOLETTE ──

IT WAS VIOLETTE'S proficiency with a gun that advanced her.

Her instructors had made no secret of their disdain for her, calling her mercurial, unreliable, and even unstable. But when weapons assembly and target practice began, she blew them all away.

There are just six left in the merged companies, of which she's the lone woman and Jack is one of the only remaining men. Jack had abbreviated SOE training early on, before his first mission, but it's become more advanced, so he wanted another shot at it. He already passed parachute training, so he's off to wireless operator school. They had no opportunities to talk of anything of substance at the paramilitary course, and Violette's dying to ask him a thousand questions, especially if he knows where Henri is. She hopes their paths cross again at finishing school. If she makes it.

First, she has to pass parachute training.

On the drive to Ringway Airport, Miss Atkins continues her behind-the-scenes instruction.

"You cannot allow yourself to become personally attached to those in your networks," says Miss Atkins. "It leads to heartache."

"But I love my company," Violette says. "They're good boys and I'd trust them with my life."

"Yes, and they're all in love with you."

"Not Jack. He's like a little brother. We work well together."

"Yes, at making mischief. I heard about the two of you and your pranks. Pretending to hold up a train full of locals."

"Oh, they thought it was funny. Once they knew we were only joking. Well, I think they were laughing as hard as we were. Laughing on the inside, that is."

"And poaching whisky from Major Sykes?"

"We were all freezing in our tents. We needed something to warm us up."

"And stealing Sykes's trousers to hike up the flagpole while he was swimming."

"Now that was Nancy Wake's idea. One hundred percent Nancy."

"Which makes it likely that none of you will be assigned together behind enemy lines. We don't need any high jinks or foolish gestures of chivalry in the field. When it comes down to it, it's every man or woman for him- or herself."

Violette chews on that the rest of the way to the airport.

They arrive at sunset. The great shadows of the airplanes perch against the orange sky like birds of prey, ready and eager for hunting.

"When we win the war, and my Tania is older," says Violette, "I'm going to take her to the Hotel Victoria and Scotland and Ringway and show her what her mother did. I'm going to show her she can do anything she wants."

Miss Atkins stares at Violette without speaking.

"I can't thank you enough for bringing me on," continues Violette. "I promise, I won't disappoint you."

Miss Atkins's gaze turns to the runway. She pulls her cigarettes out of her breast pocket and offers one to Violette. After they light up, the women get out of the car and lean against it, exhaling together, watching the planes take off and land.

"You shouldn't smoke once you're in France," says Miss Atkins. "The Nazis don't think it becoming in women. And rations don't allow for it."

"They also don't think women can shoot or keep secrets. They'll sure be surprised to find themselves on the other side of my gun, my cigarette smoke blowing in their faces, while I send them straight to hell."

"You're speaking figuratively, I hope. It is not our wish that you get to a point when you're in a firefight with a Nazi. You should leave that to the growing Resistance army."

"Then why's shooting part of my training?"

"The same reason you'll learn how to fall at parachute school and how to resist interrogation and torture if you make it to SOE finishing school. We all must have a contingency plan for emergencies."

Shooting. Interrogation. Torture.

The vocabulary sinks into Violette's consciousness, reminding her this is not a game. And for the first time since she began training, she understands that not coming back is a real possibility. She said she wasn't afraid of dying—and she isn't—but it's dawning on her, there are things worse than death, both for her and for those who love her.

TORTURE BEGINS IN a way she didn't anticipate. It starts in a wheelchair.

At parachute school, Violette learned to fall easily. She learned to jump in a hangar from one story, from two, from ten, from five hundred feet, from a hot-air balloon. Her first airplane jump was perfection—textbook—and exciting beyond words, especially when she received her shiny parachute pin. But on her second of the five required jumps, in spite of all her physical fitness, in spite of mastering the art of falling, she'd been bested by misjudging her distance from uneven ground, twisting her left ankle upon landing, and spraining it.

She's forced to sit in a wheelchair, on an indefinite period of leave from SOE training, at a convalescent center in Bournemouth, surrounded by the elderly. On phone calls to Maman and to Vera, she has to lie, telling them she fell out of a lorry on a FANY run to drive a colonel to the airport. Deceiving her loved ones is harder than she would have thought and, based on the quiet on the other end of the line, she's not convincing. This is worrisome for one training to be a professional liar.

At night, when Violette catches the shiny glint of light on the metal of her parachute pin on the side table, she punches her pillow. By day, she wheels herself moodily from one vantage to another, unable to escape her thoughts. She's slowly coming to terms with the fact that she can't afford both her flat and Tania's childcare much longer, and she still has no assurance in writing of a pension for Tania in the event of Violette's death. In the downtime, the ache to see her daughter presses like an actual weight on her chest, but Vera's house in Mill Hill is two hundred kilometers away, so there's no possibility anytime soon.

After several weeks, Violette makes the agonizing decision to let go of the flat. When she calls home to speak to Maman about the logistics, her father answers.

"Vi!" he says. "I'm glad to catch you. Maman told me about you enlisting with the FANYs, and about your injury."

Violette has a hard time finding the words to speak to her father after such a long separation.

"Look," he says. "I know we had a bad time. But I want you to know, I'm glad to hear you picked yourself up. Before you fell down again, that is."

While he laughs at his own joke, she takes a deep breath. It takes all she has in her to push her pride aside to ask for his help.

"Yes, about that," she says. "When I'm discharged from the center, I'll need a place to continue to heal, and, well, my pay isn't enough to keep the flat at the moment, and I could use help with Tania, especially with it being hard to get around."

"You're welcome home anytime."

Tears spring to her eyes. She guesses parents always feel the pain of separation from their children, even when they're grown, even when they don't always get along.

She stammers a thank-you, and he agrees to handle the selling of most of her furniture and move the rest of it to the already cramped family home.

But as cordial as the call turned out to be, by the time the taxi delivers Violette to Burnley Road, her mood is low. She loved her place in Notting Hill, and she's not feeling up to sparring with her father. She limps toward the front steps. Her heavy satchel, paired with her bruised pride, makes the short walk all the more difficult. Maman throws open the door and calls to Papa to help with Violette's bags, fussing over her and escorting her to a chair in the living room. With narrowed eyes, Papa looks Violette over from head to toe, and she senses his mood matches her own.

"Where's Dickie?" she asks, hoping her little brother will defuse the tension.

"At Aunt Florrie's," says Maman. "When do we get to see Tania?"

"I'll get her tomorrow."

"Good."

Maman chatters, trying to fill the awkwardness of their reunion with mindless conversation, but Papa soon takes over.

"How'd this happen?" he asks.

"As Maman told you, I twisted my ankle stepping out of a lorry. It was muddy."

"You expect me to believe a lynx like you, who can land on two feet jumping from a tree branch, sprained her ankle getting out of a car."

In what Violette has learned so far in training about withstanding interrogation, sticking to the truth as much as possible is best.

"I was careless," she says. "I hate myself for it."

"Who's that colonel you were driving?"

"No one to you."

"Are you dallying with him?"

"Charlie," says Maman.

"That's none of your business," says Violette. "But no, for the record, I am not."

Papa's interrogation skills, Violette thinks, *would impress the staff at SOE finishing school.*

"I hope you'll take this as a sign that you belong home," he says. "Raising your daughter. Instead of driving people around, acting like that's some kind of war service."

It takes every ounce of restraint Violette has in her to suppress the instinct to lash back at him. The silence stretches between them. She stares at her father with ice in her eyes until he looks away. An echo of Miss Atkins's voice comes to Violette's mind.

You will often be judged and misunderstood. You must learn to endure this in silence.

Violette takes a deep breath. Once she trusts her voice is steady, she turns her attention to her mother.

"Would you like to come to Mill Hill tomorrow with me to fetch Tania?"

"I would love to," says Maman.

"I need to pay Vera and discuss the terms of Tania's care when I return to work."

"If it's too much, you know we're always happy to keep the baby."

"I know," says Violette.

Her father gets up and leaves the room.

Dinner is a tense affair. A ticking clock. The clank of silverware on plates. Chewing noises. Afterward, Violette limps to the living room to retrieve her handbag. Turning quickly, she runs into her father, who trails her. The bag falls to the ground, its contents spilling across the floor. Her mother hurries in from the kitchen as Violette and her father crouch down and reach for the parachute pin at the same time.

Beating her to it, he holds it in his fingers, his scowl softening the longer he stares at it. Violette's horror at his seeing the pin—knowing that, as a veteran, Papa will understand at least in part what it is—turns to relief. After a long moment, he looks into her eyes, his own covered in a film of tears.

"Vi?" he whispers.

She can't answer him with words, but she gives him a small smile. They stand up together, and he takes her hand.

"What is it?" says Maman.

Papa clears his throat and holds up the pin.

"Vi can't tell us," he says. "But she's doing good. Real good."

His words of praise open a dam of unshed tears, and the three of them wrap their arms around each other.

30

───ᐳᐸᐸ───

─── **VIRGINIA** ───

THE KNOCK IS expected, but Virginia and Philippe are still cautious. They tiptoe to the door of the apartment and take turns looking out the peephole. Standing in the hallway is a tall man with thinning brown hair, rounded cheeks, and dark circles under his sad, wide-set eyes. Philippe opens the door.

"Do you have the parcel for Lily?" the man asks.

As the words of the code phrase Michel gave them are uttered, Virginia's filled with the excitement she feels more and more. It's a rush—a drug—and a good one. One they needed. One that has given them clarity and purpose. That night with the baker and the pilots at Nesles opened the door to their new lives, which now involve many doors, many strangers, and the realization of their shared vocation.

"We do," Virginia says. "Come in and I'll fetch it."

Last night, Michel had told Virginia and Philippe to expect a Belgian agent who had recently been burned.

"What do you mean?" Virginia had asked. "Agent? Burned?"

"We're all now a part of the newly reconstructed Comet Line,"

Michel said. "An underground network, running from Belgium to Spain, helping downed pilots and Nazi fugitives escape."

"The Comet Line," said Virginia, her voice a whisper.

"I like the sound of that," Philippe had said.

"One of the Comet chiefs—Jean," continued Michel, "was operating out of Brussels when he was betrayed and had to escape through Spain. He was just parachuted into France with a wireless operator to coordinate pilot evacuations with London by finding fields for landings around the full moon."

"Wait, slow down," Virginia said, trying to take it all in. "Parachuted in? Jean was dropped from a plane?"

"*Oui.*"

"To use some kind of radio device to communicate with London?" asked Philippe.

"An intelligence service there."

"But the device," said Nicole, "and the supplies dropped and hidden with Jean and Louis, his operator, were found by the Gestapo. Luckily, the barn where it was stored was on an abandoned property, so no one was arrested. And the men had come to Paris to rendezvous with us, here, so they're safe, for now."

"Jean will arrive at your apartment tomorrow," said Michel, "before heading to a nearby safe house to try to round up another wireless. Louis will arrive later. He needs shelter while they await orders."

"So," Virginia had said, "this Jean and Louis will try to coordinate Allied plane landings, in Nazi-occupied fields in France, to take pilots who have been shot down back to London?"

"*Oui.* The Pyrenees trip is long and exhausting. Getting them back by air is much quicker. Pilots, as you realize, are not easily replaceable."

"And these aviators are willing to hop back in the captain's seat and return to the skies over a country where they were just shot down?"

"Their bravery is incomprehensible," said Nicole.

"So, ours has to be, too," said Virginia.

In her life plan, Virginia never could have foreseen that she—a rule follower—would become an evader, a harborer of fugitives, and a resister. Nor could Philippe, for that matter. But once she and Philippe helped each other come to this place, they realized exactly why they were brought together.

Nothing has been confusing since that night at Renard's bakery. Virginia's stomach has stopped roiling. She no longer frets and feels indecisive. In spite of the strain of evolving to this place, it was worth it, and her marriage is stronger for it.

Once Jean is safely inside their apartment, his shoulders relax, and he gives them a smile.

"I smell stew," he says. "Michel told me you'd be gracious hosts."

"You came at the right time," says Virginia. "The boches only allow the gas on for an hour at noon and at six, so cooking has to happen quickly."

"Maybe my luck is changing."

Virginia invites Jean to sit at the kitchen table. She ladles a generous serving of rabbit stew into a bowl from where it's simmering on the burner, while Philippe gives Jean white bread from Nesles. Jean digs in with gusto. With a full mouth, he instructs them on his close contacts, whom they can trust.

"Lily is a Belgian girl who acts as a guide," Jean says. "She'll be in and out of Paris. Louis was just dropped with me and will arrive in an hour. But I have to warn you, his nerves are shot. Can you escort him to your country house soon?"

"Yes," says Virginia. "There's a train that leaves this evening."

"How are you able to move back and forth so freely?"

"Aside from a mighty dose of luck, Philippe's farming work pass makes it possible. We transport produce, eggs, and bread from Nesles to show them when we're stopped. Of course, we make the trip so often, the regular German MPs and French gendarmes recognize us and usually wave us through. And the rail workers, as you likely know, tend to be on the side of the good guys, and keep their noses down."

"Excellent. Do you have a phone at your country place?"

"*Oui.*"

"Good. As soon as I make contact with London and find out if we can get our hands on another wireless transceiver for Louis, I'll ring you and let you know if you should escort Louis back to Paris, or if I will come to you. I'll say either, 'Lily says you should pick up the parcel here,' or 'Lily says I should come pick up the parcel.' Got it?"

Philippe nods.

"One more thing," says Jean. "I need a second in Paris. Someone I can trust, who has freedom and reason to travel in and out of the city, as you do, and who can connect with Daniel, our other chief in the region. What do you think?"

Philippe looks at Virginia, and she nods her head.

"I'll do it," says Philippe. "We will."

Jean breathes a sigh of relief.

"If this goes well," he says, "you'll be transporting many, many parcels."

VIRGINIA'S FIRST PARCEL from Paris is trembling so badly, he's making her body shake right along with him.

Louis did not relish jumping from an airplane and having the Gestapo on his heels the moment he'd arrived in occupied France. A "burned" Belgian agent, he thought they'd be starting over in France, but the Gestapo talk, and their networks are as sophisticated as—or more so than—those of the Resistance.

Virginia has her arm through Louis's, attempting to stroll with him through the Square Montholon on the way to the Gare du Nord for the evening train out of the city. But it's freezing outside, and between the man's nerves and the temperature, by no means is it a relaxing walk.

Philippe was sick at the thought of Virginia navigating the trip with Louis, but Jean agreed that Virginia would be a less suspicious traveling companion for Louis than Philippe would. Able-bodied men in their thirties, together, caught the attention of German MPs far faster than couples.

"You'll be on the same train," she'd reassured Philippe. "Keep us in eye view if it makes you feel better. I'm not scared."

And she isn't, but poor Louis can barely put one foot in front of the other. It's less of a stroll and more her propping him up and dragging him.

"Let's sit," she says, spotting a bench at the base of the dry fountain.

The fountain has been decapitated of its crown. The Nazis insisted the massive bronze statue, *The Bear, the Eagle, and the Vulture,* be removed and melted down to become absorbed into their machinery of war.

Moments after they take a seat, two German soldiers appear around the turn on the path leading toward them. The Nazis smoke and chat, but when they spot Virginia and Louis, their expressions darken.

Louis is shaking so badly Virginia worries they'll see. At odds with the chill in the air, his face is covered in a sheen of sweat. She thinks fast and, as the Germans get closer, she yanks Louis's head and presses it into her neck. She closes her eyes, pretending she's enjoying being nuzzled, while praying the ruse will work. After a few moments, she opens her eyes a slit and sees the Germans nudging each other and smirking at the so-called lovers. Once they've passed, she removes Louis from her neck and gives him a sheepish smile, while holding his face in her hands. He looks a little dumbfounded, but he's able to manage a small smile in return.

The relief is short-lived. Virginia's eyes are drawn back to the path, where an elderly woman with yellowing hair and clawlike hands clutches her handbag and stares, her mouth open in horror. It's Mum's church friend, Madame Mollet.

All the blood leaves Virginia's body and her face burns with shame. Madame Mollet lowers her gaze and hurries away.

Louis is no longer the one trembling. Now it's Virginia who needs support. She knows Philippe will understand, but her reputation will no doubt take a hit. And there'll be no way for Virginia or Mum to explain the truth of what happened.

Virginia takes a deep breath and stands, pulling Louis along to the station as quickly as she's able without drawing any more unwanted attention to her parcel, wondering all the while if she really comprehended what she was getting into.

31

LONDON

———✦———

——— VIOLETTE ———

ONCE SHE READS over the will, Violette comprehends exactly what she's getting into.

At Orchard Court, one of the SOE's office buildings in London, Miss Atkins and Major Maurice Buckmaster, head of the F Section, witness Violette sign the sheet of paper that, in the event of her death in the field, appoints her mother the executor of Violette's small estate—including a pension for Tania—and assigns guardianship of Tania to Vera Maidment. Violette feels a pang of regret in her heart knowing how hurt her mother and father would be to learn this. Violette didn't make the decision lightly, but it's still troubling to see it typed in black and white.

I'll just have to make sure I come back, Violette thinks. *Then they'll never need to know.*

She pushes the paperwork away, with a huff of disgust.

"Are you sure about this before we file it?" Miss Atkins asks.

"Yes."

"A formality only," says Buckmaster.

Miss Atkins gives him a reproving look, but Violette smiles. Buckmaster's confidence is a welcome balance for Miss Atkins's caution and never fails to put the wind in Violette's sails. Some people call him stiff, but he's always warm with Violette.

Violette looks at her bosses, her affection growing for them by the day. They're like a dear aunt and uncle, the family she's chosen, in a sense, instead of those she was given. They each care for her in their own ways, and their instruction is making a better agent of her all the time. Violette recalls Mr. Potter and the dozens of shadowed men and women zipping around the offices and watering holes of the SOE and the OSS, some of whom she's beginning to recognize by sight, who are beginning to recognize her right back.

In spite of caution to avoid such attachments and each other, it's impossible not to admire one's coworkers in espionage. There are no outward signs of what they have in common. They come from many different places and walks of life. No one in the world outside understands them—many can scarcely understand themselves—and it's this duty to a calling that serves as a bond between them.

It's the women in the organization who most draw Violette's attention. Always on Violette's mind is the question of motivation. What brings them here? Vengeance? Conscience? Daring? A cocktail of the three? Violette's talents at curiosity, observation, and questioning give her some answers, but not others.

For instance, why is the demure Muslim woman with large doe eyes learning to be a wireless operator? How did the intimidating American woman with the limp—whom everyone from lieutenants to generals steps aside to let pass—come to join their ranks? What brought the tragic-faced, aristocratic beauty—the kind of woman who makes you stand up taller and smooth your skirt when she walks by—to the SOE? Then there's the Jewish woman, narrowly escaped from France, who dyed her hair blonde so she can return as a wireless operator to another region. That's a whole other level of courage.

On the way back to Ringway to complete parachute training, Violette can't help herself from peppering Miss Atkins with questions about the women. Violette turns in her seat, legs tucked up under her, while she interrogates her boss. Miss Atkins pretends to be annoyed, but Violette is certain Miss Atkins adores Violette the way one does a naughty pet.

"You know by now," says Miss Atkins, "I won't tell you any more than your snooping self has discovered."

"Will you tell me after the war?" Violette asks. "Promise me, all us girls will meet for a drink up at your place in Sussex and talk about every little thing?"

"I never told you I had a place in Sussex."

"Nor have you told me how you got involved in the SOE. And that's what I really want to know."

"Both are none of your concern. Perhaps you should focus on learning to fall without ending up in the hospital for months on end. If you don't make it through this round of training, you'll have to go to the cooler. You know too much. And most of that is because you're nosy."

Miss Atkins pulls up to Dunham House—the requisitioned country estate where recruits are housed, a short ride from Ringway Airport—and a guard nods at them to proceed through the gate. Seeing the redbrick facades of the grand buildings glowing in January's early sunset draws a happy sigh from Violette. The place looks like a friendly boarding school.

"You know what the SOE really stands for?" Violette asks.

"What's that?"

"Stately 'Omes of England," Violette says, putting on her thickest Cockney accent.

The side of Miss Atkins's mouth turns up but quickly returns to its neutral position.

"We're getting spoiled," continues Violette. "You really should think about more modest dwellings. Like the tents at Loch Nevis. I might get too comfortable in a place like this."

"I wish you would."

"What do you mean?"

Miss Atkins puts the car in park and grips the steering wheel, holding on like it's a life ring.

"There is no shame in stopping at any point in the training," says

Miss Atkins, still looking straight ahead. "Most recruits leave us, either because they aren't fit or because they have second thoughts. I could expedite your time at the cooler. You'd need only stay a month—"

"Stop," says Violette.

"I might even consider you for a job at Orchard Court."

"Don't say that. I won't quit."

"'Quit' is the wrong word. Making a sensible decision best for your loved ones is what recruits often say when they elect to discontinue training."

"Do you say this to everyone, or just those women with children?"

"Don't get sharp with me. Your hesitation, filling out that will, inspired this conversation."

"You've never had an agent hesitate when filling out a will?"

"I often see hesitation, and many of those people elect not to continue."

"Well, that's not me. I'm human, after all."

"Yes, very human. And you will need to learn to better control your true emotions if you are to succeed in the field."

Violette opens her mouth to respond, but then purses her lips. She knows Miss Atkins is right. It takes a great deal of effort to swallow the retort, to remind herself that she isn't arguing with her father. It pains her that Miss Atkins doesn't fully believe in her.

Realizing she still sits like a teenager in the passenger seat, legs tucked under her, Violette carefully unfolds them and turns to stare ahead. They sit in silence until the darkness rises, the winter chill creeps into the car, and their breath fogs up the windows.

"I have to be in London by six o'clock," Miss Atkins says. "Are you coming back with me, or not?"

"No," says Violette.

ENTERING THE FOYER, she almost slams into a young man being pushed outside in a wheelchair by an older man.

"Whoa," the older one says. "I didn't know a cyclone was due in tonight."

His smirk and the twinkle in his heavily lashed eyes draw a smile from Violette, in spite of her mood.

"Well, it was, and I'm here," she says before extending her hand. "Code name Louise."

"Clement."

"Robert," says the young man in the wheelchair.

Seated, Robert is almost as tall as Clement and Violette are standing. Robert's knees are up at his chest level due to his long legs. He looks like a grown man in a child's chair.

"Oh dear, Robert," says Violette, her anger evaporating. "I left parachute training the same way last time. Which jump did you do it on?"

"Oh, I've graduated the program here," Robert says. "The boches managed to shoot me in the back while I was recently trying to escape their unfortunate company, but I'm doing much better, recuperating and making plans for my next mission with my good friend and partner, Clement. Would you like to join our team? We need a wireless operator."

"Sadly, I failed to show proficiency in Morse, so I'll likely be a courier or saboteur. And though I gave an Oscar-worthy speech to Miss Atkins about wanting a better world for my loved ones, I really just want to kill Nazis."

"Don't we all," says Clement. "Robert is an expert saboteur."

"Then I think we'll get on well," says Violette.

Robert pushes the door closed and turns the wheelchair around on the parquet floor of the foyer to face Violette.

"I thought you wanted to get out for some fresh air?" says Clement.

"That was before I met our new courier-saboteur," says Robert. "Now I want to sit with her by that roaring fire and make plans for our next mission."

"I have a few training hurdles to cross before they drop me," says Violette, "but I'm all for getting right to work. And I want to hear about the shooting. Just let me put down my bag."

She starts for the stairs, but Clement calls to her.

"Has anyone ever told you, you bear an uncanny resemblance to Ingrid Bergman?"

"Yes," she says. "And has anyone ever told you, you look like the Tin Man?"

"I don't know who that is, but I'll take it as a compliment. He sounds like a soldier."

"Oh, you haven't seen *The Wizard of Oz*. Delightful American film. We got it in London at the start of the war."

"I was in France, and it seems the Nazis aren't keen on American films."

"What about me?" asks Robert. "Who am I like from that Wizard film?"

"The Cowardly Lion," Violette says, with a wink.

His fallen face gives Violette and Clement a good laugh.

She hurries up the stairs, happy to have met these men and reassured that she has made the right decision.

32

PARIS

~~∞~~

—— VIRGINIA ——

SEEING THE MOTLEY crew of lanky, ill-clothed Allied aviators emerge from the train steam at the Gare du Nord makes Virginia wonder if she has made the right decision. Each time she picks up her "parcels," she can't help but think, *Will this trip be the one that does us all in?* But her feet haven't failed to move her yet, and the joy she gets helping the pilots along to their next stop provides the antidote to the fear.

The men trail the tiny Belgian girl, Lily, whose family started the Comet Line. Lily's parents and sister were arrested and deported. Lily is desperate to find the betrayer but, for now, the fearless twenty-three-year-old, who looks barely fifteen, has not ceased her own Resistance activities, even making multiple trips guiding men over the Pyrenees herself.

Unfortunately, Jean and Louis were ordered back to London. Jean was able to find another wireless operator to report the Germans took theirs and the materials they'd been dropped with, but a spate of arrests made HQ suspicious of the pair. Mission failed, they had to leave, but once everything is cleared up in London, they'll return to France. At least, Jean will. Louis might be too unsteady.

This is Virginia and Philippe's third batch of parcels. With their contacts, they'll divide and hide the men overnight, escort them to Nesles tomorrow, and—once the men have had rest and food—send them on their way. The pilots will pass through a network of bakers, priests, widows, tradesmen, and farmers until Lily meets up with them again at the border to Spain. Then, if all goes well, it's back to London. No use dwelling on the alternative.

Virginia glances at Michelle the florist at the next table in the station café, and then nods toward the formation. Michelle finishes her coffee and closes her newspaper. Then Virginia glances at Daniel, a small Belgian man who could easily pass for a Frenchman. He stubs out his cigarette and rises.

Tiny Belgians. Tiny florists. At five feet seven inches, Virginia feels like an Amazon around these men and women of the Comet Line, but the six-footers walking toward them will tower over all of them, conspicuous as lighthouses.

Smooth as synchronized swimmers, Virginia, Michelle, and Daniel stand and discreetly fall in behind Lily's crew, threading their steady arms through the trembling men's arms and directing them toward opposite exits. Now that the team has done this together before, there's little need for the members of the Comet Line to speak. Those being conveyed upon it, however, need reassurance. They are young, harried, injured, and traumatized, but when they learn Virginia is American, it never fails to give them a boost.

The winter air slaps their faces the moment they step outside the station. Virginia scans the sidewalk and, once they're free of other pedestrians, she whispers to them—one on each arm—in English.

"Steady, boys. We have an hour's walk ahead of us."

"You're American!"

"Hush," she says, not unkindly. "I'm going to chatter in French on our walk. Nod and say, '*Oui, cousine*,' if a German looks at you. Otherwise, keep quiet."

"*Oui, cousine.*"

Virginia smiles.

She increases the pace at which they walk, making sure she looks natural and bland. She's covered her auburn hair with a kerchief and wears no makeup. Her clothing is brown and old; her shoes are sensible. Women are nearly invisible to the enemy. Nazis can't comprehend that the female of the species is as brave, intelligent, and even devious and vengeful as the male, and the stupidity of the enemy is a chink in their armor. While Virginia knows the side streets where they're less likely to run into soldiers, for anonymity it's best to stick with the crowds.

Her parcels begin to relax, their grasps loosening and their gaits growing smoother. Even though they can't understand what she's saying, she points out the tourist sites along the way, in case they've never been to Paris, which they mostly have not. When they pass the massive Madeleine church, she draws their attention to the columns that give it the appearance of a Roman temple. She walks them along the Jardin des Tuileries, nodding to the mighty golden statue of Joan of Arc on horseback that never fails to make Virginia stand up straighter. As they pass the Louvre, the men make efforts to parrot her French. She's pleased how quickly they've been put at ease, but also knows how fast things can become dangerous, and never lowers her guard.

They soon reach the busy intersection leading to Pont Royal, where they'll cross the Seine. The traffic is more voluminous than usual, and they're left to wait longer than Virginia is comfortable. The boys sense her unease and again tense up. One of them sucks in his breath when a captain in the Luftwaffe walks up next to them. Virginia can feel the heat from the boy closest to the Nazi flier, and sees her pilot's neck has turned bright red.

Steady, she thinks, trying to will calm into him.

The line of traffic is endless, and they're trapped. The Nazi flier is almost as tall as her boys, but he's older and has broader shoulders. He pulls out a pack of cigarettes, places one between his lips, and pats around his jacket pockets for a light.

Just as they're about to get a break in the parade of vehicles, a siren comes screaming toward them. The closer it gets, the more unsettled Virginia feels, and it's all she can do not to cover her ears when it passes them.

The Nazi has not found a light and turns to look at them. To Virginia's horror, the boy closest to him reaches in his own pocket and pulls out a Zippo lighter.

Time slows. Sound recedes. Everything around them goes dark. It is only she, and the American pilot, and the Nazi flier, and the cigarette, and the flashing silver of the United States Army Air Corps lighter.

The pilot on her opposite side gasps, but the one who has offered his lighter appears oblivious to his gaffe.

In agonizingly slow motion, the Nazi leans toward the flame and inhales once, twice, before standing up straight again and exhaling toward the sky. The traffic has ceased, but Virginia can't move.

The Nazi looks at the American pilot and smiles, exposing his yellow teeth that bite the cigarette. He then tips his hat at Virginia and crosses the street.

She cannot walk until he's out of sight. She doesn't breathe until they've reached her apartment.

33

LONDON

—— VIOLETTE ——

VIOLETTE, CLEMENT, AND Robert lean in toward the candle flame to light their cigarettes. They pull back and exhale toward the ceiling of the bar at the Pastoria Hotel, on Leicester Square. Close to the SOE's offices in London, agents like to stay at the Pastoria while they await mission dispatch. They're here to celebrate Violette's and Jack's graduation from SOE finishing school, at Beaulieu Estate, in Hampshire. They watch the door for Jack, who's running late.

Since their meeting at parachute school, Violette, Clement, and Robert have been inseparable, and now that they're all in London, Jack has folded right in. Whether playing poker, going to the shooting gallery, or visiting the Studio Club, the four of them have the easy banter of siblings. Clement has let on that he has a wife somewhere in France, and Robert is a Don Juan—he could never think of settling at this point. This frees them to enjoy each other's company without the burden of romance.

Violette wishes Henri could complete the tribe. Though Jack says he doesn't know where Henri was dropped, she somehow senses Henri is well. She thinks with fondness of how gentle Henri was with Tania, and Violette often finds herself humming "I'll Be Around," the song playing when they first danced. She still shivers at the thought of his kisses and hopes she can somehow find him in France.

The men are a few drinks in, but Violette sticks to club soda. She's never liked feeling out of control while under the influence, and that's more important now than ever. The fact that she's a bona fide clandestine agent is a reality she has difficulty comprehending, but that gives her fresh waves of elation every time the thought runs through her mind.

As expected, at finishing school, the SOE drama coach and weapons instructors gave Violette highest marks. In the cat-and-mouse games at the village, she was able to evade capture by mock Gestapo while successfully trapping another agent, though she couldn't catch Jack, much to her consternation. But what gave Violette the greatest level of pride was her performance under interrogation. Cultivating the quieting of mind techniques she's always naturally used to block out her surroundings when shooting, she succeeded at creating an inner place of refuge where her consciousness could retreat in the face of harsh conditions. Agents are told, if they are tortured, remaining silent for forty-eight hours is all that's needed for compromised networks to scatter to safety. Violette is confident she can last at least that long. Not that she plans on getting arrested.

But neither did Clement on an early mission.

He drains his glass of whisky and winces, touching his stomach.

"It's never been right since internment," Clement says. "I can't recommend Mauzac prison, nor do I endorse Beleyme. I've heard terrible things about Fresnes, south of Paris, but word is that Romainville is quite pleasant, though it's only a holding place before deportation."

"I'll keep that in mind," says Violette. "How'd you get snagged?"

"Another agent talked under duress and gave my safe house address before I had a chance to vacate. Luckily, we all made it out of prison. I've forgiven him. I think."

"How long were you in?"

"Ten months."

Violette groans. "How'd you escape?"

"Marie of Lyon," he says, grinning. "The one the Gestapo call the Limping Lady."

"The American?"

"*Oui.* She helped spring a dozen of us. We owe her our lives."

"Wait, you were a part of *that* prison break?" says Violette. "Instructors at finishing school used it as a case study."

"Of course," Clement says, lifting his nose and taking on a haughty look. "Come back at seven. I'll be signing autographs."

Violette rolls her eyes.

"I've seen that Marie stomping around HQ," says Robert. "She's not very approachable."

"She lost most of the men and women in her network because of a betrayer," says Clement. "Atkins won't agree to send her back because Marie's on wanted posters, so she's transferred to the OSS, under Wild Bill Donovan."

"I admire that," says Violette. "And you, for going back, after prison. Though don't let my praise go to your head."

"Too late," says Clement.

"What about me?" asks Robert.

"You, what?" asks Violette.

"Going back after getting shot. Don't you admire me?"

Violette shrugs, making Clement laugh and Robert reach over to pinch Violette's side. Their teasing is interrupted when the door to the bar opens and a blast of cold hits them. Jack arrives, with as serious a face as Violette has ever seen on him. He scoots into the booth next to her, blows on his hands, looks around the room, and leans in, drawing the small group closer to him.

"I leave tomorrow," he whispers.

"Already?" says Violette.

"*Oui.*"

"But I wanted you to come with me."

Jack looks at her briefly before lowering his gaze to the table.

"We've already claimed you, Vi," says Clement.

"But we need a wireless operator," says Violette.

"You know Atkins doesn't want you with one who's so devoted to you," says Clement.

"Jack is only devoted to trying to beat me at the game, which he never will. Except on Morse. He's got me there."

Violette nudges Jack with a smile, but he appears too nervous to return it.

"What's with you?" she says.

A waiter arrives, saving his response, and Jack orders a gin.

"Make it a double," Jack adds.

"Goodness," says Violette. "You've only just learned to hold your liquor and here you go trying to keep up with the big boys."

"Give him a break," says Robert. "He's just got nerves. Wait'll you get your orders. You've never known true anxiety until that moment. Now that I've been shot by the boches, I'll be pissin' in my pants."

"Same," says Clement. "They're making me parachute this time. Last time was a lovely civilized landing in a Lysander. This time I have to jump out of a Joe hole in a bomber."

"Oh, stop fussing," says Violette. "It'll be fun."

Robert grows serious.

"Now, why do you look like that?" says Violette.

"My doc hasn't passed me. Says my lung still isn't up to capacity from where the bullet hit it."

"How long?"

"At least two more months. Maybe more."

"So, you won't be able to go with me and Clement, either?"

"Not if you get called before then."

Violette throws her hands in the air.

"This is turning out to be quite a graduation party," she says. "What's next? A blitz?"

The pop of a champagne cork makes Robert jump. They look over to see a group in another corner laughing and drinking straight from the bottle.

"Must have had a successful run," says Clement. "As we all surely will."

Clement's voice holds a note of false brightness.

In a recent briefing, Miss Atkins told them about innumerable agent arrests. Clement and Robert await word of their network based in Rouen, the capital of Normandy. When they left, it was getting hot. Their success at sabotaging everything from a motor factory, to a power station, to a German submarine anchored in the Seine was riling up the Nazis more and more. It was thought prudent for the pair to leave, to allow things to cool down and to gather more funding for their resisters, numbering well into the hundreds. With the rumors of the impending invasion, the Nazis are becoming increasingly frantic and aggressive. As Atkins and Buckmaster never fail to remind them, they're being dropped into a nest of vipers.

Violette regrets not ordering when the waiter arrives with another round. The men grow sloppy, and darkness settles over the party. Conversation is strained. Once she's smoked her last cigarette, she pushes against Jack until he lets her out.

"I'm leaving," she says. "Don't let your lips get too loose, eh? Bonne chance, Jack."

Ignoring their protests, she walks toward the exit and out into the frigid night. It's hard to see the sidewalk, and her mood is as dark as her surroundings. She had the distinct impression that Jack was hiding something from her, and that the other two suddenly doubted her. It was all fun and games before she'd passed SOE training, but now they look at her the way Miss Atkins does. And the Scotsman did. And countless other instructors. With their stares and words, it's as if they all keep saying, "Are you sure about this?" Her anger at them for doubting her is the only antidote for the blows the looks give to her confidence.

She soon hears footsteps behind her, and Jack cuts her off at the end of the block.

"That's all?" he says. "Good luck? You might never see me again."

She ignores the guilty pang in her stomach and scowls at him.

"I don't feel as if I see you now," she says. "You're an entirely different person than I've come to know, and I don't believe that you, of all people, have nerves."

"Come on, Vi," he says. "You know I can't tell you about my mission."

"But you know I'll be on mission with Clement. You know my real name. Is Jack even yours? You know about Tania. About Henri."

At the utterance of Henri's name, Jack looks down at his boots.

"That's it," she says, realization dawning. "Jack, look at me."

He does and she tries to read him, but it's dark outside and she can't tell if his pained look has to do with worry or frustration that he's supposed to keep secrets from her.

"Is Henri alive?" she asks, steeling herself for the worst.

Jack stares at her a moment before appearing to decide something. He steps close to Violette and whispers in her ear.

"I'm being dropped to Henri's network."

Violette feels a rush of joy and breaks into a grin. Jack returns it.

"So, he's . . ."

"He's all right. Doing good work. And he wanted you, Vi. For his courier. So badly. But Miss Atkins forbade it because she knows."

"She knows what?"

The sound of a distant airplane engine briefly calls their attention to the sky, but it soon fades. Their eyes again meet. Jack gives her a small smile.

"She knows that Henri loves you."

34

NESLES-LA-VALLÉE

—— VIRGINIA ——

"THEY'RE ALL IN love with you," says Philippe, watching Virginia in the arms of Marshall, an American aviator. "I better be careful."

"Keeps you on your toes," Virginia says with a laugh. "Don't take me for granted."

"Never."

While a pilot pounds away at the piano, and another claps along, Marshall teaches Virginia to jitterbug. She loves when the boys bring a little bit of home to her in France. The aviators teach her all the latest in slang, sports, and culture, and she uses her knowledge in interrogations of newcomers. German spies posing as Allied pilots are rumored to be trying again to infiltrate the Comet Line. Lily said one got through last year, safe house to safe house, all the way down through the Pyrenees and into Spain, where he reported to the German embassy there and blew an entire line. The volume of pilots is growing exponentially, so it's more important now than ever they don't compromise security checks.

From Michelle's, to Jessie-Ann's, to Nicole's, to Mum's, the dark corners of every bedroom, basement, and business are haunted by pilots. Les Baumées has lived up to its name more than Virginia or Philippe could have imagined, and it's here they feel safest. But the Resistance is doing such fine work cutting phone and rail lines, communication between Nesles and Paris has become spotty. It's only a matter of time before they'll have to stay in Paris, but they're waiting as long as possible. They can at least spread out at Nesles, take the men on walks in the woods, eat fresh eggs, rabbit, white bread, and canned vegetables.

After getting Louis back to London to give his nerves a rest, Jean had returned to France with plenty of counterfeit coupons and francs to fund their operations, and with a new mission: Find and organize a place outside Paris to corral the pilots and the growing Resistance army once the invasion begins. Daniel—the fearless little Belgian—helped Jean find a forest at Fréteval, near Châteaudun, one hundred forty kilometers south of Paris, to set up camp. Though the German base at Châteaudun is unsettlingly close, and they have an arms dump nearby, the woods are ten kilometers by six, deep and creviced, and surrounded by farmland. It will make a good hiding place.

"Why don't they want us to keep evacuating?" Philippe had asked Jean at their last rendezvous.

"They do, for now," Jean had said. "But when D-Day arrives, that will become impossible. We'll need a safe place for the pilots to wait until the Allied armies reach us."

"Is the invasion coming soon?" Virginia asked.

"Anytime now."

Virginia had raised her eyes to heaven and breathed a sigh of relief.

In spite of the equinox, winter weather lingers and the incessant fog and rain make her feel as if she lives in London. With the spring, if the invasion comes, she knows the sun will again shine. They only have to hold on a bit longer.

Dare she think about life after the war? Living free without the shadow of Nazi occupation? Virginia would never have believed the war would still be raging in 1944. Though it has been just four years, it feels like a decade. Still, she doesn't regret staying in France. Her only regret is that she and Philippe took so long to start with the Resistance. If Virginia could have comprehended the utter joy they'd get from subverting the Nazis, she would have sought out ways to start sooner. She now realizes all her fear and doubt and impulse to so-called self-preservation were the devil on her shoulder whispering in her ear, trying to keep her from doing right by trapping her in a prison of fear. Once she learned to silence it, she fully took on her vocation.

It's funny, she reflects, how desperately she thought being a mother of a baby was what she wanted. She still does, but harboring, feeding, caring for, and cheering on all these young men has been every bit as fulfilling, maybe more so. She's tired, but not exhausted the way Jessie-Ann sometimes is. Virginia has found access to a wellspring of peace that's so deep it refreshes her even in the most difficult and dangerous situations.

"One and two, and one and two."

Marshall holds Virginia around the waist with one arm, their other arms extended, stepping her forward and back to the beat. He sends Virginia out, mirroring her kicks and hip swings, and brings her back, nice and easy, while she learns the steps. They've pushed away the furniture, and their shoes pound the floor. Virginia wears a pair of farm trousers, which Marshall insisted she change into from her dress without telling her why.

Once she's familiar with the steps, Marshall says, "Solid!"

"Solid," she parrots, filing away the new slang for future use.

Marshall calls to the piano player, "Hit that jive!"

The tempo increases from that of a slow stroll through the park, to a brisk run. Out and in he pushes and pulls, twirling her all the time, making her laugh so hard she can barely keep up with him. Nan paces the perimeter of the room, unsure of what to make of all the commotion. Philippe and the other pilot clap along to the beat.

"Ready?" Marshall asks.

"For what?" she calls.

"When I say so, jump."

Without waiting for her response, he takes her around the waist, commands her to jump, and proceeds to flip her over, demonstrating exactly why he told her to change into farm trousers.

As the hours pass, and the sun sets, and the moon rises, Virginia takes turns dancing with aviators until she's able to teach Philippe the steps.

Until she has to tell them to turn in to rest for their dangerous upcoming journey.

To command they drink water and wash their faces and scrub their teeth.

To tuck them into their beds, thinking how they look even younger than their tender years when they're wide-eyed, staring through the dark, remembering their circumstances. The men they've lost. The injuries they suffer in mind and body. The perilous road ahead.

To fall asleep in Philippe's arms thinking how there are little moments of heaven even in the midst of hell.

WHAT'S THAT SMELL?

It's a full and fragrant aroma. It stirs the dust of memory and draws forth a moan.

She sits up in bed. Philippe is not beside her.

Is it? Could it be?

"Real coffee," she whispers.

What if this were all a bad dream? The war, every second of it.

She throws off the blanket, pulls on her robe and slippers, ties back her hair, and hurries out to the hallway. On her way past the bedrooms, she sees they're tidy, the beds are made, and there's no trace that anyone slept in them.

She walks down to the kitchen and stops at the door to see the aviators wearing aprons, frying potatoes, and pulling something out of the oven. Her eyes find the French press.

"Coffee?" she asks, breathless.

"Yes, ma'am," says the pilot with the Southern drawl. "I had a little bag of it in my flight gear that I've been saving for a special occasion. And being here with you people is that occasion."

Philippe joins them from the back door, cheeks pink from the morning cold, basket full of eggs. The men's eyes light up, and Marshall fetches the eggs with a thousand thanks.

"My ma would be scandalized by the ingredients I pulled together to try to make her biscuits," says the Southern one.

"If they taste half as good as they smell, she'll be proud," says Virginia. "What can I do to help?"

They shoo her away and tell her to relax, get dressed—if she pleases—and take her time. They'll take care of all of the cooking and cleaning. They look like angels to her, standing there, doing the domestic work.

But as she leaves, she turns back to look at them again, and a chill rises on her arms. Darkness falls over her. She doesn't want them to leave. She doesn't want to take them on to the baker's house, so he can pass them farther south, all the way to the cold mountains into Spain. She forces her feet to take her back upstairs to dress, but she's unable to keep the darkness from weighing on her.

THE SUN CAN'T penetrate the low, heavy clouds. Since breakfast, they've lost their joy. Reality has returned. It wasn't all a nightmare from which they were awakened. They inhabit the nightmare.

Virginia couldn't bear to say goodbye at the house, so she accompanies Philippe and the men to Renard's. Then, she and Philippe will return to Paris to collect the next batch of parcels. Their boots squish across the fields and on the muddy forest path. A long, lonely cry of a hawk slices through the fog-muffled landscape, and the bare trees leave them feeling exposed. Once the group of five enters the deepest part of the woods, they breathe easier. But when they come around the bend of a large mossy wall of rock, they nearly run into the German officer who stays at the Fleury house. He has a string of pheasants over his shoulder and is accompanied by a hunting dog.

Like the moment with the pilot and the cigarette lighter, Virginia finds that time slows. She can hear her heart beating in her ears and feels the temperature of the men around her rising. None of these men speak French. If the German starts to question them, they're done.

Virginia's eyes flick down to where she sees Philippe clench his fist. The pilot nearest the Nazi eyes the shotgun. They'll have to over-power the German and kill him—with five of them, it's possible—but what then?

The Nazi tenses. With his finger on the trigger, he lowers the shot-gun from his shoulder and points it low, at their boots. He scans their faces, lingering on the aviators.

"Ah, a *Braque français*," says Philippe, pointing to the dog. *"Elle est belle."*

The Nazi blinks and looks at Philippe, and then down at his dog, a striking creature with a brown head, a white-and-brown-speckled body, and a brown tail. The Nazi returns his gaze to Philippe's.

"Oui."

The Nazi looks at the pilot nearest him and starts to ask him some-thing, but Philippe cuts off the question.

"How old is she?" Philippe asks.

The German turns back to Philippe.

"Nine months," the German says in bad French. "Just got her."

"May I?" says Philippe, reaching to pet her. "What's her name?"

"Berit."

The dog looks up at her master and nuzzles him, softening his posture. Philippe whistles and she turns her attention to him, sniffing his hand, wagging her tail, and allowing Philippe to pet her.

The aviators remain tense, not daring to move or breathe.

"Good you can have her here, *oui*?" says Philippe. "Get in your hunting in France?"

Virginia is surprised Philippe says this. Hitler, strangely, is a great lover of animals and has banned hunting in Germany. He thinks it's cruel to kill innocent beasts and distasteful to eat their meat. The hypocrisy—the inconsistency of one so cruel to human beings—is incomprehensible. Does Philippe say this to shame the German? He's walking a dangerous line.

To Virginia's further surprise, the Nazi's scowl evaporates into a sheepish smile.

"Yes," he says. "This is fine country, and a place I would like to make a future."

They stare at each other for a long moment. Virginia recognizes Philippe was able to take a piece of power in the exchange. The German looks at each of them once more, tips his hat to her, and walks away, Berit following.

Once he's out of sight, the ragged breathing of the others bursts forth. Philippe takes her hand, and they hurry toward Renard's place.

35

LONDON

~~⟨⟩~~

―――― **VIOLETTE** ――――

VIOLETTE HURRIES THROUGH the London streets toward Orchard Court. Miss Atkins has called her and Clement in for a briefing, and with the coming full moon, Violette knows they're about to be dropped into France.

After all these years, she thinks, *I'm finally going home.*

Violette and Clement arrive at the same time, and the doorman allows them in with an austere nod. As they pass through the lobby, she feels a rush of energy, a strong wind lifting her spirits. When they reach the back stairs to Miss Atkins's office, Violette takes the steps two at a time. She pokes Clement in the side when he arrives at the top, well after she does and out of breath.

"Better stop smoking, old man," she teases.

"Old man? I'm thirty-four!" he says. "You're starting to sound like my wife."

Clement recently confided in Violette that his wife, Maryse, lives in Nice. They've seen little of each other these war years, with him in and out of France on several missions and Maryse keeping as low a profile as possible for reasons Clement will not disclose. Though Clement has not come right out and said it, Violette senses his mar-

riage was already strained before the war. Their separation is not making any hearts grow fonder.

She can't say the same about her separation from Henri.

Since Jack told Violette that Henri loves her, the warm feelings she
had for him have grown. She doesn't yet know if she loves him. After
losing Étienne, she's guarded. But there's no denying the electricity
between her and Henri, and how she loves eliciting smiles from his
serious face. Strong, intelligent, and thoughtful, Henri is someone
Violette thinks Étienne would approve of for her, especially seeing
how sweet Henri was with Tania. Once this is all over, if she and
Henri make it through, Violette will devote herself to finding out if
their attraction was simply the product of two people desperate for
connection in a dark time, or the sweet beginnings of a future together.

"Why do you have that silly grin on your face?" asks Clement as
they walk down the hallway.

"None of your business."

"You'll have to learn to dim your radiance, doll. You're noticeable
when you beam like that."

They continue forward, weaving in and out of the personnel bus-
tling around them. Heels click over the wood floors, telephones ring,
transmitters tap, and voices rise and fall from behind closed doors.
Miss Atkins's scowling, smoking countenance briefly brightens when
Violette and Clement enter her office but falls stern when her eyes
return to the memo in her hands. She thrusts it at the cowering young
woman before her and tells the girl to "let Buck deal with it," before
ushering the pair in and closing the door behind them. Miss Atkins
crosses the room to the table and stubs out her cigarette. Then she
turns and raises her eyebrows.

"Ready?" she asks.

Violette knew this day was coming, but she could never have
imagined the exhilaration it would bring. She can't keep the smile
from her face.

"Normandy?" asks Clement.

"*Oui,*" says Miss Atkins. "Back to Rouen. Sans Robert, for now."

"We figured," says Violette.

"We'll drop him the moment the physician clears him."

Miss Atkins hands Violette a folder. Inside is a French identity card with her photo, her true birth date, a listing of her occupation of secretary, and her nom de guerre: Corinne Reine Leroy. The false middle and last names honor her mother's maiden name. There's also a packet of ration coupons and a violet-colored kerchief.

"Matches your eyes," Miss Atkins says with a wink.

She motions for the pair to sit, slips a key from her pocket, and fetches two large, worn satchels from the closet. She passes them to Violette and Clement. Violette opens hers but, though it's heavy, it only contains a hairbrush.

"Tug the label at the seam at the top of the lining," says Miss Atkins.

Violette obeys, feels around, and soon finds slim bundles of bills. Dozens of them.

"Two hundred fifty thousand francs," says Miss Atkins. "For the Resistance of Rouen, their families, and those harboring fugitives."

"*Mon Dieu,*" says Violette.

"Only twenty thousand for you, Clement, since you're more likely to get stopped," Miss Atkins says. "Working-age male, and all that. Your identity cards—updated in the new style—are in the wallets."

Clement nods.

"If you don't distribute all the money," continues Miss Atkins, "spend what's left to destabilize the economy."

"Pardon?" asks Violette.

"It's counterfeit."

"Ah."

"Of immediate usefulness to the Resistance, but long-term harm to the boches."

Violette nods.

"Do you see the hairbrush?" says Miss Atkins. "Remove the bristles."

Violette obeys and finds a file and a tiny compass.

"Don't be fooled by the size of that file," says Miss Atkins. "And be careful how you hold it. It can slice through everything from prison bars to throats."

"Will I get a revolver?" asks Violette. "Something small enough to conceal in the liner?"

"No," says Miss Atkins. "Until the invasion, we'd rather not issue firearms to couriers."

"When's that?" asks Clement.

"I'm not yet allowed to disclose the date."

She pulls out two tiny brass containers and passes them to the pair. Clement takes his and slides it into his breast pocket, but Violette stares at hers and raises her eyebrows in a question.

"L pill," says Miss Atkins. "Lethal. It's a cyanide capsule, in case you get captured. Brings about a quick death."

Violette throws it on the table as if it were an ember. Miss Atkins stares at Violette a moment before slipping it back in her pocket.

"Suit yourself," Miss Atkins says.

After a pause, she slides a map of Normandy's capital, Rouen, and the surrounding area closer to the pair and explains their location objectives. There are rumors of new development sites for the Nazis' long-range weapons—V1 and V2 flying bombs—capable of reaching England. If they can identify the locations by coordinate and Clement can get photos (he has a small camera pen in his satchel) the RAF can take out the sites. As Miss Atkins points out the railroad viaduct connecting Rouen to Le Havre that will need to be severed before D-Day, there comes a hurried knock at the door.

"Go away," Miss Atkins says.

"Urgent," says a muffled voice.

She curses under her breath.

"It had better be. *Entrez!*"

The breathless messenger rushes in with a slip of typed paper she passes to Miss Atkins. Her eyes dart back and forth over the lines, her expression turning icy and unreadable.

"What is it?" asks Clement.

Miss Atkins dismisses the messenger with a wave of her hand. Once the door is shut, Miss Atkins sits heavily on the tabletop.

"Mission canceled."

"What?" says Violette.

"You can't go to Rouen, Clement," says Miss Atkins. "And, as a matter of fact, if you do return to France, you'll need a new identity. As will Robert."

"What are you saying?" he asks.

"Your network is *brûlé.*"

Clement stands and paces to the boarded window.

"How can you be sure?" he says. "What did the message say?"

"It says, 'Clement and team can't go to Rouen. Mass arrests. Some dead.'"

Clement curses and runs his hand through his thinning hair, leaving it sticking out wildly.

"I need to get back," says Clement. "These are my people."

"While I appreciate the gesture, you are, in fact, one of our most seasoned and successful circuit organizers. You're not going. At least not until we know more."

"I can still go," says Violette. "I'm unknown in the region. I can find out if the network is salvageable."

Miss Atkins considers Violette's suggestion but soon shakes her head.

"No, not until we have more intel. It would be a suicide mission."

"If we're willing, we should be allowed to go," says Clement.

"I'm so tired of hearing that from you people."

"What, like Marie? At least she could transfer to the OSS. Perhaps I should see if I'm wanted elsewhere."

Miss Atkins twitches backward like she's been slapped. She and Clement face each other like bulls about to charge.

"Maybe it's a mistake," says Violette, attempting to defuse the tension. "Maybe the operator was wrong."

"The operator is one of our finest," says Miss Atkins. "He's united over two thousand Maquis—the French guerilla fighters—under his command, helped in their training, and coordinated over a hundred supply drops for them. And he has saved both of your lives with this message."

"Who is it?" asks Clement.

"Hilaire," Miss Atkins says.

The name rings a bell in Violette's mind, but she can't think where she's heard it before.

"You don't know him," Miss Atkins says to Clement.

Clement storms out of the room, slamming the door.

So heavy is Violette's disappointment, it's hard for her to stand. She can't believe she has to wait another month, at least. She thinks she'll try to convince Miss Atkins once more to send her, alone, but Miss Atkins cuts Violette off when she starts to speak.

"You do know Hilaire," says Miss Atkins.

The women look at each other for a long moment.

"It's Henri," says Miss Atkins. "He saved your lives."

36

—— VIRGINIA ——

THE PARCEL TRAFFIC increases by the day, and the RAF navigator standing before Virginia was brought to them from Pierre, a new man in the Comet Line. The navigator has red hair and freckles, is from the seaside town of Devon, looks all of sixteen years old, and has the dearest singing voice. He's been humming his way through three days with them, singing a song called "Paper Doll" over and over again. They adore him the way they would a beloved nephew. He lost most of his crew when they were shot down, and the poor kid didn't even complain about his injury. Virginia only found out his ear was burnt to the cartilage when she saw blood soaking through his pillow. He confessed he can no longer hear out of it, but he isn't letting it get him down.

"God gave us two ears, after all."

Virginia wants to take this one to Nesles, where Dr. Lebettre could check him out, but Lily is making the run south to Spain from Paris, and they need to pass the aviator along to her today.

Virginia stuffs the boy's pockets with wrapped bread and cheese. Philippe sorts through the pile of French clothes they've amassed until he finds a jacket that fits their charge, a nice warm scarf that will help provide a buffer from the winds of the Pyrenees, and a good hat to hide his injured ear.

"This hat was my late father's," says Philippe. "May he guard you like Saint Michael the Archangel."

Virginia kisses the navigator on both cheeks, and once he has his false identification papers and recites the assortment of French phrases they've taught him, the trio begins the trip to the Gare d'Austerlitz, where Lily will meet them with another aviator, and where Daniel waits with the men's train tickets to Bordeaux. The tickets will be wrapped in newspapers they will take as they pass Daniel's table at the station café. Lily will ride in the coach ahead of them and be their guide to the next stop on the escape.

This aviator is their fortieth. Forty men have gone through their homes. Forty men passed to them from others, passed along to others, with no way of knowing their fates. Virginia prays that the men will try to find her and Philippe after the war. She wants to know they're all well. That they've returned to their fiancées and mothers and fathers and wives and children healthy and with restored faith in humanity.

It's a cold, rainy day in a spring that hasn't yet triumphed over winter. The seasons mourn with all of them this fourth year the world is ravaged by war. In Paris, there's been a disturbing increase in German presence. Virginia and Philippe have noticed it steadily since the turn of the year and think it's in response to invasion rumors. Like the others before him, this flier says invasion is on the horizon, but it hasn't materialized, and Virginia is beginning to wonder if it will ever be so. She forces herself to keep hope alive, but it's real work, and the weather isn't helping.

By the time they arrive at the station, an hour's walk from their apartment, they're soaked and shivering. A quick scan of the crowd and café reveals everyone's in place. Daniel sips ersatz coffee, and only one newspaper remains on the table. Lily is up ahead, standing in a queue to board the train. Her man must already be on. Philippe leads Virginia and their aviator past Daniel's table, where Virginia slips the paper off and passes it to the boy. He separates from them, and Virginia and Philippe hold their breath watching the flier present his forged documents to the German MP. They let out a sigh when the boy boards the train without incident.

They're about to leave when Daniel coughs loud enough to draw their attention. They follow the direction his wide eyes stare and see a mob of Gestapo, guns drawn, pushing through the crowd, knocking travelers left and right, and boarding the train. Virginia catches sight of Lily drifting out of line and shrinking behind a pillar. Daniel disappears, but Virginia and Philippe are immobilized. In a few moments, Virginia is horror-struck to see a man dragged from the train, followed by their flier, no sign of Philippe's father's hat, red hair sticking up, and blood dripping down the side of the boy's face from his bad ear.

Virginia stifles a gasp. Philippe pulls her closer to his side.

Another group of Gestapo disembark, dragging four handcuffed men toward the exit. The remaining thugs search the crowd.

Lily slips away and falls in with a group heading toward the far exit, and Daniel has vanished. Virginia and Philippe start toward the closest station doorway, restraining themselves as much as possible so they don't obey their bodies' instincts to run.

A whistle slices through the air and there's shouting behind them.

The moment they make it to the doors, Virginia and Philippe hurry forth, ducking into the closest alleyway, and never slowing their pace until they arrive back at their apartment.

LILY LOOKS FIERCE in the candlelight of Daniel's flat. The place doesn't have a picture on the wall, nor a superfluous piece of furniture. It's dark and cold, and Daniel says it's one of three at his disposal. It's a good setup, and one Virginia and Philippe should think about employing. There's so much activity at their place, it's keeping Virginia's nerves on edge, even when the door is locked.

"Pierre is the rat," Lily says. "I'm certain."

"His bona fides check out," says Jean.

"I saw him at the station. I know I did."

"Did the rest of you see him?" asks Jean.

Daniel, Virginia, and Philippe shake their heads.

"Aren't my eyes enough?" asks Lily.

"They are," says Jean. "But before we take drastic measures, we need to be sure."

"If Lily says it's so, I believe her," says Daniel.

"Pierre did deliver our flier to us," says Virginia. "Pierre knew where the boy came from and how long he'd be with us."

"And Pierre told me that he thought he could find out who betrayed my parents and sister in Belgium," says Lily. "I never told him my family was arrested. Did any of you?"

They all shake their heads.

Jean looks from Philippe to Virginia. "You need to get a new apartment."

"You read my mind," says Virginia.

"I'll use one of my identities to rent you a smaller studio in the same building," says Jean. "Tucked out of the way. Accessible from a different entrance."

Virginia and Philippe nod.

"Good," says Lily, "but that's not enough. We have to exterminate the rat."

"I'll do it," says Daniel. "Does anyone have his address?"

"No," says Virginia. "But Michelle's his letterbox. I can leave him a message at the flower shop and warn her in the process."

"Good," says Daniel. "Tell Pierre to meet me tomorrow evening at the bistro at the Reine Marie Hotel. Four o'clock."

"That's just around the corner from our apartment," says Philippe. "We'll get a drink at the bar across the street in case you need backups. It'll be good for us to be seen there. It's a German-friendly establishment."

FROM THEIR BOOTH at the bar, Virginia and Philippe have an unobstructed view across the street to the bistro at the Reine Marie, where Daniel sits smoking and sipping from his drink at the table in the front window. Daniel doesn't look dangerous, but none of them look like thieves, counterfeiters, forgers, and lawbreakers. Virginia wonders if one can be considered lawless if the law is malformed.

She and Philippe are exhausted from the hasty move to a sixth-floor studio apartment. One bedroom, one tiny bathroom, and one open living area with two small sofas, a four-seat dining table, and a galley kitchen. They're going to get to know their fugitives very well.

It's only temporary, Virginia thinks.

Philippe told Virginia she didn't need to join him here, to watch one man assassinate another, but she reminded Philippe they're in this together.

Virginia is not violent by nature. She doesn't know if this is justice. But she felt the horror of seeing her red-haired boy being dragged away to unknown tortures, and if Lily is certain Pierre is the betrayer, he has to go. Further, Lily tracked Pierre's place to a luxurious building close to Gestapo headquarters, on Avenue Foch. Which means he's likely being paid to betray the Comet Line, and now all of them are in untold danger because of it. Jean and Daniel have suspended operations in the short term, to give the network time to cool. Virginia and Philippe and their family members await further instruction.

They got to the bar early, ate, and settled the tab so they can leave at a moment's notice. The bar doesn't operate on the black market, so the patrons are largely the French who are comfortable with or indifferent to the German soldiers sprinkled throughout the crowd. A sweet, high voice comes from behind them, where a young woman with flaxen braids, wearing a peasant costume, sings "Auprès de ma blonde." Her voice is clear and bright as a chandelier, and she has infused the song of a soldier's longing for his girl with such feeling, the room has ceased motion. Virginia turns toward the singer, noting the sea of German soldiers sitting in rapt attention before her.

Are all German soldiers evil? Virginia wonders. *Are they here against their will, or do they subscribe to the policies of the madman in charge?*

The German hunter in Nesles seemed to be trying to communicate something to them when he allowed them to take their pilots without question, when he admitted he liked the freedom in France. Should she give him the benefit of the doubt?

No, Virginia decides. *We don't have to obey. Resistance is possible for all of us. Even if the cost is high.*

Philippe touches Virginia's hand and nods toward the street. She follows his direction to see Pierre hurrying toward the Reine Marie. Pierre is a stocky man who wears glasses and dresses loudly. His bold ties, in fact, have troubled Lily since his arrival. Though Pierre knew all the right code phrases, and was verified safe by Jean's contacts in London, Lily said it was strange that, while the rest of them try to subdue their appearances, Pierre chooses to stand out. Lily's instincts proved true. Virginia realizes she has much to learn from the young woman.

Pierre joins Daniel at the table. While Daniel is still enough to be a figure in a tableau, Pierre fidgets, shifting in his seat and tugging at his tie. Does he sense the danger he's in, or is he just excitable?

The voice of the folk singer has a particular and poignant sadness-infused beauty, like the call of a white-throated sparrow through a foggy Nesles morning. It's as if the sound comes to them from a time long ago, a time when they were innocent. A time to which they'll never be able to return, especially not after this evening.

Shortly after the waiter at the Reine Marie delivers two glasses to Daniel and Pierre's table, Pierre pushes back and strides toward the back of the restaurant.

"Do you think he's making a break for it?" whispers Philippe.

"Daniel hasn't followed, so I don't think so."

"Should we go around the back of the hotel to keep an eye out?"

"I'd wait for a signal from Daniel," she says. After a few moments, a frightening thought occurs to her. She further lowers her voice. "Do you think Pierre called the Gestapo?"

"It's a possibility. We may need to find our own back entrance for escape."

While they ponder their next move, Pierre returns to the table. He's just as fidgety. Daniel remains still. Pierre reaches for his drink and drains it. Upon doing so, Daniel stands, puts on his hat, tips it to Pierre, and slips out of the restaurant. He disappears into the shadows so quickly Virginia thinks they might have imagined him.

Holding their breath, they return their attention to Pierre, who has stiffened. He tugs at his tie, and stands, knocking back his chair. When the waiter rushes over, Pierre clutches his neck and gestures between his throat and the empty glass. The waiter recoils, taking a few steps backward before disappearing. Pierre staggers back to his seat and falls forward over the table.

Virginia and Philippe stare in shock.

The song reaches its climax.

Virginia places her hand on her chest. It's hard for her to breathe and she feels hot all over. Philippe reaches for her arm, and they stand. As they leave the bar, the singer's voice recedes, and an ambulance siren howls closer and louder.

This street will never be the same, Virginia thinks as they pass over the spot where they danced to "The Man I Love" the night Gershwin died.

We will never be the same. None of us.

37

SOMEWHERE OVER FRANCE

———— ⟊ ————

———— **VIOLETTE** ————

AT THE HOLE in the floor of the B-24 Liberator bomber, Violette takes Clement's trembling hand.

Clement's face is as white as the full moon that has guided them to their landing zone, and he can't muster a smile. She's having a hard time doing so herself. Just before takeoff, Miss Atkins informed them that Henri had been arrested.

Jack got a message through to HQ that a *milicien* had betrayed Henri and one of his teams by tipping off the Gestapo to their meeting place. They were raided mid-transmission, the operator managing a quick message that they were caught before abruptly cutting off. Jack later verified the arrests and, because Henri had in his possession a false identity card with Jack's face on it, Jack was forced into hiding. His likeness is now plastered all over wanted posters in the region.

Henri's whereabouts are unknown.

Violette is more determined now than ever to help in whatever way she can to bring vengeance on the Nazis. She passed the last week with Tania at Vera's place, and knows her daughter is well cared for. They took many walks through the park, played with Vera's dog, snuggled and cuddled and giggled away the days. On her last night before dispatch, Violette went to her parents' house. She knows she should have rested but they stayed up late talking, a peace settling over the three of them unlike anything Violette had before experienced. She thinks she could die content, but she has no intention of dying.

Miss Atkins took Violette's suggestion to send her to Rouen alone, to see if Clement's network is salvageable. Clement—now using the identity of Charles—will stay in Paris, rendezvousing with contacts there to see about which regions need new chiefs, seeking information on Henri, and awaiting Violette's report to see if it's safe for him to return to Rouen.

After four hours in a noisy airplane, the red light over the cockpit finally turns green. The dispatcher salutes them. Without ceremony, Violette slaps Clement on the back and out he goes. She counts to five, takes a deep breath, and follows him into the void.

Blackness all around, wind howling in her ears—Violette loves this feeling of flying. She takes in the landscape below, coming sharper into view, rushing toward her. Soon, she pulls the cord and is yanked back as the parachute opens. The fall becomes gentle and silent. She sees Clement's parachute below in the distance and keeps her eye on it as the ground reaches ever closer to her. She brings her legs together, tucks them up, and braces herself for impact. Keeping as loose as possible, the moment her feet hit the ground, she tumbles into a graceful roll.

On contact, she only felt a slight sting in her ankle, but the parachute has wrapped itself around her, and it takes longer than she'd like to become disentangled. She goes still when she hears voices whispering.

They're speaking French.

She resumes her struggle and crouches low when she sees figures approaching.

"Corinne," whispers Clement.

She pops up when he gets closer, scaring him so he jumps. The group titters, and she grins at them all, the dear faces of the good people who were there to receive them as they promised they would be.

AFTER SEPARATING FROM Clement, Violette faces an oppressive train ride to Normandy's capital—surrounded all the way by dozens of leering, inquisitive German soldiers, returning to their posts after Easter holiday leave. Throughout the train ride, Violette mumbles replies to the soldiers and keeps her eyes down. She hopes the redness in her face is mistaken for embarrassment instead of hatred. Three hours later, she's able to escape them.

At the sole station in Rouen not reduced to rubble, Violette is roughly handled by a German MP. Then, she experiences the shock of coming face-to-face with a wall full of wanted posters bearing the faces of Clement and Robert. In the photos on the posters, her partners are clean shaven. Now they have mustaches. She can't believe how they've aged in the short time that has passed since these photos must have been taken. One minute in Rouen and it's already clear Clement and Robert can't return to this city.

The aerial photographs Miss Atkins had shown Violette depicting the bombing damage to Rouen didn't adequately convey the level of destruction, nor could they capture the air of oppression draped about the city like mourning clothes. French men and women are experiencing violence from all sides now—the Nazis, the Allies, and the Resistance—and Violette doesn't know how any of them will be able to trust once this is all over, nor how they'll muster the strength to rebuild.

Taking a deep breath and starting forward, she recalls the SOE drama coach's instruction.

"You are Corinne Leroy, a tired, young, innocent, wide-eyed virgin."

Violette had snorted at that. The woman had given her a reprimanding look.

"You cannot let an ounce of your hatred for the Nazis come through," the instructor continued. "You may act nervous around them, keeping your eyes on your shoes. You may fidget. Always speak quietly. Your French accent isn't perfect."

Violette had bristled, especially when Clement echoed the acting coach's sentiment. Mr. Potter had thought it excellent.

"No better way to perfect an accent than immersing oneself in the culture," Clement had said.

Only one way to find out.

Clement gave Violette three contacts. Denise Desveaux—a dressmaker at 12 rue Jeanne d'Arc—who housed Clement's wireless operator, Isidore. Fates unknown. Georges Philippon—a garage owner who hid their weapons and supplies—from whom Violette might procure a bicycle. Fate unknown. Finally, an old couple, Jean and Florentine Sueur—who run a clothing shop at 72 rue des Carmes—who acted as Clement's letterbox. Fates unknown. Violette thinks she'll start with the old couple, the least likely to have been arrested. Besides, between their shop and their home, they're likely to have more space to accommodate her.

Violette doesn't have to act to appear weary. Two nights without sleep and the strain of travel have taken their toll. Recalling the map of Rouen and the code phrases and knock patterns she has memorized, she sets out for the Sueurs' shop.

The dampness in the air reaches her bones. The clouds hang heavy and threatening. Pedestrians keep their eyes lowered. Nazis and the *milice* watch everyone with suspicion. The satchel slung around Violette's body is heavy, and by the time she arrives at the rue des Carmes, sweat soaks her back, and her toes burn from her tight French pumps.

For a shopping district, it's strangely empty. There's not a man or woman in sight and, thankfully, no Germans, but the air is charged. It feels the way the atmosphere does before a thunderstorm. She spots the store sign: MICHELINE. With little other choice before her, she crosses the street and tries the door. It's locked, and the inside of the shop is dark. She looks through the window and thinks she sees a figure duck behind a cash register. Violette again surveys the street before giving the Morse knock pattern Clement taught her.

There's no response.

The hair on Violette's neck stands. She'll try once more before making her way to Denise Desveaux's place.

This time, however, the door opens before she finishes. She's yanked inside by a pale, wide-eyed woman who looks to be in her thirties, with deep circles under her eyes and dark hair parted neatly down the middle and rolled back. The woman closes and locks the door behind Violette and pulls her into the shadows.

"Who sent you?" the woman says.

"Clement," says Violette. "Are you Florentine?"

Violette thinks not. The woman is too young to match the description.

"No," the woman says, stifling a sob. "Come."

Violette follows her through the shop, noting the gleaming surfaces, the chandeliers, the plush carpets, their opulence obvious even in the dark. The woman leading Violette continues to sniffle all the way to a back staircase that leads up to a storage room. Ghostly white mannequins are reflected in the mirrors lining the walls, and bolts of fabric in great rolls fill the shelves. The woman leads Violette to a settee facing the window, where they can watch the street, and gestures for Violette to sit with her.

"I'm sorry," the woman says, after she composes herself. "Florentine is my mother. She and my father, Jean, were arrested. I wasn't even allowed to visit them at the Palais de Justice. They're being deported."

The woman chokes on the word and resumes her crying.

"Oh no," says Violette.

Moved with pity, Violette scoots closer to the woman and touches her leg. Clement is going to be upset. He said the Sueurs were like surrogate parents to him.

"Do you know where they're being sent?" Violette asks.

"No. I was just here searching for money for my family and our—" She cuts herself off. "But the safe has been emptied. There are bullet holes in the lock."

The woman weeps. Violette wraps her arms around her. After a few moments, she pulls back.

"I can help you," Violette says. "Clement sent me with money."

"Oh, thank God. We're desperate. I live outside of town, and I have many mouths to feed."

Violette senses the woman refers to fugitives or resisters of some kind.

"Here," says Violette.

She reaches into her satchel and pulls out a bundle of francs. When she passes it to the woman, she gasps and thanks Violette.

"It's why I've come," says Violette. "And to see if the network is salvageable."

The woman shakes her head.

"I'm afraid Clement would be sad to learn that's not likely. I know of at least thirty arrests."

"Thirty?"

A siren roars by, coming closer. When it passes the shop, the women release their breath.

"*Oui,*" the woman continues. "It's very dangerous for you to be here. They're keeping a close eye on the shop. I hate to put you out after such generosity, but you have to go. I'll show you out the back."

"But I need a place to stay."

"It's impossible here. And my parents' home nearby is just as dangerous. I live a good hour's bike ride away, but I don't know how many more I can cram in. Did Clement give you any other names?"

"*Oui.* Georges Philippon, who has a garage where I might get a bicycle."

The woman shakes her head, her eyes misting over.

"Georges and his employee, Chevalier, were both shot."

Violette feels nauseated. This is so much worse than Clement thought. He'll be sick, especially because he holds guilt for leaving his people when the temperature started to rise. Violette is almost afraid to speak the other contact's name.

"Denise Desveaux?"

The woman stiffens.

"You can try Denise, but I don't know if she'll welcome you. She was arrested and interrogated. I don't know how she was able to get free when so many others were not."

There's a note of accusation in the woman's voice, as if she suspects Denise supplied the enemy with information. The woman stands abruptly and leads Violette back to the staircase, but instead of moving to the front of the store, she takes Violette to a back door.

"Be careful," the woman says. "I don't think you should stay with Denise. There's a little inn around the corner, on the rue Saint-Romain. Tell the proprietor I sent you. You'll be safe there. As safe as one can be in this circle of hell."

"Merci. I'm grateful for your guidance. If you're comfortable, will you tell me your name? Or at least, one I can call you. You can call me Corinne."

The woman stares at Violette a long moment before she softens.

"When I heard the knock," the woman says, "I thought I would hide. But when you peered in the window, it was as if you were illuminated from behind, like a little angel. I thought, there's La Petite Anglaise."

Anglaise, thinks Violette. *Is my accent so obvious?*

"I'm Jeanne," the woman continues.

"Is there a place I might contact you, Jeanne? I might be able to get you more funds, once I investigate Rouen."

"*Oui*, I live near the raspberry farm in Frenelles, but if you need me, come to the post office at Saussay-la-Campagne."

Violette thanks her and starts to leave, but Jeanne touches Violette's arm.

"It's I who have you to thank," says Jeanne. "You've brought me a little piece of hope."

She kisses Violette on both cheeks.

"Now, be careful, *ma petite*," says Jeanne. "And get out of Rouen as soon as possible."

TAKING JEANNE'S ADVICE, Violette decides to try to get a
room at the inn before making contact with Denise. Violette needs to
record all she's learned and, frankly, she needs to rest. She'd never have
thought such a short time on mission could be so exhausting, but she
can barely keep her eyes open. Apparently, Miss Atkins wasn't exag-
gerating about how Violette would be tested.

The half-timbered structures lining the narrow, winding rue Saint-
Romain must look the way they did when Joan of Arc was dragged
past them. Violette soon finds the inn, and its interior is shabby and
worn, like an old couch. Beams are spaced along a pitched ceiling of
chipped, cream-colored plaster, and the air smells of fire smoke and
old wood. The ancient, scowling woman at the front desk regards
Violette with suspicion.

She might have seen Joan of Arc with her own eyes, thinks Violette.

"Bonjour," Violette says, in her sweetest voice. "Jeanne Sueur sent me."

The old woman's face brightens.

"Ah, then for you, I have my best room. Close to the bathroom."

"A bath sounds heavenly right now."

"I charge extra for baths, of course." The old woman motions to
the rate board behind her. "And the gas for hot water is unpredictable."

"I understand."

"Breakfast is also extra."

"Naturally," says Violette.

"How many nights?"

"A week, to start."

Violette passes her papers to the old woman so she can register her
in the hotel guest book.

"Why are you visiting Rouen?" the woman asks as she scribbles.
"Most people are trying to flee it."

"I'm here to look for my uncle," Violette says, using her cover story.
"No one in my family has heard from him since the last bombardment. We're very worried."

The old woman studies Violette, then returns to her task.

"You make sure you keep that story straight," the old woman says in a low voice. "You'll be asked it many times by the boches and the *collabos*."

Though glad to hear the woman use the vocabulary of the Resistance, Violette keeps her expression neutral. It could be a trap.

Once she has the total, Violette passes the old woman double what she requested. Her eyes grow wide. Violette nods at her, takes her key, and climbs the stairs to her room. Once she's locked inside, Violette looks out the window. She has a view of a lovely courtyard bordered by a garden teeming with vegetables, fruits, and chickens wandering around wrought iron tables. She can't see the street from here, unfortunately, but appreciates the privacy and the proximity to the toilet.

After unpacking her clothes, she slips the rice paper tablet Miss Atkins gave her from her satchel, and records all she's learned, in code. After sliding the tablet between the mattress and the headboard, she thinks she'll lie down for a few minutes. But in almost no time at all, she jolts with a start and realizes that evening has fallen. She must have slept away the afternoon. Curfew is at seven thirty here. She has no time to waste. In the bathroom, Violette washes her face and freshens up, ties the kerchief over her hair, pulls on her worn brown jacket, and heads to Denise Desveaux's place.

Violette's glad it's a short walk from the inn, because it begins to rain. She passes the Kommandantur and notes the line out the door of very old and very young German men. HQ will be happy to hear the boches are scraping the bottom of their recruiting barrels. The men are all smoking away, puffing into the cold, wet air. How Violette longs for a cigarette, but she stifles that longing, and continues her trip.

Just before she reaches the rue Jeanne d'Arc, a soldier stops her and demands her papers. Startled, she searches through her satchel. She'd expected to get stopped only at transportation points, not simply walking along the sidewalk. When she finds them, she presents them with a shaking hand.

"Le Havre," he says in French, spitting out the address listed on her identity card. "Why are you here?"

"I'm searching for my uncle. We haven't heard from him since the last bombardment from those evil Brits. May they burn in hell."

The soldier softens his look.

Fool, she thinks.

He passes back the card and nods for her to go, but as she does, he grabs her arm and smiles, showing his teeth.

"If you need company while you're in Rouen, Fräulein, I'm staying at the Hôtel de Ville, in room 208."

She lowers her gaze to the ground, pretends to be flustered, and hurries away, his laughter following her. All the rest of the trip, she imagines the satisfaction she'd derive from stealing into his room at night and using her file to slit his white throat.

Violette soon spots the building of her destination, one of the only structures left mostly intact on a street that has suffered mightily. She picks her way over heaps of stone and dust, stopping when she sees an ash-covered arm protruding from one of the piles. She pauses only a moment before swallowing and forcing her feet to continue.

There are a few people on the street, but most are bewildered elderly men and women, picking through the ruins. She reminds herself to allow the hatred she feels for the Nazis to be masked in fatigue. At the street corner about a hundred yards ahead, there are two soldiers with their backs to her. She slips into the shadows of Denise's building and circles around the back. Once Violette finds a door, she uses a hairpin to pick the lock, and leaves the door open a centimeter to allow for a quick exit, should she need it. Then she returns to the front of the building, gives one last look up and down the street, and enters.

Walking on her toes so her heels don't click, Violette slips silently to the second floor. She notes the back stair, and once she reaches Denise's apartment, Violette uses the code knock. She soon sees an eye at the peephole, and a woman opens the door, glancing down the hallway toward the stairs, and back at Violette.

"What do you want?"

"Madame Desveaux? I was told you can repair my sweater," Violette says, using the code phrase.

The woman contorts her face in a pained expression. She shakes her head. She starts to close the door, but Violette puts out her hand to stop her.

"Please," Violette whispers. "Clement wants word of your nephew."

The woman grimaces.

"Come in, quickly," she says.

She pulls Violette by the arm and locks the door behind her. Then she takes several steps backward as if Violette has a contagious illness. It's dark and cold inside the apartment. Violette notes where a table is missing a chunk, and there are bullet holes in the door to the bedroom. In spite of Denise's anguish, Violette can see she's a beautiful woman of about forty years of age, cutting a lovely figure in her worn but well-made clothes. Clement had told Violette that over the course of Isidore's time as the wireless operator for Rouen, he and Denise had fallen in love.

"Isidore was arrested," Denise blurts.

Though Violette knew this was likely, it still stings to hear the truth.

"I'm sorry."

Denise pulls a handkerchief from the pocket of her dress and dabs the corners of her eyes.

"Please, do you know the fate of Clement's second? Claude?" asks Violette.

"Arrested. Along with his fiancée, Anne. The *milice* and the Gestapo burst in on us while we were eating dinner together and dragged us all to jail."

Denise wavers, as if she's about to faint. Violette catches the woman by the arm and leads her to the sofa.

"I'm sorry," Denise says, her hands shaking.

"Don't apologize," says Violette. "I can't imagine how terrifying it must have been."

"You've no idea," Denise says.

Once Denise composes herself, she again stands and moves away from Violette as if she's afraid of catching something bad from her. Or of giving something to her.

"I've said too much," says Denise.

Violette remains seated. She looks up at Denise with the largest, widest eyes she can muster.

"I promise, I won't stay long," says Violette. "I'm here to help you. I was sent to Rouen to see if the network could be salvaged, but it's become quickly apparent that it can't. That you all are just trying to survive."

"*Oui*. I'm afraid to go out. I have no electricity. Little food. I'm being watched all the time. We're being bombed constantly. When I think back to last year and the year before, and I remember how hard I thought it was, I hate myself. I had no idea how bad it would get. You shouldn't be here."

"I'll leave as soon as you tell me everything. The more I know, the more I can help."

Violette reaches in her satchel and removes a stack of francs, extending it.

"Here," says Violette.

Denise gasps, and she snatches the money, eyeing it like she wants to eat it.

"Now, please," says Violette. "Tell me the rest."

Denise crosses the room to the window, and peers out from behind the dusty blackout curtains. Then she returns to the sofa and sits as far from Violette as possible.

"After we were hauled in," Denise says in a whisper, "there were mass arrests and murders. Isidore's bodyguard, Broni, was taken. Broni's brother, Felix, was shot."

Denise continues to say the names of those arrested and killed while Violette mentally records the information. It doesn't take long for Violette to become alarmed. The fact that there were mass round-ups after the dinner party arrests means it's likely one of the four talked under duress. It may have even been Denise. She is, after all, the only one sitting here, instead of in prison.

Violette slips one hand inside her satchel, on the hairbrush where the file rests, preparing her body to fight if necessary.

"May I ask," Violette says, trying to keep her voice as innocent as possible, "how were you able to get out?"

Denise covers her face with her hands.

"I'm too ashamed to say," says Denise.

"You can tell me anything. I'm on your side. No one will be angry. Everyone knows what impossible circumstances these are."

Denise looks up and searches Violette's face.

"All right," Denise says. She pauses and takes a deep breath. "I promised I'd turn in Clement if he showed up."

The room is silent but for the ticking of the grandfather clock in the corner. The sound of Violette's heartbeat whooshing in her ears.

"But I didn't mean it," says Denise. "It was a lie. They told me if I would, I could get out and I could still visit Isidore."

"And did they allow that?"

"Yes. But today was the last time. He's being deported."

Denise breaks into fresh tears. Violette embraces her again, as long as she can bear it. A faraway siren grows closer.

It's time to get out of here, Violette thinks.

She thanks Denise as calmly as she's able and assures her she'll be in touch.

Outside the apartment, Violette starts toward the front stair but, once she's sure Denise is no longer at the door, she backtracks and takes the rear door to the alley, getting away from the place as quickly as she can.

38

——— VIRGINIA ———

ON JEAN'S ORDERS, they all flee Paris.

Virginia and Philippe, Mum and Grandmère, the Blanc family, and Michelle, acting as their nanny, go to Les Baumées. Nicole and Michel are at a safe house, just outside of Paris. Lily travels south, to stay with a helper near Spain. Daniel and Jean escape to the forest at Fréteval, where they'll corral the aviators once the invasion starts.

God, let it start, Virginia prays.

When Jean wants them back in Paris, he'll call the phone line at Nesles—if it's working—using their special code. One ring, hang up. One ring, hang up. Three rings, hang up. If he doesn't call within two weeks, they can return to Paris at their own discretion, but should still refrain from engaging in Resistance activity until Jean makes contact.

At Easter mass, Abbé Rabourg looks haggard and worn, no doubt burdened by the double life he leads, the Jewish families he's kept in the rectory over the years. Dr. Noël Lebettre has also aged. His help with injured pilots and the procuring of false papers leaves him little time for rest. Monsieur and Madame Renard are not in town; they're with family in Neuilly, but the dear Madame Fleury is here. Her face is pinched and drawn. Villagers shrink away from Madame, thinking her a collaborator because of the officer who stays at her house. How

Virginia longs to slap the judgment from the faces of those who look down on Madame.

But Virginia can't. None of them can say a word. They must hold in their secrets, swallowing the bile every time it rises.

Virginia hasn't felt a depression of spirits like this since before they joined the Comet Line. Watching her boy taken away, seeing the traitor poisoned, and being ordered to cease operations for the time being is a lot to take. At least she has a houseful of those she loves. Still, without pilots, it feels incomplete.

She rocks back and forth in church, arms full of Jessie-Ann's youngest. Needing a nap, the little one was squirmy in her mother's arms but happy for a change of face, and soon falls asleep on Virginia's shoulder. Her downy hair smells like powder, and her plump cheek rests against Virginia's collarbone. It's heavenly, but the thought of any danger coming to this child or her family makes it hard for Virginia to breathe. She will tell Jessie-Ann that Les Baumées is hers as long as her family needs it. No more Paris. It's too dangerous.

"Please," Virginia says, as soon as Mass is over. "Move the girls here for the rest of the war."

"We'll be all right," says Jessie-Ann, with that sweet smile. "It just needs to cool down for a little while. Then the invasion will be here before we know it."

Virginia's feeling of dread is so deep it makes her step falter. It plagues her throughout their Easter meal of stewed rabbit.

Again.

I never thought I'd miss holiday octopus, Virginia thinks.

At home, Michelle boils eggs for the girls to color, using mashed-up radishes for pink dye and ivy for green. Once the eggs dry, Michelle hides them around the property and sets the girls loose, their parents helping with the hunt. Nan hops along behind them like a giant Easter Bunny. Mum and Grandmère sit on the terrace, sharing a bottle of Jean de la Roche Sauvignon Blanc they've been saving, faces serene while they watch the young family.

The air is mild today, for the first time in weeks, and daffodils and lilies wave in the breeze. While they look on, Philippe wraps his arms around Virginia.

"It's a good day," Virginia says aloud, trying to convince herself.

"*Oui,*" says Philippe. "We needed a rest. It's been a long winter."

"Honestly, though, I hate not having any parcels," she says. "I know how scared they are. How holidays on the run must be particularly hard. And I'm so worried about our red-haired boy."

"We have to trust, Virginia. We have to do our part. Our little piece of good. The rest isn't up to us."

"You're right."

"Let's savor this day, the way Mum and Grandmère know how to do," he says. "Once we're back at it in Paris, we'll miss the space here. We'll be tripping all over each other and our parcels."

"I'm happy to trip over you anytime," she says.

Philippe nuzzles her neck, but Nan's ferocious bark calls their attention. The girls scatter to their parents, while Virginia and Philippe dash toward Nan to see what's alarmed her. The dog has her teeth bared, and she snarls in as menacing a warning as Virginia has ever heard. As they get closer to the bushes, Virginia sees a man, cowered under a hedge. Virginia holds Nan back, while Philippe advances, knife drawn. Shaking, the man removes his hands from his twig-filled, sandy hair, lifts his brown eyes to them, smiles sheepishly, revealing dimples on his dirty cheeks.

"Howdy," he says.

Virginia smiles when she catches the accent.

"Texas?" she asks.

"Yes, ma'am. Are you the American?"

VIRGINIA'S VACILLATING MOODS are giving her whiplash.

The pilot was sent to them from Abbé Rabourg, who has "no room left at the inn." After Virginia vetted the Texan by quizzing him on the latest in American sports and news given to her from the aviators who preceded him, he teaches her the lyrics of the latest popular songs, like "Shoo-Shoo Baby" and "Pistol Packin' Mama," for her future inter-rogations.

The first few nights of the Texan's stay are festive. This pilot is fresh from the London dance halls and—in spite of his harrowing journey here—he's eager to give the girls a spin. Virginia puts on a Mills Brothers record, dangerous contraband a previous aviator left behind. The pilot partners with her, with Jessie-Ann, with Mum, and even Grandmère, to the amusement of the group. When "I'll Be Around" begins, the old women and little girls take a seat to watch the married couples slow dance, leaving the pilot facing Michelle, whose face is so red Virginia thinks the girl might combust. The pilot reaches for Michelle's hands, and draws her into the center of the room. He takes her in his arms and glides her around, Michelle blushing all the time.

All too soon, Madame Fleury hangs a blue blanket on the laundry line, the signal the German is in residence. So they stick to quieter evening pursuits, like card games, jacks, and chess, eyeing the road all the time for the messenger who's supposed to bring the pilot's false papers. Managing the tension they all feel of being anxious for the papers to arrive, while not wanting to part ways with this delightful young man, is a struggle.

His sixth night with them, once the others have gone to bed, Virginia and Philippe sit by the fireside, watching the pilot and Michelle. They lie on the floor on their stomachs, throw pillows under their chests. Their heads are bent together over a piece of paper, while Michelle writes the French phrases that will help the pilot on his journey to safety. Michelle giggles over the Texan's pronunciation, and his dimples are on full display every time he elicits a laugh, which makes Michelle's face turn redder than it already is in the firelight.

Virginia and Philippe smile at each other. Virginia has never seen Michelle so taken or so lighthearted. Though it hurts Virginia's heart to know that the pilot will have to leave them, she tries to enjoy this sweet moment of budding love and says a prayer that the pilot and Michelle might be reunited after the war. What stories they would have for their grandchildren.

When Virginia and Philippe retire, they delight in each other, grateful for the sheer space at Les Baumées, the privacy that allows them to make love without having to worry about a platoon of sleeping men just outside the door to hear them. But afterward, sleep eludes Virginia.

Dr. Lebettre has not yet been able to procure false papers for the pilot. They usually pass their parcels on to the Renards after a few days, but they'll be gone for another week, and they've heard nothing from Jean. With the German officer at Madame Fleury's, and all the people in France most dear to Virginia under her roof, she's in a state of anxiety. It's much easier to harbor fugitives when it's just her and Philippe.

Tossing and turning all night long, she finds it harder and harder to breathe, and when the sound of the phone ringer slices through the dawn air, she sucks in her breath entirely.

Once. Once. Three times.

39

ROUEN, FRANCE

—— **VIOLETTE** ——

VIOLETTE KNOCKS ONCE, twice, three times, using the code.

At what's left of Georges Philippon's garage, there are bullet holes along the side of the building, and the glass in the front windows is broken. The man who opens the door to Violette is skittish, has an eye twitch, and can barely muster thanks for the extra money she pays for the rusty bike. The transaction complete within minutes, she can't pedal away quickly enough, but the hour's ride to the post office at Saussay-la-Campagne, on the outskirts of Rouen, is anything but fast. She's stopped at checkpoints three times before she makes it out of the city limits, and once along a country road intersection.

"Where are you going?" a German soldier asks.

"To my cousin's farm."

"Why?"

"To see if she's heard anything about our missing uncle. Those terrible Brits and their bombs may have taken him."

"Don't get into any mischief on the farms. They're being watched for terrorist scum."

"Oh, merci," she says. "I'll keep an eye out for the traitors. Where can I find you if I see anything?"

He happily gives her his hotel room number.

Dolt.

Violette isn't lying about watching out for guerilla fighters. She's seeking an introduction so she can fund them, alert them to the aqueduct that needs blown up, and try to get a handle on the V1 and V2 flying bomb sites.

Then I'll get the hell out of this godforsaken place, she thinks.

There have been ninety-six arrests. Most of Clement's people have been imprisoned, deported, or even shot. The rest live in terror and hiding. There's no hope of rebuilding a network here. But Violette is determined to carry out the mission to completion before she reports to Clement in Paris.

Saussay-la-Campagne is rural and the air isn't as heavy as it is in town. Still, not letting down her guard, Violette scans the rustic post office inside and out for trouble. From behind the counter, Jeanne gives Violette a small smile, but Jeanne's forehead is creased with worry.

"I'm so glad you're all right," says Jeanne.

"Don't add worrying about me to your troubles," says Violette. "I'm fine. Are we alone?"

"*Oui.*"

"Good. What you said about the network is true. But I need to do one more thing before I go. Do you have a contact in the Maquis?"

Jeanne nods.

"Could a meeting be arranged tonight?" asks Violette.

"*Oui.* My husband, Lucien, can take you. He hides in our attic by day and goes to the Maquis in the woods at night."

"Why does he have to hide? Doesn't being a farmer exempt him from forced labor?"

"He's not a farmer. We live near the raspberry farm, not on it. He was captured by the Germans and taken in a work convoy, but he escaped. Lucien's an outlaw."

Then I'll be right in my element, Violette thinks.

"You can't stay at the house, though," says Jeanne. "I'll give you directions to a barn. It has a loft where you can watch the road. I'll give you a code for when you see Lucien approaching."

"All right. Out of curiosity, why not the house?"

"Well, I have children, and there's a family with us. And, my husband, of course."

"I understand. I wouldn't want to bring greater danger to them with my presence."

"And we don't want to endanger you. We're walking a tightrope. I haven't told you all of it."

Violette looks at Jeanne with a question in her eyes.

"The boches have requisitioned our home," says Jeanne.

SITTING IN A barn loft for hours gives Violette time to reflect on her life and on the lives of the people around her.

Jeanne, a woman in the Resistance, has lost her parents. She works during the day but has to provide for many mouths at home by night. Her husband, in the Maquis, is a wanted man. A family, possibly Jewish, is staying with them. And all while they have to pass Germans in the hallways. It's incomprehensible.

And here Violette is, a widow at twenty-two, a mother, an agent for a clandestine organization, picking like a dog through the rubble of a burned network for scraps that might help the Allies.

When this is all over, will any of them know how to enjoy a simple day, going to the market, grabbing a cup of tea with a friend, taking a walk without fear of imprisonment or bombardment? Will the shadow over all of them ever recede?

Violette doesn't know the answer.

She looks out over the spring-green landscape, watching the passage from afternoon into evening. Her stomach growls. Her feet hurt in her uncomfortable shoes. She'll tell Miss Atkins to get her a better pair for her next mission. The hay smells moldy. A chill fills the air when night falls.

Still, Violette is filled with a sense of gratitude. She takes a deep breath and thanks God that she's alive, and prays Henri is, too. Empty stomach, hurting feet, adrenaline surging through her body, she's as alive as she has ever been, and certain she's exactly where she belongs.

The air has cleared and there are a million stars. Silly though it is, Violette sends the moon a thought of thanks for providing the light to guide the brave pilots. For helping the Resistance receive her and Clement. She thinks of how she and Étienne used to send each other love on the moon, and how there's no reason that ever needs to stop. She concentrates very hard and is given the gift of certainty that Étienne is with her, and that he approves of what she's doing.

Her eyes are drawn to a movement in the field. She sees the shadow of a man. As he approaches, Violette hoots four times, as Jeanne instructed her. The man pauses and snaps the stick he's carrying in response. Then he continues toward the barn.

IT'S QUITE A journey, roughly two kilometers, creeping and crawling along farmlands and roads to the forest. In spite of the hoot call Lucien gives to alert the sentry, they still have a gun pointed at their faces and the password is demanded. Before she's led deeper into the woods, Violette is forced to have a sack placed over her head. When it's removed, Violette looks around a clearing bordered by tents made from parachutes. There are no fires and no lights, only small groups of feral men, eyes white in the black, staring at Violette with a mixture of curiosity, wariness, and suspicion.

They reach a rock wall with an opening tucked behind a ledge, and Lucien makes her wait outside it. In a few moments, he returns and invites her inside a cave, illuminated by candles about to lose their lights. Four dirty men stand around a crude table covered with a map. They look at the small girl before them with incredulity written all over their faces.

First, Violette removes her headscarf. Then, her doe-eyed expression. Finally, she opens her satchel. The SOE has taught her the common language all men speak throughout the world, and not an actual word is needed. She slaps ten bundles, one at a time, on the table.

"One hundred thousand francs," she says. "Approved for your use on the black market and to purchase arms from the Maquis of the south, who've been able to receive more drops than you have here, in the belly of the beast."

Their mouths and eyes open wide. Lucien crosses his arms, smiling with pride and giving them "I told you so" looks.

Violette gets right down to business, telling them that, though she doesn't know the exact time, invasion is coming. When they hear the BBC read the first part of Verlaine's poem "Autumn Song"—*"Les sanglots longs / Des violons / De l'automne"*—they are to ready their men. When they hear the second part—*"Blessent mon cœur / D'une langueur / Monotone"*—they're to start sabotaging communication and rail lines. Barentin Viaduct, connecting Rouen to the surrounding regions, is a strategic priority. She points out the areas of the massive viaduct that should be targeted and indicates how many tons of explosives they'll need to inflict the damage. Once they're clear, the man in charge asks what she needs.

"Locations and coordinates of the sites in the region producing and launching the V1 and V2 long-range rockets," she says. "Do you have a guide who can take me tomorrow? Someone who can show me the sites while acting as my young lover, out with me for a bicycle ride?"

Three men step forward, running into each other, and knocking over one of the candles on the table.

AFTER A NIGHT spent sleeping like the dead, curled up in a tent of her very own, Violette emerges, refreshed. She's hungry enough to take the tin of cold beans from Max, the young maquisard who'll be her escort. Max has a mop of black curls that hangs over his forehead and bright green eyes. If he's yet reached eighteen, she'd be surprised, but she knows how young she can make herself look, so he's a good pairing.

It was heaven to stay with the Maquis—a relief to scrap the virginal secretary act, if only for a night. Hard as it was, she thinks back fondly to her time in commando training in Scotland, with Jack. She misses that little scamp and thinks a prayer for his safety. Then her thoughts turn back to Henri. Has he been able to escape prison? Has he been deported? Is he alive? She prays that they'll be reunited someday.

After a quick wash of her face in the stream, a brush of her hair, and the return of the kerchief, she's back in character. She loops her arm through Max's, and he grins at her, while the others throw twigs at him, berating him with jealousy for winning the escort prize.

Before she leaves the camp, Violette places two fingers to her lips, kisses them, and raises her arm with the V symbol, for victory. The men take off their hats, place their hands over their hearts, and return the gesture.

Then Max covers her head with the sack, takes her hand, and leads her out of the forest.

"MAKE SURE YOU laugh and wink at me whenever you see Germans," Violette instructs Max. "Even if we're speaking of serious things."

"Of course," he says. "But we can't ride next to each other."

"Why not?"

"The boches made a new law. They don't like people on bicycles riding side by side, where they can easily talk. They find it suspicious."

Violette files this information in her mind to report back to HQ. The laws are ever changing, and agents knowing new procedure, to blend in, is essential to their survival.

"Then, before we go, tell me which site we'll visit first and what's contained there. That'll give me time to memorize it and the landmarks leading up to it."

He briefs her, and they set off on the longest part of their journey, roughly fifty kilometers north, to Bois de Clairefeuille. A Resistance leader got through to HQ that it appeared there were long-range rocket launch sites being constructed throughout the region, with ramps facing toward London. His intelligence led to mass bombardments, but the sites keep popping up like cockroaches. The Germans are hiding the new places better in copses, and they're almost impossible to see from the air. Any guidance Violette can give on the exact whereabouts of new launch sites will be invaluable.

Violette's sharp eyes record everything she sees along the way, especially as they get closer. She notes the road signs and directions, the numbers, rank, and morale of the German soldiers they pass, and where the railroad tracks end and the dirt roads begin, to transport the large rockets.

Every time Violette and Max get close to a checkpoint, they become animated. Max looks over his shoulder at her, and Violette blows him kisses. At the first stop, Violette learns Max speaks German, and his casual greetings in the language to the soldiers get the pair quickly on their way. But hearing Max speak the language so well puts Violette on guard. It could be perfectly innocent, but when their trip is finished, she plans to lose him without a backward glance. She hopes she doesn't have to slit his throat before they part ways. He's charming company.

At the thicket across the farmland of their first destination, where German lorries rumble in and out, Violette pauses to pretend to check her tires. She looks through the spokes, estimating and taking mental pictures of the distance from the intersection where they've stopped to the launch site. Once it's impressed upon her memory, she gives Max a nod, and he starts them on the road heading southwest, back toward Rouen. When they're alone, Max explains their next stop. The quarries at Canteleu have conscripted Russians slaving over the production and storage of the liquid oxygen needed to launch the rockets.

"When the Allies take that site out, what a mighty explosion it will make," says Violette.

"Finer than a set of Bastille Day fireworks."

The mention of Bastille Day presses the wounds in Violette's heart. She recalls the Bastille Day she met Étienne, his clumsy excuse to speak to her, asking for the time while a watch was visible on his arm. Remembering his embarrassed smile brings her own, but she pushes the memory from her mind so she can remain in character.

After visiting the quarries, Violette sweats, and her thighs burn. They've been munching on hard-boiled eggs and dry brown bread throughout their journey, but it's doing little to satisfy her empty stomach. But she steels herself, for they still have much road to cover before the sun sets.

As evening threatens, they finally make it to two more launch sites in the Rouen suburbs of Bois-Guillaume and Mont-Saint-Aignan. Violette observes the châteaus the Germans have requisitioned are full of officers, well-fed and healthy in appearance. In spite of the fact that there's still a glow in the sky, they burn electric lights off their very own generators. They'll surely turn them off, once night falls, but they're wasting energy like it's nothing just above a town of exhausted, frightened, starving people who can't even boil water for coffee made of acorns.

Though her mood is low, Violette is rewarded for her efforts with a clear view of one of the newly constructed rocket launch ramps, its concrete so fresh she imagines she could press her hands in it. At a bridge with a good vantage, she calls to Max to stop. When she dismounts, Violette pulls Max's arms around her from behind, where the two may gaze out in the distance over Rouen.

It takes work for Violette to mute her anguish at seeing the full destruction of the once-beautiful city. Rouen is a broken remnant of how Monet painted her all those years ago. Hearing the German voices in the street behind them, Violette broods about their exploitation of France—their absolute violation of her. As a pair of soldiers nears them, she turns her back on the city and presses her lips into Max's. He's happy to respond and mistakes the intensity for passion.

No, dear boy, she thinks. *It's pure hatred, and you better never do anything to be at the receiving end of it.*

When she pulls away, it takes Max a moment to recover. Wobbly and blushing, he mounts his bicycle, and starts for their final stop at another quarry. But the roar of an airplane engine calls their attention to the sky. Pedestrians and soldiers stop and stare until the air raid sirens wail, sending people running in all directions.

"Take cover," Max says, trying to pull Violette away, but she's transfixed.

Are my boys going to kill me? she thinks. *Didn't HQ tell them I'm here? I won't even be able to get my intelligence to Clement.*

The curses Violette utters are real, and she clenches her hands into fists.

But it's a single airplane, moving at an incredible speed. As it darts to avoid antiaircraft blasts, it releases not a shower of bombs, but a flurry of paper flyers. Thousands of sheets drift to the ground like flower petals as the airplane makes a sharp vertical move, disappearing from view. Frenchmen and Germans emerge from their covers. Violette jumps up and snatches a paper, appreciation dawning with every word she reads.

CITIZENS OF ROUEN. EVACUATE.
YOU ARE IN DANGER.

WE WILL SOON RETURN TO BOMB THE ENEMY
OCCUPYING YOUR GREAT LAND.

LEAVE, WHILE THERE'S STILL TIME.

How much notice are they giving? she wonders. *At least a day. Hopefully more. I still have work to do.*

While the groans and curses rise around them, Violette nods at Max. They mount their bicycles, and head to the final stop.

———————

THE LAST QUARRY site was farther than she should have gone. The whole way out, Violette ignored her rising alarm, and now she might not make it back to the inn in time for curfew.

She's cross with Max for taking her there last. Because she doesn't know him and can't be certain he's safe, she tells him she needs some privacy to relieve herself behind an abandoned building, but continues pedaling back to Rouen, as fast as her legs can take her. She's determined to beat curfew, take a bath, and crawl into bed for one last night of sleep here before the coming bombardment. She's not supposed to meet Clement in Paris for another few days, but it's time to leave Rouen.

Checking her watch, she sees she'll only be a minute or two late, but when she reaches the rue Saint-Romain, a French gendarme steps in her path. She comes to a hard stop, turning her bicycle at the last second to avoid knocking into him.

"*Arrêtez!*" he shouts. "What are you doing out past curfew?"

"Is it even curfew? My hotel's right there. You can see it."

"My watch says you're late."

"Please, Monsieur, I've been all over today, searching for news about my uncle's whereabouts, with no luck. I'm so tired."

"Then you should have got back sooner. Off your bike."

Violette stares at him with the saddest, most exhausted look she can muster, but his scowl remains. He grabs her arm with one hand and walks her bike along with the other.

She's too angry at this collaborator puppet to feel afraid, but she knows how to act. She sniffles, working herself up, and by the time they reach the commissariat, she's brought forth tears. The gendarme leaves her bicycle in the lobby and drags her to the captain's office. When they enter, the captain lifts his dark gaze from a pile of paperwork on his desk to where the gendarme stands with Violette still in his grip.

"This one was out after curfew," says the gendarme.

"Not after," Violette says, voice quavering. "I would have got to my inn in time if he hadn't stopped me."

"What were you doing out so close to curfew?" the captain asks.

"I've been here trying to find my uncle. My family hasn't heard from him since the last bombardment."

"Give me your papers."

She reaches in her satchel and passes the documents to him.

"Sit," the captain says to her. "You, get back to your post."

The gendarme gives his captain a petulant look, as if he wanted more praise for bringing a girl into the station, but he obeys. As he goes, another gendarme enters the captain's office. Tall, fair, and handsome, he could be a German or a Brit or an American. He passes a file to the captain and glances at Violette, before addressing his boss, and then quickly returns his gaze to Violette's face. The man's voice never wavers, but he narrows his eyes, as if he's trying to think how he knows her. She looks down at her hands in her lap. After a few moments, she dares to lift her gaze. He continues to stare at her, now with an unmistakable intensity.

"Mademoiselle Leroy," says the captain. "I find it suspicious that a young woman would travel to Rouen, which barely has time to catch its breath between bombings, to search for her uncle."

"I don't want to be here, sir, but he's all my mother and I have left. Since my father died, my uncle helps to provide for us. Not only do we love him very much, but we need him."

She allows the tears to flow freely. The captain squirms.

"You have an accent," he says. "It doesn't come from Le Havre, where your papers say you reside."

"No, I spent most summers growing up with an aunt in the Nord. And I had my schooling there."

She's pleased with herself for how quickly she explains away her accent.

His stare is becoming colder and more skeptical.

She turns up the tears.

"That aunt has also been killed," she says. "My father, my aunt. It looks like my uncle, too. All during the war. It's too much, sir."

His scowl deepens, and he shifts in his seat. Then he pushes her papers back toward her.

"Inspector Alie will want to question you. But he's not here until tomorrow afternoon." He turns to the gendarme at his side. "Lock her up for the night."

She sobs.

"Pardon, Captain," says the gendarme. "But our cells are full of terrorists. Perhaps we could keep her bicycle as collateral. I can drive her back to her hotel, and she can return tomorrow, when Inspector Alie gets here."

The captain weighs the suggestion. The bicycle is a good bargaining chip. No French man or woman would give up such an important possession lightly. The captain sighs and nods, before dismissing them with a wave of his hand.

"Don't think about trying to escape," the captain says. "You won't get far, and your punishment will be severe."

"Of course, sir," says Violette. "I wouldn't think of it. I'll come back tomorrow."

"Two o'clock."

"Yes sir. Merci."

She gathers her papers and puts them in her satchel. The gendarme takes her by the arm more roughly than the first did and nearly drags her out of the office. Leading her through the maze of desks and police, past her bicycle, he takes her to the parking lot, to a black Mercedes. He pushes her in the back of the vehicle, handcuffs her to the door, strides to the front, and gets in, throwing the car into gear. She watches him watching her in the rearview mirror. Once they're out of sight of the station, he speaks.

"Was Madame Desveaux able to repair your sweater?"

Heart pounding, Violette shrinks into the door, thinking how she might escape if he tries to harm her.

"Please," he says. "I'm an ally."

She stares at him, trying to size him up. But she can't see his face, so she can't read him.

"You're smart to be on guard," he continues, "but, I promise, I'm on your side. Please, do you have any news of Clement or Robert?"

She flinches hearing her friends' names on this man's lips. Clement never told her about a gendarme working for the Resistance, so she won't give him anything he can use.

He sighs.

The station is not far from the inn. When they reach the rue Saint-Romain, he continues speaking.

"It's all right if you don't trust me enough to talk to me. But listen. You cannot allow yourself to be interrogated by Alie. He's the one who's been arresting and deporting Clement's people. Young and sweet as you are, I can't bear to think about what you might face at his hands. Few can withstand his questioning techniques."

You've no idea who you're dealing with, she thinks. But she appreciates the intelligence.

When they pull up to the inn, he speaks faster.

"You must leave tomorrow," he says. "There's a Paris-bound train that departs at nine. The ticket master with the white mustache won't give you any trouble if you tell him Déterville sent you. If the Allies haven't flattened the city by then, see that you're on that train. May God be with you."

He comes around to her door and unlocks the handcuffs.

She looks up at him. Believing that he's earnest, she stands on tiptoe, kisses him on both cheeks, and hurries into the inn.

AFTER SCRUBBING HER sweaty, dirty skin raw, Violette soaks in the hot water, staring at her toes wiggling on the tub's edge. Even with the rest cycling gave her feet from walking, her blisters are sore and stinging. With all the intelligence zipping through her mind, getting dragged into the police station, and knowing a bombardment could be just hours away, there'll be no sleep this night. Instead, she'll use the time to prepare to rendezvous with Clement in Paris, before they take the next SOE plane out to London. Then she'll wrap Tania in her arms, and not let go until the next mission.

Earlier, when Violette had entered the inn, Madame was sitting by the fire. She'd stood and uttered a prayer of thanks that her little boarder made it back, and covered Violette with kisses and chastisements. Violette apologized to Madame for making her worry and said she'd check out tomorrow morning, after breakfast.

"For *ma petite*, I'll have a full spread before the sun rises," said Madame. "Chicory coffee, hard-cooked eggs, and gooseberry jam on *pain caca*."

Violette had laughed. "Poo bread" is what the locals call the nasty brown stuff they make do with since they don't have access to white flour.

"I'm grateful," Violette had said. "For everything. Please, Madame, tell me you'll leave the city tomorrow. You saw the flyers, *oui*?"

"*Ma petite*, I've lived seventy years, through two wars. If I go out in a blast, that's how I go."

What could Violette say to that?

When the bathwater cools, Violette rises, dries herself, and brushes out her wet hair. She puts on the travel clothes she'd washed and hung dry earlier in the week and packs the rest of her things. She'll wait until the last possible moment to put on those tight shoes.

She counts her money. Violette still has over fifty thousand francs. After leaving Madame with a large sum tomorrow morning, Violette has orders to spend the rest, and spend it she will. A first-class train ticket to Paris, a hotel room, fine dining, gifts for her loved ones, and a little something for herself. Maybe a big something.

Violette's able to doze for an hour or two but wakes just before dawn. After she fixes her hair and puts on her kerchief and shoes, she darkens the lantern and opens the blackout curtains. The sky is navy, with a touch of violet, a prelude to the coming dawn. But the roar of an airplane engine disturbs the silence.

It's too early, she thinks. *I haven't even got a train ticket.*

Again, it's a single plane, a warning scout. In its wake, it drops hundreds of little flares, twirling down like leaves. It's mesmerizing, watching a flare make a slow spiral into the courtyard. Violette sees Madame scurry into the garden to stomp it out. The old woman squats down and picks up the small container attached to it. Violette opens her window.

"What's it say?" she asks.

"Get out, now."

The women cross themselves. Violette puts on her shoes and meets Madame in the lobby. The old woman directs Violette to the breakfast spread on the check-in desk: a cup of steaming ersatz coffee, a hard-cooked egg, bread, and gooseberry jam, just as she promised.

"Eat," Madame says.

Violette obeys, stuffing herself as full as possible, knowing there are no guarantees of when she'll get her next meal. When she finishes, she gives Madame a wad of francs from her satchel, embraces the old woman, and accepts her thanks and travel blessings.

"I'll come back and visit you once we've beat the boches," Violette says.

I'll bring Tania, Violette thinks. *We'll eat gooseberry pie at the inn, and I'll show Tania the craters that used to be rocket sites, and the place where the Maquis hid, and I'll take her to pick raspberries with Jeanne and Lucien and their children.*

Making herself as small as possible, Violette creeps along in the shadows of the empty streets, holding her breath until she makes it to the station. The man with the white mustache sells her the first-class ticket to Paris when she tells him Déterville sent her. The station fills quickly with scared travelers and with a collection of fidgety German soldiers. The heat from the crush of bodies becomes oppressive. She nearly cheers aloud when the train pulls into the station.

In the queue that forms, she's pushed against a wall, and comes face-to-face with the shared wanted poster of Clement and Robert. Among the other photographs and sketches, her friends are plastered ceiling to floor. She doesn't know what comes over her, but she finds she can't stop herself from sliding her finger underneath, where it's not affixed to the wall, peeling it away, and folding it in half, in half, and in half again. Then she reaches up, pretends to scratch her throat, and slides the paper down her neckline, into her bra.

Heart pounding, she knows this is a jailable, even executable offense. If Miss Atkins finds out, she'll send Violette to the cooler. But if Violette makes it back to Clement and Robert with this poster, she'll have bragging rights—and the respect and loyalty of her men—forever. It's well worth the risk. She suppresses a giggle at the thought of their reactions.

I must be losing my mind, Violette thinks.

She's almost certain she is when she sees the Allied bombers arrive and feels no fear. Dozens of silver birds with droppings of fire further desecrate the badly scarred city of Rouen. The explosions are large and orange and make the train shake and the travelers cry out in terror. The bombs litter the sky as far as the eye can see, and they're deployed with a relentlessness of which she didn't understand the Allies capable.

Transfixed, she can't deny the terrible, devastating beauty of it.

40

PARIS

——— VIRGINIA ———

A RUMBLING SHAKES the apartment building.

Virginia and Jessie-Ann jump from their seats at the table, where they eat dinner with the girls, and run to the tall windows looking out over Paris.

When they returned to the capital at Jean's summons, they still didn't have papers for the Texan pilot. It was a scary journey—Philippe having to give the boy an old photo of himself they'd roughed up and affixed to outdated paperwork. Luck was on their side, however, and the MPs at the station were too busy with crowds returning from holiday travel to linger over their group.

Michelle was quick to volunteer to keep the pilot at her flower shop while they wait on good papers from their Paris forger. She and the Texan didn't have to act the part of young lovers strolling through the streets.

Virginia stays with Jessie-Ann and her girls. Nicole is with her mother. Mum and Grandmère remain together. Philippe, Paul, and Michel have gone with Jean and Daniel to the forest at Fréteval, so they'll know the route to take the pilots once D-Day arrives.

Has it come? thinks Virginia.

In the distance, she sees a glint of sunset on Allied metal. She hears the scream of the bombs as they're released, holds her breath in the terrible moments that pass, and gasps when the percussion of the explosions is felt in the trembling floor.

"I thought Jean said the BBC would give us the 'Autumn Song' poem signal when invasion is imminent," says Virginia.

"I wonder if we missed it?" says Jessie-Ann.

Plane after plane drops bomb after bomb over a concentrated area across the city.

"It looks like a specific target," says Virginia.

"I hope it's Avenue Foch."

"And the Gestapo and their collaborators are burning in hell."

As Jessie-Ann turns to take the girls to the cellar, a pair of bombers come roaring in so low, the china rattles in its case. The women can't keep themselves from turning and watching, transfixed. The bombs that light up behind the Dôme des Invalides shatter the windows in the apartment. They raise their arms to cover their heads while shards of glass rain over them, the force of the blast blowing their skirts against their legs. When the assault ends, the women race to the crying girls and carry them down to the basement of the building.

As the other residents pour down, the cellar grows stuffier and more claustrophobic by the minute. Virginia shepherds the Blancs to a corner and tries to calm them. The baby is the easiest to soothe, but the three-year-old is hysterical, as is Jessie-Ann.

"I should have listened to you," she cries. "I was a fool to keep them in Paris."

"It's all right," says Virginia. "We'll get you to the country tomorrow."

"Paul will be so worried."

"We'll leave the men a note."

Virginia is unharmed by the shattered window glass. The thick dress she's wearing provided good armor. Jessie-Ann, however, has cuts on her arms. Virginia uses the linen dinner napkin she'd shoved in her skirt pocket to blot her friend's wounds. The three-year-old sobs harder to see her mother hurt, but Jessie-Ann is able to stop crying and reassure her daughter Mommy's all right.

The rumbling and shaking of the building make Virginia think they might not, in fact, be all right underground, but the bombardment is soon silenced. Once a half hour passes without an explosion, she and Jessie-Ann take the girls back upstairs to survey the damage in the apartment. Two of the four massive windows have been destroyed. The jagged glass edges frame the burning city beyond, and searchlights and sirens add to the hellishness of the scene. Jessie-Ann is having a hard time deciding what to do first, so Virginia takes charge, commanding her friend to pack the girls' things. Virginia pulls the curtains over the windows, finds a ladder from the supply closet, and uses a silver adhesive called duct tape—which Jean gave them from a recent drop from the Allies—to secure the heavy curtains as tightly as possible to the walls around the frames.

"This stuff is a miracle," says Virginia as she finishes. "Just don't think too hard about what it might do to your wallpaper."

"I'm happy we have walls left to worry about," says Jessie-Ann.

Once the girls are in bed, the women spend the night cleaning up the apartment and packing their own things. They set out at first light for the train station, but it becomes immediately apparent that the Gare du Nord was one of last night's targets. There are still fires burning, and no trains running, so they walk the two kilometers, trading off girls and suitcases, to the Gare Saint-Lazare.

Nearly faint from exhaustion, the women groan at the sight of the long lines and crowds. While Jessie-Ann keeps track of the cranky, scared girls, Virginia buys tickets for all of them to get out of town. It's not until the afternoon that they're able to get seats, and as they board, they collide with a pretty young woman on her way off the train, wearing a violet kerchief that matches her eyes. The young woman catches Jessie-Ann's oldest girl's dolly before it falls to the tracks below and passes it back to Jessie-Ann with a smile.

"You're an angel," says Jessie-Ann, thanking the woman.

"Think nothing of it," she says. "Your daughter reminds me of mine."

Jessie-Ann and Virginia smile at the woman, who looks too young to be a mother. But she's soon swallowed up by the crowd.

------ **VIOLETTE** ------

AT THE GARE Saint-Lazare, Violette knocks into two exhausted women with arms full of children. The oldest girl's dolly almost falls to the tracks below before Violette snatches it.

"You're an angel," the mother says.

"Think nothing of it," Violette says. "Your daughter reminds me of mine."

As the current of the crowd carries Violette out of the station, she feels a sharp pang, like hunger, for her sweet Tania, followed by a stab of guilt.

The mothers at the station looked haggard and worn, no doubt from caring for their little ones in the midst of war. She thinks of the dead girl on the quay at Calais, whose glassy stare matched her dolly's. She thinks of Tania in Mill Hill, with only Vera and Alice Maidment's arms to crawl into when the bombs hit. Violette feels sick that she's not there to console her daughter.

A voice like Papa's nags at Violette's thoughts.

How could you have left your baby in the care of practical strangers during a war?

But Mill Hill is a suburb, she thinks. *It's much safer from bombs than downtown London. And Vera's no stranger. We've been chums since childhood.*

Tania's already lost her father, the voice continues. *If you die, she'll be an orphan.*

Violette shakes her head to clear the accusing thoughts and turns her attention to the city around her, but that brings no relief. Ashes, smoky air, and gray faces, Paris would look like a black-and-white film, if it weren't for the screaming red swastika flags defiling the major landmarks. Nazis march about all over. The street signs are in German. Shouts and sirens make her shoulders rise and her teeth clench. There's so much assaulting her senses. It's too loud. How will she endure this until she's set to meet with Clement?

I need to get to the hotel, she thinks.

Many moons ago, Henri had told her to check in at the Reine Marie, on the boulevard Saint-Germain. She realizes now he was speaking a language she didn't understand at the time, but that he knew would bring her to her destiny.

Henri. The thought of him languishing in a Nazi prison somewhere— or worse—is a blow. She feels dizzy.

I'm coming undone.

Violette forces her feet to walk. She's memorized the routes in her mind and knows the way. It'll take her less than an hour, but the blisters on her toes throb, and the ankle she sprained protests. She'll be hobbling by the time she reaches the hotel.

As she travels along the rue Tronchet, under the newly budding trees, she sees it.

L'église de la Madeleine.

The great columns of the church rise like a Roman temple over the city.

Étienne's letter comes as his voice in her ear.

"I look forward to the day when this is all over. When the three of us will walk into L'église de la Madeleine in Paris. We'll light candles, and hear Mass, and thank God for our survival, and for our blessings. I can *see* it, Violette, and that vision assures me all will be well. Can you see it, my love?"

Tears wetting her face, Violette staggers toward the stairs, her ankle and her feet protesting all the way. For Étienne, she must go in, but will God be there?

She uses her small body to push the heavy bronze door, and when it closes behind her, she stops and breathes.

A holy silence greets her. The air is thick with the exotic fragrance of incense and the sweet aroma of Easter lilies. Though the ceiling rises to great heights, it's dark inside the basilica, like a tomb. Over the altar, the sole skylight in the dome shines down with a ray that looks straight from heaven. The altar is crowned with a large statue of Mary Magdalene being carried up to heaven by angels, her mission complete, her life a pleasing sacrifice.

Violette moves forward, toward the great organ, passing mosaics and paintings and white marble saints lit from underneath with low lights, fields of flickering candles beneath them. The faithful kneel in the alcoves and in the pews, their prayers rising on the incense, climbing to the skylight, lifting up to God.

Violette's tears still wet her face, but she has her breath again, she has her bearings, and her pulse has slowed. She finds an empty alcove, folds a large bill, stuffs it into the poor box, and lights candles, one by one, whispering prayers for those she loves.

Étienne. Tania. Maman and Papa. Her brothers. Her cousins and aunts and uncles. Tante Marguerite. Vera and Alice Maidment. Miss Atkins. Buckmaster. Clement. Robert. Jack. Henri.

As the light before her grows, her tears cease. The glow is a visible sign of her great blessings, of all those she loves and cares for and those who love and care for her. Whether living or dead, the love remains, and that's what she's fighting for. In her despair, she's reminded that good mothers don't all look the same, nor do good daughters or good wives or good agents. They're each fighting a woman's war, the way they're called to, on different but essential fronts.

I'll tell this to Tania, Violette thinks. *I'll bring her to La Madeleine, and light candles with her for her father. I'll show her where to go when she loses her way.*

Restored, Violette rises, wipes her face, takes a deep breath, and leaves the church. When she emerges, her eyes have to adjust to the brightness, her senses to the real world outside the sanctuary.

"Violette," a voice says.

She blinks and, when the face comes into focus, she draws in her breath.

"Jack!"

She's so elated to see her friend, she's unable to censor his name before it leaves her lips.

They gasp little laughs, and he pulls her into a rough hug.

"God bless you," he whispers.

She's too overcome with emotion to speak. She squeezes him as hard as she can before they force themselves apart, fleeing each other's company as quickly as they were brought together.

WHEN THE CROWD at the Gare d'Austerlitz parts around Violette, Clement's eyes light up and he shakes his head. Standing from the café table, he wraps her in an embrace and kisses her head.

"Niece!" he says. "You look so . . . demure. I hardly recognized you."

"Uncle," she replies. "Thank God. I've been searching all over for you."

He grins, his eyes crinkling at the corners, until he notices the suitcase she's brought.

"I thought we were traveling lightly?" he asks, looking between her satchel and her luggage.

"I went shopping."

He gives her a look of reprimand.

"Remember, *Auntie* told me to," says Violette. "And I always listen to Auntie."

Clement laughs, and reaches to lift the suitcase for her, grunting from its weight.

"Better let me take that," she says. "I wouldn't want you to get caught with my new lingerie."

She winks and follows him to the ticket counter, the mood falling when they have to present their documents to the young MP at the train. He lingers over Clement's papers before nodding him along and takes even longer scrutinizing hers. Violette remembers Clement and Robert's wanted poster, which she's slipped from her bra to the lining of her satchel, and the fact that she, herself, is now a wanted woman in Rouen. As the seconds stretch, she sweats. Clement is on the train but he stands waiting and watching from the shadows.

"Open your suitcase," the MP says.

Violette sets it on the table with a thump and obeys, the lacy violet bras and panties she bought arranged over the top of the piles of gifts for her family and friends. The MP's face goes red, and he mumbles a dismissal before turning to the next passenger.

Climbing aboard, she keeps her eyes off Clement's so she doesn't laugh, and follows him to their compartment. Her heart sinks, however, when she sees they'll have to share it with a German officer. If she were alone, she could either flirt with the officer or play the demure girl, but with Clement, it's hard to know how to act. Perhaps they should have ridden separately.

As the train pulls away, she keeps her eyes on the window. Clement takes out a pack of cigarettes and offers one to the German.

The twit, she thinks. *Clement's teasing me. He knows I have to be dying for a smoke.*

"Merci," says the German.

"*Bitte,*" says Clement.

Clement then proceeds to carry on an entire conversation in German with the soldier. All Violette can do to hide her surprise—and her desire not to be asked a question in a language she doesn't speak—is to ball up her jacket as a pillow, lean it against the window, and pretend to sleep.

On the journey to Orléans, where they have to catch their planes home, Violette's mind races. It's hard to keep herself from fantasizing about how she and Clement together could silently kill this Nazi, prop him up like he's sleeping, and disembark without being caught. But they're almost at the finish line of their mission. It wouldn't do to compromise their safety so close to departure.

She shifts her thoughts to all she has to tell Clement. Though it will bring him heartache, she's eager to report what she's learned from Rouen. But the German doesn't get off at any of the stops. It looks as if they'll be stuck with him for the duration.

The men finally fall silent. Violette adjusts so her head is on Clement's shoulder. He pulls out a copy of *Signal* magazine, a glossy German propaganda periodical in which he pretends to be interested. Through the slits in her eyes, Violette sees the officer take out a chocolate bar.

I know, she thinks. *We can kill him and take his chocolate. And I can give it to Dickie. He'll love to know how I came by it.*

The screeching of brakes covers the sound of her growling stomach. The officer stops chewing. Clement puts down his magazine. Violette lifts her head, and they sit and listen, wondering if it's a bombardment, until German voices get closer. Violette doesn't know what they're saying, but whatever it is causes the officer to toss his chocolate bar on the seat, rise, throw open the door, and stride out. Clement turns pale. It's killing her to not be able to ask him what's happening, but whatever it is has made her unflappable chief as unsettled as she's ever seen him.

A woman screams.

German voices get closer.

"Remove your kerchief," Clement whispers. "Do you have any lipstick?"

"I just bought some."

"Is it handy?"

"In my satchel."

"Put it on."

As she applies it, Clement stuffs Violette's kerchief in his pocket, and she shoves the lipstick back in her satchel. Two Gestapo officers arrive at their compartment. They look right past Clement to Violette. She regards them as haughtily as she's able.

"*Wen suchen Sie?*" asks Clement.

"*Ein junges Fräulein,*" one says. "*Eine Terroristin.*"

Clement laughs and nudges Violette. She, too, laughs, turning on a smile with as many watts as she's got.

"Nicht dieses," Clement says with a wink.

The Gestapo don't return the smile, but nod and leave them, continuing to barge their way into other compartments.

In a few moments, Clement passes back Violette's kerchief, which she uses to wipe off the lipstick. She ties it back over her hair before the German officer returns. In a few moments, Violette sees a woman dragged from the train and led to the woods nearby. She and Clement jump when the shot is fired.

AT THE FARMER'S house in Orléans, after they're well fed and settled in a barn, Clement lets out a sigh.

"I thought you were done for, Vi," he says.

"Don't dwell on it," she says. "You saved us. How do you speak German so well?"

"Once we've won the war, I'll tell you all about my past."

"Do you think an innocent woman was killed?" she asks.

"As you said, don't dwell on it."

Violette nods, trying to shake the sounds of the woman's scream from her memory. She turns her thoughts to lighter things and, remembering the wanted poster, reaches for her satchel.

"I have a present for you," she says.

She plucks the paper from the lining, and watches Clement's mouth open when he unfolds it. He laughs and shakes his head.

"God, Violette, this could have got you killed. And me."

"Still could."

He shakes his head and stuffs it in his own satchel.

"Robert's going to lose his mind when he sees this," says Clement. "Well done."

Violette beams. But the flash of joy is quickly extinguished, as she reports to Clement about his destroyed network and Denise's promise to her interrogators to turn in Clement if he ever returns to Rouen. He rubs his eyes and grows quiet, taking in everything she tells him.

"I'm sorry," she says.

He nods, and pulls out his cigarettes, offering her one. She stares at it for a long moment but refuses. They're so close to the finish line. No need to push the boundaries further than she has.

Silence falls over them. They check their watches frequently, waiting for the signal. Hector, the section chief and one of Miss Atkins's stars, has a well-oiled machine, so they've no worry they'll be left. They've been assured Hector's people can be counted upon to do their parts. Sure enough, at midnight, the barn door squeaks open and a shadow of a woman pokes in her head.

"Did I leave my milking stool?" she asks, using the code.

"*Oui*, by the cattle stalls," Clement says, using the response.

Clement and Violette rise, collect their belongings, and follow the woman through the darkness to the landing field, where a small team waits.

The night air is cold and damp, and the river bordering the field reflects the moonlight. Soon, they hear the welcome drone of the Lysanders of the "Moonlight Squadron." The team on the ground forms an L and shines their flashlights to the sky as the duo of airplanes camouflaged in matte black paint bumps to a landing in the field. Two figures climb down from the planes and disappear into the night, while Violette and Clement hurry to take their places. Violette blows a kiss to the drop team and to Clement as he boards his plane. Her pilot is at her side, grunting when he heaves up her heavy suitcase, and then gives her a boost so she can board. Each Lysander comfortably holds only a pilot and one passenger, behind him. While the pilot closes the hatch, she removes and stores her satchel, pulls on the helmet—still warm and smelling of something alcoholic the previous wearer must have consumed—and gives the pilot the thumbs-up.

Takeoff is smooth, but shortly into the flight, streaks of light whiz by them. Violette knows enough from working at the ack-ack battery for the ATS that they're being fired upon, and soon, they're hit. Violette gasps.

"I'm going to get us out of this," the pilot says. "But I can't have distraction."

He switches off the intercom, and though he's only just in front of her, the pilot suddenly feels a hundred miles away. He makes a sharp dip, like he's going to land again, before banking left and then climbing as fast as he can from the searchlight passing over them.

Though it's made of glass, the hatch is so close over Violette's head it feels as if she's in a coffin. Bullets ping on the outside of the plane, and it shudders in response. Violette curses, but when there's a large popping sound, she prays. She didn't make it all the way through her first mission in occupied France to die on the way home. She begs God to get them safely back, but the only responses she receives are enemy fire and severe turbulence. She soon realizes that there could be hours of horror ahead of her, and she'll die of panic if she doesn't calm herself. She takes three deep breaths and imagines walking into La Madeleine, into the tomblike church, where there are only candles and incense and silence.

She goes deeper still, imagining going to a place of peace, where Étienne waits for her. He's there in the dark and in the quiet, and he reaches for her hand. She folds one of her hands within the other and imagines his on hers until her breathing is regular and her eyes are closed, and the terror around her recedes to a place of which she's barely conscious.

She either sleeps or passes out, because she comes to with a jerk. The plane is dropping at an alarming rate, pitching back and forth, careening with terrifying speed toward the ground.

This is it, Violette thinks.

She's no longer afraid to die, only feels the regret of not being able to raise Tania.

The plane lands with a terrible crash, and Violette's head knocks the window. There's a scraping of metal on a hard surface and a spray of sparks flies up as the Lysander screeches to a stop. She tries to think where they might be.

Châteaudun? Chartres? Rouen? We couldn't have got far, with all the blasts.

Suddenly, the hatch is lifted, and a man drags Violette out of the plane. She tears off her helmet and falls on top of him on the ground. When she sees his blond hair and light eyes, she pummels the Nazi with her fists, showering him with a tirade of French curse words.

"Whoa," he says. "Honey, please stop."

Violette becomes still, her heart and head pounding. She looks at the man under her.

"I'm your pilot," he says with a grin. "It wasn't pretty, but I told you, I'd get you home."

Violette looks up. Clement, Miss Atkins, and Buckmaster run toward them, a group of men trailing.

Violette breaks into wild laughter. She howls at the moon and showers the pilot under her with kisses.

41

NESLES-LA-VALLÉE

———— VIRGINIA ————

VIRGINIA AND JESSIE-ANN hear the explosion and run outside to the terrace of Les Baumées. They watch in horror as the Allied Flying Fortress bomber hurtles in flames like a meteor toward the earth. Five parachutes dance, waving in the distance, on the other side of the woods.

Running, Virginia says a prayer of thanks there's no blue blanket on Madame Fleury's line. When she reaches the men, she says another prayer of thanks that she finds them before the enemy does. The Allied aviators are at various stages of pain, fear, and relief, scattered across the field behind the rectory like scorched hay bales. Dr. Lebettre soon meets them. He takes the one burnt worst to his office. Virginia leads the other four, pulling, guiding, holding them until they reach the house.

Jessie-Ann greets them with water—some cool to drink, the rest boiling in case sterilization is needed. Her girls recede to the shadows, sucking thumbs, holding dollies, watching with large eyes.

Nan sits in front of the girls, keeping guard.

One of the men can't stop shaking. Another can't stop crying. One is silent. One, solicitous. He helps the women help his men.

In time, their own men arrive, dirty but in good spirits. Philippe tells them the forest is ready. Paul says the invasion will be any day now.

In whispers, Virginia and Philippe agree they must return to Paris. The phone lines to Nesles are cut, so they are cut off.

It's best if Jessie-Ann and the girls stay. Paul insists. Jessie-Ann begs her husband to remain with them, and he agrees.

In three days, Dr. Lebettre delivers their forged papers and their fifth man, limping but whole. The reunion of the aviators makes the shaking man steady, the crying man smile, the silent man speak. The solicitous one remains so. Some people are imperturbable.

The goodbyes are tearful, but the couples promise many celebrations on the other side of the war. The Blancs know where the piano box is camouflaged in the woods. If the Nazis come, the family can hide amid the canned food and canteens, blankets and flashlights. And when this is over, they will all come together in the capital to celebrate their beloved city's liberation.

Virginia gives Nan one more hug. The dog's wide, sad eyes bring a lump to Virginia's throat.

The return journey to Paris with the aviators is unnerving, but fortune remains on their side.

Seven adults share the studio apartment. It's too dangerous to turn on the radio to listen for "Autumn Song." They'll have to await the news some other way. Gas is now only turned on for cooking for a half hour at midday and at night. The hamburgers are rare.

Lily is in London. Jean, a forest dweller. Michelle, forlorn; her love—one of the last aviators out—is on his way to the Pyrenees. She's being scrutinized by neighbors and can't take any pilots for the time being.

Daniel brings Virginia and Philippe two more men. When the shorter one removes the scarf covering the lower part of his face and lifts the hat covering the upper, he reveals his dark skin.

"Oh," Virginia says.

"South African," he says, an uncertain smile on his lips. "Fifth brigade. Engineer."

The taller, fair man is also from South Africa.

Daniel brings them another. A New Zealander who doesn't look old enough to shave.

Daniel's been called to help find a wireless radio so the men in the forest have a communication line to London. He leaves them.

Ten adults from four continents in a small studio apartment.

They trip over one another.

Happily.

A MOMENT'S CARELESSNESS can cost one dearly.

If Virginia hadn't been staring up at La Madeleine, distracted by the enormity of the church, she wouldn't have clipped the edge of the back steps with her front bicycle tire.

She falls, the pavement wet with rain, scraping a runway of skin off her right leg and making shreds of her already run stockings. When she hits the ground, the heel she'd almost walked off her right shoe can withstand no more abuse and falls off entirely. The basket—stuffed full of black market provisions—spills, scattering an illegal feast of real coffee and tea, baguettes, cherry jam, and sausages across the street. Facedown, she almost can't bear to lift her eyes to see who's attached to the black boots that enter her line of vision.

That's it, she thinks. *All our work evacuating fugitives will end because of my carelessness.*

She'll be arrested for the illegal food. The enemy will see her address on her papers and go to the apartment and find the men. They'll all be dragged to prison, deported, and murdered. She could weep over her clumsiness, her distractedness, her stupidity. It feels as if every bone in her body that has been collecting years of tension, anxiety, and fear in its cells decides at once to release them, like a virus. She thinks she'll just stay lying on the pavement as long as possible, inhabiting the space of the present moment before the dark future forces itself upon her.

"Madame," a voice whispers. "Are you all right?"

It takes some effort to lift her head to see a little man, barely five feet tall, in a worker's uniform, with a broom in his hand. She scans the alley behind the basilica and releases her breath when she sees he's the only person who's noticed her.

She pulls herself to standing and nods. Still shaking, she picks up her things, but she drops as much as she collects. If the little man judges her for what are clearly black market purchases, he doesn't let it show. He helps gather her supplies and reattach her basket to the handlebars.

"Merci," she says. "You're so good to help me."

And not report me, she thinks.

He tips his hat to her and resumes his sweeping.

She's so grateful for this little angel of the church alleyway, she plucks out a loaf of bread and insists he take it. When she starts forward, the basket must not have been tied on properly, because it falls once more, spilling everything they've just collected back on the street. He returns to help.

"It's all right," she says.

But it's not. She thinks she might be having a nervous breakdown. She can't stop shaking.

He waves her off, making double sure the basket is attached, and motions for her to leave. She insists he take the coffee, and the near toothless smile that lights up his face does her heart good.

"HONEYBEE."

Philippe pulls her into the apartment, fretting over her scrapes and bruises. The aviators envelop her, relieving her of her packages, her handbag, her coat. They fetch astringent and towels, ease her into the chaise, and start water boiling for tea.

"I'm fine," she lies.

Running his hands through his ever-thinning hair and pacing in the cramped space, Philippe is in a state. He looks worse than she does, especially when she explains what happened.

"If you'd been caught," he says. "If that man had been in the *milice* or the Gestapo."

"But he wasn't."

"I should've gone myself," he says. "Why did I let you go?"

She becomes still.

"Let me go?" she asks. She rises from the chair, her face hot. "You're not in charge of me."

"That's not what I meant."

"If it had been you, the street sweeper might not have been so helpful."

The boys around them slip into the kitchen.

"Don't undermine what I do by pretending it's something you permit," she says.

"You know I didn't mean it that way."

Philippe almost never loses his temper, but his voice is as loud as she's ever heard it.

"But that's how you said it," she says. "So, you must think it."

"What I think is, if anything happens to you, I'll be destroyed."

His voice catches. Guilt rises in her as she realizes Philippe must worry over her the way she did about Jessie-Ann's family. He must also be coming undone. It's all so much to take.

She sits back in the chair and covers her face in her hands. Philippe kneels before her.

"Losing you would kill me," he says. "I won't pretend otherwise. And I won't pretend I'm not in agony every time you put yourself at risk. That I don't stay awake worrying about you. I just keep my back to you in bed so you can't see my eyes, wide and fearful. I can't lie to you, Virginia. You're entitled to your feelings, as I am entitled to mine."

The teapot whistles. The whispers of the men sound like rustling autumn leaves.

When will we hear the "Autumn Song" poem?

Philippe slides his large hands up the sides of her thighs, pulling up her dress as he does.

She looks down at him, and sees his face twisted with worry as he looks over the scrapes on her leg. He leans down and kisses her wounds. She feels warmth rush down, the magnetic pull of him stealing her breath. He looks up at her with hungry eyes.

A titter in the kitchen extinguishes the heat. She releases her breath.

"I guess we know what it is to be parents after all," says Virginia.

VIRGINIA AND THE Black South African sit in the window alcove, curtains pulled enough to gaze out at moonlit Paris, but not enough to reveal their figures to anyone who might look up. They couldn't be seen anyway. There are no lights on in the apartment, where men inhabit every square foot of space. Philippe was snoring when she'd crept out to get a drink of water and seen the aviator peering through the opening in the blackout curtains. He'd snapped them closed and apologized, but she'd assured him it was all right. She drew the curtains back enough for them both to see.

"Paris is so lovely," Virginia whispers.

"Dazzling," he says.

The sixth-floor studio allows a good vantage. The familiar skyline silhouettes look like sleeping giants. Virginia pulls up her bare feet under her and slides the curtain open a bit more. He breathes out in awe, shaking his head.

"I never thought I'd see something like this," he says.

"I didn't, either. When I was growing up."

"Are you American?"

"Yes."

He smiles at her, before turning back to the scene in front of them. He can't keep his eyes off Paris. Virginia studies the man's profile. With his strong jawline, high cheekbones, easy smile, and gentleness of manner, he's attractive.

"What's your name?" she whispers. She doesn't always ask their names. She almost never tells them hers. But she wants to know this man. She'll tell her future grandchildren about him and all of them, if she's blessed enough to have them. "If you're comfortable telling me, that is."

"Ebrahim Abrams of Cape Town. You?"

"Virginia d'Albert-Lake," she says. "Of Florida. May I ask how you got here?"

"To this apartment?"

"Maybe a few steps before that."

He smiles that easy smile.

"In 1942, I volunteered to be a snapper in the South African army. Men like me are not allowed to be combat soldiers, so we support those who are with the logistics of war: building bridges, minefields, defense. But we got captured by the Germans and shipped to an Italian work camp. Then to a German camp. Then to labor in France, building runways. That's where I escaped."

"I've heard terrible things about the camps."

"I'll spare you the grim details. But I'm here now. And though I've seen the worst in people, I've also seen the best through their hospitality. I can't thank you enough for putting yourself at such risk to help me."

She reaches for his hand and squeezes it. He widens his eyes and stiffens, appearing surprised that she would touch him. He soon relaxes enough, however, to return the gesture.

"I'm glad you made it to us, Ebrahim," she says. "And we'll do everything we can to get you to safety."

42

~⊱⊰~

———— **VIOLETTE** ————

ROBERT SQUEEZES VIOLETTE so tightly she feels as if she'll pop.

"My girl!" he says.

He lifts her up to his great height of six feet, four inches, and spins her around at the door to her suite at the Pastoria, where she'll be staying a few weeks until her next mission. She kisses him on both cheeks.

"I can barely lift you, with those giant balls you have," Robert says. "A bloody wanted poster. I can't get over it."

"Put me down," she says with a grin.

"I won't. I'll never let you go. I had the worst damned feeling while you were gone. I'm afraid I fell in love with you."

"Love? Nonsense, my dear boy, you're incapable. Also, watch your mouth."

Violette nods over her shoulder, and Robert catches sight of Tania. The toddler, not quite two years old, stands sucking her thumb and twirling the dark curls growing in place of her downy baby hair. Violette had relieved Vera of her childcare duties as soon as she could, and Violette won't part with Tania until absolutely necessary.

Tania stares between Violette and Robert with wide eyes. Robert draws in his breath, puts Violette down, and crouches down to Tania's eye level.

"Actually, I've fallen in love with her," he says, his voice becoming gentle. "She's the spitting image of you. But with hazel eyes instead of violet."

"I think she looks just like Étienne."

"I never knew him, but I'm telling you, this girl is undeniably as beautiful as her *maman*. Though she doesn't look as feisty."

"Tania came into this world like a squall, but she's calmed. Far sweeter than I could ever hope to be."

"You've got your moments," he says. "Hello, Tania."

"Papa," Tania says.

Robert throws back his head and laughs, sending Tania running to Violette's skirts. Violette picks up her girl, who wraps her plump little arms and legs around Violette, like a monkey.

"It's so sad," says Violette. "She's started calling all men 'Papa.'"

"You mean, I'm not special?" Robert says.

"Not even a little bit," says Violette.

She sends him into the kitchen to fix a drink, and Clement arrives. He kisses Vi and Tania, whom he met when he dropped Violette off at Vera's, on both cheeks, and places the tray of sandwiches he brought on the counter. Violette puts on a Mills Brothers record, placing the needle at "I'll Be Around." Then she and the team settle around the table—Tania still clinging to Violette—to speculate about their mission.

"Thank God I've been cleared to go back with you," says Robert. "I was burning with jealousy that you two got to spend a weekend in Paris together."

"I had to keep reminding Vi that I'm married," says Clement.

"Breaks my heart," she says.

"Nah, we all know your heart belongs to this Hilaire fellow," says Robert. "In all seriousness, does Atkins have any word on him?"

"She does," says Violette. "Apparently, one of ours is a double agent at Avenue Foch."

"Talk about balls," says Robert.

"Exactly," says Violette. "He reported Hilaire was in Gestapo hands, undergoing God knows what kinds of interrogations, but was recently shipped out to a prison, though we don't know which."

"I hope it's not Fresnes," says Clement.

"At least he'd still be in France."

"Yes, deportation means you're done for," says Robert.

"Hilaire's the strong and silent type," says Violette. "I know he'll be all right, no matter where he is."

"If he's still in France," says Clement, "and he can hold steady, there's a good chance he'll make it to the liberation. Atkins assures me invasion is imminent."

"How many years have we been hearing that?" says Robert.

"Yes, define 'imminent,'" says Violette. "Are we talking months? Weeks?"

"Maybe days."

Violette looks at the wall calendar. It's June first.

"The full moon is—" says Violette.

"Sixth June," says Robert. "Hell, we could be dropped into our region along with Operation Overlord's Allied landing fleet."

"Could we be a part of D-Day?" she asks.

Clement looks from Violette to Tania, and back to Violette. He clears his throat.

"It looks that way."

"MOON," SAYS TANIA, her plump finger pointing at the moon visible in the daytime sky.

"Yes," says Violette. "Maman's moon."

She swallows the lump in her throat and continues walking Tania in the pram to the SOE offices for her team's mission briefing. Thinking of Henri in a dungeon at Avenue Foch has disturbed Violette and stolen more air from her balloon than she cares to admit. She knows obstinance is the antidote to wavering confidence in her, so she'll rebel

until she's again inflated to her usual self. Tania is part of that rebellion.

Violette knows Miss Atkins frowns upon the personal lives of
agents spilling into the halls of the SOE—especially their children—
but Violette won't be apart from Tania for one moment longer than
necessary. Besides, Tania is getting used to Clement and Robert, and
they're all heading to her parents' house later for dinner. Violette will
slip Tania into Miss Atkins's office with the door closed faster than she
can smoke a cigarette.

"When your Papa and I were apart," Violette says, "we used to look
at the moon and send our love to each other."

"Papa."

"Your Papa's in heaven. He's watching over both of us. And when
I have to leave, I'll look at the moon, and you can, too, and we'll think
how much we love each other."

"You go heaven?"

"No. France."

"France."

She knows Tania is too little to understand all this, but Violette
feels compelled to say it anyway.

"One day, Tania, when the war is over, I'll take you to France.
We'll light candles at the church for Papa."

"Candles, *hot*." Tania says *hot* like a whisper.

"Yes, hot. But I'll be with you, so you'll be safe. I'll always watch
over you."

Violette's thoughts turn back to Henri. He was so tender with
Tania, and respectful of Violette's life as a single mother. When the
war is over, she'll introduce Henri to her family. She'll throw him in,
headfirst, and be there to help him swim. Dare she allow herself to
hope for such a future?

Yes, I will, she thinks.

When they arrive at Orchard Court, the hallway buzz is louder
than usual. So much for slipping Tania through unnoticed. Tania is
eager to get out of the pram, so Violette leaves it with the doorman,

and follows her little one, who runs forward—the curls forming along her neck bouncing all the way. Tania parts the tide of uniform skirts and pants like the Red Sea, until she runs smack into a woman who looks as young as Violette. The woman has a high forehead, black hair, slim eyebrows, and an open, wide-eyed expression. She wears the same FANY cover uniform Violette does.

"Oh!" the woman says. "A recruit even younger than I am."

Violette picks up Tania and apologizes to the woman.

"Think nothing of it," she says. "I thought they were desperate when they signed me up, but seeing how young they'll go, now I know it."

Violette smiles.

"I'd love to introduce myself to you," says Violette. "But I think Miss Atkins would frown upon it, as she will frown when she sees I've brought my little one to the office."

"Yes, and Miss Atkins is in a state. Bad news out of France, I'm afraid. One of our chiefs, Hector, was picked up south of Orléans. He's at Avenue Foch."

"Hector?" Violette says. "His people just got me and my partner home from France."

They're falling like dominoes, she thinks.

"It's terrible," the woman says. "One of our best. One of the largest networks: *brûlé*. If you'll excuse me."

Violette watches the slender young woman disappear and proceeds, sober, up to Miss Atkins's office. When Violette gets there, Miss Atkins doesn't conceal her alarm at seeing Tania in Violette's arms. Miss Atkins ushers her in and closes the door. Clement and Robert are already there. Their eyes widen when they see Tania.

"I know," says Violette. "A mark against me. But I'm not detaching my little monkey from my hip until absolutely necessary. Tania, meet Auntie Atkins."

Miss Atkins tries to frown, but when Tania says, "Auntie," and holds out her arms to Miss Atkins, the woman of steel melts. She takes Tania in her arms.

"Now I'm certain," says Miss Atkins. "Your *maman* is not allowed to go back to France."

"Nice try, Auntie," says Violette. "I wouldn't miss this for the world."

"You continue to display an alarming level of self-confidence, bordering on the reckless."

"Reckless," says Robert. "Try crazy. Did you hear about the wanted—?"

Clement punches Robert's shoulder, while Violette scowls at them. Miss Atkins regards them all with suspicion. In a moment she turns her attention back to Violette.

"Because you exceeded expectations in Rouen, and your intelligence has allowed for not only the successful blowing up of Barentin Viaduct but the destruction of several V1 and V2 sites," says Miss Atkins, "I'll tell you the good news, even as I have second and third thoughts about your next dispatch."

"Good news? With Hector's capture, I thought it was only bad."

"My, my. News travels fast," says Miss Atkins. "But yes. For you, Violette, good news. Tania, your *maman* is going to be promoted. No longer an ensign, but a lieutenant."

Violette cheers. Clement and Robert whistle. Tania reaches for her *maman*. Violette takes Tania back and plants a kiss on her plump cheek.

"Even better news," says Robert, "I've been promoted to captain. So, I can still order you about. You'll have to call me Captain Bob once we get in the field."

"I can beat all of you, now that I've been upped to major," says Clement. "I'll be known as Major Charles."

Violette groans.

"The news is getting worse instead of better," she says. "Wait, does promotion come with an advance?"

"Why, did you spend all your money in Paris?" asks Clement, with a wink.

Violette narrows her eyes at him.

"We'll see what we can do," says Miss Atkins, eyeing Tania.

"Oh, that reminds me," says Violette.

Violette takes out a jewel box from Trois Quartiers department store of Paris, wrapped with a red ribbon, and presents it to Miss Atkins.

"What's this all about?" asks Miss Atkins.

"Just doing my part to destabilize the boche economy."

"Boche," says Tania, to the room's amusement.

Miss Atkins unties the ribbon and lifts the lid. She softens when she removes the brooch—red and green jewels with pearl drops. Violette can't be sure, but thinks she sees a sheen on her boss's eyes.

"It looked royal to me," says Violette. "And since I'm almost certain you're some secret princess or countess or something, I thought it looked the part."

Miss Atkins fastens it to her lapel.

"I recently gave away my favorite bird pin to another agent," she says. "This will take its place perfectly. I'll treasure it."

Violette beams.

"Where's my gift, Vi?" asks Robert.

"You got yours," she says. "Have you gotten it framed yet?"

He grins at her.

Pleasantries aside, they gather around the map, Tania watching as if she understands, while Miss Atkins shows them their new destination.

WITH CLEMENT AND Robert, Papa is in his element. The men smoke on the terrace with Roy, on leave, and Dickie, orbiting them, playing soldier. Papa was proud to hear about Violette's promotion, and in awe of the officers in his company. Violette chases Tania through Maman's and Aunt Florrie's legs in the kitchen, where they frost Tania's flourless, sugarless, wartime-ration early birthday cake. The evening light is sweet and golden, and laughter sparkles in the air like fireflies. Maman has put on her favorite Germaine Sablon record, and it takes Violette back to four years ago, when she met Étienne and he dined with them, and her life was forever changed.

I'll likely be in France for Bastille Day, Violette thinks. *By then, the Allies will be crushing German skulls with their boots. And I'll be there to help.*

It's almost impossible to comprehend, and Violette doesn't dwell on it too long. It doesn't feel right to think about battles and bombs when her little girl is in her arms.

And may Tania never have to think about such things once this war is won. May none of us. Ever again.

Maman kisses Violette's cheek, pulling her from her thoughts and enveloping her in a powdery cloud of the Je Reviens perfume Violette bought for Maman at Trois Quartiers. It mingles with the rich, romantic aroma of the Soir de Paris Violette bought for herself. Along with the crimson flower earrings, the white silk dress with violets, the yellow jersey, the plaid frock, the sling-backs, and the divine black evening dress, from Molyneux. Not to forget the kid gloves, ivory fan, and rouge for Maman, the ties for her father, the cuff links for Roy, the scarf for Aunt Florrie, and the paintbrushes for Dickie. Oh, and books for herself. Romances and spy thrillers.

As it turned out, Violette was happy to exploit the German economy, and her family were beside themselves over the excess. Over thirty-seven thousand francs' worth.

Tania's gift is still too large for her. With the little ones largely evacuated from Paris, the shops weren't well stocked for toddlers. Violette had fallen in love, however, with a pink Peter Pan–collared dress with puffy sleeves. Maybe next year Tania will be able to wear it.

When the night falls and the candles are lit, and they sing a noisy, raucous "Happy Birthday" to little Tania, who claps and squeals with joy, Violette can scarcely see through her tears. The candles take her back to La Madeleine and everything is blurry, and she suddenly feels very much apart from everything and everyone around her.

FROM THE NOISY belly of the B-24 Liberator, Robert nudges Violette with his shoulder.

"Why so quiet, Vi? I haven't heard you hum 'I'll Be Around' in ten whole minutes."

"Quiet? Me?" she says, shaking her head. "Never."

Violette can barely get her voice to lift. She's been fighting a funk since Tania's birthday party, further punctuated by their separation several days ago, when Violette had descended into the tube, waving at Tania in Vera Maidment's arms until Tania was out of sight.

To distract herself, Violette had spent her last night in London dancing with her team at the Studio Club. She'd worn her new black Molyneux and broken in her sling-backs on the floor for every single song, taking turns with her boys and Roy, who'd fallen in easily. But even the dancing couldn't shake the darkness that had taken over her. At least, with her new identity as a widow, she can wear the engagement ring Étienne gave her. She looks at the emerald-and-diamond ring, turning it so it catches the light.

Across from her, Clement coughs. He's pale as ever over parachuting. So is the wide-eyed boy at Clement's right. Their new wireless operator, Jean Claude—whom Robert made fast friends with at a volleyball match, and whom Clement vetted with a thorough interrogation—is an American with French parents. Over the last few days at cafés and clubs, they've gotten to know and adore their new little "pianist"—as wireless operators are called. Jean Claude is only twenty years old—and quite a looker—but Violette feels ages older than he is. She feels a rush of maternal warmth toward their new charge and is able to push her own worries aside to assure him.

"Chin up," she says. "Second time's the charm."

Jean Claude breaks into a smile, flashing those gorgeous, straight, white, American teeth.

Last night, after Miss Atkins had got them dressed and loaded, they were stopped on the runway, while picking up speed for takeoff, by a guard waving flares. A pilot who'd just come in said the weather had taken a turn and nearly killed him and his cargo on landing. Wind gusts were reported at over sixty miles per hour. So, the team had been forced to disembark, undress, and spend another night play-ing Ping-Pong at Hassell Hall.

It's now the fifth of June. The weather still isn't ideal, but the flight crew is especially eager to get them on their way, as are they. The team is headed to the Nouvelle-Aquitaine region to help support the Maquis of the Haute-Vienne, one of Hector's departments before his arrest, and unite them to those of Hilaire's old department, the Corrèze, of which Jack is now in charge. Their task is to bring together the war-ring guerilla factions—the Communist Francs-Tireurs et Partisans, or FTP, on the left, and the Armée Secrète, or AS, on the right—to be-come one army, the French Forces of the Interior, or FFI, under de Gaulle. As one, they can pool resources, sabotage rail and communi-cation lines once D-Day arrives, and harass the hell out of the SS–Das Reich panzer division when they're inevitably called upon for German reinforcement at the coast.

After three hours and innumerable cups of tea, the pilot finally comes over the speaker to let them know to prepare to drop at the landing site. They ready themselves and watch for the green light, but it remains red. The plane does a large loop. It soon steadies, and the team continues to watch the light, but it stays red. The pilot does an-other loop before making a sharp ascent.

"Is this normal?" asks Jean Claude.

"No such word in war," says Clement.

They continue to watch and wait until the pilot again comes over the loudspeaker.

"Sorry, guys and gals. We're going home. No reception committee. No lights, no drop."

He signs off.

"He can't be serious," says Robert.

"If there's no drop team to receive us, they have orders not to risk it," says Clement.

"He should leave that to us to decide," says Robert. "I know how Vi would vote."

"I don't know," she says, running her thumb over the ring Étienne gave her. "Maybe it's our guardian angels looking out for us. Steering us clear of trouble."

"Nonsense," says Robert. "Where's my Violette and what have you done with her?"

She recalls her father saying the same thing to her not so long ago.

It's funny how her growing relationship with Tania has made Violette more reflective. Now that Tania is a toddler, Violette is starting to take to motherhood. She can have little conversations with Tania, and the child is happy in a garden or a pub, as long as she's in her *maman*'s arms. Violette feels an unexplainable peace with the situation, a certainty that this night has turned out how it must.

"The reception team probably fell asleep," Robert grumbles.

"As should you," says Violette. "Rest up. Tomorrow will be different."

"That's what you said last night."

Violette yanks the side of Robert's new Clark Gable mustache, pulls off her heavy parachute pack, curls up with it as a pillow, and wraps herself in the thin blanket nearest her. She sleeps a dreamless sleep for the rest of the return journey and doesn't awaken until they've landed.

BACK AT HASSELL Hall, in the wee hours of the morning, Violette kisses her team good night. They head, grumpy, to their room and she to hers, but she's too keyed up to sleep. She takes a bath and gets a wicked idea. Once she's dressed, she posts a notice on the boys' door.

WAKE-UP CALL: 6 A.M.

Then she heads back to her room to prepare herself all over again for the mission. Through the rest of the night, she sips tea and pores over maps. At dawn, she hears a sudden shouting in the hallway. Her door bursts open, and her team accosts her. Robert throws her over his shoulder, runs her outside—Clement and Jean Claude trailing—and tosses her in a haystack at the edge of the field.

"Six a.m. wake-up call," Robert mutters. "Such a she-ass."

Violette pops up, wiping the hay from her clothes. She runs to catch them and leaps onto Robert's back.

"Ow!" he says. "You kneed me right where the Krauts shot me."

"Stop your bellyaching."

Their banter quiets, however, when they're greeted in the foyer by Miss Atkins. She's in her uniform, crisp as ever, but her eyes betray her lack of sleep. She crosses her arms and glares at them as if they're naughty children. Robert eases Violette down, and they stand at attention.

"Follow me," Miss Atkins says.

She leads them to Violette's room and closes the door behind them. Miss Atkins looks over the messy bed and map-covered table with distaste, before turning her attention back to the team.

"It's D-Day," she says.

They each draw in their breath.

"Tonight?" asks Clement.

"No, last night. Seven thousand ships, ten thousand aircraft, and over one hundred fifty thousand Allies made land on the Normandy coast."

Violette and Robert cross themselves.

"You mean, while we were flying back?" asks Clement.

"Yes, they were heading over."

"And the pilots never woke us to tell us to look out the damned window?" says Clement.

"I saw," says Robert.

"Why didn't you say?" says Violette.

"I didn't know what I was seeing. I just thought the waves, the whitecaps, were so incredibly large. The clouds, so dense. Our plane so . . ."

"Noisy," says Jean Claude.

"I can't believe we missed it," says Violette to Clement.

"You'll get to see plenty once you land," says Miss Atkins.

"Why didn't we land, by the way?" asks Clement. "Any word?"

"There was worry over a patrol in the area. We're unsure whether it was real or imagined, but it's always best to be safe."

"Safe," says Robert. "What a silly word for what we're about to do."

"Yes, and speaking of, Buckmaster sent me to ask if any of you would like to withdraw from the mission. You will not be penalized or looked down upon. I cannot stress that enough. France will be an entirely different country than the one you were in not long ago. Even the one to which you would have dropped last night."

The team is silent. Violette can feel Miss Atkins trying not to look at her, and it makes Violette's neck turn red with frustration. After a few moments, Miss Atkins makes eye contact. Violette scowls and clenches her hands into fists. The silence is interminable. After several long minutes, Miss Atkins lights a cigarette with a shaking hand.

"Very well then," she says, after her first exhale. "Bonne chance."

43

PARIS

—⟳—

——— VIRGINIA ———

WHEN AN AMERICAN pilot in their care offers Virginia his last Lucky Strike, she gives him a kiss.

Philippe is out of French cigarettes, and her nerves are shot. Their radio made a terrible burning, staticky sound, and it hasn't worked for days. How will they know when D-Day comes?

The increase in Gestapo arrests and transport of prisoners is alarming, with convoys of captured men and women being shuttled to and from Avenue Foch and the train stations at a disturbing rate. The resisters in the building and in the streets have disappeared, contracting to their hiding spaces and safe houses as Virginia, Philippe, and their people have done. It's almost impossible to sleep, and when Virginia does, she has nightmares of apocalyptic landscapes, burning planes, or Nazi soldiers like the officer from Cancaval or at Madame Fleury's place hunting Virginia.

On the morning of June 6, the phone rings, waking her from a strange dream. In it, the young woman with the violet kerchief at the train station picked up the dolly, but instead of handing it to Jessie-Ann, she gave it to Virginia. Confused, Virginia tried to pass the dolly to Jessie-Ann, but the woman said, "No. It's for your baby." Virginia had tried to explain she didn't have a baby.

Sitting up in bed, Virginia rubs her eyes and looks at the clock. It's six thirty in the morning.

Philippe grumbles and sits up, pulling on his pants and stumbling out, over piles of men, to the kitchen. Virginia puts on her robe and walks to the doorway.

"Pardon?" says Philippe to the caller.

The men who were able to sleep are waking. They watch Philippe, his expression becoming wide-eyed. He nods, thanks the caller, and hangs up, mouth agape.

"What is it?" asks Virginia.

"The invasion. The Allies have landed. At Normandy."

There's a collective intake of breath.

"How do you know?" Virginia asks.

"Daniel said Jean got a wireless message from London and called Daniel from an S-Phone."

"So, Daniel's back in Paris?"

"Oui."

"D-Day," one of the men says.

They all cheer, jumping and screaming, shushing each other and hugging, crying and laughing. As he surveys them, Philippe shakes his head and covers his mouth, his face overlaid with the worry of a father for his children.

"All right," he says. "It's time to go to the forest."

IT'S AS IF a gun goes off at the start of a race.

With the help of Michelle and Daniel, they need to get the men one hundred forty kilometers south, to the forest at Fréteval. It will take at least two days, maybe three. Philippe has made the journey and knows the way, so—in case of separation—Daniel draws Michelle and Virginia each a copy of the map to the woods, including the final complicated series of turns. In the wrong hands, these maps could result in the demise of the men already in the forest and the networks feeding them, but there isn't time for memorization.

Philippe goes out in search of bicycles, but—in addition to his and Virginia's—is able to get only one. An American aviator with a mortal fear of being in proximity to Germans volunteers to cycle with Philippe and Virginia so he doesn't have to ride the rails. Michelle and Daniel purchase train tickets for the remaining men and themselves to get them as far along their way as possible. Unfortunately, because of rail destruction by Maquis, their tickets will get them through only about a third of the journey, to Dourdan, and because of the large amounts of tickets purchased, they have to wait for three days.

In that time, they enlist Mum, Grandmère, Nicole, and Michel's help rounding up food, finding as many shoes with good soles as possible, seeking French clothes to fit the men, and teaching them as much of the language as they can. They also procure bandages to cover Ebrahim's face, and gloves for his hands. Daniel finds a photo of the darkest-eyed, darkest-skinned Frenchman he can for Ebrahim's forged papers, but it will still be a challenge to smuggle him under Nazi noses. Ebrahim offers to ride alone on the train, but Michelle reassures him she'll wear a nursing uniform, and tell anyone who asks that he's a burn patient she's escorting to his family. Michelle even has her own set of forged identity papers that list her occupation as a nurse.

That night before they embark, Daniel brings the rest of the forged papers for the aviators and one hundred thousand francs from one of Jean's drops for the journey. When he leaves, Virginia and Philippe gather the men in the tiny living room to distribute the paperwork and discuss the trip.

"I don't have to tell you how dangerous this will be," says Philippe. "We'll have to spend at least one night on the road. Possibly two, depending upon how your feet hold up and how many checkpoints we have to go out of the way to avoid."

"Once we reach the forest," says Virginia, "we'll camp there until the Allies reach us. It will also be dangerous. We'll be sitting ducks. If any of you want to stay in Paris, you're welcome to use our studio. We can give you contacts and code phrases but, with all the scattering happening and so many people unwilling to help anymore, we can't ensure they'll answer the knock."

Virginia looks at each of her men while they weigh their choices. Soon, the fair South African speaks.

"I think I'll stay here," he says. "I've been at prison camps. Death camps, really. They almost killed me. I can't ever return to that. I'm sorry."

"There's no shame," she says, putting her hand on his arm.

Philippe stares at the man a long moment before continuing.

"If any of us are arrested," he says, "we must resist divulging anything we know under interrogation for at least forty-eight hours. Enough time for the rest of the group to cover a great distance."

The men nod.

"If any of you are captured," Philippe says, "the others are not to intervene. That would gain nothing for us or the cause. Only result in more losses and more chances to expose our network."

"It's every man or woman for him- or herself," says Virginia, giving Philippe a pointed look. "Understand?"

He nods. So do the rest.

After giving two contacts to the South African who won't be joining them on the road, Virginia and Philippe go to bed. Silently, slowly, they come together. Afterward, they hold each other.

"Forgive me, but I have to ask you," says Philippe. "Will you stay in Paris? You can go to Mum's place. Take care of her and Grandmère."

"No," Virginia says. "Nicole and Michel will be here."

"You want to live in the forest, in a tent, for weeks? Months? Eating canned beans. Having no privacy. Surrounded by men? A sitting duck?"

"I want to be with you. Wherever you are. However that looks. When I stayed with the women at the beginning of the war, apart from you, it almost killed me."

"This is different, Virginia. We're outlaws. The Nazis will be brutal if they find us."

"Do you think Paris is safe?" she says. "What about when the bombers come? Or the Nazis destroy the city, on retreat? How long before they declare martial law? And the phone lines are cut entirely? And there's no food. And we have no way of knowing if the other is all right? Paris is not an option."

"Then Les Baumées. Stay with the Blancs."

"Stop."

She puts her finger over his lips and follows with a kiss. Then she turns and presses her back into him, while he curls himself around her, burying his face in her neck. The long hours of the night feel like an eternity that alternates between the bliss of being warm together in bed, and the agony of knowing the danger ahead. When first light comes, they rise, dress, and fill up on the last of the baguettes, jam, and coffee.

"I'm going after all," says the fair South African.

"You don't have to," says Virginia. "If you'd rather wait for the liberation here, you're welcome to do so."

"No, my courage has returned. I feel the hand of fortune with us."

The group is glad to hear it and continues to prepare. Philippe folds the map to the forest and tucks it in his boot, but Virginia stops him.

"Wait," she says. "It could get sweaty and fall apart. Besides, you've been there, so you know the way. I'll need the map if we get separated. Give it here."

He hesitates before passing it to her, but she shows him where she's picked the lining of her handbag to create a pocket. She folds the map up small and tucks it and the money as deeply into the lining as they will go. Followed by one extra set of clothes she's able to roll up, and minimal toiletries.

Once they're ready, an American pilot asks them to pause and join hands in prayer. They do so and, when he finishes asking God for their safety, they look up, eyes glistening.

ONCE VIRGINIA WITNESSES the final duo—Michelle as a nurse, escorting Ebrahim—make it safely on the train at the Gare

Saint-Lazare, Virginia pedals back to her apartment building, where Philippe and the last aviator wait. She's full of emotion as she goes, thrilled at knowing the finish line is almost in sight, and grateful for all the men they've been able to help, almost seventy if her count is correct.

She recalls their first, Louis, and hopes his nerves have calmed. She remembers the boy who lit the Nazi's cigarette with a United States Army Air Corps lighter, and Marshall, who taught her how to jitter-bug. She thinks of the very first group at Nesles, with the Hawaiian man, and prays they've made it to safety.

When she passes Jessie-Ann's building, Virginia prays for her friend and her family, and for Michelle when she passes the flower shop. Virginia says another kind of prayer when she pedals past the Reine Marie, where Daniel poisoned Pierre. And finally, a prayer of thanksgiving when she sees Philippe and the aviator, waiting in the alley of their rendezvous, who fall in behind her on their bikes and begin their journey.

The crowds in exodus provide an element of shelter. Because of the feared coming destruction, there are hundreds of men and women on bicycles and on foot, leaving Paris. If there were cars and babies, it would look the way it did at the start of the war. But most of the children are long gone, and the automobiles are long dry, including the blue baby, gathering dust in the barn at Les Baumées.

Thoughts of that terrible drive with Mum create a deep ache in Virginia's heart, one of fear for Mum and Grandmère's safety, along with a desire to return to Cancaval and live her happily ever after with her husband. To invite her own family, and embrace her mother and father, her sister and brother, and get to know her nephew. Will that day ever come? Will Philippe's family home be left standing? Will anything remain intact after the final battles are fought?

At each checkpoint, Virginia and Philippe allow their man to pull ahead so they're able to watch if he makes it through. There'll be nothing for them to do if he's caught—and they all understand that—but they will at least be able to report to the rest of the group.

They make it in four hours without incident to Dourdan. Virginia's heart lifts when she sees the men and their guides, scattered about the benches and under the trees of the park where they agreed to meet, eating from the rations they've packed. She keeps her smile in check, but the eyes of the others light up when they catch sight of the three cyclists.

"A hundred kilometers to go," says Virginia.

For the three on bikes, it won't be so bad, but for those who've been atrophying in apartments and in cellars for weeks and even months, some still nursing injuries of one kind or another, they will be tested.

The walkers set forth at intervals in small groups, spread apart to look as if they're not together, and the cyclists bring up the rear, shortly passing those on foot. The crowds thin and the roads clear, and after an hour, the travelers find themselves alone and tense from their vulnerability. After two hours, some of the men limp. The cyclists give the walkers turns on the bicycles to give their blistered feet in ill-fitting shoes a rest. After three hours, they groan when they see a wall of rain, like a gray curtain, on the horizon. The wind bends the wheat stalks around them, and in no time, they're exposed in a deluge.

Can nothing be easy? thinks Virginia.

Philippe circles back to the last in the pack and tells the guides he'll ask at the next farm for shelter. But he returns ten minutes later, shaking his head. Virginia asks at the following farmhouse, but the woman won't even open the door. The same happens when Michelle tries at the next farm. The fear is palpable.

When Ebrahim spots a shed in the middle of a grain field, they duck through the crops to seek shelter. Shoddily constructed, with gaps in the rotting wood, the structure does little to buffer the sideways rain and wind. The aviators and their guides huddle together for warmth, while some collapse. Two of the men remove their shoes and groan over their great, bloody blisters. They all decide to hang up their socks in the rafters to dry in the gusts. As evening nears, they know there's no way they'll make it to the forest, or even their Resistance contacts in Châteaudun, by nightfall.

"Stay here," says Philippe. "I'll cycle to the farms up the road to keep trying."

"Let me go," says Virginia. "Somehow I don't feel tired. Just soggy."

"I'll take this scouting mission," he says. "You can get the next."

Philippe kisses Virginia's forehead. She watches him cycle off, the feeling of dread rising so acutely it feels as if hands are squeezing her throat. She sits cross-legged on the cold earth. Daniel nudges Virginia and holds out a flask, which she takes with gratitude. The liquor sends a welcome warming sensation down her limbs.

The group passes the flask and Virginia pulls out her map, placing her body between it and a leak from the roof. The rain has stopped, and the sunset tries to push through the clouds, making everything glow a strange shade of yellow orange. Michelle and Daniel move in close to Virginia.

"The last sign I saw up ahead was for Ymonville," says Virginia. "Do either of you know about where that is on the way to Château-dun?"

"Here," says Daniel, pointing to the paper. "We're about forty kilometers from Dourdan."

"So, we have another forty or so to Châteaudun," says Virginia.

"And then about twenty more to the forest at Fréteval," says Michelle.

"Can you speak in miles, please?" asks an American.

Virginia looks up to the ceiling, calculating.

"About twenty-five miles to Châteaudun," she says. "Then fifteen to Fréteval."

Groans rise around them.

"I know," she says. "You must keep your eyes on the finish line, boys. Don't give up now."

Suddenly, the roar of airplanes screams overhead, and a terrible blast shakes the earth. They jump up to see what's happening, just as a formation of Allied bombers makes a frightful attack on a target on the horizon, exploding it like fireworks. The aviators cheer and clap as great bangs and whizzes shoot out at all angles. Virginia's glad they're not closer, or they'd be done for.

"Atta boys!" yells one of the aviators at an airplane that roars over them.

"Must have hit a munitions store," says another.

Virginia prays Philippe was nowhere near the bombardment.

Soon, a noise at the door and Philippe's grinning face gives her reassurance.

"Put your shoes on," he says, breathless. "We have shelter for the night."

THE FARMER KEEPING them has white hair to his shoulders, a long, yellowed beard, and very few teeth, but that doesn't stop him from smiling, even when he looks around the barn and sees the large party. Philippe had told him there would be five people.

"Easier to ask forgiveness than permission," says Philippe.

The old man struggles to carry a heavy tureen. When Ebrahim, who has slid his bandages down around his neck, rises to help, the man looks at him, wide-eyed, and begs their pardon before he departs. He soon returns with his wife, also white-haired and toothless, bearing two loaves of warm bread, made with white flour. The farmer ushers her over to Ebrahim, and the old woman kisses the young man on both cheeks and presents him with the bread. Virginia catches Ebrahim's eye, sees the sheen of unshed tears, and has to look away to keep her own from falling.

The bread and creamy potato soup restore them, as does the warmth of the barn. The farmer and his wife whisper prayers over them before they leave them for the night with as many blankets as they can round up and a freshly spread pile of hay that Virginia finds surprisingly comfortable. She's stiff when the rooster crows the next morning, but well rested and ready to take on the next leg of the journey.

Almost as soon as her team starts, however, she's sidelined by a flat tire, and when she walks her bicycle back to the barn, she finds that Philippe and one of the aviators still haven't left because Philippe also has a flat. The farmer again gives from his poverty, allowing them to stuff the tires full of hay and providing some kind of sticky adhesive for the punctures, and they again set out. When the three pass the walking teams and see they're doing well, they continue forth.

Midafternoon, a cyclist coming from the opposite direction pedals past them at a high speed. He doesn't stop but shouts something about the road ahead, before he disappears from sight. The old farmer had warned them, the radio said all moving targets are in danger. The Allies don't have the time or visual capacity to sort out civilians from the enemy. They should take cover whenever they hear planes and avoid the main routes as much as possible. At this point, they wonder if it's Germans or Allies they should fear more.

Proceeding with caution, the cyclists move to the forefront, and soon come upon a farmer's truck that has been shot full of bullet holes. Its windshield is shattered, and it has careened into a ditch. There's not a soul in sight, so they approach the vehicle, looking in to see if the driver is alive. There's no one in the truck, but Virginia releases a laugh when she spots a half-eaten coffee cake on the dashboard. She points it out to Philippe and the aviator, before reaching in to stuff it in her handbag. They pedal off as quickly as possible.

After several kilometers, Philippe, in the lead, screeches to a halt. Virginia and the airman stop behind him. A German convoy crawls along the main route, running parallel to their road. They turn back and warn the walkers, using the time to hide in a ravine and rest. They eat the hard-boiled eggs the farmer's wife had given them, along with the remnants of the coffee cake.

"What a scavenger I've become," says Virginia. "Could you ever have imagined me, at the onset of this, picking through burnt-out trucks for food scraps?"

Philippe laughs and shakes his head.

In spite of the difficult circumstances, the group is in high spirits. Michelle and Daniel have not once slowed their pace, and the men with bloody feet say the torn skin they now walk on is less painful than the unpopped blisters were. There must have been some magic of optimism in the farmer's dinner for them. Or they're becoming delirious from how exhausted they are, and how close they're getting to the end of their journey. Either way, it's a good group. They'll be easy to live with in the woods.

As they continue on, and afternoon turns to evening, in the far-off distance they spot the grand castle rising over the town of Châteaudun. Though it's not quite the promised land, they are greatly relieved to see it, especially because the Resistance here works as a link to the forest, and Jean has prepared them for the inevitable arrival of Virginia, Philippe, and their parcels. But the closer they get to Châteaudun, the more sober they grow.

The residents of the town crawl over craters, sifting through rubble. Nazis race about with scowls, pushing around women and the elderly. The guides agree to stand down, turning back and holding the aviators on farmland outside of town, while Virginia and Philippe go ahead, seeking the bakery with the rabbit's foot hanging in the back doorway, where they're to make contact with the Resistance. Though Daniel knows their man, Daniel says his own recurring presence in town has drawn suspicion, so it's best if he waits with the group.

Shell-shocked and war weary, the residents of the town pay little attention to the newcomers. Philippe leads Virginia to a winding street of half-timbered houses, to the bakery of their destination. When they knock at the back door, they're greeted by a young man with a mop of blond curls and a toddler, with the same mop, clutching the man's leg. Once Philippe gives the code phrase, the man urges them inside the back room. The aroma of bread and the man's warm smile put Virginia at ease until it occurs to Virginia how much danger this man and his son are in by admitting them.

"Jean told us to expect you," the man says. "You'll need shelter for the night?"

"*Oui,*" says Philippe. "We have a total of twelve, including guides."

The man whistles.

"We'll have to spread you out," he says. "I'll take you two to where I sleep, with the Maquis. The rest can be distributed to several farms and houses on the outskirts of town. You probably noticed, the boches are rattled."

"We did," says Philippe. "We know the danger we bring, and we're grateful for any help."

The man nods.

"Do you think we could get a wagon for the final push to the forest, tomorrow?" asks Virginia. "Some of our boys have walked the skin off their feet."

"I'll see what I can do."

The man tells them the names and addresses of three safe house contacts, which Virginia scribbles on the back of the map. He asks Philippe and Virginia to meet him behind the blown-up railway station at seven thirty, then he'll lead them to where they'll spend the night. They depart, but on their way out of town, air raid sirens wail. They pull their bicycles under a bridge and huddle together while they watch the sky. When the Flying Fortresses roar overhead, Virginia is elated to see them, all the while hoping she and Philippe don't die from Allied bombs. They exhale when the planes pass over, en route to another destination.

Philippe has a hard time standing up straight. Virginia takes his face in her hands.

"Are you all right?" she asks.

"I will be. I just had a terrible feeling I was about to lose you. Weren't you afraid?"

Virginia looks in his eyes and shakes her head.

"No," she says. "Since we've joined the Comet Line, I've had no regrets. I feel like the boys have been like children to us. And if we die in each other's arms, at the same time, neither of us will have to mourn the other."

Philippe wraps her in a hug. They hold each other a long while before they return to the group.

SEPARATING FROM THEIR friends is harder than they could have imagined, even though it's only for the night. But the blond man reassures them the safe houses are fortresses, and they will all be well taken care of. When they reach the barn, the blond man does a code knock and enters, spreading his arms open like a showman. Before them, in the lantern light, are dozens of young men, smiling, smoking, and passing wine bottles, not one among them without an intimidating-looking gun of some sort slung across his torso.

Philippe greets some by name, and they welcome Virginia as if she's one of them, sharing their cigarettes and drinks, and revealing a platter of cold chicken cutlets and rolls. She and Philippe haven't eaten as well as they have on the road in ages, and Virginia marvels at how completely one's mindset improves with a full belly.

Talk soon turns serious, however, especially once Virginia realizes she and Philippe are about to be separated. Before the sun rises, he will go to the forest camp to make contact and give advance notice of the volume of arrivals, while Virginia waits for the separated groups to reunite at a nearby farm. There, they'll await a wagon so they can make the final push to the forest.

She can't sleep, and neither can Philippe. They stare at each other through the dark, holding hands, whispering about their plans for after the war. He wants to open an antique shop, a place to preserve and sell pieces that honor France. She'll sell dolls from it—restored for collectors and for children—that provide comfort and hold memories. They'll keep trying for their own children, but if they can't have them, they'll babysit for Jessie-Ann and Paul, and spoil Nan rotten.

At first light, she and Philippe rise, pray together for the other's safety, and assure each other that they'll be in each other's arms by noon. After a long embrace, Philippe and the Maquis leave.

Virginia washes her face and hands with water from the well pump, brushes her dirty hair, and changes into the only other dress she was able to roll up and fit in her purse. Then she sets off on her bike to meet the group, desperate for this to be over.

A FLY, RELENTLESS, orbits Virginia while she waits, heart pounding, in the courtyard. Alone, she feels exposed and off balance, all of her confidence draining from her. Watching Philippe move away from her brought back that same horrible wrenching sensation of losing half her body that she'd experienced at the beginning of the war.

It's only for a few hours, she thinks.

A hand on her shoulder causes her to jump.

"Michelle," Virginia says, touching her chest. "How didn't I hear you?"

"You know what a little pixie I am," Michelle says.

Virginia smiles and pulls her friend into a hug. Then she embraces Ebrahim, hidden under his bandages, and the other South African. In a few minutes, to the great relief of all, the rest of the men arrive with Daniel. The American who got the kiss from Virginia after he gave her the last Lucky Strike asks for another kiss, and she gives it. Feeling better, she consults her map.

"Don't you need yours?" asks Virginia.

"I memorized it and burnt it," says Michelle.

"Oh, I didn't think to do so. I'm sorry."

"Don't worry. Not much farther to go."

Soon, a farmer with salt-and-pepper hair under a black beret pokes his head around the side of the entrance and says the code phrase. When Virginia answers with the correct response, he steps forward.

"For those of you who can't walk," he says, "I have a wagon. I'll cover you in hay and vegetables."

The group discusses how they'll separate. Michelle will continue escorting Ebrahim. The New Zealander elects to walk with Daniel. The American Lucky Striker will cycle with Virginia. The other South African looks the most French, and has a reasonable command of the language, so he'll ride alongside the driver. The remaining aviators will pile into the back of the wagon.

Roles sorted, men hidden, bicycles mounted, they set out.

VIRGINIA DOESN'T KNOW if it's the tension or the sun, but she and her partner are roasting. They stop at a crossroads, under an old linden tree. Virginia takes a long drink from the canteen, while the aviator removes his jacket and places it in Virginia's bicycle basket. She passes him the canteen and surveys the area. Weariness presses in on her. If only she could curl up in the shade and let the tree shelter them. She removes the map from her bag to study it.

"It looks like we're about halfway," she says. "Not bad progress, all things considered."

She tries to get a deep breath, but all her lungs will give her are shallow gasps. She thinks that's all she'll get until she and Philippe are reunited. When she looks up at her companion, he gazes on her with near worship.

"I can't tell you how much we all—" His voice breaks, and he looks away. After he gathers himself, he looks back at her. "How grateful we are for you and your husband. I almost stayed back at the apartment. I had the worst feeling. But we're practically at the forest. What a relief."

"We're not there yet," says Virginia. "These last miles will be the longest."

A movement out of the corner of her vision calls her attention to the road behind them, where the travelers on foot, followed shortly by the wagon, appear from around a turn. They're about a hundred yards away from them.

"All right," she says, stuffing the map back in her purse, and slinging it over her torso. "Let's finish this."

They mount their bicycles and start pedaling. The road narrows, and it's bordered by ravines that surround farmland. She still can't get a deep breath and feels shaky because of it. She's never ached more for her husband, or for rest and good hydration. She fantasizes about the mossy-banked stream Philippe told her about, which winds through the forest camp and pools in secret places where they might skinny-dip. After kissing her husband, the first thing she'll do is wade in, filthy clothes and all, and let the cold reach her bones.

A cloud covers the sun and, in spite of her sweat, she feels a chill. In the squiggly heat rising from the road ahead, a blur appears. She squints and sees it's not a mirage. At the intersection, a black Citroën takes the turn fast and speeds toward them.

Her heart hammers.

"My God," she says. "Germans. Pull over. Quick."

She turns her handlebars sharply and bumps over the grass at the side of the narrow road, and down into the ravine, her boy following. She pulls ahead, trying to put some distance between the two of them so it looks like they're not together. When the car reaches them, the driver—a German MP—looks twice at her and slams the brakes. She holds her breath and continues to pedal, but she hears him open the door, and shout at her.

"Halt!"

She stops.

She feels a wave of distress like no pain she has ever experienced wash over her. A weight follows it, pressing further down, making her feel so heavy she might sink into the earth.

To have come so close, she thinks.

With all the effort she can muster, she forces a bright look onto her face and opens her eyes, wide and innocent, at the approaching MP. He's a caricature of the boche—tall and blond, with a face like a bull-dog. The other MP from the car walks toward the aviator, who is only about ten feet behind her.

"Give me your papers," the bulldog says to her.

She reaches in her purse. Her hand grazes the money and the map, and it feels as if it sets her skin on fire. If this man searches her bag, not only is she done for, but so is the Resistance of Châteaudun, the blond-haired man and his little son, and every man in the forest, in-cluding her husband. It's all she can do not to collapse.

How could I have been so careless?

Hand trembling, she passes the German her identity card, while her partner does the same with the other MP.

"American?" the German says to her.

Virginia sees her boy flinch as he fumbles with his false papers.

"Yes, by birth. I married a Frenchman, though, and took citizenship here."

He narrows his eyes. The other MP asks her companion why he's traveling this route, but the American is only able to mumble, *"Oui"*—the only French word he can think of—which makes no sense in response. The MP searches him. When he pulls the dog tag out of his wallet, he mumbles a curse about POWs.

"Are you together?" her interrogator asks.

"No," she says.

"Then why is his coat in your basket?"

Out of the corner of her eye, she catches sight of the wagon in the distance. She sees the trickle of men and Michelle slipping into the hedgerow. The wagon, empty of cargo, turns back for Châteaudun. The relief from knowing her people are hiding gives her a burst of strength. She might be caught, but the rest are safe. At least, until the German finds the map.

The MP commands her off the bike and pulls the purse strap that crosses her torso. She's forced so close to him she can smell his stale breath. He grazes her breast while he puts his hand in her bag, pressing down so it pulls on her shoulder. He soon holds up the stack of francs.

"Always travel with this much money?"

She doesn't respond. He shoves it back in, then continues to search until he finds the map.

All sound around them recedes. It's only her breath she can hear. Gasps of shallow, unsatisfying air.

He unfolds the paper, eyes darting all over it, his face becoming wild with triumph. He says something in German to his partner and holds up the map. His partner laughs, sticking out his tongue like a dog.

The aviator makes a move to run. The German in front of him grabs him by the shirt collar, and a scuffle ensues. To her shock, her MP puts the map back in her purse and helps his partner to subdue the aviator. They punch her boy in the stomach, wrestle him to the ground, and handcuff him before dragging him to the back seat of their vehicle. In the commotion, she slips her hand in the purse, pulls out the map, tears it in as many pieces as she's able, and shoves the pieces in her dress pocket.

She can breathe.

Her interrogator returns to force her in the back of the vehicle. The MP in the passenger seat keeps a gun pointed at them, while he and his driver watch the road ahead, speaking in animated German, laughing all the way.

And all the way, while her boy shakes on the seat next to her, she becomes steady. Silently, stealthily, she slips each piece of torn paper from her dress pocket, one at a time, into her mouth, forcing them down her parched throat through sheer force of will.

She can read the horror on her boy's face when he notices. Without a word spoken, she knows he thinks her punishment will be severe. But she also knows she has saved her people. Her husband. Her partners and parcels. The farmer. The man with the mop of blond hair, and his toddler. The Maquis.

The triumph she feels from reversing what could have resulted in terrible consequences gives her access to a well of strength and calm she didn't know she had. She's certain she can withstand torture for forty-eight hours while they find their way to safety. She winks at her boy, reassuring him.

If this ends badly, she thinks, *I have no regrets.*

44

~~~

—— VIOLETTE ——

AFTER CLEMENT DISAPPEARS from the B-24, Violette winks at Robert and Jean Claude and jumps through the Joe hole into the black.

Knowing it's 0200 hours on Tania's second birthday, Violette feels as if luck is on her side. In the briefing, Violette and her team were told they're being sent to a thousand well-disciplined men who were given a series of targets to sabotage in advance of their arrival, and who await more arms and training. A local maquisard, Jacques Dufour, is in charge until Clement takes over. Diplomacy with others in the region will be a challenge. Their team needs to make contact with Jack—operating in the region south of where they'll be dropped—to work at uniting all the Maquis in the FTP and the AS so they're ready to fall in under de Gaulle's FFI. Jack has had a measure of success with diplomacy already, so he'll be a valuable resource.

"FTP. AS. FFI," Violette had said to Miss Atkins. "So many letters."

"And numbers. Hundreds of men in dozens of disparate groups."

"Needing thousands of weapons. Speaking of, do I get one this time?"

"Wait until you unpack the containers dropped with you. Then you'll have your pick. If you think it's absolutely necessary."

Violette does think it's necessary. As Miss Atkins said, this is a different France than the one Violette was in just weeks ago, and she had felt exposed and defenseless then. She isn't going to let that happen again.

Violette pulls the line and scans the terrain, noting Clement's parachute below hers, and what looks like a tumultuous sea beneath them both. In her mind, Violette goes through the procedures taught in the event of a water landing, but the closer she gets, she sees the swirls aren't waves, they're moonlit wheat fields blowing about in the wind gusts.

Out of the peripheral shadows, dozens of men close in on the landing area, some holding torches. Two vehicles throw on their lights and drive across the field along with them, cutting lines across the crops. From her vantage, the men and cars look like child's toys.

Was the team dropped into a trap?

Once she's within about fifty feet, she hears their voices—French, thank goodness—but she's alarmed by the amount of noise they make.

As she's about to land, a swoosh of wind blows her off-kilter, causing her feet to separate, and preventing her from moving into a roll position. On impact, as she stutters forward, there's a sting in her weak ankle. She rights herself quickly to assess the men moving toward her, limping all the while. Clement is the first to reach her.

"You all right, Tinker Bell?" Clement asks.

"Never better," she says, with a wince.

Robert and Jean Claude drop nearby, and the reception team surrounds them. At the front of the pack is a tall man with a square jawline and a thick pouf of black hair.

"Bonsoir, ma belle!" he says, arms open wide. "So good of you to join us."

He extends his hand to take Violette's and kisses it.

"Jacques Dufour," he says. "I'm chief here, also known as Anastasie. But the Krauts call me *le plus grand bandit*."

His men laugh and pat him on the back.

"I've been holding everything together since Hector's arrest," he says.

Violette narrows her eyes. This Jacques "Anastasie" Bandit looks as if he can't be more than twenty years old. With Clement now at the helm of the operation, Violette knows this cocky little rooster will soon be tamed.

"Why so serious?" Jacques asks. "D-Day has come. We have food, wine, and soon, boches, for target practice."

"Now you're talking," Violette says, sensing the need to lighten her team's mood. "And we brought the guns. Come. Let's get them."

They don't have time to remove their flight suits before the containers begin dropping. After several earthshaking bangs from those whose parachutes failed to deploy, the ones with open chutes land with pleasing thumps. Keeping an eye on the sky to make sure they don't get squashed by any strays, the Maquis hurry to unpack them into the waiting wagons, whistling and hooting every time they open one to reveal the cache of weapons and supplies. They're happy to see that even those containers that crash-landed were well padded enough inside that everything appears intact, including a few bottles of Beefeater gin, which bring as many cheers as the arms did.

Once Violette and her team are reunited with their suitcases, they load the nearest truck bed.

"Could they be any louder?" Robert whispers in Violette's ear.

"Well, they know their position on the ground better than we do, at this point," Violette says. "It must be secure here."

"Remind me," Jean Claude says. "Where exactly is here?"

"Sussac," says Jacques, stepping out from behind the truck and making them jump. "Just outside, anyway. Right on target."

He holds open the door to the passenger seat for Violette, and nods for the rest of the team to get in the back seat. Clement gives Jacques a dark look before taking his spot. Robert and Jean Claude pile in behind him. Violette sees one of Jacques's men climbing into a black Citroën, the kind the Gestapo drive. She can't imagine how the Maquis came by that.

"Hey, Alain!" Jacques says to the man. "I'm taking them to Madame Anna's."

"Wait up!"

"You wish."

With that, Jacques throws the truck in gear and speeds off, wheels skidding and slipping in the mud before lurching them forward. He bumps onto the road and skids around the first turn, laughing all the way. The Citroën soon roars into Jacques's rearview mirror.

Violette holds the handle, eyes wide, as Jacques makes a ninety-degree turn without slowing. The Citroën is right on their bumper now, lights illuminating all of their forms. Violette is afraid to take her eyes off the road ahead, but she remains as silent as her team, praying that she doesn't die in a car accident. At least not before she's killed a Nazi or two.

They barrel toward a small village, and Jacques turns off his lights before slamming his brakes and bringing them to a stop outside a bakery. The car behind them does the same, tapping them with a bump.

"Did we accidentally land on the Reichsautobahn?" asks Clement.

Jacques laughs too loudly and gets out of the truck. He and the maquisard whom he'd been racing start a raucous wrestling match in the street until a portly woman's silhouette fills the doorway, hands on her hips. It must be Madame Anna.

"Anastasie! Alain!" she yells. "Knock it off."

The boys run to her, wrapping her in hugs and kissing her cheeks, until she's giggling and shooing them away, while motioning for the team to come forward.

"Please, *les enfants*, come," Madame Anna says. "We've been waiting two days for you. The food's getting cold."

THOUGH THEIR WELCOME in Sussac couldn't have been warmer, though the spirits of the Maquis couldn't be higher, Violette still feels off, as if the ground under her feet shifts the way the wheat fields had writhed in the moonlight. She doesn't have time to dwell, however. There's much to be accomplished.

After a few hours' sleep, they meet in the dirt courtyard behind the bakery, where Violette helps Jean Claude set up his wireless. By 0700, Jean Claude gets the message to HQ that they landed and made first contact. But the limited view from the courtyard and the obvious lack of security put Jean Claude on edge. Clement insists the Maquis find their pianist a safe house, away from the fray.

"You better find one by noon," Clement says to the young man charged with the task.

Clement, or Major Charles, has assumed command and begins putting *sous-lieutenant* Jacques and his legion of bandits in their places by relegating them to errand boys. Being a member of the AS, Jacques bristles when he's told to fetch the leader of the FTP, Georges Guin-gouin.

"The Commies can go to hell," Jacques says. "We have all the man-power you need. Six hundred soldiers, and two hundred more joined after D-Day. Most of them gendarmes."

"Soldiers?" says Clement. "Not from what I've seen. And as for the two hundred who joined yesterday, I don't think much of those who've been hiding in the shadows, watching the fight like a tug-of-war match, waiting to see which side they'll throw their weight behind once the winner became clear."

"That's a hell of a charge to lay at the feet of the brave men who've been keeping their people safe while making the enemy think they can be trusted."

"'Trust' is a funny word," says Clement. "And you've not yet earned mine. You have no respect for security or authority. You think because you've managed to outsmart the boches thus far we should all be in awe of you. I've been battling the enemy since you were in train-ing pants, and once the armies are united under the French Forces of the Interior, as a major, I far outrank you. You haven't hit the targets that were supposed to be blown up before our arrival, you had no safe house for our wireless operator, and you seem to think this is all a game. The way your men race around town, it's like they're training for the Grand Prix, instead of quietly ambushing the enemy and providing protection for the innocent civilians of your region. I'm not impressed. I don't trust you. And if you don't have my trust, when General Koenig arrives to command combined forces, you sure as hell won't have his."

Jacques appears stunned to be talked to in such a manner, but Clement is on a roll. The angrier he grows, the lower his voice goes, which is more intimidating than if he were shouting.

"One more thing," Clement says. "Every weapon, every explosive dropped, every franc note delivered, will be under Captain Bob's armed guard until you comply. He won't hesitate to shoot any *bandit* who tries to arm himself without my permission. Do I make myself clear?"

Shoulders and eyes low, Jacques manages a nod and a clumsy salute, before leaving.

Violette cares little for the undisciplined youth before her. Since she heard the name, she's been in awe.

"Koenig," she says, placing her hand on Clement's arm. "Did you say General Koenig?"

"*Oui*. General Marie-Pierre Koenig. He'll assume command of the FFI, if we're ever able to get these fighting factions to form a unit."

"Koenig was like a second father to my husband. He was at my wedding. He commanded Étienne."

Clement smiles at her and takes her hands.

"And soon, Lieutenant," he says, "Koenig will command you, while you help to liberate France. Maybe that guardian angel you mentioned is Étienne."

Her emotion makes it difficult for Violette to speak, but she's able to muster a nod. Robert calls her attention with a loud sniff, and she turns to see that his eyes are as glassy as hers. At first, she thinks he's teasing her, but when he looks up to the sky, trying to keep the tears from spilling over, it's clear he's not.

"Enough of you two," Robert says. "I'm going to go blow up some shit."

They laugh as Robert leaves them.

Clement and Violette are joined by Jacques's second, Alain, for a briefing about the SS–Das Reich panzer division they're charged with harassing. The fierce panzers, twenty-five hundred men strong, are fresh from their slaughters against the Russian army at the eastern front and are now stationed outside Limoges, the largest city with a German garrison in the region. The evils Das Reich committed on both Russian military and civilians are the stuff of horror stories. Fear among the local population has increased knowing that not only will the panzers be rolling through the countryside on their way north, to Normandy, but they've been given orders to conduct reprisals on civilians for Maquis attacks.

"The boches call this area *la petite Russie*," Alain tells them, with distaste. "Because of all the Communists. And though half of us are *not* reds, they'll treat the population as if we all are."

"We care nothing about regional politics," says Clement. "Stick to what we need to know."

"Fine," Alain continues. "For every Nazi wounded, Das Reich will hang three civilians. For every Nazi killed, they'll murder ten civilians. They'll also burn any house harboring a resister. And our people are harboring many resisters and Maquis, and there's hardly enough food to feed their families, let alone the hundreds of men who've taken to the woods."

"My courier will fund them," Clement says, nodding at Violette. "Give her the addresses to memorize and she'll be able to help."

"I'll also need a bicycle," Violette says. "With a basket."

"Of course. Madame Anna can lend you one."

"I'd be grateful."

"Would you also be able to deliver explosives?" asks Alain. "Our letterbox is at a bakery near the train station in Magnac-Bourg. If we can get the owner sets of plastic explosives, she can get word to the men so they can blow up the rail line."

"Yes," says Clement. "Add it to the list."

Alain makes a crude map of five locations, including the rail station, lists the contacts at each, and the code phrase that will get cooperation at every stop. Violette takes the list up to the room where she slept and spends the next hour drawing and labeling it over and over until it's impressed upon her brain. At one point a little head pokes around the door frame, but when she smiles at the boy and tells him to come in and say *bonjour*, he disappears.

When Violette returns to the courtyard, a satchel covering her chest, a dull ache in her ankle, she sees Jacques has returned with a short man, who's arguing with Clement. Robert and Alain watch with scowls. When the men see her, they quiet.

Violette walks up to the bicycle that has appeared and lifts the lid of the basket to reveal wrapped bread, cheese, and grapes, a pile of shirts, and underneath, several plastic explosive kits. She puts the shirts back in place and raises her eyebrows.

"Laundress," says Alain. "Here."

He passes her a forged work pass showing that she's allowed to deliver clothing.

"The boches of the region have outlawed most transportation," says Jacques. "Civilians can only travel by car or bicycle if they have work papers."

"Then how do you get off zooming around in that truck?" she asks.

"I'm a bandit, remember?"

He grins at her, and she can't help but return the smile. He's trouble, but she likes his confidence.

Robert pushes past Jacques and walks up to Violette.

"Are you up for this?" Robert whispers. "We can send one of the Maquis if you'd rather. I need help finding drop fields. You can come with me—"

"Nonsense," she says. "Where's my 'Captain Bob' and what have you done with him?"

He smiles.

"Stop worrying, or I'll tell Miss Atkins," whispers Violette. "She doesn't like your level of devotion. It can make you do stupid things."

"All right, all right," he says. "Just be careful, Tinker Bell. I have a vintage bottle of Pernod I want to share with you tonight."

"You know I don't drink in the field."

"Yes, that's why you're the perfect person to share it with."

She slugs him in the shoulder and climbs on the bike, but remembers she isn't armed.

"Give me your revolver," she says, holding out her hand to Robert.

He looks at Clement. When their commander nods, Robert pulls a revolver from his belt and passes it to her. She checks the chamber, tucks it in her satchel, and climbs on the bike.

LONG AS IT was, the trip was good for her.

Pedaling the rustic, green countryside by herself, making contact with hardworking men and women, experiencing the joy of seeing their faces light up when she gave them correct code phrases, money, weapons, and assurances the end was in sight—all while gathering intelligence for her team—made her feel solid again. Even better, she didn't see a single German. She didn't let that give her a false sense of security, however. They could pop up around a turn at any moment.

She had much time to think about Tania and all the places she'd show her baby girl after the war, and Madame Anna had packed plenty of food to keep Violette well fed. Her ankle was the only thing that bothered her, but since she cycled, it wasn't as bad as walking. Tonight, once she's in her room, she'll take some aspirin from the dropped medical supplies and prop up her foot. She'll try not to draw any attention to it so she doesn't give her team any more unnecessary worry. Especially Robert, who she can tell is becoming smitten.

She smiles at the thought of Robert, but she doesn't feel an impulse to love him in any way but like a brother. It's Henri she warms to when she thinks of him. Somehow, in Henri's absence, the pull she feels to him has grown stronger. The remembrance of his touch and his kiss sends the heat up her neck and, knowing what he had been holding back while they dated, she can't wait until after the war to fall into his arms, to confess her own exploits, and to thank him for recommending her for service. She can't explain it, but she feels certain that he's alive. She'll be able to ask Jack if he's heard anything when she meets with him tomorrow.

The sky is pink and lavender as she pedals back toward Sussac. A movement in a field catches her eye, and when she slows, she sees Jean Claude waving to her from a hilltop. She scans the horizon before turning off the main road and pedals up to find her anxious pianist looking as content as she's yet seen him.

"My very own place," he says, pointing to the stone cottage hidden behind a tall hedge.

"Jacques even rounded up a radio for me to listen to the BBC broadcasts," he says.

"It's perfect," she says. "An excellent elevation for transmission."

"With a great view of the countryside. I can keep an eye out for Nazi signal tracers."

She follows his gaze, and they spot two figures she knows well, walking up the lane.

"The team's all here," she says.

When Clement and Robert see Violette on her bicycle, they both pick up their step. Robert is nearly at a run when he reaches her. He almost knocks her off the bike with his hug.

AFTER THE BBC broadcast, Robert places a sugar cube over the slotted spoon balancing on the rim of his cup. He pours the Pernod over the cube, into the glass, and uses a lighter to set the sugar on fire.

"I thought absinthe was illegal," says Violette.

"Yes, anything over sixteen percent alcohol."

"And this is forty percent?" Jean Claude says. "I regret, I must pass."

"Come on, pussycat," says Robert. "We need to put some hair on that chest."

"I don't think HQ would appreciate a drunken, passed-out wireless operator. Nor would our network here, for that matter."

"What network?" says Clement, exhaling his cigarette in disgust.

The man Jacques brought him today was not the leader, Georges Guingouin, Clement had asked for. The man was his liaison, said Guingouin had to change location frequently, and mumbled something about there being important matters to attend to. But Violette, knowing Guingouin's description from their briefing at HQ, thinks she spotted him on her travels. He was wearing civilian clothes and ducked into the back room of the bakery at the railway station in Magnac-Bourg. She told Madame there to please pass a message to her contacts that her commander awaits Colonel Guingouin and can be trusted far more than the Maquis. Clement had been thrilled with Violette's success, and all of them impressed by her particular talent for getting others to trust her so quickly.

"I have hope," Violette says. "If for no other reason, the Maquis need us and all we'll provide. They can fall in line because of either duty or blackmail. Does it really matter which?"

"I like loyalty for loyalty's sake," says Clement. "But, yes, I'll take either one."

The sugar dissolved, Robert holds out the drink to Clement, who shakes his head. Robert frowns and holds it out to Violette, who does the same.

"What a bunch of wet blankets you all are," Robert says, before taking a large swill of the drink himself. He can't hide the wince that results.

"Oh, and give me back my gun," he says to Violette.

She pulls it from her satchel and slides it across the table, where Clement has laid his piece. Packs of cigarettes also litter the surface, and the ritual pieces of absinthe service glisten in the lantern light, making a tableau of debauchery.

"I'll take one of those cigarettes," says Violette.

"In occupied France?" asks Clement. "That doesn't fit the identity of a virginal secretary."

"Ah, but I made HQ change it. I'm a widow now. No acting there, I'm afraid."

She holds up her hand, flashing her emerald-and-diamond ring. Jean Claude looks at her with a creased forehead of concern, but she doesn't elaborate. No need to divulge any more personal information than necessary when the smell of German diesel fuel is in the air.

Robert pushes his pack to Violette, and she slides out a cigarette. He lights it for her and watches her take her first long drag. He stares at her so intently she has to look away. His growing attention is starting to feel burdensome.

"Can I ask you all," Jean Claude says, "did you take the L pill Miss Atkins offered?"

"*Oui,*" says Clement.

"Wouldn't travel without it," says Robert.

"No," says Violette. "There are people who need me when this is over. And I'm confident, if I get snagged, I can withstand anything the boches throw at me. What about you?"

Jean Claude shakes his head.

"No," he says. "I hope it's not naive, but in spite of the wireless operator life expectancy of six weeks, I feel certain I'm going to make it. And suicide is a sin. Even in the face of certain death."

"And capture doesn't mean certain death. You can attest to that," Violette says, nodding toward Clement.

"True," Clement says. "I'm glad I didn't have an L pill when I was in prison. I might have taken it. And I am most certainly glad I did not."

"Then why'd you accept it this time?"

"It's a different France."

Silence falls over the table.

Violette has the sudden desire to be alone. To try to sleep well before her journey tomorrow to contact Jack, to begin the work of uniting the Maquis across the region. In some ways, it was easier when she was on mission by herself in Rouen. She doesn't know if it's because she's a mother or because she's always sought some level of male approval and attention, but she can feel the needs and desires and worries these men carry, especially because of how close they've grown.

Her team is special because of their care and awareness of one another, and she loves them all fiercely, but sensing the currents of their moods is like hearing three different radio frequencies at once. She longs to switch them all off.

Violette finishes her cigarette and pushes back from the table.

"Well, boys," she says, standing. "I need to retire. I have a hundred forty kilometers to cover tomorrow, and maps to memorize before I go to sleep. *Bonne nuit.*"

Robert rises from his chair, as if tethered to her.

"I'll walk you back," he says.

Clement joins them in standing.

"We should all go," he says. "Give Jean Claude a chance to get to work."

Violette sighs, inwardly consoling herself that she'll be alone soon enough. Jean Claude jumps up to kiss Violette good night, but knocks his chair over in the process. He turns three shades of red as the men laugh at him. She smiles, gives him kisses on both cheeks, and once more on the first for good luck.

The three of them leave, Violette walking her bike back with the men on either side of her. She keeps the bike on her right side for support, leaning away from her left ankle, which is now throbbing. It doesn't escape Clement's notice.

"That ankle still bothering you?" he asks.

"It's nothing," she says.

"Is it the one you sprained at parachute school?" asks Robert.

"*Oui.*"

"Do you think you should take a day off it tomorrow?" asks Clement.

"No, there have already been too many delays. Jack is expecting me."

"We can have Jean Claude get a message through to him to wait for one more day."

"No!"

The men stop and look at her, surprised by her vehemence.

"No," she says, more calmly. "I'm fine. Aspirin and elevation, and it'll be good as new."

The men stare at her until she continues forward, and they follow, making the rest of the walk in silence. But when they reach the main road through town, a wailing sound stops them. The noise is coming from up ahead, near the church. They proceed with caution until they get a good view of where a small crowd has gathered. A woman weeps and presses her hands to her heart while a sober-looking group of Maquis carry one of their own on a sheet toward a priest. The boy's forehead is covered in blood from a gash on it.

Violette and her men hurry toward the group, where Alain stands on the fringe.

"Is he . . . ?" asks Violette.

Alain nods.

"What happened?" asks Clement.

"The boches?" asks Robert.

Alain shakes his head.

"Car accident," he says, quietly. "Racing."

Robert curses. Clement glares at Alain. Violette can't take her eyes off the mother. She weeps and pulls at her hair, her grief radiating outward until Violette can feel it in her own mother bones.

THE NIGHT GIVES Violette no rest. She can't get the sound of the mother's weeping out of her mind. Violette knows that kind of raw grief all too well. She'd heard it from her mother, after Violette's little brother Harry died. She'd embodied it herself when Étienne was killed. Each wail had ripped another layer of scar tissue off Violette's heart, and now the wound is reexposed and burning.

Two days into her new mission, and Violette admits to herself that she regrets coming. She didn't anticipate this. She never could have imagined how unsteady she'd feel. Regret and unease are foreign sensations to Violette, and she can't get used to them. The thought of anything happening to her, and Maman again having to experience the grief of losing another child, is too much to process. The thought of Tania becoming an orphan— *No.*

Violette shakes her head and rises, washing in the basin in her room. The aspirin did little to help her ankle, but she takes more anyway. Dressing, she fastens a belt of secret money bags at her hips. Then she puts on a white blouse, a light blue suit, and flat-heeled shoes. She wonders if the virginal secretary cover might have been better, but it's too late to rethink that now. She doesn't have the papers for it, and she left her violet kerchief back in London, with her mother.

While she looks down at her emerald ring, a knock comes at the door. Madame Anna's son, Pierrot, smiles when Violette opens it.

"Bonjour, ma petite," Pierrot says.

It's funny that a nine-year-old, who isn't much shorter than she is, calls her by the name his mother has christened Violette, just like Jeanne in Rouen had. Pierrot places the breakfast tray on the sideboard and points to the bunch of wildflowers in a mason jar.

"I picked these for you," he says, looking down at his feet.

"Oh, Pierrot!" she says. "You've done my heart good. Thank you."

His ears turn red, and he runs from the room.

Violette raises her eyes to heaven, and thanks God for the boost in her mood. She was beginning to worry she might not be up for the journey.

At 0800, right on schedule, the men wait for her in the courtyard. She manages a smile for them and joins the meeting. While she and Clement go over the map, Jacques arrives. Clement barely acknowledges him and continues pointing out the best side roads to avoid the major known checkpoints.

"Jean Claude got word, Das Reich is on the move," Clement says. "It won't take them long to cross into the region. Don't let down your guard for a moment."

"Of course," says Violette.

"If only the train lines were running. I hate to think of you cycling all that way, alone."

"I can take her at least part of the trip," says Jacques. "I've got business in Salon-la-Tour. Why don't I drive her there? Then she can cycle the rest of the way."

"No," says Clement. "It's too dangerous. You're too conspicuous."

"I take that route all the time. I have Maquis and family along the way."

"Today is different. Every day after D-Day gets more dangerous."

"We have a call system," says Jacques. "They call village to village if they see any German movement."

"It's not a bad idea," says Violette. "It's a lot of ground to cover in one day."

"No," says Robert. "Not with the way you all drive. That boy died last night."

"I know," says Jacques, as serious as Violette has ever seen him. "And I take responsibility. I've set a bad example. I'll take it slow."

"It still feels like an unnecessary risk," says Clement.

Violette's ankle continues to throb. The thought of shaving off a third of the journey is a welcome one.

"Jacques knows the area," she says.

"He's got a price on his head from the Nazis, for God's sake," says Robert.

"So do you. And him," she says, nodding at Clement. "And so do I, for that matter."

Silence falls. Violette looks from one man to the next, until she arrives back at Jacques.

"Good," she says. "It's settled."

Jacques gets to work, tying her bicycle to the passenger side of the car, its wheels resting on the running board. She sees a Marlin submachine gun on the passenger seat.

"That reminds me," Violette says. "Since I won't be on a bicycle, at least for the trip there, I want a Sten gun."

"Why?" says Clement.

"Because I'm not going up against Das Reich with a revolver."

"I don't want you up against them even with a Sten."

"What, are you turning into Miss Atkins? Get me one. And a couple of extra magazines."

"Extra magazines?" says Robert. "Are you planning on taking on half the panzers?"

She gives him a look that makes him hold up his arms in surrender before hurrying to fetch her a gun from their stores. He's back in no time, and Jacques is ready to go.

"You'll be back in a day or two, *oui*?" says Robert.

"Yes," says Violette. "I won't even be gone long enough for you to miss me."

"Miss you? Hardly! I'll be able to go a full twenty-four hours without hearing you humming 'I'll Be Around.' It'll be heaven!"

She smiles and kisses him on both cheeks, followed by Clement.

"Bonne chance," says Clement. "And you, Jacques, as a lieutenant, she outranks you, so you better follow her orders."

"Yes, Major," says Jacques.

"And hurry back," Clement says to Violette. "I need you teaching the new boys to shoot."

"I can cover that," says Robert.

"I want the best instructor, not second best."

Their laughter is music. It calls Madame Anna and Pierrot out to wish them farewell. It follows Violette until she climbs into Jacques's car and they leave the village.

"GOOD THING I'M driving, with those clouds ahead," says Jacques.

Violette doesn't respond. She's having a hard time conversing from the growing feeling of claustrophobia. Jacques strapped the bicycle to her side of the car, and she feels trapped. She holds the Sten gun across her lap, but it brings her less comfort than she thought it would.

"The boys are impressed by you," says Jacques, oblivious to her desire to ride in silence. "They can't believe a girl as pretty as you would get involved in a thing like this."

She throws him a glare, but all it elicits from him is a wink.

I should have taken the bicycle, she thinks.

The road they travel is a single lane and winds through close rocky ledges, stretches of woods, and tight streets bordered by houses. Just when she thinks she'll suffocate, the road opens to farmland. But all too soon, they're again plunged into hedge-bordered country roads. After about ten kilometers, Jacques makes a different turn than she would have expected. She has memorized the best route, and this is not it.

"Why are you going this way?" she asks.

"I have to pick up a maquisard. My friend Jean. In La Croisille."

"You didn't mention any stops."

"It's mostly on the way. Don't worry. There aren't any Krauts in this little town."

"I don't appreciate changes to the plan. I wouldn't have ridden with you if I'd known you had other stops."

"This is it. I promise. And you'll like Jean. Far more than you like me."

When they arrive at a large, gray house crawling with ivy, a young man wearing glasses slips out of the garage and into the back seat. He pats Jacques on the back and nods to Violette.

"Jean, this is Corinne," says Jacques.

"Very nice to meet you," Jean says, with a warm smile.

Violette nods at him.

"What happened to Suzanne?" asks Jean.

"Nothing. Suzanne waits for me in Salon-la-Tour. Corinne is my . . ."

"Laundress," she says wryly.

The boys both laugh as if what she said was hilarious, and Jacques continues on to Salon. Once they reach the open farmland, the boys start singing a raucous version of "La Marseillaise."

"Should you roll up the windows?" Violette asks, shifting in her seat.

Her back sweats, and it's not from the heat. She hasn't stopped cursing herself since Jacques turned off to pick up his friend. And with every staring farmer they pass, it's quickly becoming clear how badly they stick out in this vehicle. She should have listened to Clement's first instincts.

The boys continue to sing French songs at the tops of their lungs. When they get to "La Madelon," she feels that familiar stab in her heart. She thinks back to her wedding day, when they were all stuck in the bunker and Étienne had danced with her.

While struggling to control her emotions, she turns and looks out the window. The wind picks up and she realizes she's squeezing the gun so tightly her hands are sore. After another twenty or so kilometers, she's finally relieved to see signs for Salon-la-Tour.

Jacques starts blabbering about how he was born there and what a darling his girlfriend, Suzanne, is, when a flash of light, like a mirror in the sun, causes Violette to squint. She shields her eyes and tries to make out what's at the crossroads. When she comprehends what's ahead, she grabs Jacques's arm.

"Stop," she says.

He looks from the road to her and back, and slams on the brakes when he sees what she does. About fifty yards ahead, at a T in the road, a group of German MPs is setting up a roadblock. When the wheels squeal, the Germans look up. Two at the front lift their rifles and start toward them, shouting at them to get out with their hands up.

"Merde," says Jacques.

"*Sortez!*" shouts one of the Germans, now forty yards from the car. "*Maintenant!*"

Violette feels a strange calm come over her. Everything around her falls away except her awareness of herself, her men, and her targets. They appear in her frame of vision like color figures on a black-and-white background. She listens to her own breath, to the beating of her heart, and readies the Sten.

"Jean, are you armed?" asks Violette, slipping the gun magazines from her satchel into her bra.

"No," Jean says, voice quavering.

"Then, when I count to three, you're going to have to run. We'll cover you."

"I can't."

"You must. *Un. Deux. Trois.*"

Jean throws open his door and takes off running. The first German shots burst forth. Jacques climbs out the driver's side, crouches, and fires back through the open window, using the door as a shield. The Germans return fire, shattering the windshield. Glass raining over her, Violette feels a sting across her shoulder. She puts her head down and crawls across the shards to the driver's side seat.

"Now, I'll cover you," she says. She crouches on the ground beside Jacques. "Go!"

Jacques takes off. Violette shoots—haphazardly to scare them, at first, but then she aims. The short MP with the thatch of black hair is her first target. She fires, sees him fly backward, and then aims for the man who has turned, running back toward the checkpoint. She fires and sees him fall face forward in the dirt. Two other German lorries squeal to the checkpoint, and dozens of men pour out.

She runs.

Jacques is at the edge of the wheat field, and fires cover shots while she races toward him. In her peripheral vision, she sees half the Nazis are on foot; the others run back to their vehicles to take the road running parallel to the fields. Her ankle throbs with white-hot pain, her shoulder stings, but she runs as she never before has.

Once she reaches the wheat, she sees an old woman step out of the barn between the fugitives and the Nazis. A soldier fires. The old woman staggers forward and lands on her hands and knees before collapsing in the dirt.

Nausea rises in Violette's throat.

Violette aims at the shooter. She hits him.

"Go!" she tells Jacques, covering him as he races through the wheat.

As his footsteps recede, all she can hear is her breath, followed by the crisp blast of gunshots.

In, out. Shot.

In, out. Shot.

She hits one of the Nazis in the arm, a spray of blood shooting in all directions.

She runs.

The wheat moves around her and around Jacques, up ahead, swirling the way the wheat fields did on her drop night. A bullet whizzes past her head.

She listens to her own breath.

In. Out.

Jacques falls on his belly and crawls. She follows.

In. Out.

The wheat scratches at her hair and her legs. She can't keep a good hold on her gun. She's out of her first round. After a quick magazine change, she sees the edge of the wheat field open up to a field with low corn and no cover. Jacques waits for her.

"Run!" he says.

She takes off.

In. Out.

Shot.

She looks sideways and sees the lorries crawling along the road, the cowards keeping to their cars, afraid of a girl and a boy and their guns. While continuing to run, she aims at a tire on the first truck in the convoy and fires. It explodes. She reaches the gnarled brambles of a hedge and covers Jacques while he races to join her.

"Keep going," she says.

Jacques breaks into a run at full speed until he reaches a grove of apple trees. He covers her and she takes off, seeing the woods rise high on the hill above them. They can lose the Nazis once they make it there. They just have to make it.

In. Out.

Shot.

In. Out.

Head up, she doesn't see the divot in the field, the hole that swallows her ankle and pulls her down. She cries out in pain and has to crawl the rest of the way up the hill, to the apple trees. When she looks down, she sees her ankle already swelling. She didn't need to see it to know.

"I'm done," she says.

"No," Jacques says. "I'll carry you. We're almost at the woods. We'll lose them."

"I'll cover you. Keep going. Here."

She removes the pouches of money from her hip bags, pressing them into his hands.

"Go," she says. "Quickly. Back to my men. Tell them they don't have to worry. I won't break."

"No, I won't leave you, *ma petite.*"

A bullet whizzes past them. It hits the leaves above them. Violette thinks of her father shooting an apple off her head. She laughs.

"You'll be all right," says Jacques, crying. "I'll carry you."

The trucks get closer. Violette lifts her gun and shoots at a windshield, shattering it.

"We'll accomplish nothing if we both get caught," she says. "It's every man for himself."

"I can't leave you," he's sobbing. "This is all my fault. I'm sorry."

"Go! That's an order."

He looks at the Germans.

"Merde!" he cries.

He kisses her savagely on the cheek, looks at her a moment, and runs.

Violette maneuvers herself so the tree trunk is between her and the Germans. A quick scan reveals at least forty of them.

Sniper-style, she shoots at the Nazis. She aims for the gas tank of one of the lorries. The men pour out and advance, returning each of her shots with their own. Bullets whiz past the tree.

In. Out. Shot.

They return fire.

It's a game.

An ungentlemanly game, she thinks. *Ungentlemanly warfare.*

She laughs.

In. Out. Shot.

In. Out. Shot.

In. Out. Click.

Aside from the sound of her breathing, there's the gift of pure silence, if only for a moment, before the hard consonants on the German tongues get louder, closer. When the first Nazi reaches Violette, he drags her to standing and points at her. When the men following see what they've been fighting, they laugh. Then they drop their eyes, faces burning red with embarrassment.

The commander arrives, moving slowly toward her, regarding her as if she's a dangerous animal.

I am, she thinks.

He bows to her, and his thick, rubbery lips curl into an ugly smile.

"Not bad," he says, pulling a cigarette out of his pocket. "We have a few vacancies, if you'd like to turn coat."

His men's laughter rises, nervous, around him.

The commander notices Violette eyeing his cigarette.

"You've earned it," he says.

He places it between her lips and lights it.

She smiles with her teeth around it. Then she spits it at him.

The back of his hand slams against her face.

APRIL 1995
FÜRSTENBERG

I COULD USE a cigarette to steady my nerves, but it feels vulgar to burn something at this place that has incinerated so many.

Nuit et brouillard. Night and fog.

In French, the words of the decree sound almost poetic. There's nothing poetic, however, about Hitler's order to arrest those who "threatened" German security and make us disappear without a trace. He thought it a fitting end for those of us who had operated in the shadows to undermine his demonic mission.

Incarceration. Interrogation. Industry. Incineration. An efficient, insatiable war machine.

In spite of Hitler's decree, we didn't all disappear. Some of us lived, and some even thrived. I'm among the blessed.

I don't know how to feel about the fact that most of the buildings are gone. When the Russians came in, they burned whatever filth the Nazis hadn't, and closed the rest behind the Iron Curtain until the Berlin Wall came down. Part of me wants to see the places where we bunked in flea-infested straw, and shit in overflowing holes with no way to wipe, and bled down our legs until our cycles stopped, and fed ourselves with the fingers that picked lice from one another's hair, and carried the bodies of our dead friends, stacking them in piles outside the crematorium.

That unholy building remains. So do the houses of the guards, pretty white places that had delicate pink flowers and thick lawns within smelling distance of our barracks. The shooting alley also stands, the wall still stained with blood after fifty years. There's nothing that will ever remove those stains. Not from the wall. Not from the perpetrators' souls.

Many of them were executed for war crimes, but killing the criminals didn't bring back our friends. There's something in me that would rather have seen our guards and torturers sentenced to the camps where they worked us to death, to live the way they had forced us to live. There would have been some justice in that.

I look up at the sky and it's so vividly blue it's somehow too much. Today would have been better overcast. Gray, like all the mornings we had to stand at *Appell* for hours, in sleet or snow, wearing the threadbare summer clothing in which we'd arrived, while our fellow prisoners wobbled and whimpered and dropped dead just feet away from us, while we could do . . . nothing.

They've set out chairs for us at the ceremony. Rows and rows of white folding chairs where rows and rows of us used to stand.

Who organized this? Why did I come?

My friend and I help each other to where we're directed to sit. Bent old women and men, and some young women and men, file in and fill the seats. A speaker walks to the microphone. I sit up straighter when I realize I know her. I knew her, anyway. Her hair is white now, and her skin is lined, but I'd know those bright eyes and that steady gaze anywhere.

I search my memory, pick back through the years, the new memories, the times of good living, until I find the bad memories, the ones I've kept locked up for a long time.

I sort through them like old clothes, like yellowed photographs.

Now, what was her name?

III

1944 – 45

Greater love has no one than this: to lay down one's life
for one's friends.

—John 15:13, New International Version

45

PARIS

VIRGINIA

"I KNOW YOU," says Virginia.

The two women are handcuffed together by the wrist in the armored van taking them from Fresnes Prison to Gestapo headquarters on Avenue Foch. Though grimy, the skin on their arms still looks young, with life hiding under the filth, only a bath away. In spite of the dirt and the hunger, Virginia can see a fire in the young woman's violet eyes, like a torch reflecting over a cave lined with shards of amethyst.

"I saw you that day at the railway station," Virginia says. "You saved the dolly from the train tracks. You said my friend's daughter reminded you of your own."

God, Virginia thinks. *This woman has a child.*

The woman stiffens at the mention of her daughter.

"That's right," she says.

"Isn't it interesting how people come and go from our lives," Virginia says.

"Do you believe it's all coincidence?" the woman asks, her voice flat and faraway. "Or does God give us who we need, when we need them?"

"I don't know," says Virginia. "But if I have to be handcuffed to anyone, I'm glad it's someone like you."

The woman stares hard at Virginia for a moment before looking away from her. Though the woman is petite and has a sweet voice, there's a coldness in those jeweled eyes. Young though she may be in years, she has clearly lived many lifetimes. Virginia wonders how the woman got here, in a prison for resisters, heading for interrogation at Gestapo headquarters. Maybe Virginia doesn't want to be handcuffed to someone like this woman, after all.

After Virginia's arrest, when she'd arrived at the Feldgendarmerie at Châteaudun, the Nazi who'd taken her in had been horrified to realize she'd eaten the map with the contact list. What saved her from certain death was the man's shame. If he'd admitted his carelessness to his superior in putting the map back in her purse, he'd have been punished severely. So he never again brought it up. Virginia and her aviator had been separated, and after a short time in the local jail, Virginia was brought to Fresnes.

With hundreds of male and female prisoners arriving by the day, the woman handcuffed to Virginia was just placed in her cell in the wee hours. Even though the cell is only about six feet wide by nine feet long, Virginia already shared it with two other women. Large-eyed, auburn-haired Janette is forty-three and has the bearing of an angel. Marie is forty-six, though she looks older, and has salt-and-pepper hair and hazel eyes. Like Virginia, they were arrested for harboring resisters. Though Virginia has just turned thirty-four, they dote on her like mother hens. If this young woman is in her twenties, as she appears to be, the women will fuss over her even more.

"I'm Virginia," she says.

"Call me Corinne," the woman says. "Do I hear an American accent in your French?"

"Yes. I married a Frenchman, but I'm from the States. Do I hear an accent in your French?"

Corrine stares at Virginia a long moment but ignores the question.

"You stayed in France for the war," Corinne says. "You could have gone home."

"My husband is my home."

Corinne flinches.

Does Corinne have a husband? Virginia thinks. *It's likely if she has a child.*

At the ache over missing Philippe, Virginia swallows the lump in her throat. If she lets even a tear out, she might never be able to stop crying.

"It was brave of you to stay," says Corinne.

Corinne turns to look out the small barred window. Virginia looks past Corinne, also trying to get glimpses of Paris. In Virginia's limited view, she sees pedestrians walking in the June sunshine, some looking at the prison van with sadness, others with pity. Most, she observes, are either indifferent or oblivious. Virginia wonders how many prison vans passed her when she was free. She never once thought to disrupt their progress or help those inside. It feels like a grave sin that she would have been so preoccupied with her own neck not to think of others'. Especially in the early years of the war when the only thing she hid was herself.

"Hide that," says Corinne.

"What?" asks Virginia, absently twirling her wedding ring.

"Your ring. If you want to keep it, you better hide it. The Gestapo took mine at Limoges."

"I'm sorry. Is your husband French, too?"

"He was. The boches murdered him in North Africa. They've taken everything from me. Almost everything."

A widow. A mother. Corinne has indeed lived many lifetimes. Virginia hears the bitterness in the woman's voice. It's a tragedy in one so young.

As the drive continues, Virginia thinks about where she can hide her ring. She uses her free hand to feel down along the hem at the bottom edge of her skirt. She's able to pick a small opening and tucks the ring in as far as it will go. Its weight there is a comfort.

Corinne becomes more agitated the closer they get to Avenue Foch. She tries to twist in her seat, away from Virginia, but that pulls on the handcuff at their wrists, so Corinne settles back. When they turn onto the street—one of the most elegant in Paris—Corinne's breath comes fast.

"I just came from this kind of thing," she says, with a shudder. "You're not a political prisoner, are you?"

"What do you mean?"

"Clandestine agent? Spy?"

"No."

"Good. You might be spared the worst because of it. You mustn't show any weakness. No matter what they do or say to you, endure it. Find a secret place inside your mind where you can curl up. We can survive anything if we have that place."

Virginia's mouth goes dry.

They pull up to a cream-colored building with black iron balconies. The back of the prison van is thrown open, and guns are pointed at them, as male guards order them down and shove them toward Gestapo headquarters. Inside the building, perfectly coiffed German men and women, uniformed and civilian, walk around as if they're in any old office building, not a place of unspeakable tortures.

In the basement, the women's handcuffs are removed, and they're pushed into a room like a holding cell, full of moaning men, with barely anywhere to sit. Corinne finds a place along a bench next to a man with his head in his hands. He flinches when her arm touches his, and when he raises his face, Virginia sucks in her breath. He has deep, angry cuts, the blood dried black in lines along his cheeks. Virginia sits next to another man with a bloody gash on his forehead and swollen lips. She sees that he's missing most of his fingernails. She averts her eyes and tries to get a good breath. The smell in here is unimaginable.

Mixing new arrivals with those who've been tortured must be a way the Gestapo try to intimidate people before the questioning begins. Seeing the results of their barbaric behavior, however, Virginia finds that she's feeling more resolved than ever not to divulge any-thing she knows. She thinks of Philippe, Mum, Nicole and Michel, the Blancs, Michelle, Jean, and Daniel. The thought of bringing this kind of pain to her loved ones puts steel in her spine.

As the hours tick by, Corinne busies herself by scratching some-thing in the wall plaster. Virginia prays for strength. The stomach of the battered man next to her growls.

"Hungry," he whispers through his puffed lips. "So hungry."

Virginia has four crackers from this week's Red Cross parcel in her pocket. She takes one and holds it out to him. He looks down at his bloody, nail-less hands, and shakes his head.

"Of course, you can't," she says. "I'm sorry."

She breaks off a piece of the cracker and feeds it through his bruised lips. He lets it dissolve in his mouth and opens it up again. Morsel by morsel, she feeds him like he's a baby, until he's eaten every last cracker. When she finishes, a tear runs down his cheek, cutting a clean line in the blood.

"Thank you."

Virginia gives him a small smile.

"American!" a male guard barks from the doorway, causing Vir-ginia to jump. "You."

Virginia rises, steady as she's able.

"And you, Violette," the guard says.

Corinne stands.

Surprised, Virginia looks at her companion. Corinne—or is it Violette?—shrugs and walks past Virginia, head held high. Virginia sees that the woman has scratched the name Violette on the wall, but doesn't have time to see if there's a last name. The women are led, at gunpoint, up the center stairwell to the third floor. Down the hallway to the left, a man's hoarse, guttural scream causes Virginia to gasp. Violette doesn't flinch.

A young, pretty German woman meets them and asks for Virginia by name. The Gestapo guard keeps the gun pressed into Violette's back, and leads her in the other direction, but not before Violette turns to Virginia and says, "Courage." The guard knocks Violette with the butt of his gun, pushing her forward.

Virginia looks at her escort. The woman is blonde and trim and wears a bored expression. She takes Virginia down the opposite hallway, opens a door, and invites Virginia to take a seat in front of a Louis XV painted desk with bronze trim. It sits in the middle of a sparsely furnished yet lavish room with high ceilings. Windows extend the length of the wall, dressed in rich golden draperies. Virginia half expects to be offered tea.

A man soon joins them from a door within, the secretary's neck turning pink when he arrives. She takes a seat at the typewriter at the smaller desk to his right. He's about Virginia's age and doesn't wear a uniform, rather an expensive tailored suit. His hands are clean and well manicured, and his thick sandy hair is neat and stylish. Taking in her own dirty fingernails and soiled clothes and knowing how greasy her hair must look and how badly she must smell, Virginia feels as much shame as she did when the officers requisitioned Cancaval and caught her in her bare feet. That she still has the instinct to feel this shame angers her. It's his fault, and that secretary's fault, and the guards, and the fault of people like them that Virginia's in this state. She somehow knows Corinne/Violette wouldn't feel ashamed, and this knowledge helps Virginia to sit up straight. Summoning all the dignity she can muster, she crosses her legs at the ankle and lifts her chin.

"I finally get to meet the American," the man says in English, heavily accented with German. "Why, pray tell, would you put yourself in a position that would result in you being here?"

Virginia doesn't answer.

The secretary, clearly able to understand English, begins typing.

The man slips a pair of glasses from his inside breast pocket, puts them on, and checks the paperwork before him, then looks back up at her.

"Surely, at some point, your husband, Philippe, must have insisted you return to America instead of putting yourself in danger during a war."

Virginia forces herself not to react when the man says Philippe's name, and steels herself for whatever he might say next.

"Did Philippe tell you to go back home before your country made the unfortunate decision to enter the war?" he asks.

"Yes. For my safety. But he didn't insist. He knew that would be futile."

"An American wife. Headstrong," he says, tapping the side of his forehead.

His calm and elegant manner is more unsettling than if he screamed at her. He's acting the part of a gentleman, but there can be no such thing in a Nazi.

"I have a certain level of admiration for you for staying by your husband's side," he continues. "But I'm mostly disappointed that a wife would not only disobey her husband's wishes, but then she would accompany him into lawlessness."

Virginia feels sick that he's speaking so much about Philippe. How does this man know her husband's name? Was it a simple check of papers and records, or was Philippe arrested? If Philippe was arrested, is he all right, or does he look like one of the men from the cell downstairs? Was anyone arrested with him?

"But it's a lawless family you've married into," the man says, sitting back in his chair. "Philippe's cousin, Michel, for example. Philippe's own mother. Do you know where your mother-in-law is hiding?"

Virginia's spirits lift, if only a little, to know Mum is safe.

"No," she says.

"We will find her," he says. "And then we'll use her to trap her son."

They don't have Philippe!

It takes everything Virginia has in her to keep from leaping from her chair with joy. She keeps her face as placid as the Rance at dawn.

"Your apartments are beautiful," he continues. "Even the little studio where you hid all those enemies of Germany. Such a shame. We didn't find much at either place—it appears Philippe made it there before we did—but we at least got the illegal stash of champagne."

She and Philippe had been saving that for the liberation. A liberation that is taking agonizingly long in coming. D-Day was weeks ago.

Why haven't the Allies made it to Paris?

As if on cue, the drone of an airplane begins. They look out the windows.

----- **VIOLETTE** -----

WHEN THE PLANE in sight is clearly Luftwaffe, the interrogator's shoulders lower with relief.

Why haven't the Allies reached the capital yet? Violette thinks, clenching her jaw.

Further upsetting, she's working through resentment that Clement and Robert didn't manage to spring her from the jail at Limoges. Hadn't Clement been a part of his own prison break? Maybe he should get Marie, the limping American, on the job.

The man at the desk before her wears a Gestapo uniform with A. SCHERER on the name patch. Another man in a lab coat enters from an interior door and places a tray of various metal instruments on a table to the right of the desk. Violette stares at the rusty speculum.

"We heard you were difficult in Limoges," Scherer says in German-accented French. "Perhaps if you don't spit and claw like a she-cat, we won't have to treat you like an animal."

She turns her cold eyes to his. He looks down at the paper on his desk.

"I see it's your birthday," he says. "Twenty-three. So young. So foolish."

She keeps her glare steady but doesn't speak.

"You had a French husband working as a slave for the English. What a disgrace to die in the desert for one's treachery."

That hurts, but she doesn't respond. Between SOE training and her natural instincts, plus the interrogations she's already survived, she's confident she won't break. Her companion, Virginia, however, worries Violette. Wide-eyed and polished, Virginia might be too soft.

"I see you are also a slave," Scherer says. "Used by an organization that dropped you into certain capture. Do you know, we have our own people within the SOE? Some very close to you. That's why I know everything about you."

This knocks Violette off balance. Who could he mean? Is it someone at HQ? Someone in the field? Clement speaks German. His last network was burned.

No. She cuts off this thinking. *Do not let them manipulate you into doubting your people.*

It's excruciating not to be able to react. It's like having to take blows in a boxing match with one's hands tied behind one's back.

"Your friend, Jacques Dufour. Anastasie."

"He's no friend of mine," she says.

"Ah, there she is," says Scherer. "Friend or not, you keep very bad company. If I were your father, Charlie, I would throw you over my knee and spank you for riding around with terrorists. However, because you're so young and immature, this kind of poor judgment can be understood, though not condoned. I have a bargain for you. If you tell us where Jacques/Anastasie hides, that will work very much in your favor."

This hurts worse than any punch.

That bastard is why I'm here, she thinks.

But no, it's not only Jacques's fault. Miss Atkins tried to dissuade Violette from dropping into France at all. Violette ignored Clement's and Robert's protests about riding with Jacques on the trip. Violette didn't obey her own instincts to get out of the car. Jacques is foolish and overconfident and impulsive—traits with which she can identify— but she can't lay sole blame on him.

"I see I've got you thinking," Scherer continues. "Where does Jacques stay?"

"I don't know."

"Yes, you do. And if you ever want to see your daughter again, you'd better tell me."

Violette feels as if all the blood drains from her body.

"Tania," he says. "It's a strange name. Wherever did you get a name like that?"

She has a flash of memory, of her and Étienne laughing, watching *A Midsummer Night's Dream.*

In agony, the only thing keeping Violette quiet now is knowing if she turns in Jacques, her men would be next, and then the good people of Sussac. She thinks of Madame Anna and of little Pierrot, and of the wildflowers he picked for her. How could she sacrifice Pierrot to go home to her daughter? She couldn't live with herself.

The minutes that stretch on are endless, but she's done this before. She knows what's next. She'll survive it again. Though there were no metal instruments last time.

Scherer pushes back from the desk in disgust.

"Fool," he says.

He nods at the man in the lab coat, then strides around the desk to restrain Violette.

46

──── VIRGINIA ────

WITH VIOLETTE SUBDUED and clearly suffering, the guard doesn't handcuff the women.

Virginia holds Violette against her side on the ride back to Fresnes and helps Violette walk up the four flights of iron stairs to their cell. When the door is unlocked, Janette and Marie rush to them, assisting Virginia with easing Violette on one of the straw mattresses as gently as possible. Violette shakes violently. Marie places her blanket over Violette, while Janette cries softly in the corner. Once they're locked in, Marie says prayers over their tiny cellmate. At one point in the night, while Marie hums French lullabies, Virginia hears Violette say, "My *maman* used to sing that to me." Her voice sounds very far away.

Virginia was not tortured, and she hasn't stopped thanking God for that. But it's another kind of torture to see how Violette suffers, to imagine what they could have done to cause her such pain, to make it so she can barely walk, for blood to stain her skirt. It's incomprehensible to think that humans can inflict such cruelty on one another.

The four women have two straw mattresses between them. Marie and Violette share one, Janette and Virginia the other. Listening to the shrieks and groans and arguments coming from other cells, Virginia doesn't know what she did to deserve such dear women. She thanks

God all through the frightening nights that pass, between fitful bouts of sleep, and the long days when they're assaulted with the noise of the iron staircases, the shouts of Gestapo prison guards, and the gunshots that ring out from the courtyard.

Each morning at Fresnes, dirty water they're told is coffee is served. Hot water thickened with enough of a flour-like substance to make one gag is the "soup" at lunch. And soggy, moldy bread is their dinner. Twice a week they're given a serving of cheese and some unidentifiable meat that brings dead horses to Virginia's mind, and makes for a lousy, humiliating next day on the toilet. But they're all so hungry, they'll choke down anything. And each day, along with the weight they lose, goes more of their dignity.

In the days following the trip to Avenue Foch, nursing Violette consumes them. They take turns untangling her hair with the comb from the Red Cross kit, wiping her with a rag soaked in cold water from the rusty spigot over the toilet, and sharing from their own meager rations. Within four days, their tiny cellmate has the fire back in her eyes. And within a week, Virginia is astonished by Violette's resurrection.

Violette leads them in exercises—morning, noon, and night—encouraging the women to squat, to do push-ups and sit-ups. She makes them line up in the tiny cell to complete jumping jacks and leg raises, encouraging even the matronly-figured Marie to join in, insisting that fitness will keep them physically and mentally strong for their escape.

Not an hour goes by that Violette doesn't talk about escape. From the outside, from the inside. How to do it, when to do it, which guards might be bribed. Violette is happy to receive a Red Cross parcel with gauze and uses it to wrap her left ankle. She says all the sitting around has helped the ankle heal, but she's sprained it a couple of times, so it's weak. She says it's what tripped her up when the Nazis were chasing her, so she needs to wrap it now in case she gets the opportunity to run in the future. What she did to make the Nazis chase her, she has not said, but—the way the guards narrow their eyes at Violette and always keep their guns pointed at her when she's in transit—Virginia knows it must have been serious.

When Violette isn't planning escape, she's singing "I'll Be Around" by the Mills Brothers, or telling crass jokes, or teaching them dances like the Lambeth Walk. She never speaks of what she endured at Avenue Foch, and they would never ask, but knowing how she bled, Virginia imagines the worst. And every day their names aren't called at 0700 for the Avenue Foch van, or at 1400 for transfer to who knows where, Violette's power grows. Her energy is contagious.

There are bright moments. The sporadic deliveries of Red Cross parcels of food and toiletries, for one, and on alternating days from the male prisoners, the women are allowed outside to walk in a loop in the courtyard. Though they aren't allowed to speak to each other outdoors, they're able to breathe fresh air and look up at the blue sky over the walls and stretch their tight limbs. Though Virginia knows how haggard and thin they look, they all agree the exercises Violette makes them do have made the four of them appear healthier than the other prisoners around them. If the liberation comes soon, their sufferings will be a faint memory.

At least, Virginia's will be.

In spite of Violette's spirit, there's a darkness in her that churns. It comes on unannounced, like the summer thunderstorms that rage through the courtyard. It mostly comes in the middle of the night, when the fleas keep Virginia awake and she sees Violette at the window, trying to find a place to see out the frosted, barred glass to look at the moon. On those nights, it sounds like Violette's whispering to someone—to an "Étienne"—telling him there's a betrayer at some HQ and to find him. Or her.

But morning brings back Violette's sanity, and—like a sleepwalker—she has no recollection of her nighttime ramblings.

—— VIOLETTE ——

FOR THE FIRST time in her life, Violette can't sleep. She should be able to—she fights perpetual exhaustion from hunger and a lack of adequate exercise—but when night falls, she can't quiet her mind.

It's on a stifling hot night in early August—she thinks it's August—that she hears it. The tapping sound comes from the pipes. At first, she's annoyed. As if the grating sounds of bars scraping metal and the horrible echo of the iron stairs aren't enough, now they'll have to add ancient plumbing noises to their torment. Soon, however, the taps start to wake something in her mind. The sounds translate into words.

"Morse code," she whispers.

Marie snores, and Janette doesn't move, but Virginia props herself up on her arm.

"What's it saying?" Virginia asks.

Violette and Virginia crawl over to the wall where the plumbing runs, and Violette cocks her head, listening.

"Sec," Violette says, sounding it out. "Sssec?"

Virginia looks at her with a question in her eyes.

"I never was good at Morse," says Violette.

To this point, she hasn't told her cellmates that she's a spy—for their protection as much as hers. But there could be any number of reasons someone might know Morse code. Violette continues to listen, whispering the letters as they come.

"S. E. C. T. I. O. N. F. S. E. C. F Section!" she says.

"What's that?"

"The good guys."

"Secret agents?"

Violette thinks a moment before answering. It's been long enough for her people to have fled after her capture, and this woman likely will not be called back to Avenue Foch.

"Oui."

Violette taps "F. S. E. C." back. She feels a little shake on the pipes. Then, she taps her code name at HQ. "L. O. U. I. S. E."

"What are you tapping?" asks Virginia.

"My code name."

Violette gets back "O. D. E. T. T. E.," then "A. M. B. R. O. I. S. E.," and then "N. A. D. I. N. E." She whispers the names aloud. She doesn't know the women by code name but wonders if she's seen any around the offices.

She types "V. S. I. G. N. A. L." and "Y. A. R. D." and hopes they understand to flash the V signal in the exercise yard when the guards aren't watching.

On their next exercise day, Violette catches sight of arms lifting and Vs flashing, and all at once, through the grime and the malnutrition, she recognizes some of her peers. The Jewish woman with the dyed blonde hair. The elegant, aristocratic woman. And finally, the one whom Tania ran into that day at Orchard Court. When the woman sees and recognizes Violette, the woman places her hand over her heart, her fingers to her lips, and blows Violette a kiss.

47

PARIS

VIRGINIA

THE AIR RAID sirens start when they're in the exercise yard.

While the guards rush about in terror, the women look up to the sky to see a configuration of Allied Flying Fortresses roaring overhead. The prisoners shout with joy.

"This is it!" Virginia says.

Her cellmates huddle together, embracing, watching some of their boys flying low enough to see the outlines of their heads. The mighty noise of the airplane engines inspires dizzying heights of joy and patriotism.

But a line of fire like a meteor blasting up from the earth hits one of the Flying Fortresses. Virginia holds her breath until she sees four parachutes pop open, their precious cargo falling to enemy-occupied land amid a firefight. Every cell in her body wants to run to them, to find the aviators, to hide them, but she's a caged animal. Another blast shoots up and explodes a Fortress. She's heartbroken to see no parachutes make it out of that wreck.

The guards hit the women with the butts of their guns, screaming at them to get back in order, corralling them. In the pandemonium, a prisoner across the yard claws at a guard's face. The guard aims at the woman's chest and fires, point-blank. Her body falls to the ground.

Virginia can't move or take her eyes off the dead woman. Violette wraps her arms around her cellmates, shepherding them.

"Come," Violette says. "We've almost won, but that means we're in more danger than ever."

Violette leads them to the prison door, and files them into the lines of women hurrying back to their cells. Once they're locked in, the screams of airplanes and the shouts in the prison continue. Violette grabs a grimy towel, wraps her elbow in it, and uses it to knock out four panes of frosted glass.

"I'll tell the guard the explosions did it," she says.

The women run to the window, each looking out a pane, watching the heavens, begging God to let the liberation come.

──── VIOLETTE ────

WHEN THE SKIES clear, the burning smell continues, but Violette welcomes it and all it means.

At sunset, Violette goes to the cell bars and sings out, leading the women in "La Marseillaise." At the end, shouts of "Vive la France!" ring out until the guards threaten the women, banging their batons against the doors.

That night, looking out the broken window at the moonlight, Violette imagines going inside La Madeleine and lighting candles, praying for those she loves. When they're liberated, she can begin to heal. All of this will have been worth it. She'll have no regrets. She'll be proud to return to Tania.

A prayer, a verse from a long time ago, comes to her mind.

"Greater love has no one than this: to lay down one's life for one's friends."

Even if one doesn't lose one's life, she thinks, *the willingness to do so is enough.*

The candles in Violette's imagination become an offering pyre. She imagines removing the memories of her torture—the beatings, the rape—from her mind and throwing them in the fire, watching them flare up and burn to ash. She thinks of those who have died—the woman in the courtyard, the pilots shot down overhead, the secret agents, networks of men and women, Étienne. She can see the flames of their lives laid down for others burning even higher and brighter than her offering. Their sacrifices aren't worth less because they've paid the ultimate price. They're worth more.

THE NEXT MORNING, after she has written a letter to her parents, Violette returns to the window.

Under a package of crackers in the last Red Cross parcel, there were small slips of paper and pencils. Virginia suggested they write notes to their loved ones, and if any of the women get called for the afternoon transport summons, that woman can hide the papers and try to get them to someone on the outside to deliver to their families. Violette finished first and slid her letter in their hiding place, the crack in the wall behind the toilet.

At the window, she's able to breathe better. Even the small glimpses of the world outside help her feel less caged. Today, she watches the men being led out to exercise. She searches the faces for other agents, but they're as grimy and pale as the women—many more so. She notes that, on the whole, the men are more injured than the women. Many are limping or doubled over, covered in dried blood, and at least half of them don't have shoes on their feet.

The Nazis' obsession with imagined hierarchies dictates their treatment of prisoners. After all this time, they still assume men are more dangerous than women, and dish out punishment accordingly. The boches are more threatened by Americans than the French, so they've treated Virginia better than Violette. Of course, Virginia only harbored fugitives instead of actively sabotaging and killing Nazis, as Violette had done.

Last night, Violette hadn't been able to sleep. She thought they'd be liberated before dawn, but no such thing happened. Now, seeing the men so broken sends a fresh wave of despair over Violette. The cruelty of human beings to one another is staggering to behold. She continues to search the men's faces, when her heart stops.

"Henri," she says.

Her cellmates look up from their letters.

Violette presses her face as close to the window as she can. The man is almost at a prison door. He limps terribly, and the deep lines along his cheekbones are even more pronounced, but she's certain.

"Hilaire!" she screams. "Hilaire, it's V! I'm up here!"

He looks up but is pushed through the door by a guard.

Marie rushes to Violette, pulling her away from the window. The other women hurry to stuff their letters in the wall.

"Shhhh, *ma petite*, hush," Marie says. "Look, you've cut your beautiful face on the glass."

Violette can't feel any cuts, only the pure elation of seeing Henri. Of knowing he's alive.

"It's him, Maman Marie," Violette says, breathless. "I know it's him."

Marie leads Violette to the spigot and wets the cloth to dab at Violette's cuts.

"Of course it is, *ma petite*. But you don't want to get yourself or him in trouble."

"You don't believe me," says Violette. "But I know it. God sends me angels when I need them. It's him. Oh, God, thank you, Henri is alive!"

Violette turns from her cell mother to her cell sisters. Virginia and Janette look at her with pity written all over their faces. They don't believe her, either.

She doesn't care. She knows what she saw, and it was Henri.

48

PARIS

—— VIRGINIA ——

VIOLETTE HAS BEEN exuberant since she thought she saw a man she loves.

Manic, really.

Violette's shouts drew the guards, and when they noticed the broken window glass, they wouldn't accept Violette's explanation, and conducted a thorough search of the room. They took all the things that rightfully belonged to the women, including the precious sliver of soap they'd been sharing. Luckily their letters weren't found.

No one is angry at Violette. It's impossible to be with a woman whose heart is so fierce. And because Virginia's ring is still safely in the hem of her skirt, she's at peace. She somehow feels like it's her lucky rabbit's foot. If she can just keep the ring, Philippe will be with her in spirit, and everything will be all right.

Virginia now has to roll her skirt at the waist to keep it from slipping off her shrinking frame. The first weeks of imprisonment were the hardest, while her body adjusted to the gnawing pain of hunger. She's still hungry, but her stomach no longer hurts, and with the approaching sound of bombs—getting closer to Paris every day—she knows they just have to make it a bit longer. If only she could adapt as well to the sweltering heat.

On August 15, they're awakened by a blast that's near enough to shake Fresnes. Virginia knows it's the fifteenth because they were supposed to be permitted to attend Mass today with Abbé Alesch. The priest has been hearing confessions, ministering to prisoners, and has been allowed to say Mass once a month. Though Virginia isn't Catholic, she welcomes a religious service not only to feed the soul, but to break the monotony of imprisonment.

In the rumbling, the women sit up and look toward the window, a crude, splintery board nailed across where the broken panes are. Virginia can barely see light in the sky through the frosted glass, but the sounds of battle are distinctly closer. Their happy whispers begin, and soon the entire prison is alive with excitement.

The women rise and dress in their sole outfits, which they wash out each night in the spigot over the toilet, wring dry, and hang on the window board. Thanks to the Red Cross, each woman has two sets of undergarments, so she's able to sleep in one set and change into the other the next morning. The clothes are always damp and smelly, but it's better this way than never attempting to wash them, like so many of their fellow prisoners. There's real strength that comes from rituals of cleanliness and exercise, and they have Violette's leadership to thank for that.

When the German shouts begin, however, their excitement gives way to anxiety. The women quickly brush their hair, wash their faces, clean their teeth, and put on their shoes. Virginia slips her hand behind the toilet and pulls out the letters, sliding them in her bra.

They become immobilized when they hear shooting in the yard. The firing isn't haphazard. There are orders to march and line up. There are shouts of "Vive la France," followed by "Fire!" Then there are blasts. By the third round of executions, Virginia and the women are on their knees, Marie leading them in prayer.

"Today, on the Feast of the Assumption," Marie says. "Our Lady will watch over us. She will cover us with her holy mantle."

She leads them in a rosary, the lifeboat to which they cling as the storm rises around them. While they pray, the scrape of iron and metal doors, the pound of footsteps, the shouts of the guards come ever closer until their door is flung open and they're ordered to their feet.

Virginia looks at her cellmates, and seeing the love in their eyes gives her strength to keep her head up. As they file out, Virginia feels very tired but also proud of herself and these women. They have made a fitting offering of their lives, even if they're cut short. It's work to put one foot in front of the other, and not to wail in despair as so many women around them are doing, but Virginia manages. All four of them do, buoyed by one another's strength.

Virginia exhales when she realizes they're not being led to the yard, but toward the prison entrance. They're filed past the processing center, where their belongings—free of any forbidden items, and looted of all valuables—are returned to them. Virginia looks in her old purse and sees her identity papers still there. One has to give the Germans their due for organization. Then they're pushed out onto the street and commanded into lines. Virginia hears the guards shouting about buses, and the knowledge that they're trying to deport them before the Allies can reach them threatens to destroy the calm she has willed in herself. At least they aren't being shot, but what will await them where they're being sent?

The distant bombs, the chaos, and the rising heat are making Virginia feel sick. She takes small breaths because larger ones gag her. She thinks she'll go mad waiting here, but a woman to her right, in the line ahead of her, loses control and tries to run, resulting in a shot to the back. Virginia can't comprehend that the bloody corpse just yards from her is real. That any of this is really happening. That the woman would have survived this long to miss freedom by such a short distance.

To have come so close.

Virginia looks up to the sky and pleads in her mind.

God, where are you?

—— **VIOLETTE** ——

VIOLETTE LOOKS DOWN at the corpse—blood pooling under the body and running like a stream into the street—and says a prayer of thanks for the woman who just saved her life. The woman made the bad decision seconds before Violette would have, which has left Violette standing. Violette had just resolved to run. She could almost hear her Scottish commander's voice from SOE training.

"If you run, you have an eighty percent chance of being hit. Of that, you have a twenty percent chance it will be a mortal injury. When in doubt, run."

But those numbers had to do with only one shooter and one prey, not legions of panicked Gestapo demons, their fates written on the walls they've bloodied. They know they're going down, and they'll take as many people with them as they can.

The guards shackle them in pairs. The metal cuffs and chains are heavy and dig into her skin. Her ankle has been better, but this won't help it. Violette is distraught not to be with one of her cell family, lined up in front of her, but when she notices the woman who has been pushed to her left, she does a double take. The woman has dyed blonde hair, the roots dark. She's clearly in poor health—all the color gone from her face—but her eyes light up when she recognizes Violette.

"F Section," whispers Violette.

The woman nods and gives a weak smile.

"Louise," whispers Violette.

"Ambroise," the woman says. "Nadine and Odette are there."

Violette looks to where Ambroise nods, and sees two other SOE agents. Nadine, the aristocrat, is being shackled to Maman Marie, and Odette, the one with whom Tania collided, has been paired with Virginia. The agents look wrung out, but they're standing.

As the buses arrive, the men the guards haven't shot file out of the prison, being set into lines like the women. Violette scans the crowd, eyes tracking each face, searching for Henri. All at once, not ten yards from her, in a sweet and holy moment of beauty, he's there.

This time, Violette doesn't cry out. She stares at Henri, trying to reconcile the tall, handsome, strong man she knew with the one now bent like an old man, half his weight, limping, and filthy. But alive.

She swallows the lump in her throat and gazes at Henri as he's led to the line two down from her, and just to her rear. She looks over her left shoulder while he gets in place and is shackled to another man. She stares at him, glowing with the warmest smile she has, until he looks up from his feet and searches the crowd for the attention he clearly senses. When Henri's eyes meet Violette's, he gasps and cries. She sees his cracked lips break into a smile and her name whispered on his lips.

She kisses her fingers, raises them to him, and mouths, "Courage," just before they're herded onto separate buses.

49

PARIS

~⌒~

—— VIRGINIA ——

VIRGINIA SEES VIOLETTE whisper and follows her gaze to where one of the men stares at Violette with open longing. Is this Violette's Henri/Hilaire? She wasn't crazy, after all.

Virginia is paired with a woman with bright eyes and a steady gaze, who calls herself Odette, who recognizes Violette, though Violette has called herself Louise. Violette is with one called Ambroise, and they recognize the woman shackled to Marie, who's called Nadine. All the names are dizzying. She's glad she's simply Virginia.

And also, honeybee, she thinks with a sting of pain in her heart.

Virginia's attention returns to her throbbing, shackled ankle. Learning to walk while chained to another woman while bombs echo in the distance and a dead person lies in the gutter is almost more than Virginia can endure. Odette loops her arm through Virginia's and the two soon find a rhythm. They're herded and loaded onto buses that are meant for fifty but are at standing room only, with over a hundred starving, stinking, frightened women and guards. Virginia holds her partner back to let Violette and hers pass so Virginia can be last on the bus, next to the driver.

He looks to be in his late fifties and like he's trying not to get sick. He uses his handkerchief to wipe his sweat, and mutters prayers.

When the guard pushing them in steps back off the bus to consult with his commander, Virginia reaches into her bra, removes her cell-mates' letters, and touches the driver's shoulder. He jumps in his seat.

"Monsieur," she says.

She holds the letters out to him. He grabs them and slides them into his shirt pocket.

"For our relatives," she says. "Please deliver them."

"I promise, I will," he says. "I'm so sorry. They make me do this at gunpoint all day long. God forgive me."

"It's all right," Virginia says. "Where are the Allies? Do we have any hope?"

"Last I heard, Rambouillet."

Odette curses.

"So close," Virginia says.

"Not close enough," says Violette.

The guard boards the bus, and shouts at the driver to go. The driver pulls the door lever and steps on the accelerator. The bus groans to life, and the women groan right along with it. The Gestapo guard shoots a hole in the ceiling, stunning them all to silence.

"For every complaint, I'll shoot one of you. If you try to escape, I'll shoot five of you."

Virginia contracts as far from him as she's able, huddled toward Odette. She can barely breathe.

The convoy of prisoners starts making its way through the streets of Paris. This time, the pedestrians they pass shout and cry for the bus to stop. Some brave souls bang the sides of it. Virginia feels as if her heart will break. At a large hill, the bus refuses to climb. The weight is too much.

"Off!" the guard shouts, pushing the chained women in pairs until only half remain on board.

At gunpoint, they walk alongside the bus. Laboring up the street in chains, Virginia thinks of Jesus climbing to Golgotha, but instead of jeers from the crowd, from their apartments the people shout words of encouragement to the prisoners and rain curses on the Gestapo, who fire at faces quickly disappearing from windows.

"You will be liberated! Stay strong!"

"Vive la France!"

The encouragement gives the women strength, but all too soon, the bus reaches the top of the hill, and they're forced back on board.

An hour later, soaked with sweat, Virginia looks up to see where they've stopped. Her heart sinks further when she reads the sign.

GARE DE L'EST.

The east. To Germany.

They're marched to the train yard, where they pass hundreds of frantic German civilians. In the chaos, a tall blonde in a yellow silk suit, carrying a white cat with a black jeweled collar, orders a porter to be careful with her towering carts of luggage and furnishings, crates of wine and artwork. When the filthy prisoners file past the woman, she wrinkles her face in disgust and covers her nose with an embroidered handkerchief. After Virginia passes her, she hears the woman shriek. Virginia looks over her shoulder and sees the woman wiping spit off her face and insisting the guards arrest the perpetrator. But the tide of prisoners moves too fast, and she's soon far behind them.

All Virginia can see is the grin on Violette's face.

—— **VIOLETTE** ——

"IT'S TOO BAD I had to waste that spit," says Violette. "I'm dying of thirst."

Ambroise can barely muster a smile, but Virginia and Odette stifle giggles.

Violette's comic relief is short-lived, however. The prisoners are lined up in the railcar yard, with the relentless sun climbing higher. Ambroise can barely stand, so Violette props up her partner. The men soon file in lines beside them, and Violette is again given the sweet reward of catching Henri's eye. In spite of his obvious discomfort, he does his best to stand up straight when he sees her. She can't imagine where they're going, but if Henri is there, she'll be able to survive it.

Violette observes her cellmates, assessing their conditions. Her beloved Maman Marie is upright, enduring the journey admirably. Janette is strangely pale in spite of the temperatures, and she and Nadine are leaning on each other. Virginia and Odette, with their bright eyes and soft smiles, look the best. Both women still have their strength.

The engine soon appears, followed by passenger compartments, followed by cattle cars. Seeing each car, Violette's spirits sink lower and lower. There are no windows in cattle cars, only small skylights at the top of each, and the signs on the side read: 30 HORSES. 40 MEN.

Virginia gasps.

"Are we meant to . . . ?" she asks, her question falling off.

Violette feels pity for her friend who is still able to be surprised by Nazi cruelty, especially because Violette senses their conditions are about to get much worse than they've been.

Out of nowhere, while dozens of wounded German soldiers are boarded onto the passenger cars, Red Cross representatives appear like angels, passing out parcels to the women, telling them there's a day's supply of water in the jugs, and whispering the transport will never reach the German border. Sadly, they run out of parcels before they get to the men.

To Violette's surprise, the female prisoners are allowed in the third-class compartments, but they're soon filled, and the men are forced into the cattle cars. In the car behind theirs, there's a walkway down the center, but the seats have all been removed, and iron bars run, floor to ceiling, on each side of the walkway. The men are stuffed into the cages, standing room only, and locked in. Henri is one of the last pushed in the car behind hers, and Violette feels sick knowing he's in such conditions. Once the outer doors are shut, closing off her view, and the armed guards are in place, Violette looks out the window, waiting for the train to move.

They sit for hours in oppressive heat. She takes the time to see what's left in her old satchel, the one that has accompanied her through two missions, two prisons, two lifetimes, really. Her false papers are gone. The linings are empty. All that remains is an official-looking

Nazi document, bearing the photograph from her forged identity card and a seal, that lists her real name, true personal information, and the words *Politischer Gefangener* handwritten in red.

Political prisoner.

She shoves the papers back in and looks at Ambroise. The woman is either asleep or passed out, her head hanging forward at an awkward angle. Violette resists opening the jug as long as possible, but when she sees Virginia take a long, satisfying drink, Violette can stand it no longer. The water is like a drug, and she can barely keep herself from finishing the entire container at once. She forces it away with a gasp and screws on the lid, pushing it back in the box and chastising herself for being such a vampire. She'll need more discipline if she's going to keep up her strength.

When Odette has the courage to ask to use the lavatory, they're all relieved to take turns—humiliating though it is, strapped to another—cooling down with the water from the sink and refilling their jugs. But the men are thirsty, and they are cooking. Violette can hear them shouting, crying out, begging for water, and the longer they sit, the more she thinks she'll go mad listening to them. Some sound as if they've already lost their minds.

When the whistle finally blows and the train lurches to life, some of the women cheer, but others, like Violette, can't bring themselves to muster excitement for deportation.

As Paris recedes from view, as the train gathers speed, shooting them faster and faster to Germany, it's all Violette can do not to break open the window and scream. When they cross a tall bridge, she's glad she's shackled to Ambroise. Otherwise, she doesn't know if she'd be able to keep herself from jumping.

She's glad she didn't take the L pill, because she might have swallowed it.

50

—— VIRGINIA ——

THE SCREAM OF the bomb, followed by the blast, yanks Virginia from sleep.

As the train lurches to a stop, Virginia and Odette reach for each other.

Another explosion falls nearby, shaking their compartment.

Guards throw open the doors to the next passenger car and push forward, shouting in German. In the rising excitement, Virginia looks out the window into the night to see the shadows of airplanes roaring overhead.

"It's the Allies!" Violette says. "I knew they'd help us."

The women cheer, but panic ensues with the men trapped in iron cages. They bang the bars and scream that they'll be burned alive. In the moonlight and the firelight, Virginia sees that a pair of male prisoners manages to escape a car farther down the line, but a guard shoots them. She and Odette squeeze each other tighter.

Able-bodied German soldiers and Gestapo guards flee the train and race for cover. Another bomb falls. Virginia closes her eyes and prays, but the explosion rocks the passenger car ahead of them, which is carrying wounded German soldiers. Some scream while others crawl off, rolling to put out the fires burning their skin.

The agonizing sound of the male prisoners trapped in the cattle car, begging for water, is something Virginia thinks she'll never be able to stop hearing. Another blast falls nearby, and in the light, she sees Violette encouraging her partner to stand.

"No," Virginia says. "Violette, they'll shoot you."

"They won't," Violette says. "The cowards are hiding, leaving their own wounded to die. We need to get our men water."

Violette leads Ambroise to the lavatory sink to fill their empty jugs. When they start for the men's car, Virginia and Odette look at each other and silently agree to help. They rise to fill their jugs at the sink, and when Violette and Ambroise return, they swap out the jugs.

Violette and Ambroise make trip after trip to give water to the dying men. Blast after blast falls, and Violette doesn't waver. A woman—barely five feet tall, who has lost her husband, with a daughter somewhere in this broken world—thinks nothing of her own safety. While most of the women cower under their seats, Violette leads Ambroise in hydrating as many men as possible. Violette makes countless trips, never losing her good cheer. Virginia can hear Violette joking with the boys, teasing them, even making some laugh while they're trapped, telling them that though she's a lousy barmaid, she expects an overflowing tip jar.

Every blast that lights up the dark compartment in reddish orange illuminates Violette's face. Her countenance reminds Virginia of the mighty golden Joan of Arc statue in the Tuileries. Virginia thinks she has never seen anyone so beautiful or so powerful in her life.

In a break from the bombing, Marie calls to them.

"The guards are coming!"

Violette and Ambroise, Virginia and Odette collapse in exhaustion just before the Gestapo return and order the women off the train. The men are unlocked from their cages, and rows of shackled prisoners are led at gunpoint—past many dead German bodies and the two of their own who tried to escape—over many miles until they reach a farm. They're sent into barns of empty horse stalls, divided down the center by walkways, with the men on one side and women on the other. At their barn, just before turning in, Virginia catches sight of a familiar face among the men. It's her jitterbug partner.

"Marshall!" she calls, in disbelief.

What a strange, sad reunion this is for so many of them.

Marshall doesn't hear her and is led farther away. Though Virginia's heart was briefly lifted to see the aviator, she's filled with sadness to know that he never made it home.

—— **VIOLETTE** ——

VIOLETTE NEVER LOSES track of Henri and manipulates her position to be kept in the horse stall across from his. After the guard pushes the women on one side and the men on the other, and keeps moving down the line, Violette sits in her doorway and Henri in his, their tired, worn partners collapsed at their sides.

They stare in wonder across the darkness, unable to find the words to convey how they feel. Unable to express their perfect happiness to be sitting across from each other, even under such terrible circumstances. It's Henri who speaks first. In spite of his haggard appearance, his voice remains deep and smooth, a gentle river bearing Violette to tranquility.

"You saved my life, *chérie*. All of ours. We would have died if you hadn't got that water."

"I owed you," she says. "For saving mine. For getting the warning to my team in time."

"But you also saved my life when you called to me, like an angel from heaven, while I was in the yard at Fresnes. I had lost my faith until I heard your sweet voice. I had just been thinking I would lunge at the guard to force him to shoot me so the suffering would end."

"But seeing you at Fresnes saved my life. I was losing my will to go on."

"Then I guess we're even," he says.

He breaks and covers his face with his dirty hands.

"I'm sorry," he says, crying. "I never loved anyone more than when I saw you knocked off your feet from a bomb and come up smiling, not spilling a drop of water, to trickle it into my lips through iron bars. You kept encouraging and joking. I've never seen anything like it."

"You'd have done the same for me," she says.

He leans his head back against the door and gazes at her, shaking his head.

"I want to touch you," he says.

Violette reaches out her hand, as he does, but they're too far apart.

Ambroise nudges Violette's leg.

"I'll move closer," Ambroise whispers.

"Thank you," says Violette.

The women shift, scooting slowly, quietly, until Violette is able to reach for Henri. When he takes her hand, she feels as if a current runs through it, pulsing a wave of peace and love through her body. She didn't know she could ever again feel such a thing. Henri whispers to his partner, who obliges his request to move closer, and Henri brings Violette's hand to his dry lips and kisses it. Violette feels the same thrill from his lips on her hand as she did from his kiss at the theater.

All through the night, exhausted though they are, they whisper, telling each other every little thing that has happened since they parted. He recounts his success growing the Maquis of his region, but how a moment of carelessness on his part—not watching out a window during his pianist's transmission—made him miss the police car. He tells her about the horrors of solitary confinement alternated with what he endured at the hands of the Gestapo. Of the near drowning water torture at Avenue Foch. But he's proud to report he never gave up a single name.

"Why are you limping?" she asks.

"I saw an open door on the Fresnes yard, and tried to escape, but they shot me in the leg. They tossed me in my cell, and all I had to get the bullet out was a spoon."

She winces.

"The area is healing because one of the Red Cross parcels had alcohol swabs. I'm considering a career as a surgeon when I leave. I do my best work with kitchen utensils."

She smiles, and then she tells him everything. From how big Tania's growing, to Violette's SOE training with Jack, to her mission to Rouen, to how she got caught on her second mission, and the Germans she killed. She can see how Henri suffers to hear what tortures she endured from the Gestapo, so censors the worst and expresses her pride at also surviving without giving up any names or information.

The words never run out. Once they've talked about the past, they shift to the future. They speak their desires aloud, daring to make plans for after the war. Once Paris is liberated, they'll fetch Tania and she can join them while they stay at the Reine Marie, and drink coffee under the red awnings at Fouquet's, and buy novels at the bouquinistes on the Seine, and shop at Trois Quartiers, and light candles at La Madeleine. And though the dawn comes, and they've had not a moment of sleep, they feel as if they're ready for whatever awaits them.

When the rounding up begins, and it's clear they'll be separated, they risk coming together. Violette presses her lips to Henri's and they wrap their arms around each other, and before he's yanked away from her, they say the words at the same time.

"Je t'aime."

51

FÜRSTENBERG

——— VIRGINIA ———

RAVENSBRÜCK.

Virginia thinks that even in German the name sounds as pretty as the pine forests that surround the camp. The word calls to mind rooks and brooks, picnics along the lake outside the fence, where in the distance the lovely church spire rises, sounding its melodic bells over the bucolic village surrounding it. But all the beauty around Ravensbrück is a cruel mockery compared to what waits inside the gates.

Though unshackled, they limp. One hundred forty-four hours in chains will do that. Virginia and her cellmates, and an ever-growing number of women whom Violette seems to recognize, hobble along the border of town, through sandy paths, past charming homes where German mothers hang laundry or clip flowers, and their children run, in knee socks, through gardens teeming with butterflies. The children stop and stare. The mothers avert their eyes.

Virginia tries to swallow; she bites the edges of her tongue, trying to produce some kind of saliva to relieve the terrible thirst. But her tongue stopped rewarding her a day ago. Now it's swollen and sore, like her feet.

They're paraded over sand roads, along barbed wire fences, and under a massive green gate, where their train guards abandon them to the most vicious-looking, stocky pack of uniformed German women imaginable. As the prisoners pass, the guards lash them with whips, kick them, beat them over the heads with batons, and allow their dogs to lunge at and bite them.

They're filed into a concrete building, where the women are recorded in a register. Upon admittance, the prisoners are given a number on a white piece of fabric. Virginia's is 57,631. She stares at it, the realization dawning that it's a tally, which means all the numbers that preceded it are women who've come before her. A slap brings her attention back to the admittance station. A scowling woman wearing prison garb, with a green triangle over her number, thrusts a red felt triangle at Virginia with a black *F* written on it. Virginia sees that the women from her cell are also given red triangles with *F* inside, except Ambroise, who's also given a yellow triangle.

"What can this mean?" Virginia whispers to Violette.

"Political prisoners. French."

"But I'm not a political prisoner. I'm not a spy."

"Would you like to file a complaint? Speak to the management?"

Violette grins at Virginia, who can't help but return it.

Thank God for her, Virginia thinks.

They continue to process out, back into the glaring sunshine, and toward another building. Their line is cut off, however, when a guard shouts at them to halt.

Virginia can't help but recoil from the stinking, shrunken, limping group of strange little men passing before them. She sucks in her breath, however, when she realizes they're not men at all. They're women. Heads shaved bald, skeletal legs covered in sores, the outline of their breasts drooped and shriveled beneath their dirt- and blood-stained blue-and-gray-striped prison rags.

Virginia's body feels frozen. It's as if rigor mortis has come over her, until a crop comes down on her shoulder, and she lurches forward, toward the next building.

"Pick up your head," Violette says in a low, steady voice.

Virginia obeys, as best she's able.

A rising buzz, like a beehive, calls Virginia's attention to the electric fence, covered in skull and crossbones notices. Just before Virginia's pushed into the next building, she sees a charred body, hanging from its black fingers, stuck to the wires. She gasps.

Violette orders Virginia to look away from it.

────── VIOLETTE ──────

KEEPING VIRGINIA AND the girls from losing their minds is the only thing preserving Violette's sanity.

She should have known this was possible. Somewhere, deep down, under the buried whispers and rumors, the stories and the firsthand knowledge of Nazi cruelty, she should have alerted her conscious mind to this potential outcome. But allowing the thoughts might have prevented Violette from operating, so she's glad she didn't understand the extent of the consequences before she jumped from the plane.

I'm still glad I jumped, she tells herself. *I'm not, however, glad I allowed myself to get caught.*

Violette has to shut that thought down every time it rises. It will do no good. She has to believe—either because of her own strength or because of the inevitable liberation—she will never look like one of those emaciated women. She must convince herself so she can convince her friends.

Once inside the next building, she sees a line of men in white coats accompanied by female prisoners in better health than the group they've just passed. She wonders why some prisoners get better treatment than others. Do they offer to be overseers? Or are they forced into service to the Nazis? Violette doesn't imagine there's much choice in the matter.

In the long, low room, the prisoners are lined up in rows facing the front. They're ordered to remove their clothes and to hand them to the prisoner-overseers, but not to lose track of their numbers and triangles.

A seasoned veteran of this kind of attempt at humiliation, Violette doesn't hesitate to strip down, nor do the other SOE agents, she notes. Virginia, however, shakes so badly she can barely manage her buttons. As do Janette and Maman Marie. Virginia looks as if she'll break when she hands her skirt over to the prisoner-overseer. Her ring must still be inside the hem. But when Virginia sees the prisoner-overseer put the clothing in a box, label it with her number, and slide it on a shelf, Virginia composes herself.

While they stand in lines, most trying to cover their private parts, a tall, fair Nazi with large pale eyes and a stupid expression on his round face strides in, followed by two male SS guards. The doctors, SS girl guards, and prisoner-overseers stand at attention. The leader slowly slides his eyes across the naked women before him.

"I'm the *Kommandant* of this camp, SS-Hauptsturmführer Suhren," he says in French. "I was alerted to the arrival of a particularly offensive group. Where are the parachute girls?"

The Parachute Girls, Violette thinks. *We'll have to use that name for our musical act at the liberation dance.*

"If you don't raise your filthy, traitorous hands," Suhren continues, "I will find each one of you, and personally cut them off."

He pulls his bayonet out of its sleeve.

Violette raises her hand. Odette, Ambroise, Nadine, and a number of others follow.

"Step forward," says Suhren.

Violette leads. The others fall in behind her.

He saunters over to Violette and looks over every inch of her body. She gives him a stare that doesn't censor an ounce of the contempt she feels for him. He sneers at her before giving the other women the same scrutiny.

"Turn and kneel."

The women do so and are met with lashes from the SS girl guards. Five each on their bare backs. It takes several seconds for the shock of each lash to wear off before the searing pain begins.

Violette doesn't make a sound. She won't give them the satisfaction.

She won't look at her observing cellmates, who gasp and whimper more pathetically than the women being punished do. She contracts to her secret inner place that none of them can touch.

"The sight of all of you offends and sickens me," Suhren says, when it's over. "It is my sincere hope that the work here will rehabilitate you and make a new creation of you. And if you won't yield to it, I hope that it will slowly, painfully destroy you."

52

FÜRSTENBERG

—— VIRGINIA ——

WITNESSING VIOLETTE'S UNDISGUISED hatred for the *Kommandant* fills Virginia with dread for her friend. Violette could make a target of herself.

After the horrible spectacle of the whipping, they all have to endure a medical exam, legs spread wide with a team before them. Then it's off to a cold shower and a spray with disinfectant that stings her eyes and draws forth curses from Violette and the women who were whipped. For some reason, their heads aren't shaved, and Virginia doesn't know why, but she could weep with relief. The women are sent to pick through piles of old clothing in the building next to the crematorium, where a fine layer of ash covers everything, and where the smell coming from the rotting bodies whose bony feet spill out of the doorways makes even the guards gag.

Still miserable from thirst, still hot in spite of the cold shower—though starting to numb in other ways—Virginia and her friends select the lightest garments they can find.

"I guess they're running out of prisoner uniforms," says Violette. "Maybe they should be more selective in their admissions."

Some of the women can manage a smile, but Virginia doesn't know if she'll ever smile again. She doesn't know how Violette can put one foot in front of the other, with the obvious pain she must feel, let alone find it in herself to joke. But she senses Violette is trying to prop them all up in whatever way she can.

Virginia pulls on a worn, light green voile dress, and Violette selects navy cotton—to hide the bloodstains—with puffed sleeves. It looks like its last wearer was quite young, but Violette is so small it's the best she can do without a neckline so wide or low that it hangs down to her breasts.

The barracks are arranged in two long rows. Their group is led to Block Five, where a plump dark-haired prisoner-overseer wearing a red armband with a *P* on it distributes a needle and thread, bowl, spoon, and cup to each woman. She tells them to sew their triangles and numbers to the left front side of their garments, once they've claimed a bunk. The women spread out, but the SS guards yell at them to pack in, three to a slat that's hardly wide enough for one on each three-tiered bunk bed. A prisoner in the back of the pack tells an SS girl guard she can't find her number.

"Walk to the showers to look for it," the guard says.

When the prisoner's not three paces away, the female guard shoots her in the back.

Stunned to silence, Virginia and Janette hurry as far from the entrance as they're able. They scramble to the top of the wooden bunks, where Odette joins them. Violette, Marie, and Ambroise take the next, while Nadine can only manage to collapse on the bottom bunk, next to several women they don't know.

Virginia doesn't know why the guards bothered to disinfect the women. The hay is jumping with fleas. They have to crouch to sit up and sew because the ceiling is so close to the top bunk. She can see into the toilet, and there are only three stained latrines and one sink. It's so hot in the block she can barely get a good breath, and the smell of the women—even though they've just showered—is pungent. The top bunk was the wrong choice.

Groups of women continue to squeeze in, hundreds and hundreds, now from outside their transport, until not another body can fit.

There's crying and whimpering and some nasty hisses, but her friends remain silent while they stitch.

There's nothing to say.

ONE CAN NEVER get used to pretty things in proximity to hell, Virginia thinks.

The white cottages with flower boxes and perfect green lawns, the bright blue sky reflected in the lake just outside camp, the beautiful Alsatian shepherds who look like Nan—yet are possessed by Cerberus—mauling women to death who attempt to flee. A clean, new bread truck from the nearby men's camp that delivers black rolls, each woman getting one a day. Shiny modern kitchens that only produce the weakest ersatz coffee to start the morning and only enough thin rhubarb soup to allow for a half pint per woman—spread between lunch and dinner—a day.

The contrasts keep her perpetually off balance. As do the days that begin at 0330 with the banshee wail of the siren. They are forced to stand at *Appell*, roll call, for hours, shivering in the predawn, before twelve-hour workdays of farming, painting, laundry, food preparation, manure hauling, digging, and construction of a massive tent to house new arrivals, coming in waves each day. The Nazis must be deporting every prisoner they can as the Allies advance through France.

There are some prisoners of note among them. Geneviève de Gaulle, niece of the general. Also, a tiny girl who looks like Lily, who turns out to be her sister, Andrée, the very woman who helped start the Comet Line. How happy Lily would be to hear her sister is alive. The parachute girls, as Violette and women like her are known, are minor celebrities, whispered about for their courage and daring by some, their insanity by others.

Because Ambroise is both Jewish and a political prisoner, she wears both the yellow and the red triangles. They're happy she hasn't yet been relegated to the Jewish bunk, where the conditions are even more miserable than theirs. Purple triangles are for Jehovah's Witnesses, and black triangles are to mark the so-called asocials: lesbians, prostitutes, and Romani, some of whom have children. They all try to keep away from the prisoners with green triangles, because they are criminals: thugs, thieves, and murderesses, many of whom enjoy the power and privileges they receive as prisoner-overseers, or *Kapos*.

Their own *Kapo*, Julia, holds a leather crop she likes to slap against her thigh, but they've never seen her use it. She seems to crave their approval, and some even say she can get people medicine or extra food, but Virginia does not yet know how or why that is. All she knows is that the labels are sick methods of division to create hierarchies of distrust among the prisoners. Like the devil, the Nazis know that to divide is to control and conquer.

Trembling at *Appell* one morning, three weeks after she's entered into the hell of Ravensbrück, Virginia feels an overwhelming dread. It's only September and the thin frock she chose after the stifling hot journey is already not enough to protect her from the chill. What will it be like in October? November? The last batch of prisoners said the Allies were still in France. Though losing ground every day, the Germans are putting up enough of a fight to keep the prisoners' saviors away. Virginia doesn't know if she'll be able to last if this goes on until Christmas. By the way her dress has loosened, and how shriveled her hands are becoming, she can tell she's already lost a lot of weight, and it hasn't even been a month.

On the way back to their block for so-called breakfast, Virginia spots a familiar form in line for the medical entrance exam.

"Michelle!" Virginia says.

She's both elated to see her friend, the florist, and also saddened to see Michelle was arrested. When Michelle catches sight of Virginia, she brightens. Virginia slows her step, and Michelle looks around before speaking.

"Philippe is all right," Michelle says.

Virginia covers her mouth.

"He escaped to London and got word to Jean that he was well. The whole forest is safe."

"Thank God," Virginia says, raising her eyes to heaven in thanks. An SS guard steps between them and pushes Virginia forward. Virginia mouths over her shoulder, "Courage."

—— VIOLETTE ——

VIRGINIA'S GOOD NEWS about her husband's well-being gives all of them a needed boost.

Just this morning, shivering in the cold, Violette felt a wave of exhaustion like she hadn't experienced since she was pregnant with Tania. She can't remember the last time she had her period and, while she's glad not to experience the humiliation of blood running down her legs as so many women around her have, she's sick with the thought that she might be expecting, especially because the child would be born of Nazi rape.

Between the Gestapo of Limoges and those of Avenue Foch, there's a chance, and trying to imagine pregnancy under conditions like these is incomprehensible to Violette. She has seen women with large bellies in the distance, and the Roma pulling their sickly children along behind them. She's also heard the rumors of abortions and forced sterilizations and the killing of babies on delivery in the medical building, but most of the women who've gone in for such procedures have never returned to their blocks to tell about them.

When the idea dawned on Violette that she might be pregnant, she had an impulse to throw herself at the electric fence. But once the sun rose, and she heard Virginia's good news, and she remembered her Tania, Violette returned to her right mind. She won't worry about being pregnant unless she is. And even then, there's nothing worrying will do to change it. It might even get her extra food rations from sympathetic friends.

Violette is grateful for her cellmates, particularly for the love and affection of Maman Marie. Like in a family, Violette has observed, the moods of one deeply affect the others. Ambroise is perpetually depressed—ever mourning being separated from her fiancé and worried about his whereabouts—and Nadine is growing weaker by the day. She gags over the soup so she can barely choke it down, resulting in even less nutrition than the others. The rest are holding up in mind, body, and spirit, especially Virginia. At the start, Violette was skeptical about her friend's endurance, but Virginia is the most even-keeled in the group. She possesses a quiet strength and a strong capacity for hope.

While Violette hugs Virginia, thrilled for her friend's good news about her husband, their overseer, Julia, approaches. They quiet and separate. The woman looks hungry to share in the affection of others, but there can be no affection for a *Kapo*, no matter how mildly she behaves.

"Good news," Julia says. "Because of your group's good health and discipline, you've been selected for work at a subcamp at Torgau."

Her companions' excited whispers give Julia the response she's looking for, but Violette is suspicious. She's seen the busloads of women shipped out to never return.

"When do we leave?" she asks.

"In an hour. But first, you'll be allowed showers and a change of clothes," says Julia.

The women cheer.

"You have to hurry, though. You'll have to restitch the numbers and triangles."

Violette remains skeptical. She trusts no one with any kind of power at Ravensbrück.

AFTER THREE DAYS in cattle cars, several hundred women are escorted from the train station to the subcamp at Torgau, two hundred thirty kilometers south of Ravensbrück. Their guards are strangely lax. They appear as relieved as the prisoners to be away from Ravensbrück. The mood is better than it has been in weeks, and it climbs higher for the women when they pass a POW camp on the outskirts of town. At a fence bordering an old stone building, men run toward them, calling out to them in English and French. Violette's heart lifts.

"How are ya, boys?" says Violette, in English.

"Never better, now that you're here," says a Brit.

"Say, when are the good guys gonna reach us?" Violette says.

"Soon! The Joes just crossed the frontier."

Violette translates and the women around her cheer. Many excited conversations in French and English erupt, and the men run along the fence to keep up with the women. If only Violette could join the well-fed, smiling, joyful group of French and British POWs. If she'd been a man in uniform, the Geneva convention would have applied to her. It occurs to her that these men might somehow get to contact London before her. She slips as close to the fence as she's able.

"Fellas," she says, whistling and putting on her highest megawatt smile. "Garçons."

In spite of how she must look, the men still respond to her as men always do, like puppies at her beck and call. When they get close, their hands holding the fence, she leans toward them.

"If you get to London before I do," Violette says in English, "I need you to remember this. Go to the Sanctuary Buildings on Great Smith Street, near Westminster. Leave this message for E. Potter. 'Louise, Ambroise, Nadine, Odette, Alice, Rose. Fürstenberg to Torgau.'"

She repeats the message in French.

"Got it?" she says.

The men nod. The guards intercept, pulling Violette back in line and hurrying the women along. The prisoners wave goodbye to each other, blowing kisses and promising to meet up after the liberation.

Violette is electrified, full of new will and spirit. Surely, once they get word, HQ will send someone directly. Maybe even a whole rescue mission. Her excitement soon turns to worry, however, when she sees Maman Marie about to faint.

"It's all right, Maman," Violette says, coming to her side. "We're almost there."

Maman Marie gives Violette a weak smile and leans heavily on her.

When they've been walking for about forty-five minutes, they spot a factory in the distance. Violette is the first to see the name on the sign.

"Heinkel," she says.

"Is that . . . ?" asks Virginia.

"Munitions."

The group becomes silent, and the pace slows. Knowing they'll be working to make weapons for the Nazis sobers them. When they reach the gate, a German officer waits and holds his arm to let them pass, as if he's inviting them to a dinner party. After walking by a row of outhouses, they step into the barracks. When Violette enters, she draws in her breath.

The room smells of lemons, and rows of individual cots are organized neatly, laid with two clean, folded blankets and one pillow on each. There are steam heaters at both ends of the room, and a long, white, deep sink.

Is this a mirage? thinks Violette. *Or a trap?*

It's not until the officer invites them in further that she starts to believe it's real.

"Welcome," he says. "I think you will find conditions here favorable. I insist upon order and cleanliness, and I expect you to keep yourselves and your spaces as tidy as possible. If you cooperate, you will find it not intolerable here."

There are sighs, and happy cries.

"*Appell* is at six o'clock each morning. Work is from eight a.m. to seven p.m. Sundays are for rest and religious services, Catholic and Protestant. We'll serve dinner in the yard in an hour, then you should wash up and go to bed to ready yourselves for work tomorrow."

With that, he nods and leaves them. Two armed SS guards remain at the door.

Happy as children at Christmas, most of the women run to claim their beds. Violette helps Maman Marie to a cot in the corner, as close to a steam heater as possible, while others jockey for beds near the sinks or the windows.

When she takes her own cot next to Maman, Violette feels a disturbance in the atmosphere. She scans the room and sees two young prisoners remain near the door. They wear petulant expressions and watch the rest of the room with their arms crossed over their chests.

WHILE HER GIRLS take turns cleaning themselves, Violette tracks the pair. She sees them whispering with small groups of women, who then whisper with other groups. Like the darkness of a heavy London fog, when the whispers reach each ear, brightness disappears from faces, brows furrow, shoulders sag.

Though the pair have not yet reached her girls, Violette walks over to see what's going on.

"If you have a conscience, you mustn't cooperate," says one of them.

"We can't have the blood of our comrades on our hands. Not even if it costs our lives," says the other.

"If I were an Allied soldier," says a woman in the group, "and my loved one was in this position, I would want him or her to cooperate. I would know it's not their fault."

"How can you say that?" says the first. "What if a bomb you helped build takes out a village full of children?"

Violette feels a pang in her heart at the thought of a weapon made with her hands resulting in the death of anyone, let alone a child like her Tania. Like Dickie. Like Pierrot. Mood darkened, Violette returns to her group.

"What are they arguing about?" asks Virginia.

"Conscience," says Violette. "Specifically, can you sleep in this cot at night knowing your hands help make a bomb that kills our men? Or innocent civilian women and children?"

She sees the faces and shoulders of her friends fall the way the rest of the group's have fallen.

Before they can discuss it among themselves, the pair of women call for the attention of the room.

"Women of goodwill," says the younger of the two. "I, Jeannie, and my friend Martinette beg you to resist. These Nazis are trying to numb us with the promise of full bellies and clean cots. But at what cost? I'll tell you: the blood of innocent men, women, and children on your hands."

"Sit down, you Commie," shouts one woman.

"What she says is true," yells another.

"We should turn the reds into the Nazis," calls yet another voice.

Jeannie is a striking woman—tall and beautiful. She raises her hands to shush the crowd.

"Martinette will secure a piece of paper," Jeannie says, "demanding those who object be placed in areas away from munitions. There are kitchens here. There's cleaning that needs to be done. There is no reason anyone who doesn't want innocent blood on her hands should have to participate. Think about it. Make your decision by *Appell* tomorrow morning. And to those who don't resist: May your gods have mercy on your souls."

53

FÜRSTENBERG

—— **VIRGINIA** ——

SHIVERING, ARMS CROSSED over her chest, puffs of breath clouds evaporating in the October air, Virginia cannot pull herself from the black hole of bitterness she's felt since they were forced to return to Ravensbrück. At least the cold emotion has made ice of her, her tears frozen. Everyone knows, the ones who cry at night are dead the next morning.

The revolt at Torgau resulted in their banishment.

After an agonizing night of debate, by *Appell* the next morning, most of the women—including Virginia, Maman Marie, and the parachute girls—had signed the protest paper. But at the last minute, Janette convinced them all to get their names off that paper, that their husbands and children and mothers and fathers needed them to come home, that the war was almost over, so the weapons wouldn't get used anyway. Hadn't the POWs said the Allies had crossed the frontier into Germany? Assured or, rather, unable to defeat their basest survival instincts, Virginia and the others had scratched out their names. But the damage was done.

Once presented with the paper, the stunned German officer had acquiesced, allowing all the women in their tent to work at digging and peeling potatoes for the kitchen instead of on the weapons assembly lines. He also, however, sent the protest paper to Kommandant Suhren at Ravensbrück, and within a month, they'd been called back. They went from the relative comfort of Torgau back to the torture of Ravensbrück. Every last one of them.

On return, the ringleaders—Jeannie and Martinette—had been sent to the solitary confinement dungeons. Violette—who'd been caught planning escape once she realized they'd be shipped back— was whipped with ten lashes. They were all told to await transfer to another subcamp, where, Suhren said, he was quite sure none of them would make trouble.

It has been two weeks since their return. They've been crowded even worse into their block, with five to a slat, but at least they weren't forced into the newly finished tent, on the dirt, with the thousands of incoming prisoners—Jewish women from Hungary and Polish women from Warsaw ghettos—who die by the dozens each day in the mud. The bodies, the overflowing latrines, and the disease have made Ravensbrück smell worse than it did before, which Virginia couldn't have imagined possible. Each time she's forced to comprehend some new level of horror, Virginia thinks back to the time before, when she thought she'd seen the worst. But there is no limit to worse when it comes to Nazis.

Nadine can barely stand up straight. Janette has turned a sickly yellow color. Marie is coughing blood. At *Appell*, women are starting to fall—to simply collapse, in heaps of bones held together by skin. If the prisoner doesn't get up by the end of roll call, the guards make those around her drag her to the crematorium. Virginia will never forget the first time she heard screams as the oven was being fed with a woman who was not quite dead. Virginia had thought that was the worst. It was only a new threshold.

The night Violette had returned from her whipping, her amethyst eyes had gone black. She'd started mumbling about revenge on the rebellion leaders, the Nazis, the German people in town who pretend not to know what the prisoners suffer in the camps. Between bloody coughs, Marie cautioned Violette and all of them not to allow the darkness to overtake them. She said it would kill them faster than starvation or slavery.

"I'm sorry, Maman," Violette had whispered. "Can we at least burn the camp to the ground on liberation?"

"Yes, my dear. We may do that. As long as there are no people in it."

"How can we call them people?" Violette had asked. "How is such evil possible for people?"

"Because the devil leads people off the path with bread crumbs," Marie had said. "It never happens all at once. Just a little at a time."

Virginia hasn't stopped thinking about these bread crumbs that lead one to evil. Marie is right. Indulging in dark and vengeful thoughts is another kind of lure off the path of goodness. But it's so hard to overcome the feelings of hatred and hopelessness in the ever-falling temperatures, before the sun rises.

When the pug-faced guard passes them, she pauses at Nadine, who's almost bent in half. She slams Nadine with the butt of her gun. Nadine moans but forces herself upright. The guard watches her with suspicion, and once she's satisfied, continues down the line. When the guard is about ten yards away, Nadine wavers and starts to fall. Ambroise props her up, but looks around pleadingly, unsure what to do. If Nadine collapses, she'll be fed to the fire.

Soon, the guard starts back toward them. Ambroise releases Nadine and returns to her spot, begging her friend to stand tall, just for a little while more. Nadine continues to wobble. It's all Virginia can do to stay in place, but raw, animal fear cements her. The guard again catches sight of Nadine, and tracks her, almost daring Nadine to fall while she watches.

Suddenly, a humming sound distracts them. Virginia looks to the left, where Violette stands. Violette sings and does some kind of rock step dance in place. Virginia shoots her gaze back to the pug-faced guard and is alarmed to see that Violette has caught the woman's attention.

"You'll find us all," sings Violette, "doing the Lambeth Walk."

Is she going mad? Virginia wonders.

Virginia shushes Violette, but her friend winks at her. She doesn't stop singing.

When Nadine starts to slump forward, the guard's attention returns to Nadine. Then Violette's voice grows louder. Her movements get wider. The guard ping-pongs her stare to Violette.

Realizing what Violette is doing, Virginia starts to hum along to the melody. Soon, Odette and Janette join the singing. And in a few moments, voices from up and down the rows join in singing "The Lambeth Walk" while the guard shouts at them to stop. Nadine tips forward, but Ambroise is able to right her before the guard notices.

Violette strides forward, arms swaying, singing "The Lambeth Walk" at the top of her lungs. The guard storms down the row with another who has come to see what the commotion is. While Ambroise holds up Nadine, the women's voices sing the chorus.

The guards pounce on Violette and drag her off toward the solitary cells.

Violette sings the whole way.

—— **VIOLETTE** ——

ANOTHER WHIPPING. A stint in solitary.

I'd do it again, Violette thinks. *Nadine is still alive.*

Another train journey.

Her girls are happy to again leave Ravensbrück. Many appear to have forgotten that Kommandant Suhren promised they would pay for their insubordination. It doesn't take long for them to remember.

Violette hears the howl of the wind over the plain before the cattle car doors are scraped open and the blast of cold assaults them.

Virginia has a coat. She'd felt guilty for finding it, grabbing it from the pile of dead women's clothing after their transfer showers. Violette had told Virginia to stop feeling guilt in places such as these. If Virginia died, Violette would be the first to peel the coat from her body. Sad at the loss of her friend, but guiltless. It's every woman for herself. Just like Violette told her team, like she'd told Jacques "Anastasie" Bandit all those many lifetimes ago. Or has it been only five months?

Far beyond the black and white and gray landscape of their new hell are the red roofs of the town of Königsberg. Pretty red roofs over pretty homes, cozy fires burning in stone hearths. Soft quilts and warm sausages and wool stockings and mothers tucking daughters into bed.

Will I ever again get to tuck in my baby girl?

The barracks are down a steep hill, where the rain runs in rivers, turning the yard to mud. Their barracks have metal roofs with rusted holes where sleet and snow drip in, and rain rattles, and there are no fires, and no sausages, and Violette's bed is dirty straw. And Tania is far away, being tucked in by Vera Maidment.

Is Vera tucking Tania in nice and snug as a bug, like I do, blankets up around her tiny ears? Does she give Tania, who's prone to coughing, a hot-water bottle on cold nights?

Violette can't stop thinking about Tania. And Henri. And Tania. And Robert and Clement and Jean Claude and Jack. And Tania. And Maman and Papa. Her brothers and cousins. And Tania.

I will not bring Tania here after the war, Violette thinks. *Not even to show her what her mother survived.*

She hopes the planes of the Allies bomb every last town and every last person in Germany to ashes. She would assemble the bombs herself. She wonders if Henri is alive. She wonders if her message has got back to London with the POWs. Will they rescue her and the parachute girls? The last place she told them was Torgau, but Königsberg is closer to the frontier than Torgau. So here, they'll be liberated first.

"Are we in Siberia?" Violette jokes.

Her work detail has to clear land for runways and rails. The dirt is frozen solid, and yet they must fell trees, pickax roots, and pry them from the icy earth with gloveless, frostbit, bloody hands. They must level the ground, chipping away at mud clotted with ice veins. They must pile the dirt shards—sharp as glass—into wagons, and haul the dirt to holes, and fill them in and tamp them down.

"Where is Jeannie? Or Martinette?" Violette asks. "Should we ask them to draw up protest papers? Refuse to build the runways for the boche planes to take off and drop bombs on our boys?"

"Shhh," Virginia says. "The guards will hear you, *ma petite*."

"They can't hear me over the wind."

It's relentless.

The flash of light on metal draws Violette's attention. She squeezes her eyes closed and open again. The flash is like a mirror in the sun, and it causes her to squint. She shields her eyes and tries to make out what's at the crossroads.

"Stop," she commands.

The women cease motion and look up. But all Violette can see are Germans. The ones that Jacques ran into. The ones she shot. She feels her dormant trigger finger twitch.

"It's the soup truck," says Virginia. "Come."

But the Polish and Russian brutes elbow their way into line first, like they do every day. These women somehow remain hearty and stocky with red rosy cheeks and fists they aren't afraid to use when it comes to food or bedding or clothing or washing at the trough. There are thieves among them. Virginia has lost her coat to one of them, and there's nothing she can do to get it back. She can't weigh more than ninety pounds.

The sound of a thick, wet cough draws Violette's attention to the old woman behind her.

"Maman Marie," Violette says. "Are you all right?"

"I'm all right, *ma petite*."

When it's their turn, Violette helps Maman carry her soup bowl to a knoll where they might sit. She helps her camp mother, whose hands shake too much to bring the spoon to her mouth, which is crusted with blood, to eat the thin soup. She gives Maman the bit of potato Violette finds at the bottom of her own bowl. She thinks of her real mother.

"My *maman*'s name is Reine," Violette says.

"Yes," says Maman Marie. "A queen."

"She is. One day, you'll meet her. My papa is a loudmouth, but I miss him. He'd be very proud to hear about the Germans I shot. And my brothers are a hoot. But Tania, oh, Tania."

"Your darling girl."

"Yes, my baby. You will love her, Maman Marie. She's a good girl. She got the best of me and her father."

"You are the best, *ma petite*. The very best. I can't imagine better."

"Then you don't have much imagination."

They laugh. It helps Violette get a good breath.

But that night, Maman can't get a good breath. In the morning, Violette looks out at the fresh blanket of snow and insists Maman go to the infirmary. Violette hates to leave Maman there, where there are no more cots, and Maman must lie on the floor without a blanket, and there's no medicine, and gray women at various stages approaching death moan, but at least it's out of the elements.

Violette steels herself before opening the door, but one can never get used to the bitter wind, the snow sliding in wooden clogs where feet have no socks, and legs have no stockings, and bodies have no undergarments, hands no gloves, heads no hats. No scarves. At least it's too cold for her tears to fall.

The ones who cry are always dead by morning.

54

—— **VIRGINIA** ——

JANETTE WON'T STOP crying and tearing out what thin wisps of hair she has left. The cold is driving her mad. It's driving them all mad.

Virginia guides her friend through the shin-deep snow to the small fire their German guard has granted. They're only allowed five-minute breaks once an hour at the fire, but it's the difference between life and death. Leaving the fire is such agony, however, that Virginia wonders if it's better not to have it at all.

Once Janette is calm and their break is over, Virginia helps her back to where they're digging in dirt, hard as concrete, to lay the railroad track sections that take twenty of them to lift.

"Herr, can you please get us some clothes?" Virginia begs the foreman.

He's a French-speaking German civilian, conscripted to oversee the prisoners. When the SS guards aren't watching, he's prone to bouts of sympathy.

"It's only November and you can see our fingers are turning gray," Virginia says. "We'll work better and faster if you find some gloves or scarves for us. They'll reward you for managing us well. Please, I beg you."

He pretends not to hear her, but a few days later, when he isn't being watched, he fetches a basket of clothes he'd hidden in a wagon and dumps it on the ground. The women in his detail descend upon it like a pack of wild dogs, tearing through, grabbing stockings, underwear, mittens, scarves, and thin sweaters made from ersatz yarn. It's more than they could have hoped for, and they're so grateful to each have a few pieces to help insulate them, he has to order them to stop thanking him and get back to work.

Virginia slides off her cotton underwear and pulls on the woolen, then stretches the cotton of the old underwear over her head and to her neck, making a scarf.

What an animal I've become, she thinks. *No, what an animal they've made of me.*

It takes an act of will, but Virginia stifles the dark thoughts. She spends the rest of the morning asking God to bless their foreman and whatever women worked in secret to knit these things that might keep them alive a day or so longer.

SOME WOMEN HAVE started praying to get sick so they can rest in the infirmary; others pretend. Janette rejoiced when she got a fever that reached over a hundred, but she was in despair two days later when it returned to normal. Marie remains in the infirmary, still coughing blood. Nadine couldn't get out of bed one morning, so she had to be carried there. Ambroise was also admitted. The sores on her feet are infected.

When they started here, their group of French had more than two hundred fifty in it, and there were at least as many between the Russians and the Poles. Now, *Appell* takes less and less time. At work, all along the road where they lay train tracks and level land for runways, bodies lie. Women collapse throughout the day and are pushed to the side, and sometimes they're not discarded before the next day, so their dead bodies watch the living through empty eyes, mouths slack and stiff, covered in dustings of snow. Virginia sees them so often now she feels no emotion about it. She's become used to it. And that terrifies her.

What an animal I've become, she thinks over and over again.

No, what an animal they've made of me, she reminds herself.

Violette continues to lead the ones who are able in exercises. None of them have their periods any longer and, while that is cause for some celebration, it has also taken away some of their health, their womanhood, along with their ever-shrinking breasts. Violette had told Virginia that she was worried she carried a Gestapo baby from the rapists, but her stomach has only shrunk, so now she thinks not.

When the recurring darkness doesn't overtake Violette, she jokes and encourages and pushes their girls. But sometimes her eyes go black, mostly in the nights. When that happens, Virginia whispers to Violette, reminding her about Tania and Henri and all the things they'll do after the war.

Christmas is agony. The little tree on the edge of the yard they decorate with scraps and things from nature is less a festive reminder and more a mimicry of the season, as is the sad Nativity Janette makes from bark and twigs. It's the mothers who suffer worst, thinking of their babes who will wake up with nothing. With no tree and no mother and often no father. No chocolates or lights or carols or midnight masses with pretty candles. Virginia's own mother would be in agony to know what she's living through. Virginia wonders if, somehow, her mother senses it.

Virginia realizes the baby she miscarried would have been four years old by now. Would she and Philippe have joined the Resistance if they had a little one? She thinks of Jessie-Ann and Violette and many of the women around her and hopes she and Philippe would have, even with the resulting circumstances.

When Violette's sweet voice leads them in the Latin "O Come, O Come, Emmanuel" on Christmas Eve, Virginia has to stop singing so she doesn't break wide open. The criers continue to extinguish themselves by the very act of it.

On the twenty-ninth, they see the full moon start its climb before the sun sets. As it rises, Violette points it out to Virginia.

"A day moon," she says. "Little Tania saw one the day I left her, just before her second birthday. I told her it was Maman's moon. Do you think she'll remember me?"

"Of course she will, *ma petite.*"

"I hope so," Violette says.

When New Year's Eve comes, they're all in better spirits. As the second hand of the clock over the barracks in the yard gets closer to midnight, the women count down. Under the glow of the waning gibbous, they cry out with joy because they know—*they know*—they have entered the last year of the war. If they can just hold on a little longer, they will be free.

——— VIOLETTE ———

HOW MUCH LONGER can we hold on? Violette thinks.

In addition to the living hell of their daily reality, the nightmares are coming with more frequency. In spite of the icicles formed on the inside of the barracks windows, Violette had woken up covered in sweat.

In the dream, the Germans from the checkpoint at Salon-la-Tour were pursuing her on foot. All she could hear was her own breath, until she could hear his breath as he overtook her. It was SS Scherer from Avenue Foch. He launched at Violette from behind and wrestled her to the ground, where she put up a violent fight. Just as he'd worked himself on top of her, forcing her legs open, she'd found the garrote in her pocket and got it around his neck. She pulled with all her might, strangling him, watching his eyes bulge, his fingernails scratch at his neck, his body shudder until it went limp, heavy over her.

Violette had shot up in her cot and looked for her anchor, Maman Marie. Maman was forced out of the infirmary. Even though she has pneumonia, all of the patients have been barred from rest by the new female SS guard they call the Aryan witch, a pale, cruel beauty who is rumored to have just returned from a mental institution. She's a soulless devil who takes delight in making the sick stand in punishment in the snow for hours for their "laziness," and in working the women to death.

Maman Marie's breathing is labored. Violette prays the dear woman makes it. Violette doesn't know if she could have come this far without Maman Marie's love and care, and is determined to give it back, even if it takes every drop of her own soup or the very clothes off her own bony back.

Violette can't believe they're almost through January and the Allies still haven't reached them. In the SS guards, she's observed an increase in frantic whispers, brutal punishments, and fear on their faces when they think the prisoners aren't looking. The Allies have to be getting close, but if they don't liberate them soon, there will be no one left to liberate.

At *Appell* on the twentieth of January, the Aryan witch opens an envelope and tells the women whose names are called to step forward.

"Denise Bloch," the witch says.

Ambroise, Violette thinks.

"Lilian Rolfe."

Nadine.

Violette's heart lifts, hearing the next.

"Violette Szabo."

There are whispers, confusion as women who are known by one name to some, by another to others, answer the call.

As Violette steps forward, she tries to suppress a smile. The POWs from Torgau must have gotten the parachute girls' names to London.

Miss Atkins and Buckmaster have come to the rescue. She doesn't know why the Aryan witch didn't ask for the other women, but Violette doesn't dwell on it.

She's going home to Tania.

KNOWING SHE LEAVES tomorrow, it's easier to work.

"Once each of us is liberated," Violette says to Virginia, "this will all become a faint memory. We'll heal fast. Hold on. I'll make sure our men come for you."

Virginia is strangely quiet. Violette keeps catching Virginia staring at her with a worried look in her eyes. Come to think of it, they all keep looking at Violette that way. It was the way Miss Atkins looked at Violette before the second mission.

Nadine wears her usual blank expression, but Ambroise can't stop weeping.

"Why are you crying?" asks Violette. "London knows where we are. They're coming for us."

Ambroise won't answer. She just keeps crying.

The cold is as brutal as it has ever been, and the women who are stuck here are dropping left and right in the knee-high drifts. The Aryan witch has been assigned to their detail. She won't take her eyes off Violette. When the sleet begins, a woman drops her pickax. She stares ahead for a moment, then starts walking toward the forest.

"Halt!" says the witch.

The prisoner doesn't stop walking. Violette thinks the woman must be out of her mind from the cold. She appears to only be driven by the thought *I must get to the woods*.

"Halt," the witch again demands.

The prisoner continues to stagger away from the work detail.

The witch sighs in disgust, draws her pistol, and shoots the woman in the back. The sound echoes across the field, and hundreds of heads turn slowly to see who got shot. The snow grows red under the body. The prisoners turn back to their tasks.

Nausea rises in Violette. For that woman to come this far, to suffer this long, and not be given the gift of liberation is a tragedy. Violette hasn't cried yet, but this threatens to undo her.

Maman Marie has a coughing fit. When she gets through the spell, she spits. More blood stains the snow. When Maman sees Violette watching, the woman smiles weakly, as if trying to reassure her camp daughter that she's all right. Mothers never want their children to know how they suffer. Violette will never tell Tania how she suffered.

A wave of despair crashes over Violette.

How can I leave Maman Marie to die? Violette thinks. *To be so selfish. To tell the POWs about the agents but not the others. The mothers, the daughters, the sisters, the wives, the friends.*

Violette feels the tears hot on her face.

"Oh no!" she cries. "No, I can't cry. I'll be dead by morning."

"No," says Maman. "You get to leave tomorrow."

"I'll die. The ones who cry all die. And I will die—of heartbreak—having to leave you."

Violette breaks down, sobbing. She looks at the dead woman in the bloody snow.

"To have come so close to the liberation."

Maman wraps her arms around Violette. Violette doesn't know if it's her shudders or Maman's coughs that are shaking them.

VIOLETTE SITS IN the iron-stained washtub in the infirmary, Maman Marie scrubbing Violette's hair with the tiny sliver of soap she was given and helping to pick out the lice. The Aryan witch is at the doorway. She whispers with a male SS guard. The way they speak, it looks as if they're flirting. It's sickening behavior in such a place.

"I'm so sorry, Maman," Violette whispers. "I was selfish to just tell the POWs the names of the parachute girls. To leave you with these beasts."

"Shhh," says Maman Marie. "I won't hear you say that again. You are the leader, *ma petite*. It's only fitting you are in the first wave of the liberated."

Maman pours the lukewarm water over Violette, and the sensation is welcome on her frostbit skin.

"Would you like to sneak in a bath when I'm finished?" asks Violette. "Those two are distracted. Save some soap for yourself."

"I will have plenty of soap and baths when the war is over. Let's just get you ready. You have some new clothes to put on. New shoes. New to you."

The tub hurts Violette's bottom. There's not an ounce of padding on her body to cushion her from the hard, cold porcelain. She shivers. One can never, ever get used to the cold.

"All right, up you go," says Maman. "Before you catch a chill."

Violette sees the outline of her reflection in the window glass. She can't believe the skeleton in silhouette is her. She looks down at her knobby hands, her shriveled arms and emaciated legs. She's never been a large person, but she used to be muscular. Powerful. A swimmer, a runner, a climber of trees. Will she ever get the strength back for such things?

The Aryan witch looks in and wrinkles her nose in disgust. She turns back to the man in front of her. Violette thinks she'll find this woman after the war, and see that justice comes to her and all who are like her. She and Miss Atkins can hunt the war criminals together.

Violette wasn't given a towel, so Maman uses Violette's new, clean brown jacket to wipe her body. The jacket can hang overnight to dry, and Violette can wear the pink blouse and the brown skirt they gave her until the morning. The clothes are too big, so Maman Marie helps Violette roll and cinch, tsking all the time about how thin she is.

"At first, you must eat slowly," says Maman. "If you eat too fast, you'll tear your stomach."

"How do you know so much, Maman? You're so wise."

The old woman looks at Violette and gives her the saddest smile she has ever seen.

Violette's heart begins to race. She gets a frantic feeling, like when the Nazis pursued her. All at once, she realizes why the others have been looking at her with such pity. Why she has been so heavily guarded since the names were read.

She's not going to be rescued by HQ. The Nazis are going to execute her.

Violette collapses into Maman's arms, and sobs.

"They're going to kill me, aren't they, Maman?"

"No," Maman says, but she's crying.

"Tania won't remember me. My mother's heart will break. My father. Henri. My men."

"No, you mustn't say such things."

Violette pulls back. She scans the room until she sees a label on an empty medicine bottle. She rips it off.

"Find me something to write with," Violette says, frantic.

Maman looks around, but Violette spots the pencil first, lying across a file cabinet. She fetches it, scribbles her parents' address, and shoves the paper into Maman's hands.

"My parents' address in London. Charlie and Reine Bushell. Hide it. Quick."

Violette watches the guards and pretends to continue fastening her buttons while Maman rolls up the paper.

"Your hem," whispers Violette. "Hurry."

Maman breaks into a fit of coughs that keeps the witch away for a few moments more, while she slides the paper in her skirt with a shaking hand.

The door soon bursts open, and they're escorted at gunpoint back to the barracks.

All through the night, Violette whispers to Maman that she must tell Charlie and Reine that she loves them both very much, and all her brothers, and her cousins and aunts and uncles. But most of all, Maman Marie must tell Tania that Violette will always watch over her, and to think of her *maman* and papa when she sees the moon, and how very much her *maman* and papa love her.

55

~⚭~

—— **VIRGINIA** ——

WHEN THE SIREN wail awakens them to prepare for *Appell*, the women gather around Violette. Her purple eyes are wide like an owl's, peering through the dark. After they dress, Violette gives each of them a hug, but for her beloved Maman Marie, Violette also has many kisses. She says they're for her parents, her brothers, her cousins, and her Tania.

Virginia watches, willing herself not to cry. She cannot. Not if she's going to make it. It's not certain the worst will happen to her friend or the other parachute girls, but if it does, Virginia can't think about that now. She needs to stay well in mind and body for Philippe. The Allies will come any day. She must not break before that happens.

The truck arrives at dawn. Violette leads them. Nadine has to be half carried. Ambroise limps on a foot that looks as if it has gone gangrenous. The rest of their little camp family follows. Violette helps her partners into the lorry, and just before she climbs in herself, she looks back over her shoulder at Virginia.

"Courage," Virginia says.

Violette winks, and then she's gone.

The taking of the parachute girls pulls some hidden foundation from under the camp. The earth quakes. Is it Allied bombs or God's

anger? The wind howls. Intermittent sleet stings them. Odette—
unsure if she's relieved or crushed not to have been taken away—
coughs as badly as Marie. Janette's body starts to bloat.

At work detail, the ground trembles. The guards run to meet in
groups, shouting at one another in German, watching the horizon
more than they do the women. Virginia senses something unholier
than ever before has been unleashed, and she feels the tension of
knowing the end is coming but—to survive this apocalypse and get
back to Philippe—she must be stronger and more careful than ever.

Midday, while they're at their workstations, a lorry comes speeding
and sliding over the mud. The driver shouts at the guards in German
and, though it's not even noon, the women are commanded to release
their shovels and pickaxes, line up, and return to the barracks. They
march the women as fast as lines of skeletons can go. Those who fall
behind are beaten, the dead left in the snow. When they arrive at the
barracks, the Germans force them inside and tell them to stay, or
they'll be shot. Terrified, excited whispers fly around the room. Janette
collapses in bed. Marie has a coughing fit.

The ground shakes harder.

"Is it?" breathes Virginia.

"It is," says Odette.

The women hug one another, exclaiming with joy, but the sounds
of shots in the yard above sober them and keep them in place. They
stay inside, watching and waiting, taking turns looking out the windows, though all they can see is the muddy hill they have to climb to
view the rest of camp.

Throughout the afternoon, there's rumbling and honking and
shouting and the sounds of motion. The women aren't fed. They lie in
their bunks, wasting away, watching the light move over the ceiling,
turning dark in the early setting sun. They dare not turn on the electric
bulbs. Maybe they'll just hide until the Allies come.

But maybe no one will find them. Or maybe they will die before
they're reached.

By nightfall, it's silent outside the barracks. Virginia sits up, dizzy, starving. She rises and puts her feet in her shoes, but the bottom of the right one falls off. She takes her feet back out and flinches over the ice-cold, filthy concrete to the door.

"Don't," someone hisses. "They'll shoot you."

Frosted ice trails sparkle over the surface of the window, winking in the light of the waning gibbous. Virginia thinks of Violette.

Courage.

A movement catches her eye. Prisoners—Poles and Russians—are running down the hill. Their hands are full of cans. Virginia hurries back to her friends.

"The Germans are gone. Prisoners are looting. Will anyone come with me?"

Janette mumbles, delirious and bloated. Marie can't stop coughing. Neither can Odette, but she rises.

"I will," Odette says.

"Take my clogs," says Marie.

Virginia thanks Marie, and then Virginia and Odette wrap their scarves like turbans around their heads. Odette leads Virginia across the room and looks out the window. Odette then crosses to the door, listens, and opens it a crack. When no shot is fired, she opens it a crack more. She waits a few seconds before she nods to Virginia, and they're off.

IT'S TERRIFYING OUTSIDE the barracks. The hangar at the airfield is on fire. The guard housing building is lit up like a torch, daring them to come inside.

They do.

The mess hall has plates of half-eaten food—boiled carrots, potatoes, and meat. Virginia and Odette stop to stuff themselves, as do a few other women along the tables, eating like pigs at a trough. Odette places her hand on Virginia's arm.

"Slowly."

There's a radio playing German songs, coming from the dormitory hallway. They tiptoe, alert, passing rooms with emptied drawers hanging open like surprised mouths. In one room, Virginia spots a pair of thick-soled shoes and a jacket. She puts on the jacket and shoves the shoes in its pockets. Odette finds a sweater and fills her pockets with socks. They each grab blankets to drape over their shoulders. Then they turn their attention to the storage cellar.

A pair of Russian women pass them on the stairs, making motions as if to say, "Don't go," but Virginia is sure it's only because they want more for their comrades. In the cellar, they can't find a light switch, but in the shafts of moonlight coming in through the windows above them at ground level, they spot buckets under a sink. They start filling them with as many provisions as they can carry. Cans of jam and vegetables, jars of honey, crackers. Virginia searches drawers until she finds a can opener. Their buckets full, they're about to return to the barracks when a sudden shouting upstairs stops them. Shots are fired. Boots pound overhead.

Frantic, Virginia and Odette shove their buckets and blankets on a low shelf and search for cover. In her haste, Virginia knocks over a tin of utensils that go clacking over the concrete floor.

There's shouting in German, and the boots pound down the stairs. Virginia and Odette look at each other in horror. They crouch lower, under the counters, desperate for a closet, a pantry, anything that might hide them.

"Come out!" the voices shout in German-accented French. "Or we'll shoot!"

A wink of moonlight on a beer keg beckons Virginia. She leads Odette to a wall of kegs and pushes with all her might to hide among them. A few months ago, she wouldn't have been able to fit, but they've all lost a staggering amount of weight. Odette just makes it in after Virginia when a flashlight passes over them. They stop moving and hold their breath.

One of the Germans says something and runs back upstairs, while the other continues to shine his flashlight around the room, under shelves and back across to the kegs. Virginia's heart pounds so loud, she wonders how he can't hear it.

It feels like hours, but he finally turns and climbs up the stairs. Once Virginia and Odette are alone, they exhale, staying in place until all sound recedes. When some time has passed without noise, they creep back to the buckets and blankets they shoved under the shelf. They hoist them, struggling with the weight up the stairs, and sneak out the back door. When they return to the barracks, Marie cries out with relief.

"We thought you were done for," she says.

"We're all right," says Virginia, trying to catch her breath. "Look what we have for you."

The feast is met with joyful exclamations. Virginia wraps Janette in a blanket and returns Marie's clogs. Virginia puts on the Nazi girl guard's shoes. Though they're a little large on Virginia's feet, they'll do. They pass out the underwear and socks, and then the food, re- minding each other to take it slowly though they're ravenous. Some of the other women in the barracks venture out to get more, and all night they feast, sharing in a liberation banquet.

VIRGINIA AWAKENS TO the sound of retching. There's a line for the outhouse. Women clutch their stomachs and whimper, paying for their overindulgence.

Once Virginia has worked through a bout of stomach cramps, she gathers the strength to walk back to the dormitories. Based on the lack of prisoners wandering around, they're all suffering from last night's gluttony. That, and fear of German patrols. Virginia feels like she's moved past fear. She feels very little emotion, in fact. Mostly a faint curiosity about what will happen once the Allies arrive.

Like a sleepwalker, she heads down the hallway of the guards' dormitory to their lavatory. It's heaven to use a real flushing toilet, and when she sees the shower, she can't resist the call of cleanliness. There's even a sliver of soap on the shower floor.

But first, new clothes.

The dress she wears is so foul she can't bear to put it back on after a washing. Virginia returns to the female guard's room to see if she can find any underclothes to add to the spoils she's already taken. There is an SS woman's uniform, which certainly won't do, though the thick-lined jacket is a temptation. She moves to another room, and a row of framed photographs catches her eye. There are groups of young people in a meadow, staring, stiff and serious, at the photographer. There are three little girls, dressed in fine clothes, with an elegant older woman in a garden. It's incomprehensible to Virginia that any of these demonic guards would have framed pictures of family or friends. Where does one life end, and another begin?

I'm taking too long.

She hurries through the women's dorm, which has been scavenged to the bones, until she finds a light blue sweater at the top of a closet, and a long gray wool skirt folded underneath it. She carries her new clothes back to the lavatory and reaches for the shower handle, but not a drop comes out. She looks in the toilet she flushed, but it hasn't refilled. Either the Nazis turned off the water before they left, or a main has been hit.

Her shoulders sag and she rolls her eyes to the ceiling.

She still changes into her new, clean, warmer clothes, puts her jacket back on, and is about to grab the soap to stuff in her pocket, when a movement by the sink catches her eye. She jumps when she sees the woman staring at her. Bulging eyes, sunken cheeks, skin clinging to every bone and sinew, she's a frightening sight.

Through the fog of her mind, her understanding catches up to what she sees.

It's a mirror.

Virginia still won't cry. At least she has her hair, patchy and brittle as it is. She doesn't have time to dwell.

A rumbling draws her to the window, where she sees a line of lorries racing toward camp.

The SS have returned.

IT'S PANDEMONIUM.

The SS guards from Ravensbrück give them five minutes to pack. Some of the women can't stop vomiting. Janette begs to use the latrine. She's refused, and has to void her bowels in the yard, squatting in the dirt.

Virginia can see by the wild, frightened look in the guards' eyes that the prisoners are in great danger. She does her best to contract, to become a compliant shadow. She prays the others can do the same. Especially Janette. Her friend is raving and mumbling. Janette's strange bloating has gone down, leaving her looking like a deflated balloon, but that's somehow more terrifying than when she was swollen.

"March!" the guards shout.

The women obey—if the way they limp, drag, and stumble can be called marching. Virginia can't wait to get to the train station. She doesn't know how some of these women will manage to make it, let alone climb in a cattle car. But they don't stop at the train station. They keep going.

Do they mean to walk us to Ravensbrück?

The train took three days to bring the women here. It must be over four hundred kilometers.

Virginia looks to the sky, but it's gray, and the air smells of snow.

My God.

56

FÜRSTENBERG

—— VIOLETTE ——

VIOLETTE CAN'T REMEMBER the words to any prayers. There's a constant ringing in her ears, and whenever she moves, she sees flecks of silver racing around the edges of her vision like Allied bombers.

To have come so close.

The isolation cell on the punishment block is a hole of darkness, coldness, and filth, where her only companions are the ravings of the other prisoners in solitary, the rats that walk over her hair when she tries to sleep, and the *Kapo* who brings her once-daily allotment of water and black bread. The *Kapo* looks familiar, but it's too dark to see clearly.

"Violette," the woman whispers. "I was able to get you some soup. Quick."

Quick.

Funny, Violette thinks.

But she pushes herself up off the floor and crawls over to the bars.

The *Kapo* slides in the soup and a spoon, but the spoon looks so heavy. Violette laps the soup up like a dog. The woman leaves with her lantern, as if she can't bear to watch.

I will not show Tania this place.

As the soup depletes, she's able to tip the bowl, drinking the rest. She feels around the bottom of the bowl and finds a little piece of something. She eats it, rolling her eyes to heaven over the perfect goodness of a morsel of sausage.

Thank you, she thinks.

There, a prayer she can remember.

57

FÜRSTENBERG

———— VIRGINIA ————

SIXTY. SIXTY WOMEN are left, from two hundred fifty, from five hundred, from countless thousands. The others lie dead, along the roads and rails from Königsberg to Ravensbrück.

When they hadn't got far, they'd watched the Russian fliers bomb the airfield and the camp. Virginia had thought—had hoped—the guards would abandon them there. Why would they want all these women to drag and coerce and kick and beat and shoot all the way back to Ravensbrück? All these stinking, bleeding, bloated, sick, starving, wailing women?

Blessed, saintly, courageous women. Sharing, carrying, enduring, all the way back to hell.

Janette is only bones and skin and feverish love.

With strength that can only come from the grace of God, Virginia hoists her dear, dying friend into her arms, and carries her to the Ravensbrück infirmary. Odette and Marie lean on each other and collapse, coughing, on the ground. Not a bed is open. Barely a space on the floor. Virginia eases Janette onto the ground next to Odette.

"There, there," Virginia says, touching Janette's burning forehead.

Janette's hands have turned blue. The blue travels up her arms. Her eyes are glassy, and a smile of serenity rests on her pale lips.

"It will be all right," says Virginia. "Soon the weather will turn, and you can pick cherries with your *maman*, and we'll picnic while the blossoms flutter down over us."

Janette can only smile at Virginia, but she feels the love from her friend pulsing out like sunshine. Virginia will not let it penetrate the ice. She cannot.

"I love you," Virginia whispers. "My friend."

A shrieking sound calls her attention to the door. It's Michelle, the florist. Michelle is bloated and raving the way Janette was just days ago. Odette can't stop coughing and Marie is mumbling, begging for Virginia to find Violette. Virginia can't stay here for one more moment.

But there's more hell outside the infirmary.

The fire rages in the crematorium, but it can't keep up with demand. Piles of corpses spill from the morgue in a grotesque cornucopia. Skeletons in rags dig graves, but some collapse into their own holes. There's no room in the tent, but that's where they're ordered to go. Stepping over sick bodies in piles of filth from dysentery, over dead bodies. Ferocious, inhuman women slap and kick while others try to find a way through the masses, to claim some small piece of real estate.

She can't stay in the tent. On the way out she runs into Julia, the *Kapo*.

"The parachute girls?" Virginia asks. "Are they . . . ?"

"Barely."

Julia points to the punishment block, where the solitary confinement cells are, but the guards there look murderous. More so than usual. And there is no order. And there is nothing Virginia can do to help them. Julia hurries away, and in her wake, in Virginia's swimming vision, the building where she first checked in all those months ago appears. All she can think of is her wedding ring.

That will protect me, she thinks.

"Philippe," she whispers.

Courage.

Inside, she finds it. The Nazis, so organized, have kept the boxes filed by number. She tears the box open and sees her old clothing, feeling the hem of her skirt until she's rewarded.

She won't let herself cry.

She pushes the ring over her swollen knuckle. It spins on her claw-like finger, sparkling in the light.

58

FÜRSTENBERG

─── VIOLETTE ───

THE LIGHT FROM the flashlight hurts Violette's eyes.

She still can't remember prayers, but she's been humming a song from many lifetimes ago and it has brought her comfort.

The sound of the key in the lock, the scrape of metal, hurts her ears.

The sight of the men hurts her heart.

Suhren and a line of four—two in uniform, two in lab coats—stand there.

To have come so close.

She pushes herself up to standing, smooths her hair and her skirt, and steps forward without being told.

Her only weapon remaining is contempt. She wields it, piercing each man with her stare, assuring them that she will haunt them forever. Not one can keep his eyes on hers. Not even Suhren.

Nadine and Ambroise can't stand. They're loaded onto stretchers.

Violette follows Suhren. The others follow her.

Outside the punishment block, the wind is cold but gentle. It makes her feel awake. The quarter moon glows down over her in benediction. She sends her love up through the satellite to Tania. To her family. To her men and Henri. But then, she feels Étienne, his hand on her shoulder, his peace in her heart.

Courage, he whispers.

The alley by the crematorium isn't wide, but it's enough for the women in one row, the men in another. A directive of execution is read. Violette stares at the reader. When he looks up at her, he nods at her as if to salute her courage. It's a strange kind of diplomacy for the moment. A flare of darkness toward the man swells in her heart, but Étienne's presence pushes it away.

No more of that.

Ambroise can't stand, but she can kneel, facing away from the man with the revolver. He cocks it, presses the gun to her neck, and shoots.

Violette thinks of the altar at La Madeleine, how it shows Mary Magdalene being carried up to heaven by angels, her mission complete, her life a pleasing sacrifice.

Nadine is too weak to kneel. They lay her down on her stomach. The man clenches his jaw, cocks his gun, leans down over her neck, looks away, and shoots.

Violette is taken back to the first night she and Étienne met.

A Midsummer Night's Dream. Titania. Tania.

Now am I dead, Now am I fled; My soul is in the sky. Tongue, lose thy light; Moon, take thy flight. Now die, die, die, die, die.

Violette turns and faces the wall.

Étienne whispers in her ear.

When the war is over, we'll live in France in a little chalet, and our feet will be stained from grapes, and our bellies and hearts will be full.

Faraway, she hears the cock of the gun, feels the steel on the back of her neck.

I look at the moonrise each night, as you instructed me, and I send my love. Do you feel it? Look up tonight. Send me yours.

Violette raises her eyes to heaven.

59

—— **VIRGINIA** ——

BY THE THIRD gunshot, Virginia knows.

She goes numb in the knowing.

She tucks Violette and Ambroise and Nadine and Janette into a locked place in her heart. One she may never open again.

Virginia runs her hand over her bald head. Shorn and shaved by a cruel guard, just because. Because the guard had asked the women who would like showers, and she had foolishly raised her hand, and there was no shower. Only a barber with a pair of clippers who cut her scalp while the guard held her down as she struggled in vain.

Humiliation complete, Virginia cowers in the corner, shaking, covering her cold head with her hands, forgetting about her ring until the guard says, "Where did you get that? Give it to me."

Virginia snaps. She raves and screams at the woman. Possessed.

"You've taken everything," Virginia shouts. "From Tania, from Henri. From the French, the Hungarians, the Russians, the Polish. But I'm an American. And you will pay for what you've done to me. You will pay dearly."

Her words stop the struggle. The guard's eyes widen. She looks from the barber to Virginia.

"You're American?"

"Yes."

Everything changes.

"PUT HER WITH de Gaulle," says the secretary.

Once they've given Virginia the shower she'd come for, doused her with anti-vermin powder, and layered her with clean clothes topped with an orange jacket, she's led by a polite female guard to a holding cell of some kind. In it is a private lavatory, a clean couch, and a table, with a pitcher of water, glasses, and a plate of cheese and crackers from which the niece of the next leader of France nibbles. When Geneviève—still in reasonably good health—sees Virginia, de Gaulle's manners are not good enough to mute her horror at how repulsive her companion looks. A little bald woman in dead prostitute's clothing. Virginia thinks back to the creatures she'd thought were men when she had arrived at Ravensbrück. She'd looked at them the way Geneviève looks at her.

Before the guard leaves them, Virginia says, "Pardon. What's happening?"

"You're leaving."

Virginia gasps, choking back the tears. Forcing them to remain in her eyes. There can be no crying. Not yet.

"For where?" she asks.

"A Red Cross camp. Near the Swiss border. Your train departs at half past four."

Virginia's breathing becomes labored. She still holds in her tears, but she's trembling badly. Geneviève helps her to sit.

"It's all right," Geneviève says. "We made it."

We made it.

The words become a mockery over the next six days while three young SS guards—two men and one woman—try to navigate travel with special prisoners—one half-alive—through bombed station after bombed town, even through an actual bombing.

We're not going to make it, Virginia thinks, all the long night at Ulm, while fire rains down upon them from Allied planes.

To have come so close.

But they do. In this war of a thousand journeys, they make it all the way to the picturesque town of Meckenbeuren, nestled along Lake Constance in view of the Swiss Alps, where the good doctors and nurses of the Red Cross camp called Liebenau fuss and fawn over their seventy-five-pound American patient, who saved sixty-nine pilots and watched many hundreds of women die, and who just wants to get home to her one dear and loving husband.

Over the next two months, Virginia is nursed back to health. It's extraordinary what nutritious food and air and rest and care can achieve in a very short time. Though she doesn't know if they will reach her loved ones, she writes letters to Philippe, and to her mother and father, and to Mum, and Jessie-Ann, and everyone she can think of. Her hair is slow in growing—it's like peach fuzz—and she keeps her head wrapped in a turban.

The nights are hard, plagued with memories of gunshots, and screams from crematoriums, and Janette's glassy eyes, and women lying dead in the snow. Virginia is tortured by guilt, by surviving when so many did not. When she awakens and sees herself, still so very skinny, she wonders if Philippe will be able to love her again. In her conscious mind, she knows the worry is ridiculous, that her husband will always love her, but it's hard to remember that in the dark.

On April 21, the camp is officially liberated. The French are the first to reach them. That night, they hold a liberation dance, and though Virginia is still weak, she dances to every song but one. When "I'll Be Around" comes on, she can hear Violette humming it, and Virginia cannot allow herself to think of dear Violette right now.

The spring has never been lovelier. Virginia's health continues to improve. She's up to eighty-five pounds, and her leg sores are gone, as is the ringing in her ears.

They get word that Hitler committed suicide.

Geneviève is the first to leave. She gives Virginia kisses on both cheeks, and tells her how lovely she is, admitting that when she'd first laid eyes on Virginia, she thought her a very old woman. Geneviève promises Virginia that she will pursue justice for every Nazi she can and is quite sure her name will give her a lot of pull.

It's on a day perfumed with floral breezes that the mail brings Virginia the sweetest gift she has ever received. She holds the envelope with her husband's handwriting on it with trembling fingers. She kisses the letter and presses it to her heart before tearing into it. Eyes racing over the words, she reads Philippe's agony poured out, turning to a joy he didn't think possible. He told her of the torture of learning she'd been arrested—how Daniel and Jean had to hold him down on the ground so he didn't go out searching. He wrote of his terrifying escape over the Pyrenees, his trip to London, his return to Paris after the liberation, his position in the Free French Forces and the intelligence service. Of the anguish of not being able to find her, not knowing her fate for so long. But that this is the Easter of their lives, the spring of their resurrection, and he can't wait to take her in his arms. He'll never again let go.

At the end of May, it's Virginia's turn to be repatriated. She's ninety pounds. Her hair is an inch long, wrapped in a kerchief with little bangs out the front. Her cheeks are sun-kissed. The bus takes her to the border, and when she crosses into France, she gets a breath like she hasn't had in a year. A deep, cleansing breath that leaves her with the utmost sense of peace.

It's at the repatriation center at Strasbourg that a French colonel on his way to Paris tells her he'll give her a ride. He's gentle and solicitous and helps her in the car with such care she thinks he must fear breaking her.

If the death camps didn't break me, she thinks, *nothing will.*

60

PARIS

—— **VIRGINIA** ——

VIRGINIA KNEW SHE had to come off the mountaintop, and the closer she gets to Paris, the more agitated she becomes.

The countryside and its population still bear the terrible scars of war. They will for a long time. Like the land, she is much reduced. It's been almost a year since she saw her husband. Her health is not entirely back. She still needs rest. Philippe never knew her when she needed rest.

How will we learn to live normally again? Is there any such thing?

She shifts, trying to get comfortable, her bones still poking through her skin, making it painful to sit for long periods. The colonel gives her a sad smile.

"Almost there," he says.

When they see the skyline, she has to work not to cry. She cannot cry yet or she won't stop.

She draws in her breath when she sees the moon. Though there's still light in the sky, the full moon is visible, even before the sun has gone down. It's huge, appearing close enough to touch. A day moon.

Don't cry yet.

The moon has never been so magnificent. Nor has Paris. It's more breathtaking than she remembered. Everything is so achingly beautiful.

"They preserved her," the man says. "Hitler had given the order to leave Paris in ruins on retreat, but his military governor disobeyed. He had fallen in love with her. As we all do. How could he execute her?"

How, indeed.

They drive past La Madeleine, and the Joan of Arc statue, and the Louvre, and Jessie-Ann's place, and the florist shop, and the Reine Marie, and finally, they reach the apartment building. Virginia has to put both hands on the dash to steady herself. She takes several deep breaths.

"Are you all right?" he asks.

"I think so. I will be. I am."

He turns off the car and comes around to open her door, offers his arm, and helps her out. She looks up at the lavender sky and sees the moon glowing in benediction. It's as if Violette is at her ear.

Courage.

On the envelope, Philippe had written the address of their old apartment, so that's where they go. She climbs three flights and is winded when they reach the door. She sees that it has been broken and repaired. The new lock is smaller than the old. It exposes the unfinished wood the other lock used to cover. There are blows that cut deep into the grain. She runs her fingers over them. It's battered, but it still functions.

She stares at the door a long moment, thinking of all the people who've knocked on it, who've hidden behind it. How are her boys doing? Did they all make it? Is Marshall all right? Will Michelle return? There are so many whose fates she doesn't know. It tires her to think of all the stories they'll hear, and the inevitability of the ones that didn't end well.

She tries the knob, but the door is locked. She doesn't know what comes over her, but she uses the code knock, the one that Jean gave them. And before she can finish, the door is thrown open. And there stands Mum.

Mum covers her mouth, but not before she shows her shock at Virginia's appearance. She takes Virginia in her arms. Virginia can't help but look over Mum's shoulder for Philippe.

"Oh, dear girl!" cries Mum. "Oh my God."

She kisses Virginia on both cheeks and helps her inside. Virginia can't find any words. She'd expected Philippe to open the door. She loves Mum. Virginia's so happy to see Mum alive and well, but where is Philippe? Terror suddenly comes over Virginia. What if he's not all right? What if something has happened?

There's an awkward farewell with the French colonel, whom Mum sees out, while Virginia sits on the couch trying to put together a question. She's finally able to manage something.

"Is Philippe . . . ?" Her voice trails off.

Virginia feels foolish for assuming he would be all right. For assuming anyone would. She had a letter, but what if something bad happened since it was sent?

"Oh, yes, yes," says Mum. "Philippe is well. Very well, darling. He just left, not a half hour ago, to celebrate with Marshall. You remember Marshall? He said he's the aviator who taught you the jitterbug."

"Marshall?" Virginia feels like a confused child.

"Yes, he was at a camp, too. And he, too, survived. He showed up at the door before you did. Philippe will be devastated. Who would have thought you'd both arrive on the same day? Such a coincidence."

"Do you know where they went? Or when they'll get back?"

"I don't, darling, but I will feed you, and you will rest, and when you wake up, you will be in your husband's arms."

Virginia slides the kerchief off her head. A look of pain and pity flashes over Mum's face. She swallows and stands abruptly, walking to the kitchen.

"Would you like tea or biscuits?" Mum calls. She returns to the door. "A glass of wine?"

Virginia shakes her head no.

"All right, dear," says Mum. "Would you like to rest?"

Virginia nods.

"Good girl."

Mum helps Virginia to walk to the bathroom and, when she finishes, takes Virginia to her and Philippe's bedroom.

Virginia inhales the scent of her husband's aftershave. The bed is made, nice and tight, the way he learned in the army. There's a Bible on his nightstand with wrinkled edges, and a picture of Virginia next to it.

I'm not that woman anymore, Virginia thinks.

She feels a deep sorrow settle over her.

Mum takes Virginia's coat and kerchief and helps her to the bed. She tucks in her daughter-in-law and kisses her on the forehead. Before she leaves Virginia, she stands in the doorway, her silhouette lit from behind.

"Thank God," Mum whispers, her voice cracking.

IN HER DREAM, Virginia is with Philippe at Bussière-Galant, when they were reunited in the Unoccupied Zone, after the phony war. The moonlight comes in the circular window like a boat porthole. They wrap themselves around each other, waking up a hundred times in the small hours to reassure each other they are together, and unwilling to disentangle to get a proper rest.

Philippe kisses her neck.

She opens her eyes.

Philippe is weeping and kissing the back of her neck.

Thank God.

Her tears start.

She rolls toward him and takes his face in her hands.

"Honeybee," he whispers.

She smiles and kisses him, tasting the salt from their mingling tears. She can't tell who's crying harder. It doesn't matter. They are one, returned to each other. And they will never be apart again.

He gently slides his hand up her spine. She can feel him taking measure of her. He runs his hands over her short hair. His tears come harder.

"Can you love me this way?" she asks, burying her face in his chest. He smells like wine, good enough to drink.

"I love you all ways," he whispers. "Always."

After another kiss, she turns and burrows her back into him. They face toward the window that looks over Paris. They face the future.

She has been in hell. They both have. Even with all she has lived, however, the terrible things she has seen, she has also witnessed the best in humanity.

The thought of Violette, glowing golden in the night, as she took water to the men in cattle cars, comes to Virginia. And Violette spoon-feeding Maman Marie. And Violette doing the Lambeth Walk to distract the guards from Nadine.

The tears fall so hard, Virginia can't see. Philippe cries with her. Will they ever be able to stop?

But when the dawn comes, Virginia thinks of her people—the Comet Line. She thinks of Ebrahim and Marshall and every one of those dear boys. Even if Marshall is the only pilot who made it, it was worth it for him to live. But he's not the only one, of that, she's sure. And if she had to do it all over again, even to save only one life, she knows she would.

APRIL 1995
FÜRSTENBERG

THE DAY MOON is there again. I remember my little one's plump arm pointing at it while I took him on a walk.

One year to the day after I was reunited with Philippe, we were given a miracle. A baby boy—sweet Patrick—the joy and light of our lives. He was our hope after the time of hopelessness, a gift we never expected.

Nicole and Michel had two little ones of their own. From the moment the cousins could walk, they loved to run over the lawns at Cancaval, and sail in the Rance, and climb up the dovecote, searching for the ghosts of old corsairs.

Philippe became a dealer in antiques while I worked with dolls. As the stories came to me about the women—those lost and those who survived—I found dolls to replicate them, restored them, and sold them, tucking little name cards in the boxes and shipping them all over the world. I gave them names like Janette and Denise and Lilian and Marie. Names like Violette, the one I first met because she'd rescued a doll. I can still see her purple kerchief, her amethyst eyes.

Michelle wraps her wrinkled arm around mine a little tighter. In spite of her bloating and mental deterioration, Michelle somehow survived, regained her health, and went on to marry several times, including her pilot. She had no divorces, only widowhoods, but she likes to joke about how her third husband drives her batty.

We nestle together to watch Yvonne Baseden—whom we knew as Odette, with the bright eyes and steady gaze—tell us about the parachute girls, the women of the SOE, and the plaque that honors them. I try not to think about the gunshots, but instead, to recall their sweet voices joined to ours, singing on Christmas Eve, the exercises Violette made us all do to stay as healthy as possible, her constant jokes and songs, and that day at *Appell* when she did the Lambeth Walk and saved Nadine's life, if only for a time.

It took a long while for me to seek information about the women. Perhaps I was wrong to suppress the memories, or perhaps it's how I survived. It wasn't until many years later, when a film based on a book came out about Violette, *Carve Her Name with Pride*, that I read in the papers about her family. When Violette's little Tania was four, she was invited to Buckingham Palace, and King George pinned the child with her late mother's George Cross. Tania was apparently wearing a dress Violette had bought for her in Paris, shortly after the first time I crossed paths with Violette. The child was initially with a friend of Violette's, but the friend turned Tania over to her grandparents, who raised her. Violette's father, Charlie, wrote a beautiful poem about his daughter that the paper published.

Letters from the pilots we'd helped started coming immediately after the war. Philippe and I attend reunions, and some of the men and their families have come to stay with us at Cancaval or in Paris, and their enduring friendships are some of the greatest gifts of our lives. I never found Ebrahim, and pray he's well, but sometimes Marshall and I still jitterbug, for old times' sake, though we haven't done the lift in many years.

Two years ago, the wife of Alfred Wickman, the pilot with whom I was arrested, found me from a *Reader's Digest* article, and wrote to me to say that Al had died. It was a sad letter because he hadn't told her much about his escape, our arrest, or his time at Stalag Luft 1, the camp where he'd been interned. He'd always harbored guilt, blaming himself that I had been detained. If only he had reached out to me, the way the others had, I could have given him every assurance that it wasn't his fault, that I was thrilled he'd survived, and that I would do it all over again, even knowing the outcome.

There has been pain over the years. Jessie-Ann and her family stayed at Nesles until the liberation, and we were able to resume our close friendship after the war. We were saddened Paul took a job at the French embassy in Washington, DC, and they had to leave us, but we made promises to keep in touch. In 1947, however, when the family was on vacation in Solomons, Maryland, one of their daughters disappeared beneath the surface of the river where she was swimming. Jessie-Ann jumped in to save her, and they both drowned. The loss was unimaginable.

My greatest heartbreak—the reason Mum had to step away from me when I had returned—came when I learned my mother died of leukemia days before Liebenau was liberated. Once my mother received Philippe's cable that I had been arrested, she had worked tirelessly, writing letters to everyone from the secretary of state, to the Red Cross, to the war department and the Office of the Provost Marshal General of the Army Service Forces to find my whereabouts and negotiate my release. It was in large part because of her efforts that I was able to leave Ravensbrück when I did. Mother never knew that I had been freed, and for that, I will be forever haunted.

We all carry our ghosts with us.

The ceremony comes to a close, and I reflect on how remarkable the endurance of the human spirit can be. I'm convinced to my bones that Violette, and others like her, did not die in vain. Violette couldn't have lived with herself if she'd sat home always wondering if her talents would have helped win the war in some way. She laid down her life for others, and we all know in our hearts what we've been taught, that there is no greater love.

We're each given a flower to place on the lake, where the ashes from the crematorium were dumped. We walk to the shore and toss the blooms, watching them bob away on the surface toward the center. Violette is under here with the others. It's a pretty resting place, though I hardly think of Violette as resting at all. I think of her flying on a strong wind under a full moon, singing and dancing across the heavens. The thought brings a smile to my face.

I'm glad I came. I would still do it all over again. The what-ifs are much harder to live with than the consequences of action inspired by a desire to help. Inspired by love and a need to serve.

I will keep the chamber where I've stored these bad memories open to air it out. To share the stories with others. Though I was not incinerated by the hellfires of war, those who were consumed are no less than I. They are more. They will live on in me if I remember them. They will live on if I promise to tell their stories.

I see now the duty before me. The next mission is in the remembering and the telling. The redemption. It will be hard to speak of some more than others, but I must. We all must. And though we can't do it ourselves, grace can come in to help shoulder the burden.

I think of Violette and how pleased she would be for her story to be known. She would wink at me and grin, and when my step falters or the words get backed up, she'd remind me what I need to have in spite of all my fears.

Courage.

AUTHOR'S NOTE

VIRGINIA D'ALBERT-LAKE AND Violette Szabo entered my radar while I researched my previous World War II novel, *The Invisible Woman*, about SOE/OSS agent Virginia Hall. Their stories all spoke so deeply to me, I tried to put them all together, but it was too much. I thought I'd spread the stories out over three novels, but when I attempted to write Violette's story, it hurt too much. I placed her scenes aside and turned my attention to Virginia d'Albert-Lake.

One day, deep in research, I found some of Virginia's comments on a fellow prisoner who'd inspired and led the women, one who had been executed. It was Violette. I still tried to avoid Violette, but her pursuit was relentless. In a series of three dreams, her story came alive for me. First, I dreamt I was Violette, being chased by a Nazi, whom I wrestled to the ground and strangled. Then I had the horrible dream of her execution. I again was Violette, led to the alley at Ravensbrück, and I was shot, feeling the gun go off on my neck. Finally, I dreamt that Violette came to me, upset, saying I'd abandoned her story. I told her it was too sad, but she begged me to tell it. She said it wasn't sad, because she was proud of herself and didn't regret it, and her memory should live on.

I gave in.

As it turned out, weaving the stories of Violette and Virginia together brought balance to each. Both had good partners, and families, and friends who loved them well, even when they challenged them. Violette's and Virginia's journeys came together naturally and created a multifaceted jewel showing the different ways that women, in particular, are called to serve. How each of us has a vocation, and we cannot have peace until we become who we are meant to be. Also, ultimately, they show us that none of us can operate alone. We are all called into a community of people working together for good.

NOTES ON HISTORY
AND CHARACTER CHOICES

VIRGINIA AND THE COMET LINE

- Early in the story, when Virginia drove Mum to Cancaval, the women took two cars. I put them together for simplicity.

- In Nesles, a house near Virginia's was requisitioned by a German officer who liked to hunt, but I couldn't find out exactly whose house it was. I assigned the soldier to Madame Fleury's inn. It also wasn't clear if Madame was a widow by that time. I made it so to suit the story.

- To consolidate characters, Michelle, the Paris florist, was a composite of two women: Andrée Donjon (actual florist, code name Michelle) and Vera Aisenberg (Russian, Comet Line guide, widowed by a Russian and a Belgian pilot and then married to an American). I picked Michelle for the name because there were already two Veras in the book, Vera Maidment and Vera Atkins, whom I call Miss Atkins.

- Lily (code name Michou) is Micheline Dumon. Her father, Eugene; her mother, Marie; and her sister, Andrée, started the Comet Line out of Belgium. After their arrests, Eugene died in prison, but Marie and Andrée survived Ravensbrück. Lily made it safely out of occupied France to London. They are a family of great courage and heart.

- Daniel (Albert Ancia) didn't accompany Virginia, Philippe, and Michelle on the trip to the forest at Fréteval. Two other guides, Gérmaine Melisson and Jeannine Piguiet, did. Because those women weren't featured anywhere else in the book, for simplification, I used Daniel.

- Pierre (Jacques Desoubrie), the double agent, survived the poisoning by Daniel, but was eventually captured—with the help of Lily and Jean—and executed for his war crimes.

- I couldn't find many details about the physical and personal characteristics of couples Nicole and Michel and Jacqueline "Jessie-Ann" and Paul Blanc. I hope any liberties I took honor what admirable and courageous people they were.

- Janette is Jeanne Marie de Boissard, imprisoned for her work with the Resistance in Saint-Front, France. Little is known about her but what Virginia tells in her diary of her dear friend, whom she described as an angel.

- Virginia was a few cells down from Violette at Fresnes, was moved briefly to another prison, and traveled to Ravensbrück on a separate transport from Violette. I kept them together the entire time for simplicity of plot.

- If Virginia was aware of Violette's execution at the time it occurred, it is not documented. I made it so for purposes of story.

- There were many ceremonies at Ravensbrück over the years, but I was not able to find the exact one that Virginia attended, or the exact women who were there when she went. I chose the fifty-year anniversary of the liberation of the camp, and paired Virginia with Michelle (actually Vera Aisenberg, who stayed a lifelong friend), and featured Yvonne Baseden (code name Odette) as the speaker.

VIOLETTE AND THE SOE

- I don't know that Vera Maidment, childhood friend of Violette and caretaker of Tania, was in the ATS with Violette, but I included her for purposes of story and consolidation of characters.

- Violette was recruited for the SOE because of a number of referrals. Henri (Harry) Peulevé and Jack (Jacques Poirier) likely referred her, as did a man named Georges Clement, whom she spent time with at London dance halls. (Henri and Jack both survived the war, and excellent accounts of their experiences can be found in the selected bibliography.) Violette's time in the Land Army and the ATS, her command of the French and English languages, and her work on the film *In Which We Serve* all helped get her name to the right people. E. Potter (Selwyn Jepson) was a writer and SOE recruiter. He forwarded Violette's information along to Vera Atkins.

- Clement (Philippe Liewer) and Robert (Bob Maloubier) were devastated about Violette's arrest. They came down hard on Jacques Dufour, and tried to spring Violette from jail at Limoges, but they were misled by a prison guard who was a crook. Ultimately, Jacques proved himself, becoming a more disciplined maquisard, and the group had many successes, including the liberation of Limoges. Liewer died of a heart attack in Casablanca in 1948. Maloubier went on to live a long and adventurous life of much daring, many adventures, and several marriages.

- Maman Marie was Marie Lecompte. She survived Ravensbrück but lost the skirt hiding Violette's parents' address. It took Marie thirteen years to find the Bushells, but she was able to track them down after the release of the film *Carve Her Name with Pride*. Her relationship with the family, especially Tania, brought great comfort to all of them.

- Yvonne Baseden (Odette) of the SOE did meet Tania in passing at the SOE offices, and ended up at Ravensbrück. It is unclear if she is the "Yvonne" Virginia mentions went "looting" with her when Königsberg was falling apart, but I made it so to suit the story.

- Violette was tortured by the thought that there was a betrayer at SOE headquarters. As investigations after the war got closer to the truth, a fire (likely arson) at the SOE offices broke out in January of 1946, burning 85 percent of all agent files. Suspected betrayers included Nicolas Bodington and Henri Déricourt. The infamous Abbé Alesch, chaplain at Fresnes Prison, betrayed agents who confessed to him to the Gestapo for money. He was executed shortly after the war.

- Vera Atkins was haunted by the loss of Violette and so many other agents. Atkins's tireless hunting of war criminals and testimony at the Nuremberg trials resulted in the imprisonment and execution of many Nazis. When Atkins interviewed the hideous Kommandant Suhren of Ravensbrück and one of his deputies, both expressed admiration for the bravery of Violette, Lilian, and Denise. The cowards apparently regretted they had to carry out the order and wished the Gestapo had been forced to do it.

- Finally, inspired by my editor's comments in her first read-through of the book, I've included a short list of situations that involve Violette that seem unbelievable but are true.

   › Violette's father did play the "apple on the head" shooting game with Violette.

› Violette did steal Clement and Robert's wanted poster from Rouen.

› Violette did take Tania to the SOE offices, and Yvonne Baseden (Odette) saw them.

› Violette did run into Jack outside La Madeleine. Incidentally, Jack was hidden for a time at Virginia and Philippe's building by writer-resister André Malraux, but there was no natural way to work that into the story.

› Violette scratched her name into the wall of cell number forty-five at Fresnes Prison.

› Violette, shackled, did bring water to Henri and the men on the transport to Germany during an Allied air attack.

› Violette did get punished for doing the Lambeth Walk at *Appell* at Ravensbrück.

ACKNOWLEDGMENTS

To Patrick d'Albert-Lake, for kindly speaking to me from France and answering many, many questions on calls and over email about his incredible parents.

To Judy Barrett Litoff and Jim Calio, editor of and consultant on *An American Heroine in the French Resistance: The Diary and Memoir of Virginia d'Albert-Lake,* for their conversations and insights.

To my agent, Kevan Lyon, who steered me well in the early drafting stages and cheered me along every step of the way.

To my editor, Amanda Bergeron, whose warmth, understanding, and expertise helped shape this story to fully honor those on its pages.

To the team at Berkley—Claire Zion, Craig Burke, Jin Yu, Sareer Khader, Jeanne-Marie Hudson, Lauren Burnstein, Brittanie Black, Michelle Kasper, Emily Osborne, and Alison Cnockaert—for all their work producing the book and getting it into readers' hands.

To my father, Robert Shephard, and my in-laws, Richard and Patricia Robuck, for their boundless enthusiasm and support.

To Frank Damico, for his eagle eye in copyediting, and to Frank and his wife, Sheri, for their support and friendship.

To the archives and resources made available from the United States Holocaust Memorial Museum, the Violette Szabo Museum, the

Air Forces Escape and Evasion Society, the Frank Falla Archive, and cometeline.org.

To Olivia Beattie at Biteback Publishing, for permission to use the epigraph from Maurice Buckmaster's *They Fought Alone*.

To my husband, Scott, and our three sons, for their love and encouragement, and for enduring at least one conversation a day that I start with "You know, back in World War Two . . ."

And to God, for helping me find Violette and Virginia and all of the brave women and men whose stories must be told.

SELECTED BIBLIOGRAPHY

Fleming, Thomas. "Deliver Us from Evil." *Reader's Digest*, August 1991.

Guiet, Jean Claude. *Dead on Time: The Memoir of an SOE and OSS Agent in Occupied France*. Stroud, UK: History Press, 2016.

Helm, Sarah. *Ravensbrück: Life and Death in Hitler's Concentration Camp for Women*. New York: Anchor Books, 2015.

Litoff, Judy Barrett, ed. *An American Heroine in the French Resistance: The Diary and Memoir of Virginia d'Albert-Lake*. With afterword by Jim Calio. New York: Fordham University Press, 2006.

Maloubier, Robert. *SOE Hero: Bob Maloubier and the French Resistance*. Stroud, UK: History Press, 2015.

Minney, R. J. *Carve Her Name with Pride*. Barnsley, UK: Pen and Sword Military, 2013. First published 1956 by George Newnes (London).

Ottaway, Susan. *Violette Szabo: The Life That I Have*. London: Thistle Publishing, 2002.

Perrin, Nigel. *Spirit of Resistance: The Life of SOE Agent Harry Peulevé, DSO MC*. Barnsley, UK: Pen and Sword Military, 2008.

Poirier, Jacques R. E. *The Giraffe Has a Long Neck*. London: Leo Cooper, 1995.

Rochester, Devereaux. *Full Moon to France*. New York: Harper and Row, 1977.

Rossiter, Margaret L. *Women in the Resistance*. New York: Praeger, 1986.

Rothman-Le Dret, Catherine. *L'Amérique déportée: Virginia d'Albert-Lake de la Résistance à Ravensbrück*. Nancy, France: Presses Universitaires de Nancy, 1994.

Stevenson, William. *Spymistress: The True Story of the Greatest Female Secret Agent of World War II*. New York: Arcade, 2007.

Szabó, Tania. *Young, Brave and Beautiful: The Missions of Special Operations Executive Agent Lieutenant Violette Szabó*. Stroud, UK: History Press, 2015.

Tartière, Drue. *The House Near Paris: An American Woman's Story of Traffic in Patriots*. New York: Simon and Schuster, 1946.

Watt, George. *The Comet Connection: Escape from Hitler's Europe*. Lexington: University Press of Kentucky, 1990.

SISTERS of NIGHT and FOG

ERIKA ROBUCK

QUESTIONS FOR DISCUSSION

1. Who do you align with more—Violette or Virginia—and why? In what ways are the women most different, and what common threads do they share?

2. What did each woman have to overcome before she became a part of the Resistance? During? After?

3. Discuss how Virginia and Philippe both complemented and challenged each other.

4. Discuss how Violette and the men she loved—Étienne and Henri—complemented and challenged each other.

5. Do you think Virginia should have gotten involved earlier in the Resistance? Why or why not?

6. Do you think Violette should have gone on her missions to France? Why or why not?

7. Do you think you would have joined the Resistance in some capacity?

8. Both women had to weigh their family ties and responsibilities when deciding to become involved in Resistance work. How would those factors affect your decision if you were in their places?

9. Would you have worked in the munitions factory at Torgau?

10. Discuss the lowest moments for each woman in the book. Discuss the most triumphant.

11. What aspects of the book will resonate longest with you?

Photo by Nick Woodall

ERIKA ROBUCK is the national bestselling author of *Receive Me Falling, Hemingway's Girl, Call Me Zelda, Fallen Beauty, The House of Hawthorne*, and *The Invisible Woman*. She is a contributor to the anthology *Grand Central: Original Stories of Postwar Love and Reunion* and to the *Writer's Digest* essay collection *Author in Progress*. Robuck lives in Annapolis, Maryland, with her husband and three sons.

CONNECT ONLINE

ErikaRobuck.com

f ErikaRobuck

𝕏 ErikaRobuck

◎ ERobuckAuthor

Ready to find
your next great read?

Let us help.

Visit prh.com/nextread